Praise for Elin Hilderbrand's

Here's to Us

"It must be summer: Hilderbrand is back with a new beach read."
—Jocelyn McClurg, *USA Today*

"Beautiful people, dysfunctional families, and Nantucket: that's Hilderbrand territory, and it wouldn't be summer without a visit.... Just the thing for a day by the sea."
—Kim Hubbard, *People*

"The perfect summer book.... I fell in love with all of these characters.... The perfect mingling of forward action with excerpts from the past make for an engrossing story, as each chapter contains more revelations than the one before.... Fans of delectable summer reads and romances with a touch of tragedy will love this latest Hilderbrand novel, a perfect companion for a sunny summer morning and a bowl of something sweet."
—Tara Sonin, *B&N Reads*

"Hilderbrand is the queen of the summer beach read and she keeps the title with another light-as-air Nantucket-centered tale."
—*New York Post*

"The must-read that will be in everyone's beach bag this summer."
—Brenda Janowitz, *Popsugar*

"Absolutely addictive.... *Here's to Us* is written with such exquisite attention to detail, you'll practically smell the salt air and feel the sand beneath your feet."
—Georgea Kovanis, *Detroit Free Press*

"The book immediately draws you in with its scenic descriptions of the island and the Page Six–worthy life of a famous rock-star chef. A comfy beach chair and *Here's to Us* make the perfect recipe for a delectable reading experience."

—Bronwyn Miller, Bookreporter.com

"Hilderbrand is a master when it comes to writing the quintessential summer read and her offering this summer, *Here's to Us,* is no exception."

—Laurie Higgins, WickedLocal.com

"Elin Hilderbrand knows the recipe for a delicious literary drama, and *Here's to Us* is one of her most delectable yet."

—Kimberly Nelson, WorkingMother.com

"Queen of the summer beach read."

—Lambeth Hochwald, *Parade*

"No one captures the flavor and experience of a summer place—the outdoor showers, the seafood, the sand in the floorboards—like Hilderbrand." —*Kirkus Reviews*

"Hilderbrand writes another juicy, beachy family drama set against the beautiful backdrop of Nantucket. Her stories are as alluring as the island itself and as delicious as the included recipes, such as the one for champagne cake."

—Melissa DeWild, *Library Journal*

"Fans of that crazy four-letter L-word will find themselves caught up in this emotional story right away. Make sure to keep a box of Kleenex close by, because this one works its way up to being a real tearjerker.... A fast-paced and satisfying read." —Jaime A. Geraldi, *RT Book Reviews*

Here's to Us

ALSO BY ELIN HILDERBRAND

The Beach Club
Nantucket Nights
Summer People
The Blue Bistro
The Love Season
Barefoot
A Summer Affair
The Castaways
The Island
Silver Girl
Summerland
Beautiful Day
The Matchmaker
Winter Street
The Rumor
Winter Stroll
Winter Storms
The Identicals

Here's to Us

A Novel

Elin Hilderbrand

Little, Brown and Company
New York Boston London

Little, Brown and Company
Hachette Book Group
1290 Avenue of the Americas
New York, NY 10104
littlebrown.com

Little, Brown and Company is a division of Hachette Book Group, Inc. The Little, Brown and Company name and logo is a trademark of Hachette Book Group, Inc.

The publisher is not responsible for websites (or their content) that are not owned by the publisher.

Printed in the United States of America

Originally published in hardcover by Little, Brown and Company, June 2016
First Little, Brown and Company mass market edition, June 2017

10 9 8 7 6 5 4 3 2 1

For Anne and Whitney Gifford:
Thank you for "a room of my own."
xoxo

Here's to Us

PROLOGUE: ONE PERFECT DAY

Deacon Thorpe is thirteen years old and still more a boy than a man when his father, Jack, tells Deacon they're taking a day trip out of the city, just the two of them.

Deacon is intrigued by the idea of a day trip out of the city. They rarely have money for anything other than minute-to-minute survival. Jack works as a line chef at Sardi's in Times Square, and he gets only three days off per month.

Deacon is even more excited about the phrase "just the two of us." Jack is the king of Deacon's world, primarily because he is rarely available. Deacon anticipates time with Jack the way astronomers anticipate a comet or an eclipse.

Jack wakes Deacon at four in the morning. They leave Deacon's mother and his sister, Stephanie, asleep in the apartment. At Jack's instruction, Deacon is wearing his swimming trunks, and Jack is wearing a bright-yellow collared shirt that Deacon has never seen before.

Jack plucks at the shirt with a smile of pride. "Bought it specially for today," he says.

For the trip, Jack has rented an Oldsmobile Cutlass. Deacon didn't even realize his father knew how to drive. They live in Stuy Town, and if they need to go somewhere—work, school, the park—they take the subway or the bus.

"Now this," Jack says, "is one classy vehicle."

His father is suddenly full of surprises.

Deacon naps for much of the drive, waking up only as they cross a bridge that looks as though it has been made from a giant erector set. Elton John is on the radio, singing "Don't Go Breaking My Heart." Jack sings along, *"Oh, honey, if I get restless..."*

"Where are we?" Deacon asks.

"Cape Cod," Jack says. Then he sings, *"Whoa-ho, I gave you my heart!"*

Cape Cod. It has a mythical ring to it, like *Shangri-La.*

Jack turns down the radio and says, "I want one perfect day with my son. That's not too much to ask, is it?"

By nine o'clock, they are sitting on the top deck of a ferry, drinking coffee. Deacon has never been allowed to drink coffee before; his mother believes it will stunt his growth. Jack doesn't seem to think twice about ordering a cup for Deacon. He says, "You may want to add some cream and sugar to that, mellow it a little." But Deacon chooses to take it black, like his father. Some of his Jewish friends at school have had their bar mitzvahs, and that's how Deacon is viewing this day trip—as a rite of passage, in which he will learn some things about becoming a man.

The ferry delivers Deacon and Jack to a place called Nantucket Island. Jack insists they stand at the railing as soon as land comes into view. They pass a stone jetty where seals are sunbathing. Real seals! These are the first wild animals Deacon has seen outside a zoo. The ferry cruises into a harbor filled with sleek, elegant power yachts and sailboats with tall masts and elaborate rigging. Gulls circle overhead. Deacon sees two church steeples, one a white spire, one a gold dome, and clusters of gray-shingled buildings.

Jack says, "Today we are going to live the life on Nantucket."

On the wharf, Jack rents another car—an army-drab Willys jeep, which is like nothing Deacon has ever seen in the city. It has no top, no windows, no doors, even. It is basically two seats and a gearshift, four tires and a motor. This is not a classy vehicle—it's as far from the Cutlass as you can get—but Jack looks happier than Deacon has ever seen him.

"Hop in!" Jack says. "I'll give you the grand tour."

They drive over cobblestone streets, past a general store called Hardy's, which has a charcoal grill and a lawn mower in the plate glass window with a male mannequin wearing a collared shirt just like Jack's, standing between the two. *He'll cut the grass first,* Deacon thinks, *then grill up some burgers outside.* It's like a scene from *The Brady Bunch.*

They pass a pizza parlor, then a restaurant called the Opera House.

Jack points at the restaurant. "My old stomping ground," he says. "There's a real British phone booth in the dining room, where I used to kiss my French girlfriend, Claire."

Deacon feels himself redden. He can't imagine Jack Thorpe kissing anyone, not even Deacon's mother.

They drive out a long road that twists and turns. They pass gray-shingled cottages draped with roses, they pass fields with horses grazing alongside split-rail fences. To the left, Deacon catches glimpses of the blue harbor. The sun is starting to get very hot, and Deacon's stomach rumbles. All he has had to drink so far today is the coffee and there's been nothing in the way of food.

A lighthouse comes into view. It's white with a fat, red stripe in the middle. They pass a wide pond; on the other side of the pond, Deacon can see the ocean. Jack takes a left at a sign that says HOICKS HOLLOW.

"Good old Hoicks Hollow Road," Jack says. "Used to be my home away from home."

"It did?" Deacon says.

"Funny name for a road, isn't it?" Jack says.

Deacon doesn't know how to respond.

"Funnier than East Twenty-Eighth Street, anyway," Jack says.

They wind around until they reach a place called the Sankaty Head Beach Club. PRIVATE, the sign says. The air smells deliciously of French fries, and Deacon wants to believe they will eat lunch here, but the word "private" makes him ill at ease. The Thorpes aren't a family that belongs anywhere private. Not at all. Deacon figures that in another thirty seconds or so they will be told they are trespassing and will be asked to leave.

But surprisingly, Jack Thorpe is not only welcomed at the door, he is *celebrated*—by a heavyset, red-faced man wearing a name tag that says *Ray Jay Jr., Manager.*

"Jack Thorpe!" Ray Jay Jr. says. "God, you're a sight for sore eyes. How long has it been?"

"Too long," Jack says. He introduces Deacon to Ray Jay Jr. "I told Deacon I just want one perfect day with my son. That's not too much to ask, is it? How about some lunch, for old times' sake?"

"You got it, Jack," Ray Jay Jr. says. He ushers Jack and Deacon into the club. They pass signs that say LADIES' LOCKERS and GENTLEMEN'S LOCKERS. Through a swinging set of

Dutch doors with thick, white paint, they emerge outside. Ray Jay Jr. seats them at a table overlooking the swimming pool, which is an alluring lozenge of deep, turquoise water. Along both sides of the pool are cabanas with chaise longues where beautiful women in bikinis work on their suntans and towheaded children lie on navy and white striped towels. Waiters deliver iced teas with wedges of lemon, beers, and fruity cocktails to the chaise longues. At the far end of the pool is a wooden fence draped with red, white, and blue bunting, probably left over from the bicentennial celebration.

Over the loudspeaker, that song, "Don't Go Breaking My Heart," is playing again.

Jack holds an imaginary microphone under his chin as he sings along in falsetto. Then, to Deacon, Jack says, "You can go ahead and jump in. I'll order for you."

Deacon understands that this was the reason for the swim trunks; he shucks off his T-shirt. He approaches the edge of the pool. A few kids are splashing around in the shallow end while an older gentleman does freestyle laps. The only other swimming pool Deacon has been to is at the community center on Avenue A, where the water is too warm and stinks of chlorine and is always jam packed with shrieking kids and bullies who dunk Deacon, keeping his head under water long enough for him to panic. By comparison, this pool is cool and serene, like a pool in paradise.

One perfect day with my son. The phrase makes Deacon's heart soar. For the first time in his life, he feels as if he matters.

Deacon jumps in.

Lunch is a double bacon cheeseburger with French fries, a frosty Coke, and soft-serve ice cream. Ray Jay Jr. checks in to see how their food is and to offer Jack a beer, but Jack declines.

"I have my boy here," Jack says.

Deacon has never seen his father turn down an offer of a beer, and certainly not a free beer. Jack has an alcohol problem, Deacon's mother says. She calls it an occupational hazard, because he works in a restaurant, where alcohol is an ever-present temptation. When Jack drinks, bad things happen. He flies into rages for no reason, he throws things and breaks things, he screams profanities at Deacon, Stephanie, and their mother—and then, always, he cries until he passes out. But today, Jack seems to be a different man. In his yellow collared shirt, he fits right in with the members of this private club. The radio plays "Afternoon Delight."

"You know what this song is about, don't you?" Jack asks with a wink.

Deacon lowers his eyes to the scattering of salt across his plate. "Yeah," he says.

Jack slaps him conspiratorially on the back. "Okay then. Gotta make sure you're up to speed."

Deacon thinks they might stay at the pool all afternoon, lounging next to the women in bikinis, but Jack says, "We're off to the beach. Can't come to Nantucket and not go to the beach."

They get back into the open jeep with a couple of the navy and white striped towels that Ray Jay Jr. slips them on the way out.

As Jack pulls away he says, "I worked there fifteen years ago. I was the fry boy, and Ray the grill master. I should have done what he did. I should have stayed and lived the life on Nantucket."

Deacon nods in agreement, although he suspects that if Jack *had* stayed and lived the life on Nantucket, then he,

Deacon, might not exist. This unsettling thought evaporates once Deacon sees the beach. It is a long stretch of golden sand. The ocean is bottle green, with rolling, white-crested waves. Jack and Deacon set out their towels. Jack goes charging into the water, and Deacon follows.

They bodysurf in the waves for well over an hour, then they collapse on their towels and nap in the sun. When they wake up, the light has mellowed, and the water sparkles.

"Here it is," Jack says. "The golden hour."

They sit in silence for a few minutes. Deacon has never experienced a golden hour before, but he has been to church once, with his friend Emilio's family, and this feels sort of the same, peaceful and holy. In his life in the city, he watches too much TV, and he and Emilio and Hector set off bottle rockets in the alleys behind Stuy Town. Jack walks off down the beach, and Deacon senses that he wants to be alone, so Deacon goes to the water's edge and finds a perfectly formed clamshell with a swirl of marbleized blue on the inside. He'll take it home, he decides. He will keep it forever.

He throws rocks into the ocean until Jack returns with a dreamy, faraway look on his face. Deacon wonders if he is thinking about his French girlfriend, Claire.

"What do you say we start heading back?" Jack says. "I have to return the jeep by six."

Deacon nods, but his heart is heavy. He doesn't want to leave. The remainder of the day is shadowed by melancholy. They drive back into town, roll the jeep over the cobblestone streets, return it to the rental place. It has cost Jack forty dollars, which seems like a fortune.

On the wharf, Jack buys an order of fried clams, two lobster rolls, and two chocolate milk shakes. Deacon and his father eat their feast on the top deck of the ferry as the sun sets, dappling the water pink and gold. Jack hums some amalgam of "Don't Go Breaking My Heart" and "Afternoon Delight."

"Now, that was a perfect day with my son," Jack says. "What do you say we go downstairs so you can get some rest?"

Deacon nearly protests. He wants to stay outside and watch the lights of Nantucket fade until they disappear, but the breeze picks up, and Deacon shivers. He follows his father downstairs, where they secure a section of bench. Jack rolls up the two striped towels—there was never a doubt in Deacon's mind that Jack would keep them; he's thrifty that way—and places them on one end of the bench for Deacon as a pillow.

"Thank you," Deacon whispers.

He tries with all his might to stay awake, but the gentle rocking of the boat is like that of a cradle, and he feels himself succumbing. His eyelids grow heavy and eventually drop like anchors. Deacon knows somehow that more than just one perfect day with his father is ending. It's as though he can see the future: a week later, Jack will leave his family for good, taking the last scraps of Deacon's childhood with him. There is nothing either of them can do to stop it.

BUCK

John Buckley had performed some astonishing feats in his thirty years as an agent, but nothing compared to the miracle of assembling Deacon Thorpe's entire family at the house on Nantucket so that they could spread Deacon's ashes and discuss the troubling state of his affairs.

Buck realized he should be parsi
congratulation. He hadn't gathered the
had stubbornly chosen to remain in Savanna
stay, Buck supposed, until she realized the m one.
At some point in the near future, Buck assumed, uld look down, like Wile E. Coyote in the old cartoons, believing himself to be standing on solid ground but seeing nothing below him but thin air. They were sure to hear from her then.

Six weeks had passed, but John Buckley still couldn't believe that his first-ever client and his best friend, Deacon Thorpe—the most famous chef in America—was dead.

On May 6, a call had come to Buck's cell phone from an unfamiliar number, and, since Deacon had been incommunicado for nearly forty-eight hours, John Buckley took the call, thinking it might be his friend. He was in a chair at the Colonel's, the last old-time barbershop in New York City, where cell phones were expressly not allowed.

Buck knew he would never be granted an appointment with Sal Sciosia (the colonel, Battle of Khe Sanh, Vietnam) again if he took the call, but he had no choice.

An unfamiliar number could have meant anything. Most likely: Deacon had gone on another bender, even though he had *promised,* he had *sworn,* he had practically pricked his index finger and matched it with Buck's own in a solemn vow, that he would never again have an episode like the one two weeks earlier. That rager had most likely cost Deacon his marriage. Scarlett had withdrawn Ellery from La Petit Ecole, one of the most prestigious private schools in New York City, and taken her down to Savannah, leaving Deacon contrite and chastened, a new passenger on the wagon.

But people were going to act exactly like themselves. If Buck had learned one thing from thirty years of agenting, it was this. Now this call would either be from the NYPD or from the bartender at McCoy's, where Deacon had passed out facedown on his tab.

Buck *had* to answer.

"Hello."

"Mr. Buckley?" a voice of authority said. "My name is Ed Kapenash. I'm the chief of police in Nantucket, Massachusetts."

"Nantucket?" Buck said. Deacon owned a huge, ramshackle summer cottage on Nantucket called American Paradise, a name that Buck secretly considered ironic. "Is Deacon there?" His voice conveyed more impatience than he wanted it to, and probably not the full respect due to a chief of police. "Sir?"

"Yours was the number we found on his phone listed under his emergency contact," the chief said. "I take it you're a friend...? Of Deacon Thorpe's?"

"His agent," Buck said. And then, sighing, he added, "And yes, his best friend. Is he in jail?" Deacon had never gotten into any kind of trouble while on Nantucket, not in all these years—but as far as Deacon was concerned, there was a first time for everything.

"No, Mr. Buckley," the chief said. "He's not in jail."

Buck had walked out of the Colonel's half-shaven.

His best friend of thirty years was dead.

"Massive coronary," the chief said. "An island man named JP Clarke found him early this morning and phoned it in. But the M.E. put the time of death about twelve hours earlier—so maybe seven or eight o'clock last night."

"Had he been drinking?" Buck asked. "Doing drugs?"

"He was slumped over at the table on the back deck with a Diet Coke," the chief said. "And there were four cigarette butts in the ashtray. No drugs that we found, although the M.E. is going to issue a tox report. You have my condolences. My wife was a big fan of the show. She made that clam dip for every Patriots game."

Condolences, Buck had thought. That belonged on Deacon's Stupid Word List. What did it even mean?

"I'll leave it to you, then, to contact the family?" the chief asked.

Buck closed his eyes and thought: *Laurel, Hayes, Belinda, Angie, Scarlett, Ellery.*

"Yes," Buck said.

"And you'll handle the remains?"

"I'll handle...yes, I'll handle everything," Buck said.

Massive coronary, Buck thought. *Diet Coke and four cigarettes.* It was the cigarettes that had done it in the end, Buck guessed. He had *told* Deacon...but now was no time to indulge his inner surgeon general. Deacon was gone. It wasn't fair. It wasn't *right.*

"Thank you, Chief," Buck said. "For letting me know."

"Well," the chief said, "unfortunately, that's my job. My thoughts to the family."

Buck hung up and watched his arm shoot into the air. A taxi put on its blinker and pulled over. Everything was the same in the world, but then again it was different. Deacon Thorpe was dead.

The death had been devastating enough, but as the executor of Deacon's estate, Buck was then required to delve into the paperwork that inevitably followed. He started with the obvious: Deacon's will. He had left the restaurant to his daughter Angie, which made sense, although Harv would continue to run it for the foreseeable future. And Deacon had left his other major asset—the house on Nantucket—to the three women he had been married to, Laurel Thorpe, Belinda Rowe, and Scarlett Oliver, to be owned in thirds, with time split in a fair and just manner, as determined by the executor.

Great, Buck thought.

As Buck sifted through Deacon's marriage certificates to Laurel, to Belinda, to Scarlett; the divorce agreements from Laurel and from Belinda; the deed to the Nantucket house, which turned out to be encumbered with three mortgages and two liens; the LLC paperwork for Deacon's four-star restaurant, the Board Room, in midtown Manhattan; the contracts with ABC (ancient, defunct) and the Food Network; and his bank and brokerage statements, he'd been thrown into a tailspin. All Buck could think was, *This has to be wrong.* He rummaged through every drawer of Deacon's desk at the restaurant and meticulously checked the apartment on Hudson Street, a task much more easily accomplished without Scarlett around. Every piece of paper Buck found served to make the situation worse. It was like a game of good news, bad news, except this version was called bad news, worse news.

Deacon hadn't paid any of the three mortgages on the Nantucket house in six months, and he was three months behind on the rent for his apartment on Hudson Street. Where had all of Deacon's money *gone?* Buck found a canceled check for a hundred thousand dollars made out to Skinny4Life. *Skinny4Life?* Buck thought. *A hundred large?* This sounded like one of Scarlett's "projects"; there had been the purses made by the cooperative of women in Gambia and, after that, an organic, vegan cosmetic company that absconded with fifty thousand of Deacon's dollars before going belly-up. Before Scarlett decided she wanted to go into "business," she had studied photography. Deacon had spent a small fortune sending her to University College downtown—which, Buck had pointed out numerous times, was neither a university nor a college. Deacon had built Scarlett a state-of-the-art darkroom in the apartment and bought her cameras and computers and scanners and printers, the collective price of which could have paid for a Rolls-Royce with a full-time chauffeur. All of the equipment now sat dormant behind a locked door.

Buck found another canceled check, this one for forty thousand dollars and made out to Ellery's school, along with a check to the co-op board of Hayes's building in Soho. Buck had wondered how Hayes had been able to afford such a place, and now he knew: Deacon had paid for it. From the looks of things, Deacon had also been cutting a check to Angie every now and again—three thousand dollars here, twelve hundred dollars there—with a memo line that read *Buddy fun money.* And there was a canceled check for thirty thousand dollars made out to someone named Lyle Phelan, which also went in the question-mark pile.

Even with all that cash out the door, Buck was puzzled. Deacon took only one dollar in salary from the Board Room in order to keep down operating costs, which were, famously, the most outlandish of any restaurant in the country. But the residuals from Deacon's two TV shows—*Day to Night to Day with Deacon* and *Pitchfork*—should have kept him solvent despite all his expenses.

Then Buck came across the wire transfer, dated January 3. A million dollars from Deacon's brokerage account with

Merrill Lynch to...the Board Room, LLC, the company that owned the restaurant. Buck remembered Deacon telling him at Christmastime that he'd had an investor pull out; it had been Scarlett's uncle, the judge from Savannah. The judge—Buck had met him ten years earlier at the wedding—had gone to the Board Room for dinner, and apparently something had gone awry. Deacon had never told Buck exactly what happened, but the judge had called the very next day, saying he wanted his money back, pronto. And Deacon hadn't argued.

Deacon had seemed panicked about the funding, but the following week he'd called Buck and said he'd found a new investor who shared Deacon's vision. *This guy is all in,* Deacon had said. *Vested.*

The guy, Buck now knew, had been Deacon.

Buck discovered a life insurance policy worth a quarter of a million dollars, with Scarlett and Ellery named as the beneficiaries. That would probably pay the rent on the Hudson Street apartment and the tuition at Ellery's school for a couple more years. But Deacon's beloved Nantucket house was going into foreclosure; the bank would repossess it at the end of the month unless the estate could come up with $436,292.19, the sum total of the amount overdue on the three mortgages, plus the liens. And then, even if someone paid what was owed in arrears, there was still a $14,335 monthly payment to grapple with.

Buck had never seen such a mess!

He had contacted Laurel and Hayes, and Belinda and Angie—and he'd left a detailed message for Scarlett's mother, Prue, to pass along to Scarlett, who refused to take

Buck's calls. They would gather on Nantucket to spread Deacon's ashes in Nantucket Sound, and then it would be Buck's job to inform Deacon's family that unless someone stepped forward to save the house, the halcyon days of their island summers were coming to an end.

PIRATE TAXI
508-555-3965
"Pirate" Oakley
AHOY, MATES!

Deacon's Stupid Word List

1. protégé
2. literally
3. half sister (brother)
4. oxymoron
5. repartee
6. nifty
7. syllabus
8. parched
9. brouhaha
10. doggie bag
11. giddy
12. unique
13.
14.

New York Post, *Saturday, May 7, 2016*

Popular Television Chef Deacon Thorpe Found Dead at Age 53

Nantucket, Massachusetts—Deacon Thorpe, 53, chef-owner of the Board Room, in midtown Manhattan, and host of the popular Food Network program *Pitchfork,* died of a heart attack at his summer cottage Thursday evening, according to Nantucket police chief Edward Kapenash.

Thorpe arrived on Nantucket Island on a Thursday-morning ferry, officials at the Steamship Authority confirmed. He was found by island resident JP Clarke on Friday morning.

"I stopped by to pick him up," Mr. Clarke said. "We had plans to go fishing."

Mr. Clarke said that the front door to the house, named American Paradise, was standing open and that after calling numerous times for Mr. Thorpe, he entered. He found Mr. Thorpe's body slumped over a picnic table on the back deck. Mr. Clarke called 911. The island's medical examiner concluded that Thorpe had died of a heart attack sometime the evening before.

Deacon Thorpe graduated from the Culinary Institute of America in Hyde Park, New York, in 1985. After serving in externships at the Odeon and the Union Square Café in New York City, Thorpe landed the chef de cuisine position at Solo, the landmark restaurant that helped turn the Flatiron District into the dining hotbed it is today. Thorpe worked at Solo from 1986 to 1988. During his tenure, he was offered a half-hour late-night television show on ABC entitled *Day to Night to Day with Deacon,* which is widely considered to be the forebear of reality TV. *Day to Night to Day with Deacon* ran for thirty-six episodes, from 1986 to 1989. In 1989, Thorpe left New York for Los Angeles. In 1990, he became the executive chef of the Raindance restaurant chain, overseeing outposts in Los

Angeles, Chicago, and New York. While at Raindance, Thorpe developed the recipe for his signature clams casino dip. In 2004, it was named recipe of the year by *Gourmet* magazine. In an appearance on *The Late Show with David Letterman,* Thorpe made the dip, and Letterman said, "I literally cannot stop eating this. What's *in* it?" To which Thorpe famously replied, "A teaspoon of crack cocaine." This elicited an angry statement from the Partnership for a Drug-Free America accusing Thorpe of "glamorizing drug use." Thorpe later apologized. In 2005, Thorpe was tapped to host a show on the Food Network entitled *Pitchfork,* and in 2007, the show was nominated for a Daytime Emmy for Outstanding Culinary Program. Also in 2007, Thorpe opened his own restaurant, the Board Room, on the Upper East Side of Manhattan, which was distinguished in *Bon Appétit* as being the most expensive restaurant in America. The nine-course menu changes weekly according to what is fresh and available from the twenty-seven local purveyors hand-selected by Chef Thorpe. Over half the courses are cooked over a hardwood fire—Chef Thorpe preferred using majestic hickory from Nova Scotia, which cost him north of five thousand dollars a week. Other signature touches at the Board Room include six-hundred-dollar cashmere throws available for each diner, and a menu of eighteen handcrafted cocktails created by his mixologist, David Disibio, who holds a doctorate in botany. The prix fixe nine-course dinner costs $525 per person, or $650 per person with cocktail and wine pairings. Frequent diners included George Clooney, Derek Jeter, and Bill Clinton.

Deacon Thorpe was nearly as famous for his life away from the stove as he was for his life behind it. He was married to his high school sweetheart, Laurel Thorpe, from 1982 to 1988. The couple has a son, Hayes Thorpe, 34, who works as the hotels editor at *Fine Travel* magazine. In 1990, Thorpe married Academy Award–winning actress Belinda Rowe; the couple's daughter, Angela Thorpe, 26, worked for Mr. Thorpe at the Board Room in a position unique to the restaurant called the fire chief. After divorcing Rowe in 2005, Thorpe married Scarlett Oliver, causing a tabloid sensation, as Ms. Oliver had for many years served as Chef Thorpe and Ms. Rowe's nanny. The couple has a nine-year-old daughter, Ellery Thorpe.

Mr. Thorpe's agent and longtime friend, John Buckley, issued a statement on Friday afternoon that said, "Everyone who knew Chef Thorpe is shocked and saddened by the news of his death. The country has lost not only a culinary genius but also a cultural icon. The friends and family of Mr. Thorpe ask simply for privacy and respect during their time of mourning."

Clams Casino Dip with Herb-Butter Baguettes (Courtesy of Deacon Thorpe)

SERVES 4 TO 6

8 slices thick-cut bacon, chopped
1 green bell pepper, diced
1 red bell pepper, diced
1 sweet onion, diced
½ teaspoon smoked paprika
¼ teaspoon freshly cracked black pepper

4 garlic cloves, minced
1 cup of minced or chopped clams (fresh or canned and drained work)
2 blocks cream cheese, 8 ounces each, softened and cubed
8 ounces fontina cheese, freshly grated
4 ounces Parmigiano-Reggiano cheese, freshly grated

Preheat the oven to 400°F. Spray a 9-inch round baking dish at least 3 inches deep with nonstick spray.

Heat a large skillet over medium-low heat and add the bacon. Cook until the bacon is completely crispy and the fat is rendered. Remove the bacon with a slotted spoon and place it on a paper-towel-lined plate to drain excess grease.

Keep the skillet with the bacon grease over medium-low heat and add the peppers and onions. Add in the smoked paprika and black pepper. Stir well to coat and cook until the vegetables are soft and golden, about 6 to 8 minutes. Stir in the garlic and the chopped clams and cook for another 2 minutes. Remove the vegetables and clams with a slotted spoon and add them to a large bowl. Add the cream cheese, grated cheeses, and bacon into the bowl. Use a large spatula to mix, and stir until everything is combined, distributing the cream-cheese cubes as you go. Spoon the mixture into the baking dish. Bake for 25 to 30 minutes or until golden and bubbly. Serve immediately with the herb-butter baguettes.

Herb-Butter Baguettes

1 large ciabatta baguette, sliced into ½-inch rounds
4 tablespoons unsalted butter, softened

⅓ cup freshly chopped herbs (I used cilantro, basil, thyme, and oregano)
½ teaspoon flaked sea salt

Preheat the oven to 400°F. Spread the softened butter on the baguettes. Cover the butter with the assorted herbs (use whatever herbs you like!). Bake until the baguettes are warm and golden and toasted, about 10 minutes. Remove from the oven and sprinkle with the flaked salt. Serve immediately.

Friday, June 17

ANGIE

It was her eleventh day back working as fire chief, although she tried not to think in those terms—eleven days back at work, forty-three days since Deacon had died. Instead, Angie tried to think of it as just another Friday night at the Board Room, the busiest night of the week. The world had been shocked silly by her father's death, and so Harv, the general manager—the only one with the stones to make the tough decisions—had closed the restaurant for a month. The front windows had been sheathed in black curtains, which Harv felt was appropriate. People—customers, fans of the shows, random New Yorkers—dropped off bouquets of flowers and hand-lettered signs, poems and stuffed animals, candles and crosses. When Angie saw these offerings, her throat ached. She wanted to cry, but the tears wouldn't come. She was bone-dry.

Angie had thought that the restaurant's popularity might wane or that it would veer off course like a ship without a captain. The Board Room was Deacon's creation and vision—from the wild-strawberry caprese salad, which was sourced from a boutique farm upstate and which he'd put on the menu two days before he died, to the gleaming copper tables and the caviar sets made especially for the restaurant by a descendant of one of the Russian czars, to the limited-edition Robert Graham shirts he liked Dr. Disibio to wear behind the bar. But bizarrely—or maybe not; Angie wasn't a great judge of human behavior—the frenzy for reservations had more than doubled, which hardly seemed feasible. The wait for a table was six weeks already.

Angie was grateful to be busy. Bring on the weeds, ticket after ticket piling up: the pineapple-and-habanero shrimp, the smoked maple-glazed salmon, the "sexy" scorched octopus. The Friday-night pace had just ratcheted up from screaming breakneck to white-hot roller-coaster ride when Joel came up behind Angie and whispered in her ear, "I'm telling her tonight. I'm leaving, baby."

Angie grabbed hot tongs instead of cool ones and burned the bejesus out of her hand. She sucked the webbing between her thumb and index finger. "Can we talk about it later?" she asked.

Tiny, whose job it was to stoke and tend the cooking fire, keeping it at just the right level and heat for Angie at all times said, "Buzz off, Joel. We're in the middle of feeding people here."

He was telling her tonight. He was leaving.

Angie couldn't concentrate on work; her tickets piled up until she was buried and Julio, the expediter, swore at her.

Tiny said to her sotto voce, "Are you okay, Angie? Did Joel say something to upset you?" Tiny was a gentle giant, nearly seven feet tall. He had been the one in charge of taking Angie's emotional temperature since the restaurant reopened.

"I'm fine," Angie whispered.

Joel had said the words Angie had been waiting to hear since they had slept together after the restaurant's Christmas

party, six months earlier. He was going to leave
make his relationship with Angie official. Angie's
kited all over the place, soaring, zooming, catching wind, then dipping suddenly.

The night that Deacon died had been an unseasonably warm Thursday in May, one of those spring days that make people think about the joys of summer—strolling through the park, eating alfresco. Deacon had played hooky from work. He'd told Harv he was going up to Nantucket for a few days to fish and clear his head, which Angie had thought was a good idea. Scarlett had gotten fed up with Deacon's drinking and recreational drug use, and she flew back home to Savannah—for good, she said. She had pulled Ellery out of school and everything. Angie had reassured Deacon: they would be back. Scarlett was prone to tantrums—Angie secretly thought this was because she didn't consume enough calories to inspire reason—and besides, she had taken only two suitcases. That wouldn't last her more than two weeks, and it had already been ten days. Deacon had said, *I messed up again, Buddy...marriage number three, and I torched it. It's all my fault. Everyone leaving has always been my fault.*

Angie had nearly said that marriage the institution seemed to have been invented in order to trip Deacon up, but she refrained. He was extremely upset, which Angie, frankly, found strange. His marriage to Scarlett wasn't much more than a pretty shell. Every Tuesday night, when the restaurant was closed, Deacon had dinner with Angie because Scarlett went to bed at eight o'clock, and she didn't eat anything, anyway. But when you didn't want to spend your one night off with your wife? Well, that pretty much spoke for itself.

*

…oel had driven Angie home from …heir routine. They'd had a drink after …t of the staff, as usual, and then, as usual, Jo… …ye first, and Angie followed five or six minutes … …eeting Joel on the corner of Sixtieth Street and Madiso…, where she climbed into his Lexus and they headed uptown to Angie's apartment. They made love quickly and then, after Angie poured them each a cognac, once again more slowly.

When Joel had risen to leave on that Thursday, Angie had clung to him and begged him to stay.

"Hey now," Joel had said. "You know I can't."

Joel lived in New Canaan, a place that Angie had never seen but that she imagined as hill and dale, a place where bunny rabbits nibbled the emerald grass in front of a white clapboard house with black shutters. She suspected that everyone in New Canaan was white. If Angie ever showed up at Joel's house on Rosebrook Road—and she fantasized about this all the time—the neighbors would think she was there to clean, or to clean them out.

"Please?" Angie said. She wasn't sure where the desperation was coming from. For twenty-six years, Angie had lived as an emotionally carefree, blissfully independent soul. She had worked in kitchens with men since she was eighteen and had slept with a few, but no one who mattered after ten o'clock the next morning. Angie had fallen in love with Joel Tersigni the instant Deacon hired him, two years earlier. Joel was handsome in a way that seemed custom tailored to Angie's tastes—the dark hair, the goatee, the sly smile, a voice with a smoky, seductive edge. He had a commanding, charismatic presence. He knew exactly what to say to each person who walked in the door, whether it was Kim and Kanye or a school janitor from Wichita, Kansas, about to spend his life savings on dinner.

And after seven or eight cups of Dr. Disibio's double-dare dragon punch at their Mandarin-themed holiday soiree, Joel had led Angie by the hand into the dry pantry and charmed the pants right off her.

More than four months had passed. They had their "things" now: inside jokes, catchphrases, gestures. Every Saturday, Angie paid a Jamaican woman from the prep kitchen fifty bucks to do her cornrows, and every Thursday, Angie took them out and gathered her hair in a frizzed ponytail. Joel loved the ponytail. She was exotic to him, she knew, being half-black. Joel had grown up in Pigeon Forge, Tennessee; his parents had operated something called the Biblical Dinner Theater. Joel had escaped to Manhattan, which his parents thought of as a city of sinners.

"I have to go, Ange," Joel said. She loved the way he said her name, she loved that he called her Ange. The only other person who called her Ange, was her brother, Hayes. Angie gave Joel a long, luscious kiss that made him groan but would not, she knew, make him stay.

After she closed the door behind him, she'd thought, *I would give anything to make him mine.*

Buck had called the very next morning.

Your father...? Buck had said. *Deacon...your dad...*

Angie said, *Yeah, what's up?*

He went to Nantucket..., Buck said.

I know, Angie said. *Harv told me. He went to fish.* She had thought briefly of fresh striped-bass fillets marinated in a little olive oil and chili powder, thrown onto the hickory fire until just opaque, and then drizzled with lemon juice. Sheer perfection.

Angie, Buck said. *He had a heart attack. He's dead.*

Angie hung up without a word, as though Buck were a crank caller.

Her eleventh night ended without fanfare. Or maybe there had been fanfare and Angie hadn't noticed. The bandanna she had tied around her head felt like a crown of fire, her feet had turned to bricks in her clogs, and her stomach felt like a ball of rubber bands. She flung a salmon fillet onto the fire but was too distracted to savor the hiss, or the cloud of sweet maple smoke.

Joel was leaving. But maybe she had misheard him or misinterpreted the meaning of "leaving"?

"Are you okay?" Tiny asked.

"I'm fine," Angie whispered.

Joel seemed edgy in the car, overhyped—he was probably coked up. He sometimes partook with Julio, the expediter, in the dry pantry, she knew, even though Harv had instituted a new, zero-tolerance drugs rule upon reopening. *We're going to clean things up around here,* he said. But, as Angie knew only too well, people were going to do what they were going to do.

Joel said, "I'm telling her as soon as I walk in the door. I'm finished, we're through, I want a divorce."

"Yes," Angie said. "Okay." She tried not to think of the

phrase "home wrecker." Joel was miserable with his wife, Dory, who worked as a mergers-and-acquisitions attorney a few blocks south of the restaurant, a career that paid for everything, as Dory reminded Joel on a daily basis. Joel was ten years younger than Dory, and he had adopted her twin sons, Bodie and Dylan, who were now teenagers who played lacrosse on the manicured fields of New Canaan High School.

"We haven't had sex in three months," Joel said. "She's never home. We have no quality of life."

Three months? Angie thought. So...Joel and Dory had gone at it in bed, even after things had started between him and Angie? Angie touched the tender blister that had formed on her hand. Joel probably felt okay telling her now because it was accompanied by the news of his imminent departure.

"Why tonight?" Angie asked. "Did something happen?"

"She's been acting funny," Joel said. "Like she might already know. I want to leave before I get caught. There is a difference, you know."

"I know," Angie said. For the past four months, she had lived in mortal fear of getting caught, not only by Dory, but also by Deacon. Deacon would not have approved of Angie dating Joel, and that was the understatement of the year. Deacon would have gone profane Dr. Seuss—*Apeshit batshit catshit bullshit*—if he'd found out that Joel and his daughter were sleeping together. His first objection would have been that Joel was married. His second objection would have been that Joel worked at the restaurant, and if things went belly-up, it would be awkward for everyone. There would probably have been a third objection, that Joel wasn't good enough, somehow. He was too old (at forty, fourteen years older than Angie)—and, Deacon might have argued, Joel was also a morally bankrupt snake charmer who had taken advantage not only of Angie's youth but also of her naïveté in the ways of love. Deacon knew Joel too well; they had gotten drunk together too many times and revealed too many flaws. If Deacon *had* found out, he might have tried to punish Angie somehow—stopped writing her slush checks or, worse, taken her off the fire. Those worries were gone now, of course; they had been replaced by the red, raw sadness at his absence.

"Besides," Joel said, "I want to take care of you."

Joel wanted to "take care" of her—the words were like a narcotic. And just as he said this, their song came on: "Colder Weather," by the Zac Brown Band. Angie had been endeavoring to keep one foot on the ground when it came to Joel. Men never actually left their wives; that was an urban myth. But with that one simple line—*I want to take care of you*—Joel Tersigni had executed a Karate Kid–like move and swept her leg. She fell. There was, she feared, no way back.

There were no parking spots on Seventy-Third Street.

"Should I drive around?" Joel asked. "And come up?"

Instinctively, Angie shook her head. She was leaving the next day for Nantucket. The whole family was gathering. They were going to spread Deacon's ashes. Angie was going to spend three days under the same roof as her mother for the first time in a very, very long time. It was too much, all of a sudden.

"Should I forget about leaving her?" Joel asked. "Do you not love me?"

"Of course I love you," Angie said quickly. She told Joel this all the time; she told him way too often. Belinda would have advised her to create some doubt, cultivate some mystery. But Angie operated without guile. She had waited a long time to find a friend of her heart, someone she could tell everything. "But it's late, and I'm beat."

"Sleep in tomorrow," Joel said.

He never really listened unless she was saying exactly what he wanted to hear.

"I have to pack," she said.

He gave her a blank look.

"I'm going to Nantucket?" she said. "Remember? I'll be back Tuesday."

"That's even more reason why I should come up," he said. "How am I going to last four days without your body?"

She wished he had said "you" instead of "your body." But then she remembered back six weeks ago: As soon as Joel had learned that Deacon was dead, he drove into the city to see Angie. He had held her, absorbed her shaking; he had brought her a cognac; he had drawn her a bath and sat on the bathroom floor, holding her hand. He had answered her phone and the knocks of her concerned (nosy) neighbors, telling everyone kindly yet firmly that Angie wasn't ready to see anyone. He had stood by as she snapped her precious collection of wooden spoons in half—some of them more than a hundred years old—until they lay on her kitchen floor like so much kindling, and then he swept the pieces up with a broom and dustpan. He went down to the corner store for cigarettes and then somehow managed to open the giant window that had been stuck since Angie moved in so that she could smoke without leaving the apartment. He watched her pull apart the loops of her whisk until it looked like some awful, postmodern flower. He didn't tell her she was acting crazy, he didn't tell her she should quit smoking, he didn't ask why she wasn't crying. Joel Tersigni had done everything right, every single thing, except he still went home to Dory each night. But now, that would end. He was leaving.

"Drive around," Angie said. "I'll wait for you upstairs."

LAUREL

She had a long list of tasks to tackle before she flew to Nantucket in the morning, and yet she found herself distracted by the blushing-pink envelope sitting on top of her in-box. It was a birthday card from Deacon that had arrived promptly on May 2; despite the many ways he'd failed her, he always remembered her birthday. Laurel had been too busy to open it on May 2 or the days following, and then on May 6, Deacon was dead, and Laurel was afraid to open it because when she did, it would be the last time she heard from him, and she wasn't ready for that.

She tore her eyes from the envelope; she would open it later today, she decided. Tomorrow, she was traveling back in time. She hadn't been to Nantucket since she and Deacon had split so many years ago.

Across from Laurel sat a woman named Ursula, who had three school-aged grandchildren. Ursula and the kids were homeless and waiting for Laurel to find them a placement. Ursula's daughter, Suzanne, the children's mother, was a drug addict who had robbed Ursula of all her worldly goods and then forged her rent checks, getting them evicted from the Silverhead projects, which was virtually impossible.

Ursula picked up the framed photograph on Laurel's desk.

"This your boyfriend?" Ursula asked.

The first time a client had asked Laurel this, she'd blanched, but it happened so often now that Laurel had grown used to it.

"My son, actually," Laurel said. The photo was of her and Hayes on the floor of the Knicks game, a slice of Carmelo Anthony's jersey and powerful arm visible in the frame.

"Your son?" Ursula said. "He look old enough to be *with* you. I thought maybe you was one of them cougars."

"No," Laurel said. She was allergic to that term.

"You got a husband?" Ursula asked.

Laurel stared at her computer screen. There was a hotel on 162nd Street where she could put Ursula and the kids for three nights. That would have to do, and it would be better than a shelter.

"Not presently," Laurel said.

"But you were married?" Ursula asked.

"A long time ago," Laurel said. She smiled at Ursula in a way that, she hoped, put the topic to bed.

"But you divorced now?" Ursula asked.

"Yes. Divorced." She didn't dare mention that her ex-husband was none other than Chef Deacon Thorpe. One thing about Laurel's clients: they watched a lot of TV. Ursula might have been a devoted Deacon fan, one of millions who had sobbed upon hearing the shocking news of his death.

"Your husband cheat on you?" Ursula asked.

Laurel said, "I can put you in a unit at the Bronx Arms Hotel until Saturday, two double beds and a cot. How does that sound?"

"You don't have to be embarrassed," Ursula said. "All men cheat. That what they do."

Laurel had five other families to place before the end of the day, but the unfortunate conversation with Ursula kept Laurel preoccupied.

All men cheat. That what they do.

Laurel ordered herself to *stop thinking* about Deacon. This had happened nearly every day for the past six weeks:

he took up residence in her mind and refused to leave, like a squatter.

She opened the birthday card. It was Snoopy dancing with his nose in the air, and a message that said, *Someone Special Is Having a Birthday!* On the inside of the card, in his nearly illegible scrawl, the card was signed, *Forever love, D.*

Forever love: high school, Hayes, culinary school, the first TV show, divorce. Most people would stop there, Laurel realized, but her relationship with Deacon, no matter how bad it got—and it had gotten really bad those first few years with Belinda—had always been set on a foundation of unconditional love, laid at a tender age. Her love had been a staple for him, like flour or salt in his pantry. When he moved back to New York and Belinda was away on location, Laurel occasionally met Deacon at Raindance for a drink. Those nights had always ended chastely, but Laurel loved that Deacon kept them hidden from Belinda. And then, years later, when Deacon and Belinda had the big fight and Belinda stormed off to Los Angeles in anger, who had Deacon called?

Laurel.

She and Deacon had spent five days together in the Virgin Islands. This was a secret Laurel guarded with her life. Nobody knew—not Buck, not Hayes, nobody. Laurel pictured the secret as an obsidian marble, dense and black, nestled in a remote pocket of her brain. Every once in a while, it slipped out and rolled around, and Laurel would remember the sun in St. John, the sailing, the sex.

Later still, once Deacon was married to Scarlett and the father of a baby again, he and Laurel had settled into that place where all divorced couples would like to eventually end up—a place of peace and, yes, love, and appreciation for each other, and gratitude for the past they'd shared, and respect for the things they'd learned and the ways they'd grown side by side. Laurel had always had a bit of the Pollyanna in her, she supposed, which made coming to a place of true forgiveness with Deacon easier. In the past ten years, Laurel and Deacon had talked once a week, they had seen each other on holidays with Hayes, they had served as each other's emotional backstop. When Laurel had ended her last relationship—with Michael Beale, a public defender she'd met through work—she had called Deacon to vent. And, only a couple weeks before he died, Deacon had called Laurel and told her the whole sordid story about the stripper and the Saab and leaving Ellery at school until it was so late that the headmistress was forced to contact Buck.

Deacon had told Laurel then that he would stop drinking. Laurel told him that his best bet was a program—she had seen it with clients too many times to count—and that there were fifteen daily AA meetings within a four-block radius of his apartment on Hudson Street. *You just walk in,* Laurel said. *I'll go with you.*

Nah, Deacon had said. *I'm going to lone-wolf it.*

That won't work, Laurel had thought but not said out loud. She had learned that coercion didn't work with addicts. Deacon would go when he was ready; he would go when he'd hit rock bottom.

When Buck called to say Deacon had died of a heart attack, she had immediately thought: *Cocaine.* But the tox report came back squeaky clean. Deacon had apparently been on the back deck of American Paradise, smoking a cigarette, drinking a Diet Coke, and watching the sun go down, when his heart quit.

She read the card again: *Forever love, D.* And then, although she really didn't have time, Laurel dropped her face into her hands, and she cried.

HAYES

Sula's brothers wanted to take him spear fishing; the Australians wanted him to surf the left break on the far side of the reef. Hayes wanted to lie in the yellow sand with Sula and shoot up. The dope was plentiful on Nusa Lembongan; there was a drug lord on the other side of the island who intercepted shipments from Lombok to Java and skimmed off the top. The drug lord wanted American dollars; Hayes wanted to stay high for the rest of his natural life.

His father had been dead for a month and a half. He'd had a massive coronary, a phrase Hayes found chilling. The death had been sudden, unexpected, violent.

Hayes's mother was destroyed; his sister Angie had been rendered bloodless, limbless, blind, deaf, and dumb; and Buck had called insisting he needed to talk to everyone "as a family" about "Deacon's affairs." At first, Hayes had thought Buck was referring to Deacon's actual affairs, which seemed indiscreet, but then Hayes decided he meant the will, money, and stuff, which might have been a beacon of hope except for the ominous tone of Buck's voice. Scarlett was still in Savannah, apparently—at least, that was what Hayes *thought* Buck had said. The reception had been poor.

The upshot was that Hayes was flying out tomorrow. He

would land in New York after a twenty-hour journey and drive Angie up to Nantucket.

He didn't want to go.

And so, he would ignore it for now.

Hayes and Sula lounged in her bedroom, one of six teak buildings in the family compound. In the room was a mattress on the floor sheathed in a white silk sheet that was rapidly growing grubby with their sweat, and a Buddhist shrine in the corner. The room smelled like dying flowers and rotting fruit.

Sula's family—her father and her three older brothers—was the second-wealthiest family in Nusa Lembongan, after the drug lord. Sula had been to university in Australia and spoke perfect Aussie-accented English, which charmed Hayes. She had suede-brown skin and syrupy brown eyes, and she shot Hayes between the toes with the sweetest dope he had ever known short of the pure opium he had smoked in the Jiangxi Province of China. The old Chinese man who had offered Hayes the opium pipe had done so with a few words of warning (Hayes had been unable to understand the dialect, but he could tell from the man's inflection that it was a warning). Probably: *Once you try this, you will be its slave.*

Slave.

Addict.

Dope fiend.

Deacon's death should have been Hayes's wake-up call. *Get clean! Take care of yourself!* We are given only one body per lifetime, and Hayes was systematically poisoning his. He should be eating more green vegetables, practicing vinyasa yoga; he should quit all controlled substances and limit his alcohol intake to a glass of red wine on Saturday nights. After all, Hayes had a life that most people would murder for. He traveled the globe reporting on the world's finest hotels. He had arrived at the Six Senses in Oman via hang glider; he'd taken high tea at the Mount Nelson in Cape Town at a table next to Nelson Mandela; he had breakfasted on fried rice and fresh watermelon juice on the banks of the Chao Phraya River at the Mandarin Oriental in Bangkok. He'd written features about the Palácio Belmonte in Lisbon, the Gritti Palace in Venice, La Mamounia in Marrakech, Hotel D'Angleterre in Copenhagen. Hayes could one-up just about anyone anywhere. That should have been a high in and of itself.

He had to be so, so careful. If he was careful, he'd be okay. This was the rationalization of an addict. Hayes recognized this even as he used the words to reassure himself.

He was functioning, or sort of. He could go six or seven hours without, until the itching started. He had scratched himself so fiercely on the left shoulder blade that he broke the skin. All of the bespoke shirts that Hayes had tailored in London were now speckled with blood.

Sula rose from the bed. She went to the kitchen to prepare the fish that her brothers had speared; she would serve it with *satay* sauce for dinner. Hayes wrapped a batik sarong around his waist and ventured outside to smoke a hand-rolled cigarette. (He should, absolutely, quit smoking. He and Angie agreed on that.) Hayes watched the Australian surfers loping down the shore toward him, their wet suits hanging off their torsos like shed skin. They looked exhilarated as they checked their GoPros.

"Hey, mate!" one of the surfers, a kid named Macka, called up to Hayes. "Epic day, man. You should have joined us."

Hayes felt a pang of regret. He should have gone out today. Or he should have fished with Wayan and Ketut so that he could have claimed a contribution to dinner; the smell of ginger and sesame oil from the kitchen where Sula was cooking was *insane.*

But Hayes had preferred to float along the cloud ridge and gaze down on the world from above—the green water, the swaying palm trees, the ghost crabs scuttling across the sand.

High.

Higher.

Sula served Hayes, her brothers, her father, and the Aussies at a communal table in the courtyard, where they could enjoy the reflecting pond and the fountains. Sula's father was so wealthy that he hired a three-man gamelan band to play each night at dinner. The band sat atop silk pillows on a raised platform in a corner of the courtyard; sounds of the flute and marimba floated through the air.

The fish was steamed in banana leaves, then smothered in peanut sauce and served over jasmine rice. Heroin eradicated hunger except for that of more heroin, but even Hayes found himself gorging on this meal. The fish was moist, the peanut sauce hot and pungent.

Richard, sidekick of Macka, said to Hayes, "So you leave us tomorrow, then, mate?" He cast a hungry, sidelong glance at Sula as she set out dessert—a platter of fresh papaya, mango, rambutans, watermelon, and baby bananas.

Hayes could see what would happen. He would leave, Richard would move in on Sula. It was disturbing enough to make Hayes reconsider his plans. He could come up with any number of legitimate-sounding excuses: impassable swells made it impossible for Hayes to catch a longboat back to mainland Bali; there was political unrest in Jakarta aimed at American journalists; he had made a booking mistake with his flight from Singapore to Heathrow (he should have had his assistant, Mallory, double-check), but now he couldn't make it back to the States in time for the weekend on Nantucket. He was sorry to miss it. He would catch up with everyone later in the summer.

They would simply have to understand. Hayes was at the mercy of unpredictable circumstances.

Scarlett wasn't going, and she was Deacon's *wife.*

But could Hayes miss Nantucket? Really?

He thought about his father. Deacon hadn't been perfect. He had left Hayes and Hayes's mother for a flashier life with Belinda in Hollywood, but as Hayes grew older, Deacon had become more comfortable as a father, more available—both emotionally and financially.

A year or so earlier, when Hayes's using became a serious issue—every spare dollar Hayes made went to his dealer, Kermit—he had fallen behind on the payments of his loft in Soho. The loft had been a stretch as it was, and with so much of his discretionary income going to his habit, Hayes had to approach Deacon for help. Four thousand dollars a month. Deacon had written the checks without blinking an eye or making Hayes feel bad about it. Deacon had said, "You're an up-and-coming tastemaker, man. We can't have you living in an efficiency in Hell's Kitchen." Then he'd said, "I'm always here for you, whatever you need. Only when you're a father yourself will you realize how good it feels to help out your children."

Deacon's own father had left when Deacon was thirteen and had never returned.

My parents didn't want me, Deacon used to tell Hayes. *It was like they were waiting for me to get old enough to take care of myself so they could move on.*

And then often—always, if Deacon was drinking—he would take Hayes's face in his hands and say, *But I want you. Always remember that. You're my son and I love you and I am so, so proud of everything you do.*

Deacon had said this the last time Hayes had seen him—at Easter dinner at the restaurant. When they all said good-bye out on Madison Avenue in the chilly spring nighttime air, Deacon had grabbed his thirty-four-year-old son's face and said, *I love you, Hayes, and I am so, so proud of everything you do.* He had kissed Hayes on the forehead, which had always been his thing—as a teenager, Hayes had found it embarrassing, but now, well, what Hayes wouldn't give to feel his father's embrace, his father's lips alighting on his brow.

"Yes," Hayes said to Richard. "I leave tomorrow." And with that, Hayes stood up from the table and strode across the courtyard. Sula bowed to her father, her brothers, and the Australians, and then she followed him.

BELINDA

Her phone didn't ring until seven thirty, which in L.A. constituted sleeping in. When the East Coast got up and moving, the West Coast had to follow suit or be left behind.

Belinda rolled over to check the display. It was her husband, Bob. It was ten thirty in Kentucky and a Friday, which was when Bob did speed work with the yearlings. If he was calling now, then something was wrong. Belinda wasn't sure she could handle any more bad news. Had something happened to one of the girls? Had Beetle, the skittish Appaloosa, gotten spooked by the farm tractor again and thrown Laura to the ground or dragged her, foot caught in the stirrup, around the ring? Had Mary sustained a kick to the head?

The news about Deacon six weeks earlier had come as

such a calamitous shock that even now, Belinda could barely think about anything else. She obsessed about horrible, random acts of God befalling the other people in her life that she loved.

Her phone continued to quack like a duck. Maybe Bob was calling to say he was leaving her for Stella.

Or maybe he was just calling to tell Belinda he loved her, he missed her, he couldn't live without her.

Belinda answered, but she had waited too long; the quacking ended. Before she could decide what to do, Bob called back. This was very bad, Belinda decided. Bob Percil was the most sought-after Thoroughbred trainer in the world; he didn't waste time pursuing anyone.

"Hello?" Belinda said, trying to keep the anxiety out of her voice. She willed herself not to revisit the phone call of six weeks earlier, but it intruded anyway: John Buckley calling to say Deacon had had a heart attack. When Belinda had said, *What do you mean, he had a heart attack?* Buck had said, *Deacon is dead, Belinda.* And then Buck had broken down crying, but Belinda still hadn't quite been able to process what he'd told her. It was too ghastly.

To Bob, Belinda said, "Darling, how are you?"

"Did I wake you?" Bob's voice had an accusatory edge, she thought, or maybe she was just being sensitive. Bob rose at four o'clock every morning; that was how he was wired. If Belinda had thought that marrying her, a famous actress, would change him, she was wrong. And yet his refusal to compromise his way of life was one of the things she loved most about him. Bob didn't kowtow. He loved her, but he wasn't impressed with anything as ephemeral as fame.

"No," Belinda said, though her froggy voice probably gave him a clear picture of her still sprawled across her king-size bed in her suite at the Beverly Wilshire, and possibly also suggested that she'd been out drinking and smoking with Naomi Watts the night before. "Is something the matter, sweetheart?"

"I just had a chat with Joan," Bob said. Joan was Mrs. Greene, their housekeeper and nanny, a woman cut from strict schoolmarm cloth. She looked a little like Betty Crocker, but with slender, steel-framed spectacles. Belinda knew that Mrs. Greene's first name was Joan, but, unlike Bob, she had never been invited to call Mrs. Greene by her first name.

"Did you?" Belinda said. She felt as if the bed were tilting. Mrs. Greene was Belinda's harshest critic. She constantly judged Belinda's parenting and constantly found it lacking.

"I did," Bob said. "She informed me you're going to Nantucket this weekend? I told her she must be mistaken, but she insisted."

"She's correct," Belinda said. "It's the memorial I told you about? The family is going to spread Deacon's ashes. I told you this, Bob."

"I thought you were in L.A., working," Bob said.

"That's where I am now," Belinda said. "I leave for the East Coast tonight."

Silence from Bob, then an exhale. She imagined him accepting this news, cigar clenched between his teeth. In the background, Belinda heard the horses on the track. She pictured Bob checking out Stella's ass, raised pertly over Skyrocket's back. Seven years earlier, Belinda had demanded that Bob fire Carrie, at which point he had hired Jules. When Belinda ordered Bob to fire Jules, he hired Stella, who was by far the most alluring of the three, with her South African accent, those big, green eyes, and that ass.

"What about the girls?" Bob said. "Today is the last day of school."

Belinda was, frankly, astonished that Bob knew this. The girls, Mary and Laura, and the details of their schedules, were Belinda's domain.

"They'll have to stay put," Belinda said. "I mean, I can't bring them."

"Why not?" Bob said. "They're not 'family'?"

Belinda couldn't believe he was picking a fight with her. Deacon was *dead*.

"Not that family," Belinda said archly. She had played a number of coldhearted bitches in her day, starting with Lady Macbeth in tenth grade and then again twenty years later, on the big screen. And she had been nominated for the remake of *Cleopatra*.

"Who's going to be there?" Bob asked. If Belinda wasn't mistaken, Bob sounded jealous. Was that possible?

"Well, Angie, I guess, and Hayes and Laurel," Belinda said.

"Laurel hates you."

"I realize this, Bob." Frankly, Belinda had been shocked when Buck invited her to the memorial weekend. Her first question had been, *Will Laurel be there? Yes,* Buck had said. Her second question had been, *Does Laurel know I'm coming? Yes,* Buck said. *And she's okay with that?* Belinda asked. To which Buck responded, *Laurel is an adult, Belinda.* That wasn't really an answer to Belinda's question, although Belinda had accepted it as such at the time. Maybe Laurel's feelings for Belinda—anger, resentment, dark, stinking hatred—had vanished when Deacon died.

What did the past matter now?

Belinda thought back to the first time she had ever met Laurel. Belinda had gone with Deacon to return Hayes, who had been seven years old, to Laurel's apartment on West 119th Street. It was late autumn and growing dark at four thirty on a Sunday afternoon; Deacon and Belinda were flying to Los

Angeles the next day. Deacon seemed to be having mixed feelings about leaving—happy to be starting a new life with Belinda, inconsolable about leaving his son. He didn't think it was a good idea for Belinda to come up to the apartment, but Belinda insisted. She said, *If I'm going to be in your life, I have to meet her.* She had also been banking on her fame to save her. Laurel would naturally hate her, but Belinda thought she might also be a little star struck. Most people were.

Laurel had opened the door to the apartment, and Hayes rushed into his mother's arms. Laurel had eyed Belinda over Hayes's shoulder. "Don't come in here," she said.

"I'm Belinda," Belinda had said. "Belinda Rowe." She had offered her hand.

"You're a thief," Laurel had said, staring at Belinda's hand as if it were a slimy newt. "A shameless thief." Laurel had then looked at Deacon. "Don't you come in, either. You two go. Please, just go."

"Laurel...," Deacon had said. His voice, Belinda remembered, had been full of tears and contrition and something else. It had been full of love, Belinda realized now. But at the time, thankfully, she hadn't recognized this. She had taken Deacon's arm and led him to the elevator. When they were safely down on the street, Belinda had said, "She's just angry. She'll get over it."

Belinda didn't see Laurel again until Hayes's high school graduation. Laurel had refused to speak to Belinda; she wouldn't even say hello. It had been an afternoon filled with toxic looks, and Belinda had been intimidated—not because she feared Laurel, but because she knew Laurel had every right to hate her. Belinda had skipped the party at Laurel's apartment afterward; she had gone around the corner to get her nails done while Deacon made an appearance.

Things were marginally better when Hayes graduated from Vanderbilt. There was at least an icy hello, and Laurel had agreed to sit at dinner at Margot Café with Belinda, albeit at a long table crowded with Hayes's college pals and Deacon and Angie. Laurel had sat at one end and Belinda at the other end, facing the same direction, so no conversation was required. But after dinner, as everyone was getting ready to leave, Belinda had bumped into Laurel in the ladies' room, and they had locked eyes in the mirror. Belinda had consumed enough wine that her fear had mellowed. She was ready to clear the air, finally! Laurel had held Belinda's gaze for a long moment before giving a tiny smile, which seemed to be an acknowledgment that she was ready to forgive. But no words came forth. Laurel washed her hands, snapped a paper towel out of the dispenser, and left.

"I don't understand why you would willingly enter a combat zone," Bob said. "I thought you were all about peace, love, and yoga."

"I am," Belinda said. "But there are extenuating circumstances. Deacon is *dead*, Bob."

"Have you talked to Angie?" Bob asked.

"Not since she's gone back to work," Belinda said. Belinda had called Angie every day for the past six weeks, but Angie often banished Belinda to voice mail, like a queen sending an infidel to the dungeon—which, when Belinda thought about it, meant things were returning to normal. Belinda's relationship with Angie had been strained ever since Belinda married Bob and discovered she was able to have children after all. *Clearly I'm not enough,* Angie had said. *Clearly you wanted your own children, white children.* Belinda had pointed out that Deacon had had another child as well, but that fell on deaf ears. Angie loved her father blindly.

"Just be careful," Bob said. "They're probably going to ask you for something. Money, or a favor. Or both."

"Why do you have to be such a cynic?" Belinda said. "Isn't it possible someone would want me around just for the joy of my company? Not everyone wants something from me, Bob."

"If you feel you have to go—and obviously you do—then I advise you to say your good-byes and cut ties with those people and with that place once and for all. I mean, come on, Belinda—you don't even swim."

"I'll find other things to do," Belinda said. "Like I did in the past."

"Ah, the past," Bob said. "That's what this weekend is really about, isn't it? Reliving the past. Going back to the house you shared with Deacon."

Definitely jealous, Belinda thought. She couldn't believe it. She felt a surge of something like triumph. In the ten years of their marriage, it was always Belinda who had been the jealous one—ever since she had first caught Bob in the tack room with Carrie. It was refreshing to see the tables turned.

"I'll be back next week," Belinda said, trying to sound like the most influential woman in all of antiquity. "Mrs. Greene can handle the girls."

"Whatever," Bob said. And he hung up.

Belinda took the red-eye to Boston first class, on United. She put on her Dodgers cap and her Tom Ford sunglasses, although it was impossible to disguise her strawberry-blond mane and her milky skin. When she took her seat, the flight attendant gave her a sad smile and squeezed her forearm.

"I'm sorry for your loss," the flight attendant whispered. "We all cried when we heard the news."

My *loss?* Belinda thought. Was it possible that this flight attendant hadn't read *People* magazine in ten years? Everyone in America knew that Deacon had divorced Belinda and married their nanny, Scarlett Oliver.

The two of them had carried on all through the final years of Belinda and Deacon's marriage. He had taken her on a trip to the Virgin Islands while he and Belinda were still married! Belinda shuddered when she thought of all the times Deacon and Scarlett had traveled together under the auspices of "visiting Belinda on location."

Belinda's next question to Buck had been, *Will Scarlett be coming to Nantucket?* Laurel was one thing...but Scarlett was completely another. Belinda could *not* spend one second in the same house as Scarlett.

No, Buck had said. *She refused my invitation. She's staying in Savannah.*

Of course she is, Belinda thought. Scarlett would be holed up in the decaying family manse with Mummy and a quartet of her fellow debutantes, who would provide Scarlett with freshly pressed handkerchiefs. And the old boyfriend would be there—what was his name? Belinda couldn't remember. She had tried to banish everything she had once known about Scarlett from her mind. Scarlett was a genteel Southern girl through and through, although she'd lost all her wide-eyed innocence. No one who fell in love with Deacon Thorpe remained innocent for long.

* * *

At Logan, Belinda transferred to a Cape Air flight, a nine-seater Cessna with dual props. In the fifteen years she had gone to Nantucket, this was always her least favorite part of the trip. How many times had she accused Deacon of wanting her dead? Belinda was terrified of small planes, despite growing up around them. Her grandfather had been a barnstormer outside Iowa City, and her father had delivered the air mail for all of eastern Iowa; he had met his fiery death one frigid January night—ice on the wings. The only reason Belinda had ever agreed to fly was that she couldn't abide arriving by boat. Belinda was more terrified of the water than she was of fire and earth.

Bob didn't understand why she was choosing to spend a weekend in Nantucket (with *those* people, in *that* place) when she was afraid of the water. She might have replied that in her first adult relationship, with director James Brinegar, she had traveled to Aspen, Jackson Hole, Sun Valley, Telluride, Whistler, Vail, Breckenridge, Alta, Snowbird, and Tahoe, all so that Jaime could ski higher and more challenging mountains. She, Belinda, had sat in the lodge, dressed in snug snow pants, a Fair Isle sweater, and fur-lined boots, drinking hot toddies and reading in front of the fire, *looking the part*. She also might have replied that for the past ten years, she had lived on a horse farm without ever once mounting up for a ride. Belinda had been brought up without any skills except the ability to pretend that she had skills. She was an actress!

Belinda boarded the plane with eight other souls, none of whom seemed concerned in the slightest about catching wind shear and crashing. Belinda buckled herself in and listened to the (female) pilot's spiel about emergency exits and what to do in the event of a water landing.

In the event of a water landing, Belinda would drown. She had never learned to swim.

Never learned to swim, Deacon said so many years ago, as though she had said she had never learned to play the zither.

She had shrugged. *I grew up in the heartland.*

Planes don't crash anymore, Belinda thought. Unless they were hijacked or tampered with by terrorists. Belinda looked around. She saw a man in Nantucket Red shorts, a blue and white striped oxford, and loafers; a severe-looking blond in naughty-librarian glasses; a couple in their eighties whose skin was as brown and wrinkled as tobacco. Everyone seemed appropriately Waspy and East Coast. They could probably all tie ten nautical knots and make a mean gin and tonic. No terrorists here.

Belinda dry-mouthed an Ativan, plucked discreetly from her bag. None of the other passengers had overtly seemed to recognize her, but she figured at least half did and were simply too well bred to gawk. But if, say, Naughty Librarian had seen Belinda take the Ativan, she might very well find herself outed on the front page of the *National Enquirer* as a pill popper.

Belinda took some comfort in the fact that the pilot was a woman. She imagined it was Mrs. Greene flying the plane. Mrs. Greene was far too competent a human being to ever let it crash.

The engine revved. The plane careered forward, gaining speed, gaining speed, and then...they took off.

Saturday, June 18

ANGIE

She had kept her phone on all night expecting to hear from Joel—he had said he was going to tell Dory the second he walked in the door—but he hadn't called. He might have punted, she thought, and simply gone to bed, then decided to tell Dory when they woke up. But by ten thirty, when she hadn't heard a word—not one call, not one text—she went down to the corner deli for cigarettes. The city streets were a cauldron. Summer had arrived like a panting dog.

What was happening in New Canaan?

Angie stared at her phone, willing it to ring. She *hated* feeling so powerless. She imagined Joel and Dory screaming at each other, she imagined Dory vomiting in the hatbox toilet of their master bedroom (Joel had confided that Dory had an eating disorder, which was why she was such a stick figure). She imagined Dory demanding to know the *real* reason why Joel was leaving her. Would Angie's name be mentioned? Would Dory call Belinda? No, not Belinda. Belinda was too famous to bother, even over a question of the egregious behavior of her daughter.

Angie couldn't call Joel; she couldn't text Joel. He said Dory had been acting "funny," as though maybe she already knew. What if she did already know? What if Joel had tried to leave and Dory had begged him to stay? What if she had apologized for being distant, for being preoccupied with work, for placing him below the family dog in order of importance? What if Dory wanted to start over? Once the boys left for camp, she and Joel could take a vacation, just the two of them—to Yellowstone, to Bar Harbor. Joel and Dory would start seeing a therapist; they would patch things up. Joel would have to forsake Angie. Joel and Dory would start going to church regularly—St. Mark's Episcopal—and Joel would volunteer to serve as a reader. He would stand in the pulpit, erect and righteous.

Angie finally succumbed to her hunger and walked down the block to the Burmese place to get some *momos*. She sat down at one of the sticky tables, inhaled two orders, then felt sick. She hated acting like such a *girl.*

Her head was alternately aswirl—Joel, Deacon, Dory, Belinda, Deacon, Deacon, Deacon—and empty. She had too many thoughts; she had no thoughts at all. She felt herself about to fall into a big pool of Feeling Sorry for Herself. Her father was dead.

She had a few daddy's-little-girl memories: Deacon holding her hand as they crossed Broadway to get to Zabar's, where, inevitably, Angie would ask for a black and white cookie and Deacon would make her taste olives. Or Angie riding on Deacon's shoulders at the San Diego Zoo—a day trip they had taken from L.A., where her mother was working—so that she could better see the giraffes. But mostly, Angie remembered herself older, thirteen or fourteen, not Deacon's little girl anymore but his sidekick, his apprentice. He always called her Buddy except when they were in the kitchen, when he called her, simply, Thorpe—and then, after she graduated from the Culinary Institute, Chef Thorpe. Deacon was the one who had taught Angie how to cook an omelet (no brown spots, or they threw it away), how to make a soufflé that wouldn't fall, how to roast a chicken until it was golden and juicy. She had loved nowhere better than the kitchen with Deacon.

As she climbed the stairs to her apartment, her vision started to splotch. She was roasting in her jeans. When she attacked the fifth flight of stairs, she thought she saw a man's feet in flip-flops sticking out in front of her apartment door. She *hated* this building! Indigents walked in off the street every day with the mailman, or they pressed each buzzer button on the chance that someone would succumb to indifference and let them in. But few made it up to the sixth floor.

Is it Joel? Angie softened with relief.

She loved him.

As she crested the stairs, however, she realized the man wasn't Joel. This guy had a head of shaggy hair and four-day scruff. Angie's neck tensed. She clenched her fists, although she didn't have the strength—physical or mental—to fight anyone off.

The man locked eyes with Angie, and in those eyes, Angie saw her father. The face, nearly the same as Deacon's, made her think: *Werewolf, doppelgänger, ghost, reincarnation.* Had Deacon returned to her in the form of this junkie off the street?

"Angie?" the man said.

Angie's eyes widened. *"Hayes?"* she said. Her brother. Or, technically, her half brother, she supposed, although Deacon had put "half brother" and "half sister" on the Stupid Word List.

Wow, he looked terrible.

Hayes got to his feet and collected Angie in a fierce hug. Then he broke down crying. She envied him that.

"Here," she said. "Let's go in."

She disengaged herself from Hayes's tight embrace and unlocked the apartment door.

"I completely spaced what time you were getting here," Angie said. "I was busy thinking about something else. How did you get in the building?"

"I explained who I was," Hayes said. "Deacon Thorpe's son, your brother. The lady in Three B knows you."

"Right," Angie said, "Mrs. Lopresti." Hayes really looked god-awful; Angie couldn't believe it. She and Deacon (she could not separate their personhood, not yet) lived a life of occasional glamour—for fifteen or twenty minutes each night of service, they trooped out to the dining room to greet the VIPs. They also worked a circuit of benefit dinners—events for the James Beard Foundation and for the favorite charities of other elite chefs. But they agreed that their lives did not hold a candle, in allure or sophistication, to Hayes's life. Hayes crisscrossed the planet in the first-class cabin of Singapore Airlines or Emirates, drinking Dom Pérignon and eating foie gras. When he landed, he was whisked by private chauffeur to the finest hotels in the world. He had his *own table* at the Tiffin Room at Raffles, and he had once called Angie from a suite at the Burj Al Arab, in Dubai, where he was enjoying the service of four butlers, including a "bath butler," who provided any one of fifty bath salts from around the world, along with rose petals, a cold glass of vintage Krug, and strawberries.

Are you calling me to brag? Angie had asked him then.

No, Hayes said. *I'm calling because I miss you.*

He could have been such a prick, Angie and Deacon agreed, but he was a sweet and genuine soul who always let Angie know how much he loved her. There was nothing "half" about their relationship; Hayes had treated Angie like a whole real-deal sister since her earliest memory.

"What happened to you?" Angie said. "You look like a cadaver."

"Thanks," Hayes said. He flopped onto Angie's sofa and sank his shaggy head into her feather pillows. "What happened to me is, I got my ass home from an island off the coast of Bali. I took a longboat to Nusa Dua, then a bus to Denpasar, then a puddle jumper to Jakarta, then another puddle jumper to Singapore, where I had a brief layover. Then I flew to London, and from London I flew here. I haven't slept in, I don't know, twenty-four hours?"

"Oh," Angie said. She was relieved that that was his answer. He was indistinguishable from any tweaker plucked off Ludlow Street, and he was scratching the hell out of his shoulder, which set off alarms in Angie's mind.

"I'm packed," Angie said. "Are we ready to go?" She said the words enthusiastically despite her anxiety about Joel—why didn't he call?—and the fact that all Hayes looked ready to do was take out the trash at the homeless shelter.

"Back to Hoicks Hollow Road," Hayes said. "Our home away from home."

"Where we will be living the life on Nantucket," Angie said.

LAUREL

American Paradise: it was exactly as she remembered it. She wasn't sure how to deal with the cornucopia of confusing emotions she was experiencing. As she pulled into the driveway in the cherry-red Jeep that she had rented at the airport, she sucked in her breath. This was *her* house, *their* house, a house that she and Deacon had picked out together, a house they couldn't afford, but Deacon had wanted it *so badly—Hoicks Hollow Road!* he'd cried out. *It's like magic!*—that Laurel had made concessions.

They had spent three idyllic summers in the house together, the kind of summers people sang about. Hayes had been young—four, five, six. He'd started out a chubby little boy who by the end of the summer had been as brown as a berry, with a mop of hair so blond, it was practically white. And during their last summer, he had learned how to ride a bike. Laurel could picture him, tires wobbling at first, before he gained confidence and straightened the bike out as he pedaled off down Hoicks Hollow Road.

Had the three of them ever worn shoes? Only to go into town at night to get ice cream cones, and the one or two times per summer that she and Deacon hired little Charity with the braces from down the street to watch Hayes so that they could go to Thirty Acres for drinks. The rest of the time, they had walked over the dune to the beach. They had swum and napped and eaten simple sandwiches wrapped in wax paper, and Laurel had read novels on a blanket while Deacon taught Hayes how to skip rocks at the water's edge. In later summers, they took Hayes out onto Sesachacha Pond in a canoe. They always stayed at the beach to enjoy the golden hour, that hour when the sun sank low enough to spangle the water and make everything look as if it had been dipped in honey. Then there was a race to the outdoor shower; the last person in received a cold shock halfway through. Most nights, Deacon grilled fish that he had bought from the fishermen on Straight Wharf at sunrise. They ate the fish with boiled sweet corn and field tomatoes from Bartlett's Farm, a green salad, some fresh herb rolls from Something Natural.

They rode bikes everywhere; Deacon's bike had had a tagalong seat for Hayes, and Laurel's bike had a wicker basket so that she could buy wildflowers from the woman who sold bouquets at the Sconset rotary. Once, they were out exploring and found a thatch of blueberry bushes. They ate the fruit until their tongues turned purple.

Their second summer, Deacon had bought a 1946 Willys jeep; it looked like something out of *Hogan's Heroes*. It was a close match for the jeep that Deacon had ridden in with his father on their last day together. The jeep was old and bare-bones—more go-cart than car—but somehow, it always started. It didn't have seat belts, so Laurel clutched Hayes in her lap, and the three of them would putter along, Laurel's long hair blowing all over the place in the wind.

They had treated the sunset like a Broadway show every night, getting their seats early—on the back deck, with wine and a bottle of beer, Hayes with a box of animal crackers to keep him satiated until dinner. When the sun set over their backyard vista—the golf course, the lighthouse, the moors—they would applaud. And they never missed a thunderstorm. Laurel could remember waking in the middle of the night and racing out onto the deep wraparound porch to watch the rain come down in sheets and the lightning dance across the ocean. Her much-younger, Pollyanna self had marveled at the breathtaking natural beauty of the island. Holding on to the hands of her handsome, talented husband and her adorable son, she would think, *I'm the luckiest woman on earth.*

She was glad she had gotten to the island a few hours before Buck. Being back in this house again was something she needed to experience on her own.

The inside of the cottage hadn't changed one bit, not even under the influence of two very strong women. Laurel had assumed that Belinda would hire architects and painters, tile guys to renovate the bathrooms, and Philip Bergeron, her decorator, to pick out carpets and fabrics and add design elements, thereby ruining the simple perfection of the house and blaspheming everything Nantucket stood for.

But miraculously, Deacon had stood his ground: nothing in that house was to change unless deemed necessary for the house's survival—a new roof, an updated septic system. He was against any "improvements," a philosophy he had also upheld since Scarlett became the third Mrs. Thorpe. Because of this, the house looked just as down at the heels as it had in 1986, when Laurel first saw it.

She wandered upstairs, taking it all in: the nightstands topped with crocheted doilies, a vase holding a bouquet of dusty plastic daisies, the bookshelves crammed with paperback novels—Peter Benchley, Robert Ludlum, Judith Krantz. The same faded watercolors hung on the walls alongside the amateurish oils done by Mrs. Innsley, the previous owner. In the hallway at the top of the stairs was a map of Nantucket, Martha's Vineyard, and Cape Cod circa 1838. There were the old baskets of seashells, and mason jars filled with beach glass—untouched, probably, in thirty years. The beds were topped with the exact same thin quilts over pilled blankets over bare mattresses. Laurel really hoped there were new sheets.

She claimed the master bedroom for herself. This was the room where she and Deacon had slept every night under one thin cotton sheet that had dried all day on the clothesline so that it smelled like clover and sunshine. Laurel took the room because she had had the foresight to arrive first—and to the victor went the spoils. It was the only room with a queen bed and an attached bath. She assigned the adjoining room to Buck; it had a double bed with a scrolled headboard and footboard. Buck was tall; he would have to sleep diagonally, but Laurel wasn't willing to relinquish the queen, even for him. The other rooms each had two twin beds, as if the house had formerly been a convent or a monastery.

Down the hallway was Hayes's room, with the sailboat wallpaper.

Angie's room had a pink tulip border, peeling now along the ceiling, and an old Victorian dollhouse. That dollhouse had been here when Laurel and Deacon bought American Paradise; it had belonged to one of the Innsley daughters. Laurel crouched down to study its tiny furniture: a refrigerator that opened to display a dozen eggs in a carton, and a pizza the size of a dime; a grand piano; the white canopy bed in the triangular attic room, the canopy now frosted with dust. Laurel remembered the real estate agent telling her and Deacon that the dollhouse was the most valuable thing in the house, and Laurel had hoped that she and Deacon would someday have a little daughter to enjoy it.

That had never happened—thanks to Belinda.

The next room was narrow and cramped. It was the nursemaid quarters, which had been occupied by a woman named Clara, who had worked for the Innsleys for decades. Laurel would stick Belinda in there.

And finally, at the end of the hall, the "good" guest room—it had an antique luggage rack with embroidered straps, tucked all the way back in the closet, as well as the Eastlake beds and matching mirror—for Scarlett and Ellery, if they showed.

The house was exactly big enough to hold Deacon's entire, variegated family. What would he have thought about having them all here together? He probably would have grabbed Buck and gone to the bar.

Laurel smiled. *Deacon.*

She found a linen closet full of sheets, and she ran six sets through the laundry, thinking that the most threadbare ones would go on Belinda's bed. She made a pilgrimage to the grocery store, where she lost herself among the sunburned, sandy-legged families shopping for bologna and bing cherries and Popsicles. She felt woefully out of place and out of sorts. She was shopping for a family in mourning—did that mean bananas? A whole pineapple or honeydew melon? They had to eat, and dinner that night would be up to her, so Laurel loaded up her cart: coffee, milk, butter, sandwich bread, peanut butter, potato chips, grapes, three zucchini, a bulb of garlic, a box of cherry tomatoes, salad greens. Was Belinda a vegan? Probably. Laurel got a rotisserie chicken, steak, eggs, an expensive block of Parmesan, a stick of expensive Italian salami. She bought frozen garlic bread and pigs in a blanket. The store was freezing cold, and Laurel imagined that this was a sign of Deacon's disapproval.

Frozen garlic bread? she heard him chiding.

You no longer get a say, she thought, and she headed to the checkout line.

* * *

Next, the liquor store. She bought a case of St. Pauli Girl, since Buck was coming, and a case of wine for everyone else—six bottles of the Cloudy Bay sauvignon blanc that she knew Deacon loved, and six bottles of the Luigi Bosca Malbec that Hayes had turned her on to.

She could survive the weekend as long as she was sufficiently armed.

Laurel felt relieved when Buck showed up. He would be able to help her with the unbearable load of her grief. Buck was tall and as lean as ever, his face still boyish, with unclouded green eyes and the vestiges of childhood freckles, his red hair peppered through with some gray, which, for all Laurel knew, had appeared only in the past six weeks. He had come to Nantucket in a suit and tie, which made Laurel chuckle. Buck had been raised in a strict, formal Irish Catholic family on the Upper East Side of Manhattan. His manner was as straight and correct as the grid of city streets he'd grown up on; "laid-back" wasn't in his lexicon. His only relaxed aspect had been his friendship with Deacon.

Laurel took him immediately out to the back deck. It was raised about three feet over the yard, which consisted of crabgrass and scrub brush. But the views across the island were stunning. The neighbor's house was modern and flashy now by comparison. It had a swimming pool.

They both looked at the picnic table. This was where Deacon had been sitting when he'd died. He had been watching the sun go down, the tradition that he and Laurel had started eons before. Laurel could picture the exact way he sat: leaning back, legs splayed or one ankle resting on his opposite knee, cigarette in one hand, drink in the other. The drink had been a Diet Coke. He had been so careful about the alcohol and the drugs—but ironically, it hadn't mattered in the end.

"Let's sit on the step," Laurel suggested.

Buck nodded in agreement. He stopped to remove his jacket and folded it neatly over a chair, then he loosened his tie and rolled up his shirtsleeves to the elbow. Laurel didn't think she had ever seen John Buckley in such a state of *undress.* She sat down next to him and leaned her head on his shoulder.

Buck pulled her in tight. Laurel had forgotten how good it felt to be held by a man; it had been a while. She was hugged every day by grateful welfare mothers and dozens of children, and she was averaging one date every six months. Her assistant, Sophie, had posted a profile for Laurel on Match.com, but Laurel found the choices underwhelming. She wanted someone both strong and compassionate—compassion was mandatory, in Laurel's line of work. She wanted someone employed, age appropriate, and full of life. Once she ruled out men whose profile included the words "fantasy football," there was almost no one left.

"What are we going to do without him?" Laurel asked.

"I'm not sure," Buck said.

Buck sounded bereft and far away, like a little boy floating down a river on a shoddily built raft. Laurel raised her face to look at him. His eyes were red and filled with tears. Laurel had never seen Buck cry until six weeks earlier; she had never imagined that he was capable of such an act. Deacon, however, had cried all the time. He cried when Hayes was born, he cried when he told Laurel he was leaving her for Belinda Rowe, he cried in 1986 when the Giants won the

Super Bowl. He cried when his sister, Stephanie, died of breast cancer, and again four years later when his mother died, even though his mother had abandoned him. Deacon had carried a core of sorrow within him—his father leaving, his mother leaving. Laurel had known this since the first time she talked to him, in the Dobbs Ferry High School cafeteria—he'd been sitting all alone, wearing a Black Sabbath concert T-shirt with a hole in the neck. Laurel had never been able to rid him of his sadness. He became very successful and very popular—he had been nominated for a daytime Emmy; he had cooked for President Bush and then President Obama—but that hadn't made his demons go away.

"He loved you," Laurel said to Buck. "He was lucky to have a friend like you."

"He loved *you,*" Buck said. "I will never understand why he left you."

"That's very sweet of you to say, Buck," Laurel said.

"I'm serious," Buck said. "If he hadn't been my best friend, I would have snapped you up myself."

Laurel laughed a little, but when she turned her eyes to Buck, his expression was earnest. He leaned in, and Laurel thought for a moment that he might kiss her, the way that a man kisses a woman.

"Hello?"

What? Laurel thought. No. She pulled away from Buck and stood up. "Wait a minute. I think…?"

"Hello? Hello?"

Laurel heard clomping footsteps in the house, and an instant later, a woman in a giant straw hat and cat-eye sunglasses popped out onto the deck.

Belinda.

Laurel had known she was on her way, but still, she felt woefully unprepared for the shock of seeing her.

Buck stood up and turned around. "Hello, Belinda," he said.

Belinda took a deep, dramatic breath, and then she started to sob. Here she was, then: the woman who had stolen Laurel's husband, and this house, and her summers, and her happiness. Laurel had spent years and years hating Belinda, until eventually the hate faded into contempt and then distaste and then, finally, indifference.

I don't care about her, Laurel told herself. *She has lost the power to hurt me. She is no longer able to make me feel worthless and unloved and ugly and clumsy.* But, watching Belinda cry, Laurel felt a surge of the old rage. She was older and wiser now, though. She had been to college and graduate school; she had built a worthwhile career in which she made real differences in people's lives. She could control her emotions. She could be the bigger person.

Grace, she thought. What she needed here was grace.

"Hello, Belinda," she said.

Intermezzo:
Deacon and Laurel, Part I

Jack Thorpe leaves for work on August 21, 1976—it will end up being the hottest, most unpleasant day of the summer, not only for the Thorpe family but for everyone in the city—and he never comes home. The manager at Sardi's, a man named Fitzy, says Jack's work duds are hanging in his locker, as usual. Fitzy says, *He probably just went on a bender. Give him a few days.*

Deacon's mother, Priscilla, goes on a rampage through every one of Jack's known haunts: the White Horse Tavern, Milano's, 169, Blarney Stone. Nobody has seen him. After twenty-four hours, Priscilla calls the police to report a missing person. An officer named Murphy comes to the apartment and asks Priscilla a lot of questions about Jack's routine and habits. He asks about drug and alcohol use, and Priscilla says, "He's a beer and whiskey man, always has been," and Officer Murphy nods as if he approves. Officer Murphy asks if Jack had been acting strangely. Any changes of behavior? Deacon watches the lightbulb come on over his mother's head.

"He took a trip with my son last week," Priscilla says. She narrows her red, watery eyes at Deacon; she's been doing a lot of crying, more crying than Deacon would have expected. "Where did you go, again?"

"Nantucket Island," Deacon says.

"What did you do on Nantucket Island?" the officer asks.

Deacon shrugs. He's afraid that if he describes it, it will sound regular and nothing like the unforgettable day it was. "Had lunch," he says. "Went swimming."

"Do you think that your father had plans to return to... Nantucket Island?" Officer Murphy asks.

"No," Deacon says. He's pretty sure his father is anywhere but Nantucket. He's pretty sure the purpose of the trip was to see it one last time before... well, before what, Deacon doesn't know.

A second day passes, then a third. By the end of the week, Priscilla has procured a prescription bottle filled with Valium. Deacon steals eight pills, then three more. He takes the first pill before bedtime and falls into a dreamless sleep. He takes the second pill a few mornings later, after his mother leaves for her waitressing shift at the South Street

Seaport. The pill slows everything down. It gives Deacon a relaxed but powerful feeling, almost as if he's levitating.

Wow, he thinks. With Valium, every hour is the golden hour.

He steals five more.

The following year, 1977, Priscilla meets a man named Kirk Inglehart and announces that she's moving with him to Bermuda and that Deacon and Stephanie are being shipped up to Dobbs Ferry to live with Auntie Ro. The Valium pills, of course, are long-gone, but Deacon has picked up three shifts a week working as the trash boy at Sardi's—Fitzy, the manager, felt sorry for him once it was evident that Jack wasn't coming back—and in the dregs of the kitchen, there are all kinds of drugs: pot, angel dust, whip-its, as well as dented cans of warm Schlitz. Deacon says yes to everything.

His first day of school in Dobbs Ferry is the Tuesday after Labor Day; he is a freshman. He wears jeans and a ratty Black Sabbath T-shirt that he bought down on Canal Street for fifty cents. He loves Black Sabbath, although he's never come close to seeing them or anyone else in concert. His auntie Ro takes umbrage at the shirt. She went shopping and bought him a nice blue Izod, but Deacon refuses to put it on.

He says, "I will never wear a shirt with a collar." He doesn't mention the yellow shirt with a collar that his father wore to Nantucket. The thought of it pains him and makes him long for the big, fat joint that Bub and Marcos, the dishwashers at Sardi's, gave him as a parting gift.

Auntie Ro must sense something, because she capitulates quickly. "Suit yourself," she says.

Having a big, fat joint tucked away in his top dresser drawer makes going to a brand-new school, where he knows no one, bearable. He is able to ignore the dirty looks; the raised eyebrows because his hair is too long and nobody has taught him to shave, so he has a shadowy mustache; the shoulder bump from a guy so huge, he must be the entire offensive line for the football team. Deacon's new teachers talk, they pass out something called a syllabus (what a stupid word!): English, world history, algebra. Deacon hates school. He dreams about finding a secluded spot along the Hudson and toking up.

He figures the worst part will be lunch, and he's pretty much correct about that. He goes through the line and takes a sad-looking burger, some limp, greasy fries, a chocolate milk. Then he faces a sea of kids, yipping and yapping like so many Chihuahuas. He has no choice but to sit alone at an empty table in the far corner. The good thing is that the table is next to the exit. If things get really bad, he can just run.

He has neglected to get ketchup, and when he turns around to figure out where a person might procure some, he sees a girl headed toward him. Long blond hair, no makeup, white blouse and jean skirt, normal-looking and actually kind of pretty. She smiles at him and says, "You're new, right? Okay if I sit with you?"

He is so stunned, he can't answer. She sits down and says, "I would love to see Black Sabbath in concert, but my mother is strict. She would never, ever let me."

"Oh, I haven't seen them," Deacon admits. He figures he has probably just blown away this girl's sole point of interest in him. "I bought the T-shirt because I love their music. I got it down in the city."

"You moved here from the city, right?" she says. "I heard that."

He nods. "I lived in Stuy Town. East side."

"That's cool," she says. "I love the city, but I'm only allowed to go in *with* my parents, which sucks."

He notices that her tray is loaded with food—a cup of vegetable-barley soup, a turkey club sandwich that she has slathered with mayonnaise, tater tots, a dish of some cabbage salad called chow-chow, two cartons of chocolate milk, and red Jell-O with whipped cream. She takes a big bite of her sandwich. "Everyone complains about the cafeteria food," she says, "but I like it."

Deacon lifts his burger. He's afraid if he gets up to find ketchup, she will disappear.

She says, "Is your tattoo real?"

He nods. He got the tattoo in Chinatown from a man who didn't bother asking Deacon's age. "It's a seal."

"Yes, I can see that," she says. She spoons in some soup, then takes a bite of chow-chow. She pops in a tater tot. "I'm Laurel Simmons," she says. "What's your name?"

"Deacon," he says. "Deacon Thorpe."

They're at the homecoming game, Dobbs Ferry versus Irvington, and the senior players and cheerleaders are being announced on the field, along with their parents. Deacon and Laurel are in the stands, huddled together under a plaid car blanket. Laurel asks the question Deacon has been dreading. They've been dating for two months; he supposes he should be grateful it has taken her this long.

"I know you said your mother moved to Bermuda," Laurel said. "But what about your father?"

Deacon stands up and heads down the aluminum bleachers, his hands crammed into his pockets. He doesn't want to talk about it. His sister, Stephanie, goes to the school psychologist, but Deacon has refused to do this because he really just doesn't want to talk about it.

Deacon walks to the parking lot, leaving the lights and the noise of the game behind him. He misses Laurel already. They are together every second after school until curfew. She's a friend like he's never known. His mother's departure made sense: she left them for a man. But Jack Thorpe left because...because why? Because watching Deacon and Stephanie grow up wasn't worth sticking around for?

Deacon sits on the concrete steps that lead up to the road. He could walk home, but it's far, and Auntie Ro will be here to pick him up after the game. He hopes that Laurel will come looking for him, although why would she? He's a weirdo and a loser, unable to answer a simple question. He is worth nothing, as his father so deftly proved. The thing is, Deacon knew. He sensed a requiem in his father's manner, in his father's reminiscing. He saw good-bye written on his father's face as he walked toward Deacon down the beach.

One perfect day with my son. That's not too much to ask, is it?

All that Deacon is left with is the memory. And the clamshell.

He spies the shine of blond hair from a hundred yards away, and out of the mist, her form becomes clearer. When she gets closer, he sees she's crying. He's made her cry. He is an awful, terrible person. When she sees him shivering on the steps, a look of immense relief crosses her face.

She loves me, he thinks.

She holds out her arms to him. "You don't have to tell me," she says.

"I'll tell you," Deacon says. They've been separated all of seven or eight minutes, but he can't describe how relieved he is to have her back. "I'll tell you everything."

She sits in his lap on the steps.

He's not sure where to start. "Have you ever been to Nantucket?" he asks.

It's Christmas break of their senior year when Laurel gets her early acceptance to Vassar. She has straight As and could have gone anywhere—Duke, Stanford, Yale—but she chose Vassar because she wants to stay close to Deacon. He will be only miles away, in Hyde Park, at the Culinary Institute of America.

Deacon gets Laurel a necklace for Christmas, a silver chain with a heart pendant made from leaded crystal. Laurel gets Deacon three albums—*London Calling, Back in Black,* and *The River*—and a sweater. They exchange presents on the morning of the twenty-sixth, but as soon as they finish opening them, Laurel announces that she doesn't feel well. Two seconds later, she pukes in his lap.

They decide it must be the excitement of Christmas, the rich food, or some bug that's going around.

Laurel gets sick on the morning of the twenty-seventh and then again on the twenty-eighth. On the twenty-ninth, they drive Laurel's mother's station wagon to the next town over, Irvington, to buy a pregnancy test.

Positive.

Laurel cries while Deacon sits in wonder, staring out the windshield at the white sky. It's almost 1981. Since the day Laurel sat next to him at lunch, Deacon has been a boy in love. Love has saved him. And now, it appears, he's going to be a father.

Or maybe not. Laurel can't stop crying. A baby will ruin her future, she says. She won't be able to go to Vassar, as she planned.

She says, "I want to get an abortion."

"Okay," Deacon says. His heart is soft now, like a flat tire, but he's afraid to voice his feelings. In history class, they held debates, and one of the topics was *Roe v. Wade*. Deacon was only tangentially involved, but he did gather that choice was a privilege granted a woman, not a man.

Late that night, however, Laurel calls Deacon's house, crying. She can't go through with it, she says. She is going to have the baby.

"Okay," Deacon says. He can't believe the joy that envelops him. "Let's get married."

In 1986, everything is good. In fact, everything is great. Deacon has two jobs. He is the chef de cuisine at Solo, on Twenty-Third and Fifth, and he is the star of a late-night TV show called *Day to Night to Day with Deacon,* which has garnered what studio execs call "surprisingly respectable ratings." Because he is now "on TV," he gets recognized on the street, and every afternoon, a small cluster of fans gathers on the sidewalk outside the employee entrance of Solo, waiting for Deacon so that they can get his autograph. Some of these fans are women, hot women, and some of them hand Deacon their numbers. *Call me, baby.* Deacon takes all the numbers home to Laurel. She is making a scrapbook of Deacon's successes—his review by Ruth Reichl in the *Times* (two and a half stars), his review in *New York* magazine, an ad for the show in *TV Guide*—and she pastes the women's phone numbers in. She isn't jealous at all; she thinks it's funny and cute and sexy that he's wanted by every woman in America.

"Not every woman," Deacon says. "Besides, I only love you."

Laurel knows this. She is the one who saved him. His first and only love, the mother of his beautiful son.

The show becomes so popular that Deacon is offered two more seasons, with a substantial pay raise. The advance comes in one lump sum, and when Deacon and Laurel open the envelope, they stare at the check together. It's more money than either of them had expected to make in a lifetime.

They don't know what to do with it. They have just bought the apartment on West 119th Street; it's filled with light and is well suited for the three of them, and the rest of their existence is frugal: the subway instead of cabs, staff meal nearly every night at the restaurant. They should save this money, they know, invest it with Kidder or Drexel. But the check demands to be spent in some kind of large, lavish, life-changing way. They both feel it.

"You pick," Laurel says. "You earned it."

Deacon picks Nantucket. He calls the local newspaper, the *Inquirer and Mirror,* and asks for the real estate section to be mailed to him. All the houses pictured, however, are too big and too expensive. They're meant for men who wear pinstripe suits and trade junk bonds, men who carry briefcases and play squash. But then Deacon sees a listing that catches his attention: YOUR "AMERICAN PARADISE" AWAITS ON HOICKS HOLLOW ROAD.

The hair on the back of Deacon's neck stands up.

Good old Hoicks Hollow Road. Used to be my home away from home.

The description reads: *Classic, well-loved summer cottage on exclusive Hoicks Hollow Road. Steps away from the private idyll of the Sankaty Head Beach Club, this cottage, which has remained in the same family for five generations, is in need of a thoughtful, caring owner who will appreciate its many charms. Back deck offers sweeping views over the golf course, lighthouse, and moors. Enjoy distant ocean views from the front farmer's porch. Offered fully furnished.*

The price is more than he and Laurel had wanted to pay, but it's doable. He is struck by the way the description in the paper makes the house sound like an orphan. Like Deacon himself.

His hands are shaking as he shows the listing to Laurel. "Hoicks Hollow Road," he says. "It's like magic!"

They buy the house in July and move in right away. Solo closes for six weeks over the summer, and Deacon doesn't start filming the new season of the show until September. It's meant to be.

He thinks he understands how his father felt bringing Deacon to Nantucket, because Deacon is filled with a thrilling elation. *I can't wait for you to see it,* he tells Laurel and little Hayes. *It's the best place on earth. It is,* he says, *an American paradise.*

When they pull into the driveway, Deacon has second thoughts. The front porch of the house sags in the middle; the white trim badly needs paint, and the yard is a patchwork of dirt and crabgrass. They walk up the rickety front steps and pull open the screen door. The house smells like cleaning products, with undertones of something salty and marshy, although not unpleasant. Sunlight streams through the windows, catching dust motes. The furnishings are at-the-beach shabby. Deacon figures the cushions of the sofa have been sat upon by hundreds of wet bathing suits, and a once-prized collection of hermit crabs has probably decomposed under the front porch, where some wise child placed them to protect them from the sun.

Deacon isn't sure how Laurel will react. For all the money they paid, she is probably expecting something much grander.

She follows him inside, carrying Hayes. She looks around with wide eyes and takes a deep breath.

"I love it," she says.

HAYES

Hayes visited his dealer, Kermit, on 125th Street before he picked Angie up at her apartment, but there was a problem. Kermit had been raided earlier in the week. He had some product, but not enough.

"Just sell me what you have, man," Hayes said. Traveling clean for twenty-four hours had nearly undone him. He shot up right away behind a row of garbage cans in an alley—*Ahhhhhh!*—and nirvana was restored to him. He had bought enough dope to last two days, plus half a dozen Vicodin, which he could pulverize and put in his coffee each morning for extra help. He had promised his mother Saturday to Tuesday; she had said something about waiting for the ashes to arrive in the mail. Hayes would have to score some product on Nantucket; otherwise, he would find himself in a sorry state.

They were going to spread the ashes in Nantucket Sound, which was what Deacon had always said he wanted. Even the doorman at Deacon's apartment building on Hudson Street knew this. Thinking about Deacon's physical being turned into ashes gave Hayes a moment of existential contemplation that being high did nothing to ameliorate. His father's sinewy muscles, his full head of black hair with the forelock that always fell in his eyes, all of his vividly inked tattoos—the seal, Rich Uncle Pennybags from Monopoly, partial lyrics to "Train in Vain" by the Clash, a steaming cauldron, the vanda orchid, the striped bass that took up most of his upper back—all of that personhood would be reduced to unrecognizable rubble.

One day a few weeks earlier, on a flight from New York to Quito, Ecuador, Hayes had indulged his grief and had binge-watched his father's shows. He started with *Day to Night to Day with Deacon.* His father looked so *young* in that show; he was really just a kid, barely twenty-five, nearly ten years younger than Hayes was now. He scowled a lot, narrowed his eyes, dropped the F-bomb as if it were his cool second job—it was bleeped out every time, obviously, although there were black-market unedited versions floating around out there—flexed the muscles in his forearms, did some circus tricks with his sauté pan, and generally perpetuated the stereotype of chef as badass. Actually, Hayes thought, his father had invented that stereotype. He, after all, had been on TV long before Ramsay or Bourdain. The cameramen followed Deacon downtown after service and shot footage of him drinking Guinness chased with Jameson all by himself in the shadows of any number of dive bars—Milady's was a popular one because of Deacon's banter with the geriatric bartenders, Doris and Millicent. And then, once properly lubricated, Deacon went looking for dinner. The show portrayed him as a lone wolf—hungry, hunting, an orphan, an R-rated Mowgli. He liked to eat deep in the heart of Chinatown; when that became too mainstream, he sought out Little Ethiopia and Little Burma. He loved *momo*s.

After he'd eaten, Deacon would take the subway all the

way back up to West 119th Street. This was where the camera work got artsy—Deacon in silhouette on the train, headed home with all the other poor souls who worked the third shift, the sun coming up over the East River; the juxtaposition of Deacon in his white jacket, houndstooth pants, and clogs with men in three-piece suits headed to their jobs on Wall Street or Madison Avenue.

The best part of the show for Hayes, of course, was watching for glimpses of himself at the end. He was just a little guy, usually shown in footy pajamas, scurrying down their long hallway to greet his father at the door; his mother, barefoot, her hair loose, belting her robe, followed behind him. This was the moment of salvation: Deacon—who looked first so angry and then so lonely—had a family!

The second show, *Pitchfork,* was shot in a Food Network studio kitchen. Deacon wore jeans, an Hermès belt, and a $450 black Rick Owens T-shirt. The edgy yet insanely expensive outfit was a wink and nod to Deacon as grown-up. He had manned the helm at Raindance for more than a decade; he had been married to the highest-paid actress in Hollywood. He had done things the Deacon way, and that had more or less worked out. He made his unorthodox recipes—the clams casino dip, the mesquite-smoked lobster-tail *momo*s, the champagne caramels with potato-chip salt—and he tossed his forelock and scowled at the camera every time an egg didn't break cleanly. He pretended to have retained his fierceness, but it was obvious to viewers that the good life had softened Deacon. He was a sexy teddy bear now. The only point of real controversy was that he still drank like a third-year senior at Jameson University. Each episode of *Pitchfork* ended with Deacon and his producers and cameramen and key grips doing a shot together.

As Hayes watched show after show after show, he marveled at how a man could be so alive on the screen, cursing and laughing and measuring flour and chopping onions and popping a whole clove of garlic in his mouth as if it were a piece of Dubble Bubble, for the *ewwwww* effect—and now he was dead. Never coming back.

As Hayes and Angie walked to the parking garage, Hayes said, "Dad loved you more than me."

"Shut up," Angie said.

"You know it's true," Hayes said.

"He was better with girls," Angie said.

"You two were way closer," Hayes said. "You were friends."

"I logged in the hours," Angie said. "We worked together every single day. Any idea how mentally exhausting it was to handle that much Deacon?"

"I'd trade places with you," Hayes said. Before he could say, *I didn't get enough of him,* he started to cry. *I didn't get enough of him, and now he's gone.*

Angie threw an arm around Hayes's shoulder. "Are you *okay?*" she asked. "I mean, do you *feel* okay, Hayes? Because, I'm not kidding, you look like hell. You look..."

He knew what was coming. *You look like a junkie. Are you* using?

"You look tired," she said. "Maybe I should drive."

"Yeah," Hayes said. "Maybe you should."

BELINDA

Upon first seeing Laurel and Buck, she had had a dramatic emotional moment, but for the first time ever, the person she was playing was herself. She shed real tears, uncontrollable tears. There were so many feelings where Deacon was concerned: guilt, ecstasy, sadness, regret, love, desire, guilt, more guilt, love, heartache, confusion. Belinda couldn't talk to anyone about these feelings—not yet, anyway. Maybe ten or twenty years from now, with the help of a good therapist, she could address them lucidly in her memoir. When Belinda was acting, she always tried to keep her character's *motivation* in the front of her mind. What was her motivation in coming to Nantucket? What did she expect to achieve?

She wasn't sure. But when she saw Laurel and Buck, she realized that she had had a leading role in Deacon Thorpe's life, too, and if she had stayed in Los Angeles or returned to Kentucky, there would have been an absence, a vacuum, an empty space, where she should have been.

Or maybe she was just being narcissistic, as always.

She was back in American Paradise after a twelve-year hiatus. It looked exactly the same, and it *smelled* exactly the same. That was what really transported Belinda back in time—the smell, the comforting scent of cedar from the two front closets, mixed with the musty, marshy odor of the shipwreck furniture, mingled with the green fragrance of freshly cut grass, blown in off the golf course by the breeze. Good or bad, it smelled to Belinda like summertime, and, even more disquieting than that, it smelled like her marriage to Deacon.

She had had an ambivalent relationship with the house. She hadn't wanted to go to Nantucket at all, but Deacon had worn her down. When he left Laurel, he moved with Belinda to L.A. and then announced that it was only fair for Belinda to give him three weeks—just three weeks—in his favorite place in the world. Nantucket Island.

But it's the beach, she said. *And I don't swim.*

It's more than just the beach, Deacon said. There was a town filled with shops and restaurants and charming churches and stately homes that used to belong to whaling captains, all of them with polished door knockers and window boxes bursting with summer flowers. The streets were paved with cobblestones. The island was understated and old-fashioned, the polar opposite of Los Angeles. She would love it, Deacon assured her. There were hundreds of acres of moors to hike through, and miles of paved paths for her to bike along. There were two theater companies, two movie houses, a museum dedicated to the history of whaling. There was a tiny hamlet on the east coast of the island called Sconset, where all the cottages were blanketed with roses. There were two bookstores and a big library in the center of town called the Nantucket Atheneum. There was a restaurant called the Club Car, where they served caviar and where in the back a piano player took requests when everyone gathered after dinner to sing. *I've never known you to pass up a chance to belt out "Send in the Clowns,"* Deacon said.

She couldn't articulate her real objection, which was that Deacon had bought the house and moved to Nantucket with Laurel. All his memories—short of the one perfect day with his father—were forged with Laurel. Belinda would be Laurel's replacement, and Belinda worried that she wouldn't be as good at Nantucket—did that phrase make any sense?—as Laurel had been. Deacon had solid gold memories of the place, and those memories were—they had to be—inseparable from the person he created them with. Belinda yearned to pick a new place, a place that had no history—Montauk, maybe, or Long Beach Island, if he had to be near the ocean.

Even Martha's Vineyard! But Deacon was dead set; Belinda at least had the perspicacity to realize this. If she wanted to keep Deacon, she would have to go to Nantucket and make the best of things.

Living in a house once occupied by Laurel was even more difficult than she'd anticipated. The furniture, Deacon said, had come with the house, and Belinda could tell—it all looked as though it had washed up on shore sometime during the Great Depression. But there were little things that Laurel had left behind—a hairbrush, a white tank top in the top drawer of a dresser that Deacon had said would be Belinda's—and there was a framed photograph on a side table in the front room of Deacon, Laurel, and Hayes at the beach, their faces bathed in the rose-gold light of the sunset. Belinda had taken the photograph out of the frame, torn it in half, and buried it in the kitchen trash.

She remembered the first time she did the laundry, throwing towels and her underwear and shorts into the washing machine and then, an hour later, realizing there was no dryer. She had gone to find Deacon, and he had said, "We don't have a dryer, so we normally hang stuff on the clothesline."

Belinda had stared at him. The "we" he was speaking of was he and Laurel.

"Let me buy a dryer," Belinda said. "Please."

"No," Deacon said. One thing about Deacon: when the man said no, he didn't waver and he didn't negotiate. "The clothesline is a part of the experience. It's summertime. We dry our clothes and the sheets and the towels on the line. We aren't getting a dryer."

He'd eventually discovered that the picture of him, Hayes, and Laurel was missing—Belinda would have been well advised to have tossed the frame as well—and he confronted Belinda.

"What happened to this?" he asked.

Initially, she shrugged. He gave her an incredulous look until she said, "I threw it away."

She had been stretched out on the bed, reading a script. Deacon sat next to her.

"Listen," he said, "I know it must have been painful to see..."

"You don't know," she said.

"I do know," Deacon said. "Your place in L.A. is filled with pictures of you with other men—you and John Lithgow, you and Pierce Brosnan, you and Brian Dennehy..."

"That's not the same," Belinda said.

"It is the same," Deacon said. He took her hand. "We both have a past, right? A path that brought us to where we are now. I'm going to honor your past and try not to feel threatened or jealous, and I'd like you to do the same, okay?"

"Okay," she'd said. But inside, she was glad the photograph was gone. If Deacon had sorted through the trash, he would have found that she'd torn it in half, right down the middle of Laurel's face.

There had been other things Belinda had wanted to change. Frankly, she would have liked to have gutted the house and remodeled from the studs—or, better still, have sold the house and bought a house in town. She had a favorite: 141 Main Street. She had enough money that she could have knocked on the front door and made the owners an offer. But she had known better than to ask Deacon what he thought about this idea.

During the years she spent with Deacon, she had grown to love Nantucket for all the reasons he had listed, but also because on Nantucket, no one hassled her. Everyone knew she was Belinda Rowe, obviously, but she had never been followed by paparazzi, never been interrupted while at dinner, never been hounded by fans except the occasional autograph seeker. Belinda had been able to belt out "Send in the Clowns" at the Club Car and receive a good-natured round of applause without worrying about her picture appearing on Page Six of the *Post*. It was a welcome change, the opportunity to relax.

Once Belinda had dried her eyes, blown her nose, removed her hat, and shaken out her hair, she dealt with the pragmatic reality of her situation. Laurel had gotten here first, and she moved around as though she were completely at home, even though it had been nearly thirty years since Laurel had lived here.

"Where am I sleeping?" Belinda asked. That was officially the longest sentence Belinda had ever dared say to the woman.

"Clara's room," Laurel said.

"*Clara's* room?" Belinda said. Clara had been a nursemaid to the Innsleys' children back in the 1950s. Her room was hardly bigger than a closet! Of *course* Laurel had assigned Belinda to Clara's room, with its ascetic twin bed, meant for a bony-assed spinster. "Who's sleeping in the master?" Belinda asked, though she could easily predict the answer to *that* question.

"Me," Laurel said. "I'm sorry if you don't like Clara's room, but the guest room is big enough for two people, and I wanted to save it in case Scarlett and Ellery show up..."

"*Scarlett?*" Belinda said. "I thought..."

"She's in Savannah," Laurel said. "But Buck left word with her about this weekend, and I'm still holding out hope that she'll come."

Belinda was speechless. If she had known there was even the slightest chance that Scarlett Oliver would show up, she would have gone home to Kentucky.

"Clara's bathroom has a tub," Laurel said. "I thought you might like that."

"Does the tub work?" Belinda asked.

"Honestly, I didn't check," Laurel said.

"Well, it didn't work twelve years ago," Belinda said. Instinctively, she pulled her phone out to check if there were any flights back to Boston tonight. From there, she would fly to Louisville and take Bob by surprise. But she had no cell signal. "Is there no cell service out here? Still?"

"My phone works at the end of the driveway," Laurel said.

"It's 2016!" Belinda said. "Coming back here is like a time warp."

"Tell me about it," Laurel said wryly.

"What about Buck's phone?" Belinda asked. "Buck must be pissed." She bit off this last word; Mrs. Greene did not tolerate vulgar language around the girls.

"He fell asleep in the front room," Laurel said.

"Fell asleep?" Belinda said.

"Yes," Laurel said. "He's exhausted. Can I offer you some iced tea? Or a glass of wine?"

Belinda didn't like the way Laurel was playing hostess. This wasn't *her* house; it hadn't been her house since the administration of George H. W. Bush. Furthermore, Belinda had been married to Deacon for fifteen years and with him for seventeen, whereas Laurel had been married to him for six years and with him for eleven. But Laurel had always enjoyed a certain sense of entitlement because she had been Deacon's first wife and therefore—due to some calculus Belinda didn't understand—knew him the best.

Belinda would never have agreed to come if she'd known Laurel was going to act like the lady of the manor.

"I'll have wine," Belinda said, though it was only quarter past twelve. Mrs. Greene was judgmental about the amount of alcohol that Belinda and Bob drank. Belinda imported cases of Les Monts Damnés from the Chavignol region of Sancerre, which she tucked away in the custom-made wine cave she'd had built in the root cellar. And Bob drank bourbon, obviously—they lived in Kentucky! Bob's clients, the filthy-rich men who owned the Thoroughbreds, brought him bottle upon bottle of Pappy Van Winkle—ten-year, thirteen-year, twenty-three-year.

Mrs. Greene was slightly gentler in her disapproval of Bob's drinking, probably because he was a man. If Belinda popped a cork before five, Mrs. Greene cleared her throat and eyed Belinda over the tops of her spectacles. Mrs. Greene was, quite naturally, a teetotaler.

"I have red or white," Laurel said.

"White, please," Belinda said, thinking, *Please don't let it be pinot grigio.*

Laurel pulled a bottle of Cloudy Bay sauvignon blanc out of the fridge, and Belinda blinked. That had been Deacon's favorite wine. He and Belinda had consumed...oh, six or seven thousand bottles of it over the course of their marriage. Belinda couldn't bring herself to drink it after the divorce. But now she realized that Deacon had probably drunk that exact wine with Laurel—and with witchy-poo Scarlett!

Laurel poured two glasses. *There's no point in refusing it now,* Belinda thought. The three of them were finally on equal footing. The man was dead.

Laurel held up her glass. "To Deacon," she said.

"To Deacon," Belinda said. As she and Laurel touched glasses, she thought, *Deacon would not believe this if he saw it.*

Belinda wondered how to ask about Angie. When was she due to arrive?

"So," Belinda said. Her tone of voice, against her wishes, indicated that a *big question* was coming. She was an actress, but she couldn't seem to convey nonchalance when it came to the thorny issues of her personal life. "When are the kids getting here?"

"This afternoon," Laurel said. "They got a late start, I guess, but they're supposed to be here in plenty of time for dinner."

"Oh," Belinda said. "Okay, good."

"Have you not spoken to Angie?" Laurel asked.

"Not in a few days," Belinda said, "a few" meaning ten, which was probably more like fourteen. "I've tried calling, and I got her voice mail. She and I... well, we aren't as close as we used to be. "

"But surely now... ?" Laurel said.

"Surely now what?" Belinda said. She sat on one of the kitchen stools and twirled her wineglass. "Angie is so stubborn."

"That she is," Laurel said. "But this... well, it's big. She's going to need you, Belinda."

"Is she?" Belinda said. She took another sip of wine. She didn't like Laurel's preaching. "After I married Bob and got pregnant with Mary, she accused me of not wanting her. Can you imagine? I don't think a child has ever *been* more wanted. I gave up the lead in *Ghost* so that I could fly to Perth and then take a ten-hour ride in a Land Rover to the middle of godforsaken nowhere to get her. I went alone.

Deacon couldn't get away. He had just accepted the executive chef position at Raindance."

"Wow," Laurel said. "That seems like a long time ago."

"Twenty-six years ago," Belinda said. She had been twenty-six at the time herself. Was that possible? She became a mother at the same age that Angie was now? Well, Belinda had seemed much older. In 1980, she had seen the movie that changed her life, *Ordinary People*—and with the money she'd saved working the lunch counter at Pearson's Drug Store in Iowa City, she had moved to L.A. By the time she was twenty-one, she had made eight movies. She met Deacon when she was twenty-three. He had been hired to cater an Oscars party Belinda had attended the year that she was nominated for Best Supporting Actress for *Between the Pipes*. She had been so busy chatting and accepting consolation ("You should have won, you were way better than Meryl...") that she had neglected to eat anything, and after endless flutes of champagne, she stumbled into the food tent, sat on a stack of milk crates in her shell-pink Calvin Klein slip dress, kicked off her rhinestone stilettos, and said, "Can somebody please feed me?"

Deacon had appeared instantly, the sleeves of his chef's jacket rolled up to reveal some pretty vivid tattoos; he was smoking a cigarette.

Belinda had batted her eyes at him. "I know *you*," she said. "You're the bad-boy chef who's on opposite Carson."

"And I know you," Deacon said. "You're the prima donna who lost tonight."

Belinda had then tried out her pout. "I'm not a prima donna."

"And I'm not a bad boy," Deacon said.

Belinda pressed herself up against him and wrapped her arms around his neck. "Oh," she said, "but I bet you are."

Deacon had lifted her arms as if they were a couple of poisonous snakes. Belinda wasn't used to being rebuffed in such a manner, or any manner. She wasn't quite sure what to do.

Deacon said, "If you're actually hungry, follow me."

He led her to a section of the tent that she would later think of as the Land of a Thousand Sandwiches. There had been towers of tea sandwiches—egg, cucumber, radish, and butter—and artful stacks of double-decker turkey clubs and thick, messy Reubens oozing cheese and sauerkraut and Russian dressing; there had been platters of neat, rainbow-spiraled veggie wraps. There had been tuna salad on pumpernickel, chicken salad on nutty wheat, egg salad on glossy brioche rolls. There had been buttermilk biscuits loaded with ham and smeared with apricot chutney and grainy mustard; there had been cheesesteaks, and Mexican chicken studded with jewel-toned peppers, and rosy fillet of beef drizzled with creamy horseradish sauce on French baguettes. A choir of voices in Belinda's head chanted *Eat! Eat! Eat!* Belinda lifted the biggest, messiest Reuben she could find and took a lusty bite.

"I recant," Deacon said, taking the last drag of his cigarette and grinding it out under his kitchen clog. "No prima donna eats like that."

She studied him over the top of her sandwich. She had seen several episodes of his show because she suffered from chronic insomnia and was always awake at midnight, when his show, *Day to Night to Day with Deacon*, aired. The show never included much cooking that Belinda could see. Deacon chopped something, threw a piece of whatever it was at his sous-chefs, called his sous-chefs names so profane that he got bleeped, flexed his muscles, flipped the dark shock of hair that perpetually fell into his eyes, then executed some theatrics with his sauté pan. The better part of the show, in Belinda's opinion, was watching Deacon Thorpe prowl the city, looking for places to eat and drink after service was over. It was kind of sexy, Belinda thought, the way he roamed the dark city blocks like an animal. She envied his sang-froid. It was clear from watching the show that Deacon Thorpe didn't care what the world thought of him. He didn't care if people thought he was a foul-mouthed dirt merchant, he didn't care if people thought he was a good cook, and he didn't seem to care if he got held up at knifepoint in Alphabet City. He didn't really seem to care about anything.

"This is *so good,*" Belinda said through a mouthful of corned beef.

He nodded once, then he produced a clean linen napkin from the pocket of his houndstooth pants and gently wiped the corner of Belinda's mouth.

Belinda had finished the sandwich and returned to the party. The next day she called her agent, Leif Larsen, and asked if he could somehow get Deacon hired as the caterer on her new movie, *Gypsy Red,* which started filming in New York two weeks hence.

Leif had said, "He's not a movie caterer, Bel. He's a chef, and if you're having impure thoughts about him, I'm telling you now that he's also married. Do you not watch the end of each show? He goes home to his hot wife and their little boy. Those aren't actors, babe. They're real people."

"You think his wife is hot?" Belinda asked. "I don't think she's that hot."

"She's hot," Leif had said.

"There's no way he's *faithful,*" Belinda said. "*Is* there?"

"Belinda," Leif said. "Don't."

"Okay," Belinda said. "I won't."

But two weeks later, when she was in New York to start

shooting *Gypsy Red,* she paid Deacon a visit at Solo. John Buckley had been the maître d', although at the time Belinda hadn't known who Buck was other than an awkwardly tall ginger with a cowlick who crumpled in the presence of Belinda's fame and ushered her right back into the kitchen, albeit with the caveat, "Does he know you're coming? He's pretty busy. It's the middle of service."

"No," she said. "This is a surprise visit."

"Oh, okay?" Buck had said. "My name is John Buckley, and I'm also an agent. So if you need representation . . . ?"

"I have representation," Belinda had said, and she slipped through the double doors to the kitchen.

She found Deacon at a gleaming stove in his chef's jacket, sleeves pulled down properly, a navy bandanna tied around his forehead. She had tapped him on the shoulder, and when he whipped around and saw her, he seemed nonplussed, almost as if he didn't recognize her.

"Hey," he said finally.

"It's me," she said. "The non–prima donna, Belinda Rowe."

He blinked. "Are you eating in the restaurant?" he said. "I can send something out."

"No," she said. "I just stopped by to say hello. And to give you this."

He turned halfway around. Belinda handed him a slip of paper with her room number at the St. Regis written on it. He took a second to read it, then he stared at her hard for a second.

"I'm married," he said.

Belinda nodded once, her body growing stiff with mortification. She was an Academy Award–nominated actress. Leif was always telling her to keep her nose clean. Her career was on a crescendo; if she ended up on the front page of the tabloids for dating a married man, the leading-role offers would evaporate. And yet here she was, propositioning bad-boy chef Deacon Thorpe. She was devaluing her brand with every second she stood in this kitchen. And it wasn't even that good a restaurant! Ruth Reichl had given it only two and a half stars in the *Times,* and she herself said that the half star was a donation because *Chef Deacon Thorpe shows so much promise.*

Deacon handed Belinda back the slip of paper and returned to his duties at the stove. Belinda had no choice but to slink out of the kitchen.

Later that night, she had crawled into her large, soft bed at the St. Regis, and she had castigated herself. She was a moron! She had acted like a teenage girl with a crush! She had behaved like a wanton floozy! What if Deacon Thorpe called up Liz Smith and said, *Belinda Rowe walked into my kitchen to proposition me?*

He wouldn't do that, she was certain. He was too cool for that. He was way cooler than anyone else Belinda knew. Or so she had somehow convinced herself. But what, really, did she know about him?

I'm married.

There had been something in his eyes, she thought, that made her think he had wanted her. She recalled the tender way he'd wiped the corner of her mouth; it had felt like a kiss. But maybe she had misinterpreted that gesture. Maybe he didn't want her and *that* was the attraction. Belinda had dated three men since moving to Hollywood—an actor (Stew Knightley, needy and narcissistic), a producer (David Gordman, rich and controlling), and, predictably, her director from *Between the Pipes*, James Brinegar (Jaime had been the most pompous, self-important ass she had ever met, and he was of course the one she had fallen in love with and was trying to get over). Deacon Thorpe was nothing like Stew, David, or Jaime. Deacon Thorpe might actually have known how to make proper love to a woman.

Belinda wondered about the wife. Leif thought she was hot, but she reminded Belinda of a low-rent Cheryl Tiegs, minus the boobs. Maybe Belinda had missed something.

Finally deciding that she had made a grave error in judgment but, she hoped, not one that would come back to haunt her, she closed her eyes.

And then her eyes popped open. Someone was knocking on her hotel-room door.

Belinda drank some more wine. "I know you hate me, Laurel," she said. "I know you think I stole him from you."

"You did steal him from me," Laurel said. "But 'hate' is a strong word. I hate men who beat their wives and children. I hate drug dealers and pimps and people who walk into a movie theater and shoot innocent citizens. You could even say I hate lima beans. But I don't hate you, Belinda. I don't care enough about you to hate you. You fall beneath my consideration."

Wow, Belinda thought. That was nicely done. Swiftly, cleanly, Laurel had sliced Belinda's self-esteem off at the head. *You fall beneath my consideration.*

"Besides," Laurel said. "I got back at you."

"You did?" Belinda said.

Laurel gave her a long, level look. Laurel's eyes were a clear gray-blue, like river stones. "Would you like to walk to the beach?" she asked.

"To the beach?" Belinda said. She wondered if this was part of some grand murder plot on Laurel's part. Possibly she planned on drowning Belinda in the ocean as payback for her treachery. Revenge was a dish best served cold—and this would be *really* cold. Nearly thirty years had passed, and the husband Belinda had stolen was now dead. What did Laurel *mean* when she said she'd gotten back at Belinda? Was there a rattlesnake nesting in the bottom of Clara's bed?

"Buck isn't much of a beach person," Laurel said, "and I've been wanting to go."

"I'm sure I make Buck look like Aquaman," Belinda said. "I grew up on the prairie."

"Just come with me," Laurel said. It seemed an order rather than a request.

Reluctantly, Belinda got to her feet, but first she poured herself more wine. There was no way she was walking to the beach with Laurel without wine.

Laurel eyed her wedge heels. "You're wearing those?"

Laurel is turning out to be quite the control freak this weekend, Belinda thought. "I have sandals, but they're buried in my suitcase," Belinda said. "These'll be fine."

Again, the level gaze. Laurel's face was lightly tanned and pretty much unlined. *Did she have work done?* Belinda wondered. She didn't think there was a social worker alive who went in for plastic surgery, so probably not. Laurel was wearing a pair of turquoise rubber flip-flops, the kind you bought at the five-and-dime.

Belinda said, "I came here straight from L.A."

"What about sneakers?"

"No sneakers."

"Do you not work out?"

Belinda shrugged. "Yoga."

"Do you wear your wedge heels to yoga?" Laurel asked.

Belinda didn't want to tell Laurel that Belinda's yoga instructor, Skyler, came to her suite at the Beverly Wilshire. In Los Angeles, Belinda was very conscious of her status, her lifestyle, and her perks. But Laurel was such a do-gooder—she was a *social worker* in the *Bronx*—that Belinda would have felt embarrassed admitting that she had a personal yoga instructor who paid house calls.

She said, "I have sneakers in Kentucky. Obviously." Then she wondered if this was even true. Belinda wasn't athletic. On the rare occasions that she went out to the horse track (unfortunately, a picture of Bob banging Carrie in the tack room presented itself), she wore Wellies.

"Maybe you should go barefoot," Laurel suggested.

"No," Belinda said. She would also be embarrassed to admit how much money she spent each week on spa pedicures, and she was *not* going to ruin her toe polish or invite rough patches on her heels by going barefoot. "I'll just wear these."

"Okay," Laurel said with a shrug.

Belinda put on her sunglasses and her wide-brimmed straw hat. They tiptoed past the front room, where Buck was snoring on the couch, and they headed out the door.

Belinda did better than she thought she would going down the driveway; she didn't spill a drop of wine. They crossed the road, and Laurel headed up the white sand path that led through tall beach grass. Belinda stopped and slugged back some of her wine for fortification. Laurel took off her cheapie flip-flops and kicked through the sand barefoot. From the back, Belinda thought resentfully, Laurel still looked like a girl. She wore her sandy blond hair long and straight, and her arms were nicely toned. She was wearing jean shorts and a white sleeveless blouse.

Belinda had to admit that she was jealous. Not of how

Laurel looked, exactly, but of how little effort her beauty seemed to require. Did she go to the hairdresser to get the gray taken out of her part? Did she work out at a gym with a personal trainer to get those arms?

Belinda stopped again: more wine. The sand was white, deep, and very soft. Her left wedge wobbled and threatened to turn. She sighed. She would have to sacrifice the softness of her feet.

"Hold up," she called out. "I have to take my shoes off."

Laurel gave her a look.

"Never mind, go on ahead if you want," Belinda said. "I'm way out of my comfort zone here."

Laurel waited for Belinda—which was decent of her, Belinda thought—and together they trudged up the hill until they came to the battered wooden snow fence that funneled them straight down to the beach. The ocean was in front of them: dark blue, loud, and majestic—and, to Belinda, totally terrifying. She had accompanied Deacon—and then Deacon and Hayes, and then Deacon and Hayes and Angie and Scarlett, the nanny—to this beach a handful of times each summer. She would sit on a chair underneath an enormous umbrella and read scripts while everyone else swam and splashed and loudly announced how *delicious* the water felt. That had been Scarlett, Belinda remembered now, cavorting around in her teensy red bikini—because of her name, she always wore harlot red—calling the water *delicious.*

Laurel stripped off her shorts and blouse; she was wearing a floral bikini underneath. Her body looked amazing. Her stomach was flat and smooth. How was this *possible?* It was as if she had never had children! Well, only one child, almost thirty-five years earlier. When you had a baby at nineteen, Belinda supposed, your body snapped back like tight elastic instead of bagging out. Belinda had given birth to Mary at forty-two and to Laura at forty-three, and she had been doing battle with her tummy ever since.

Laurel gave a rollicking whoop and went racing into the water—high-stepping first, shouting, "It's cold! It's cold!" until finally diving in. Belinda sat in the sand with her wine.

"Come on in!" Laurel shouted.

"No, thanks," Belinda said. "I'm good."

As Laurel swam, Belinda's mind returned to the fateful night almost thirty years earlier: She had given Deacon her room number at the St. Regis, and against all odds, he had shown up. He had thrown her onto the bed; he'd torn her paper-thin T-shirt right off her. When he kissed her, he had tasted like tequila.

After it was over, Belinda had offered him a glass of ice water, which he gratefully guzzled down. She said, "Why did you come?" She figured he was just drunk, or maybe the ginger-haired maître d' had talked him into it because she was Belinda Rowe.

Deacon said, "When you came into the kitchen, you looked so...I don't know...lonely, I guess. You looked the way I felt."

She had traced her index finger along his clavicle. "You're lonely?"

"Always," he said.

Later, as they were walking back—Belinda out of wine and Laurel dripping wet, holding her clothes—Laurel said, "So you got married again, and you have two girls?"

Belinda nodded. Those factoids could be found on Wikipedia, but even so, Belinda's guard went up.

"I married Bob Percil," Belinda said. "He's a Thoroughbred trainer. Our daughters are Mary, nine, and Laura, eight."

"I was pretty surprised when I saw a photo of you in the tabloids, pregnant," Laurel said. "I thought you weren't able to have children."

Belinda blinked. *It's none of your fucking business,* she thought. This wasn't going to be one of those weekends when every secret was confessed and women who previously hated each other forged a new bond due to the death of their mutual ex-husband.

But she didn't want to start a fight. Not yet, anyway—she had just gotten here.

"No one was more surprised than me," she said. She needed to turn the tables here. "How about you? Are you dating anyone?"

"No," Laurel said.

"I find that hard to believe," Belinda said. "You're so pretty."

"Please don't patronize me," Laurel said.

"I'm not!" Belinda said. "I was checking you out earlier. You look fantastic."

Laurel narrowed her eyes.

"Why don't you date Buck?" Belinda said. "He's single, right? And you know he's always had a crush on you."

"Stop," Laurel said.

"It's true," Belinda said. "Deacon used to tease him about it."

Laurel smiled down at her feet, and Belinda thought: *Advantage, Rowe.* She had gotten her enemy to smile. Belinda had noticed Buck and Laurel looking pretty cozy on the deck when she arrived. Something was definitely going to happen there, which would do wonders in lightening up the melancholy atmosphere of the weekend.

Belinda sat down on the big rock that Deacon had long

ago painted with a green *33*, marking the start of the driveway. "You can go on up. I'm going to put on my shoes."

"Okay," Laurel said. "I'm going to take an outdoor shower, then head into town for a bit."

The outdoor shower! On her first trip to Nantucket, Belinda had bemoaned the sad state of the indoor plumbing. The showers worked in only three of the bathrooms, each of which produced a lukewarm spritz of water—enough to mist one's face—but Deacon frowned upon using them, anyway. It wasn't how things were done on Nantucket. It was summertime; one showered outdoors! He had been right: Belinda had grown to love showering with the late-afternoon sun streaming down and the pure-blue sky above her head, the vista of the rolling moors just visible over the top of the shower door.

Belinda stood up, not bothering with her shoes. She had to hurry; otherwise Laurel would use up all the hot water.

Intermezzo:
Deacon and Laurel, Part II

He can't believe he's doing it. He would like to blame it on the three shots of tequila he did with Buck after service, but he's never felt sharper. His vision is crystal clear. He wants this. He convinces himself that if Laurel finds out—and he will do everything in his power to make sure she doesn't—she will understand.

It's Belinda Rowe.

He enters the lobby of the St. Regis and finds the elevator. He pushes *18*.

* * *

He falls under her spell. How this happens, he's not quite sure. Part of it is the fame, the money, the lifestyle, her confidence, her glamour. She has kissed Steve McQueen, Robert De Niro, and Paul Newman on screen. She lives in a room in a five-star hotel and calls up bottles of Dom Pérignon and silver dishes of long-stemmed strawberries as if it's her cool second job. Deacon sips champagne out of her navel; he feeds her the berries. She buys him a watch that he knows costs north of five thousand dollars. *So you'll know when it's time to be with me,* she says. He lies to Laurel about the watch and about where he is every time he goes to the St. Regis. He tells Laurel he's with Buck. He hates himself for the lying, but he can't stop.

He does go out with Buck one night after service, and he confesses everything to his friend; then he gets so drunk, he blacks out. Buck delivers him home to Laurel, and in the morning Deacon worries that Buck has told Laurel his secret. Buck, Deacon knows, wants Laurel for himself. Somewhere in his confused mind, this stirs up an accusation that Laurel is sleeping with Buck behind Deacon's back.

Laurel doesn't get mad. She doesn't see the accusation for what it is: an admission of Deacon's guilt. Instead, she laughs in his face.

"Me and Buck?" she says. "Hahahaha!"

He wants to get angry at her for laughing, but he can't summon the energy. He is an awful, horrible, evil, damaged human being for lying to his angelic wife. He starts to cry, and Laurel does what she always does when he cries: she pulls his head into her lap and strokes his hair.

* * *

He loves Laurel. He will stop seeing Belinda. Belinda is heading back to L.A. in another week anyway. Deacon goes to the St. Regis after service, and right away, before there is any time for funny business, he tells Belinda it's over. It was a mistake, he says. He is married. He has a son.

Belinda stares at him, and then she crumples to the floor. Deacon can't leave her in a sobbing pile. He doesn't *want* to leave her. He loves her—not because she's famous or glamorous or rich. He loves her because inside she is broken, just as he is. She is lonely, just as he is.

Belinda wants Deacon to move to L.A. She will be able to introduce him to people. His career will really take off. She will buy him his own restaurant. He can be his own boss.

Leave Laurel? he thinks. Leave New York? Leave his job at Solo? Leave Hayes, the little boy he's raising the way he wished he'd been raised? He can't imagine doing any of this, but he becomes convinced that he's meant for bigger things. Because they blew the entire advance check on the Nantucket house, he and Laurel still live on a budget. If he goes with Belinda, things will be better for all of them.

He picks Belinda up off the ground and carries her to the bed. He still can't believe she chose him, Deacon Thorpe from Stuy Town, when she could have had any man in the world.

"Come with me," Belinda says. "Please, Deacon."

He can't say no. It's as if he's turned over control of his sensibilities. It's like black magic.

"Yes," he says. "I'll tell her tomorrow."

BUCK

He fell asleep on the mildewed but surprisingly comfortable cushions of the bamboo-framed sofa and dreamed of kissing Laurel. He had almost gone through with it on the deck. He had been this close.

But then Belinda had shown up, ruining everything. Buck wondered how to create another situation in which kissing Laurel might be possible. He had been married twice, but most days it felt as though he had absolutely no experience with women.

What would Deacon have thought if he did kiss Laurel? He would either have said, *Way to go, buddy!* or he would have been explosively angry and jealous.

Buck woke up from his nap unsure of where he was. Then he remembered. He was "living the life on Nantucket." He had been to this house only once before, in the summer of 1987, and that had been awful enough to ensure that he wouldn't return in the thirty years of his friendship with Deacon. This house, with its damp, rickety yard-sale furniture and its persistent smell of a salt marsh, had been about as far from Buck's idea of "paradise" as a place could get. When Buck visited before, it had rained all weekend long, leaving Buck to alternately play tedious games of Monopoly with Deacon, Laurel, and Hayes and then twiddle his thumbs while Hayes napped and Laurel and Deacon had sex upstairs. Buck and Deacon had gone on an "outing" to the liquor store in the 1946 Willys jeep that Deacon had bought as an "island car." The jeep had no top and no doors. Buck had held an umbrella while Deacon drove, but the umbrella had inverted in the wind, and Buck had returned to the house soaked and chilled to the bone, which no amount of time standing under the outdoor shower had remedied.

Buck got to his feet. He needed to relieve himself, and he was starving. He couldn't remember which door would reveal the bathroom. The first door he tried was a closet that held someone's yellow rain slicker, a pair of rubber pants with attached suspenders, and an assortment of umbrellas. Buck tried to imagine what circumstances would require rubber pants—fighting a fire? He tried another door and found paper towels, cleaning supplies, a broom, and a mop. Finally, he stepped out the sliding door and, finding no one around, peed off the back deck. He was still wearing half his suit, but he managed to feel some connection with nature. He was a little more relaxed, a little less citified, now that he was here. Buck closed his eyes for a second and heard a distant roar, which he realized was the ocean.

It was pretty overwhelming for a boy who had grown up with yellow cabs and ambulance sirens.

Buck stepped back into the kitchen. In the fridge, he found cheese and crackers and green grapes and a rotisserie chicken. He pulled everything out onto the counter and started stuffing his face. He couldn't remember being *this* hungry in all his life. He didn't even have the patience to put the cheese and crackers together; he just crammed them into his mouth separately. He ripped the drumstick off the chicken and mowed through that and then, thirsty, he checked the fridge for beer. Drinking in the middle of the day was something he had only ever done with Deacon.

On the bottom shelf, he discovered a case of St. Pauli Girl. Laurel must have bought it, knowing it was Deacon and Buck's favorite beer. Deacon used to call St. Pauli Girl "the girl we share."

The girl we share. Buck thought about kissing Laurel. Deacon would *not* have liked it one bit, he was now certain.

Buck pulled out a bottle of St. Pauli Girl and twisted the top off with his forearm, a trick that Deacon had taught him and that it had taken Buck only eight or nine years to master. He raised the bottle into the air and said, "Here's to us, two selfish bastards." And then he drank.

"Buck?"

He swung around as Belinda sauntered into the kitchen wearing just a towel—and because this was American Paradise, where *pitiful* never went out of fashion, the towel was thin and threadbare and only just long enough to cover Belinda's famous ass. Buck turned his attention back to the chicken.

He said, "I just woke up. I was hungry."

"Yes," Belinda said. "You took quite the power nap." She sat on one of the bar stools. "I'll take a beer if you're offering."

Was he offering? He was too much of a gentleman to tell her that she was interrupting a rare moment of John Buckley introspection and that he would rather be left alone to finish stuffing his piehole and to mourn the loss of the best friend he would ever have. So instead, he ducked into the fridge and took out two more beers—one for Belinda, another for him. Again, he twisted the tops off with his forearm. The first time, when he was alone, had been to impress Deacon, he supposed. But this time it was to impress Belinda.

She raised her eyebrows and accepted the bottle. "Thank you," she said.

He couldn't look at her without his eyes traveling down to the place where the towel was tucked into her cleavage. He could see her erect nipples through the thin terry cloth. When she brought the beer bottle to her lips, the material loosened at the top; the tuck threatened to come untucked. *Oh dear God.*

"Where's Laurel?" he asked. The kitchen clock said two

thirty; the kids weren't due to arrive until five thirty. He needed Laurel to save him.

"She went into town," Belinda said. "Bookstore to browse, she said, then to Flowers on Chestnut for a bouquet for the dinner table."

Buck nodded. *Come home, Laurel,* he thought. *I need you now.*

He said, "You know, I have some business to discuss with you and Laurel."

Belinda shook her head; the towel loosened a little more. "We aren't talking business now, Buck. This weekend is about honoring the memory of the man."

"Oh, I know...," Buck said. "I don't mean to be crass or mercenary, but there are things that you and Laurel need to be aware of."

"Why do I need to be aware?" Belinda asked. "Deacon and I divorced a dozen years ago. We have no common interests except for Angie."

"That's not true," Buck said. "The will..." He trailed off. He needed to proceed cautiously here. In the Alcatraz of Buck's brain—where he kept thoughts he didn't want to escape—was this: Belinda was the only person in Deacon's "family" who could save this house. She could pay the $436,292.19 to get it out of hock and then maybe come up with a way to pay the mortgage. That would be shoe money for her. But Buck was afraid to ask. She was intimidating and dismissive. Maybe if he just told her a third of the house was hers, she would offer to help. She might think him an uncouth boor for bringing up Deacon's money troubles when they were supposed to be mourning—but then again, they were *real* troubles. This house was going to be repossessed in less than two weeks, and the treasure chest of happy-go-lucky Thorpe summertime memories would go with it.

"The will?" Belinda said, and she laughed. "Did Deacon leave something to *me?* I find that very hard to believe."

She stood up, holding her beer bottle with both hands, and that did the trick—her towel fell to the floor.

"Oops," she said. "My towel." But she made no move to pick it up or to shield herself. Belinda Rowe was naked before him.

Buck felt an uncomfortable stirring in his pants, and he cursed himself. He was getting hard. He couldn't help it; he was a man. He didn't even find Belinda particularly attractive! She was nowhere near as beautiful as Laurel. Well, correction: Belinda Rowe was beautiful, iconically so, but she was too much of a china doll for Buck. He liked his women real.

Belinda walked over to him.

Oh no! he thought. He didn't like where this was headed. Belinda was no dummy; she knew what she was doing. The blush traveled up his neck, to his cheeks, involuntarily. It was the curse of an Irishman, along with the ginger hair, the freckles—his fair skin gave every emotion away.

"Very hard to believe," she said. She gently pried the beer out of his hand and set it down on the counter. She then wound her arms around his neck and pressed herself against him. He couldn't help himself; he groaned. It had been a while since he'd been with a woman, and, although he in no way wanted anything to happen with Belinda Rowe, he couldn't ignore her naked body pressed up against him, nor her long, strawberry-blond hair and her intoxicating scent. She shifted her hip so that it grazed his erection.

Okay, this is awful, he thought. But that got rolled over when she dropped to her knees before him and undid his zipper.

Belinda, no, he said. Or maybe he didn't say that. Maybe he just thought that as she took him in her mouth and licked and sucked him until he came in explosive bursts, crying out quietly twice.

Belinda returned casually to her stool and re-secured the towel around her body.

Buck hurried to zip his pants. "I thought you were married," he said.

"I am," she said.

Buck was suddenly exhausted and very, very disappointed in himself. He couldn't bear to think of Laurel in the hushed, rarefied atmosphere of the bookstore, selecting a novel off the shelves, reading the blurbs on the cover, and carefully replacing it before selecting another novel. If she found out what had just happened, she would...lose all respect for him? Call him base? No, she would understand; that was the crushing thing. Laurel had it in her head that Belinda was prettier and more desirable, certainly more famous and celebrated. She would say, *Of course you let her, Buck. It's okay.*

But it wasn't okay.

It made Buck love Laurel all the more.

Buck started cleaning up the food and putting it away. He said, "I don't usually drink in the middle of the day."

"No, me neither," Belinda said. "But desperate times call for desperate measures." She finished off her beer, then set the bottle down for him to clear. "I'm off to shower."

ANGIE

They took the four o'clock fast ferry. When Angie saw the church steeples and the gray-shingled buildings and the sailboats in the harbor bathed in the late-afternoon sun, she felt a little better. She was home.

They disembarked and walked down the wharf. Hayes hailed a taxi; taking care of travel arrangements was his specialty, she knew, but still, she envied his confidence. He was comfortable in the world; she was comfortable in the kitchen.

The taxi was a black Lincoln Continental with suicide doors. Their driver was dressed in a long velvet coat and wore a three-cornered hat with a plume; he had a patch over one eye. He stuck his hand out to Hayes. "My name is Pirate," he said.

Angie thought, *Oh dear God, let's find another taxi.* But Hayes's face lit up. He was a big fan of street theater, Angie remembered now. He always volunteered.

"No way," Hayes said. "A pirate on Nantucket."

"The one and only," Pirate said. He opened the back door with a flourish and bowed deeply, indicating that Angie should climb in. "Where you headed?"

Hayes said, "Hoicks Hollow Road."

Pirate headed through town. The top on the Lincoln was down, and Pirate commanded so much attention that Angie felt as if she were in a parade. Everyone on the street waved. Little kids cried out, "Pirate! Pirate!"

Hayes said, "I don't think I've ever seen you before, man, but you seem like a local celebrity."

Pirate was too busy showboating to answer. Angie sank down in her seat, but over the top of her sunglasses, she checked out the surroundings. Pirate turned them up the cobblestones of Main Street. They passed the white-columned Hadwen House and the Three Bricks, which in Angie's mind always evoked the nineteenth century, men heading out on whaling expeditions, women wearing hoopskirts. People were everywhere, just as they were everywhere in Manhattan, but the Nantucket crowd was as homogeneous as the cedar-shingled buildings. Nearly everyone was blond, tanned, attractive, well dressed.

"What number on Hoicks Hollow?" Pirate asked.

"Thirty-three," Hayes and Angie said together.

Pirate hit the brakes, and Angie grabbed the seat in front of her.

Pirate eyed Hayes in the rearview mirror. "Are you a friend of Deacon Thorpe's?"

Hayes put his arm around Angie. "We're his kids."

Pirate puzzled over this, taking a glance at Angie in the rearview.

"I'm adopted," Angie said.

Pirate frowned skeptically, the way people had been doing all of Angie's life. She'd had one instructor at the CIA who hadn't believed Angie was Deacon Thorpe's daughter until Deacon had shown up at graduation.

Pirate said, "I'm very sorry for your loss. Your father was a good man, a generous man. I drove him from the ferry to the house when he came out the last time."

"You *did?*" Hayes said. Hayes was in a chipper mood, but of course he had slept for the entire drive, laid out in the backseat, his head resting on his soft suede travel duffel. Angie had tried to snooze on the ferry while Hayes smoked cigarettes and drank Bloody Marys with a very sophisticated couple who owned a cheese shop in Yountville, California. Angie had heard Hayes say, *I adore Auberge du Soleil; really, there's no other place that compares in Napa or Sonoma. A glass of Stags' Leap chardonnay on that deck in the four o'clock sunshine—well, I'm sorry, but it just doesn't get any better than that.* And she thought, *The man can talk to anybody about anything.* Hayes leaned over the seat so that he could more easily converse with Pirate.

"Really? So you were one of the last people to see our father alive, then?"

"That, I wouldn't know," Pirate said. He seemed suddenly uncomfortable, and Angie realized he might not want that distinction.

She was happy to get out of the cab, much as she dreaded all that lay ahead.

Hayes said, "Do you have a card, man? So we can party with you later?"

"Party with you later"? Angie thought. Was Hayes on *drugs?* There wasn't going to be any *partying* later. All that was happening *later* was a lot of painful interaction with family.

Pirate handed Hayes his card—it had a skull-and-crossbones motif, very original—and then made a grand production of extracting their luggage from the Lincoln's trunk.

"Please call me," Pirate said. "I would love to be your driver while you're on-island." He and Hayes shook hands, Hayes gave him thirty dollars, and then Pirate leapt over the driver's side door, into the seat. Angie rolled her eyes, then turned to stare at the front of the house with dread.

She suffered a positively dismaying memory of her father and Scarlett's wedding. Angie had been sixteen years old and had *not* wanted to attend. She had loved and worshipped Scarlett once upon a time. But in Scarlett's second appearance in Angie's life—as her soon-to-be stepmother—she had had far less appeal. Angie's nanny—who had let her swim in Bethesda Fountain in Central Park and helped Angie throw a full-blown Halloween party in the middle of April—was now the same woman making all the screaming sex noises coming from her father's bedroom.

The wedding had been held in Scarlett's hometown of Savannah, Georgia, during the sweltering first week of July.

The air in Savannah had smelled like a swamp, and the trees had hung heavy with Spanish moss, which Angie had never seen before; it reminded her of hair tangled in a drain. The fountains in the squares were dry; the river was stagnant and a breeding ground for mosquitoes the size of sparrows. The old mansions in town were pretty, but Angie couldn't get past the fact that they had most likely been built by slaves. Scarlett's parents lived in the prettiest house in Savannah; even Angie had to admit that this was true. It was a yellow clapboard Victorian with gables and a magnificent wrap-around porch, complete with lush hanging ferns—possibly the only greenery thriving in the entire city—and a swing and a line of rocking chairs. When Deacon and Angie had knocked on the formidable front door, a black maid in a turquoise uniform and a pristine white apron had answered.

She had looked at Angie first, then at Deacon, then back at Angie. "Can I help y'all?" she asked.

"I'm the groom!" Deacon had exclaimed.

"Let me go fetch Mrs. Oliver," the maid had said.

Deacon and Angie had remained on the front porch. It was the first of a thousand times Angie had wished to go home.

Mrs. Oliver had turned out to be Scarlett's mother, Prudence, known to her familiars as Prue; Angie was certainly not the woman's familiar and decided never to call her anything, not even Mrs. Oliver. Prue was simply an older version of Scarlett, with the same black hair, hers pulled back in a chignon; the same pale skin; the same vermilion lipstick. "Deacon," she said, making the name rhyme with "bacon." "You're here."

"That I am," Deacon said. He shook Prue's hand, then ushered Angie forward, like a hostess gift. "And this is my daughter, Angie."

"Yes," Prue had said. "I've heard all about Angie."

Angie assumed this meant Prue had long ago been warned that Angie was black.

There had been many offensive things about Deacon's wedding to Scarlett. Angie had been the only family member to attend—Hayes had gotten a pass because he was on his first assignment for the magazine, in Switzerland—and the only other person to attend from Deacon's life was Buck, who had served as best man.

"Rewind, repeat," Buck said to Scarlett's uncle, the appeals judge who married the happy couple. "I was Deacon's best man the last time around as well."

The ceremony had been held in the meticulously landscaped back garden of the yellow mansion. Angie had roasted in the long-sleeved lavender lace dress that Scarlett had picked out for her. It was Givenchy, but who cared? It was sadistic to put a dark girl in long-sleeved scratchy material in a sickening color when it was a hundred and ten degrees out.

Worse than the heat and Scarlett's relatives (who were self-proclaimed Confederates and therefore, Angie assumed, racists), or the fact that the Thorpes were so woefully outnumbered, was that Deacon was trying so hard to make Scarlett's family like him, to accept him, to consider him good enough. Angie didn't understand the dynamics at play. Scarlett had been their *nanny;* she had worked for *them.* But when Angie tried to make this point, Deacon said, "Scarlett comes from an old Savannah family, sweetheart. She was raised as a member of society."

Deacon had worn a seersucker suit and a bow tie, and Angie had barked out a laugh and said, "What did you do with my father?"

It wasn't bad enough that Angie was losing her father;

apparently, he was losing himself. Gone was his cool self-confidence, gone was his devil-may-care attitude, gone was what Angie had thought of as his essential superiority to every other man in the world. When he was conversing with the judge uncle and Scarlett's parents—Prue and Scarlett's upright corpse of a father, Brace—Deacon sounded downright obsequious. He must have mentioned sixty times that Angie was getting straight As at Chapin, "a prestigious girls' boarding school on the Upper East Side of Manhattan," and that his own "five-year plan" included "opening my own place somewhere in midtown, just as soon as I cultivate the right group of investors."

Angie thought, *Since when do you have to brag about my grades or state your goals?*

The worst of the worst, however, happened during the champagne toasts that preceded the cutting of the cake. By this time, Angie was rip-roaring drunk herself, thanks to a fraternity boy from Ole Miss named Burt, who slipped a liberal amount of rum into each of Angie's Cokes.

Deacon had raised his flute and said, "Scarlett and I have an announcement to make."

Angie had thought, *What kind of announcement?* They were already married. What was left?

Scarlett said, "I'm pregnant."

There was an ambiguous reaction from those assembled—some grumbles, some hear-hear's with glasses held aloft. Angie's own reaction had been clear-cut: she had vomited in the grass at her feet.

Now, she and Hayes ascended the steps to the front porch in near-perfect unison. A board on the floor of the porch in front of the welcome mat was loose, and Angie nearly stumbled over it.

Hayes pulled a couple of white pills out of his pocket. He threw one back, washed it down with a sip of the watery Bloody Mary he'd been nursing since they got off the ferry. He held the other pill out to Angie.

"Vicodin?" he said. "Take the edge off?"

Angie stared at the pill. There were multiple loci of her pain—her father's death, Joel's puzzling silence, and then... whatever waited inside this house. But Angie surprised herself by realizing that she didn't *want* to take the edge off. She wanted to feel everything. Mostly, she wanted to cry.

"No, thanks," she said.

Hayes shrugged, pocketed the pill, and held the door open. "After you," he said.

Laurel and Buck were sitting on stools in the kitchen, having drinks. When they saw Hayes and Angie walk in, they jumped to their feet.

"You made it!" Laurel cried out. She hugged Hayes, and Buck hugged Angie.

Angie wanted to grill Buck with a thousand silly, insecure questions: *Did my father love me? Did he think I was talented? Did he think I was smart? Was he proud of me?*

Did he know about me and Joel?

Did he love me as much as Hayes or Ellery?

Buck released Angie; he and Laurel did a little dance step and switched partners. Buck gave Hayes a man hug, while Laurel embraced Angie.

"Oh, sweet Angie," Laurel said.

"It's so weird being here without him," Angie said. She had been coming to this house with her father every summer of her life. Just behind Laurel's head was the spot on the door frame where Angie, Hayes, and Ellery had all been measured with pencil marks at the end of each summer. *Home is where the hash marks are,* Angie thought. Deacon used to do the measuring on the last day of their stay, and he always said the same thing: *My, my, look how you have grown!*

"I haven't been here in nearly thirty years," Laurel said. "It looks exactly the same as it did the summer we bought it, or nearly. I'm sure it's difficult for you. I'm sure you expect him to pull into the driveway any second in that crazy jeep."

"The jeep died for good last year," Angie said. "We all thought *that* was the end of the world, but no. This is."

"Angie?"

A different voice.

Oh no.

Angie turned to see Belinda enter the kitchen.

"Mom?" Angie said. She had known her mother was coming, obviously—Buck had told her, and Belinda had confirmed it herself in the two dozen voice mails she had left on Angie's phone—but Angie had been positive Belinda would back out because of Laurel. Belinda and Laurel hated each other, and Belinda also hated Scarlett. Although Scarlett wasn't present—Buck had said she wasn't coming at all—this was, technically, Scarlett's house now, and how could Belinda be expected to deal with *that* gracefully, when Scarlett used to be the nanny?

Angie was an idiot; she should have accepted the Vicodin.

"Darling," Belinda said. She moved swiftly into Angie's arms. Belinda was so much smaller than Angie that it was as if their roles had reversed and Belinda was the child and Angie the mother. Angie could have picked Belinda right off the ground. Instead, Angie gave her a halfhearted hug. Deacon's dying hadn't changed the fact that Belinda was a conniving, vainglorious disaster.

"Vainglorious": that was a Deacon word. He had loved it—but he'd only ever used it to describe one person.

"When did you get here?" Angie asked.

"This morning," Belinda said. "I took the red-eye from L.A. But I should have gotten here earlier. Then maybe I would have gotten a decent bedroom." She cut a glance at Laurel.

"Why, what room are you staying in?" Angie asked.

"Laurel assigned me to Clara's room."

Angie couldn't help herself: she smiled. She tried to picture Belinda Rowe, the most celebrated actress of modern times, sleeping in the narrow convent bed of Clara's cramped room. Deacon had made up colorful stories about Clara Beck over the years; she had been the nursemaid for the five Innsley children, and for Mr. Innsley himself before that. Deacon had portrayed her as very homely and very strict. As such, Clara's room had been used as a place of punishment. When Angie, at five or six, had thrown sand at another child on the beach, she had been whisked right up to the house and made to sit on the bed in Clara's room for twenty minutes. It had seemed an eternity. When Angie was seventeen, she had come home from a bonfire at Gibbs Pond completely smashed and stoned, and Deacon had made her sleep in Clara's room. The walls had seemed to close in on her as the bed spun. That night, Angie had seen the ghost of Clara Beck. She was dressed in a high-necked ivory gown, and her hair was rolled up in pink, spongy curlers. Angie had been too drunk to be afraid; she had closed her eyes against the apparition, then puked into the wastebasket.

"Yes, I'm sure you find that very amusing," Belinda said. "But the fact is, this used to be my house. I was married to Deacon longer than either Laurel or Scarlett, and I deserve respect."

She delivered this last sentence with her usual dramatic flair, as though it were a line she was rehearsing. There were *so many things* about the woman that bothered Angie. She would have had an easier time listing the things about Belinda that she found inoffensive.

Her mother had nice hair.

She had great taste in clothes.

She had once hosted *Saturday Night Live,* and she had been much funnier than Angie had expected.

Once upon a time, Belinda had discovered a maternal streak inside her—like a vein of pure silver running through rock—and she had traveled through the dusty, dry forever of the Australian outback, where Angie had been left to be raised in an "orphanage for native peoples."

But this maternal streak had dried up or disappeared at some point during Angie's youth, when Belinda had chosen her career over parenthood again and again and again—on location, on location, on location. She had filmed in Vietnam for *The Delta* for four months! She eventually won the Oscar, but who cared?

"If you're that unhappy," Angie said, "why don't you move to a hotel? Call Cliffside."

"I want to be here with you, darling," Belinda said. "And I wanted to say a proper good-bye to your father."

Hayes, Buck, and Laurel tactfully wandered out to the back deck, leaving Angie and Belinda alone in the kitchen.

"A proper good-bye to your father"? Most likely she had come to make certain that no one was talking about her.

"There's nothing you can do for me," Angie said. "I mean, you can't bring him back."

Belinda twisted her hair in her hands and held it to the top of her head. This was her nervous gesture; Angie had always thought it revealed the conceited little girl Belinda must have been. "I know exactly how you feel, darling. I lost both of my parents."

"You *don't* know exactly how I feel," Angie said. "You *left* your parents right after high school and you never spoke to them again. Your father died in a plane crash, and Dad had to force you to go back for the funeral. You didn't attend your mother's funeral because you were on location in Scotland. All you have ever cared about is your career, Mom. You never cared about your parents. You never loved either of them the way I loved Deacon."

"You and Deacon were very close," Belinda said, as if she were conceding a point. "But it was a little..."

"A little what?"

"A little unnatural," Belinda said. "You two were together all the time, night and day, at work, at home, at your Tuesday-night dinners together. You had one night off a week! You should have spent it with friends or a boyfriend. You should have been out dancing or going to the movies, not tending to your father's emotional crises."

"I didn't tend to his emotional *crises,*" Angie said, though her voice faltered. That had been exactly what she did, week in and week out. They cooked for themselves and drank too much, and when the clock struck eleven or midnight and Angie told Deacon he should go home to Scarlett, he had said, "I can't go home this drunk. She'll kill me." And then he would drink some more.

But her mother's being right, or partially so, only served to infuriate Angie. "I'm not doing this. I'm not going to have you tell me that you know what I'm *feeling* because you lost your own parents! You hated your parents, and you *hated* Deacon, and I'm sure you're *glad* he's dead!" She swallowed. She was cotton mouthed and really needed a glass of water.

"Angie, please," Belinda said. "Lower your voice."

"Don't tell me what to do!" Angie said. She couldn't handle another piece of emotional baggage. She missed Deacon. She needed Joel to call. Angie stormed out of the kitchen. Her roller bag was sitting at the bottom of the stairs. She had packed things for three days, but could she reasonably stay in a house with her mother for three days?

She pushed open the screen door, enjoying the sound of it smacking the frame of the house behind her. She nearly tripped on the rotting board in the floor again and almost went flying down the steps of the porch headfirst, but she managed to steady herself. She ran down the driveway, but at the bottom, she was at a loss, and the sun was hot. She was thirsty. This wasn't the city—there was no corner deli, no Burmese place, no Starbucks. Down the road a bit was the Sankaty Head Beach Club; it had a vending machine out back that they used to sneak sodas from as kids. Or Angie could go back to the house and take the antique pickup truck that Deacon had bought to replace the Willys jeep. The truck was in the garage, but the keys were hanging on a peg in the kitchen, and Angie didn't want to go back inside.

She pulled out her phone. She would call Joel. She wanted to hear his voice. She wanted to hear him call her Ange. Was it possible that she had fallen for the man simply because of the way he said her name? Did that happen to other people?

All her life Angie had felt as though her heart was a rock, dense and impenetrable. But with Joel, the rock had broken open and revealed itself to be a geode, lined with glittering crystals.

She dialed Joel's number. Her call went immediately to voice mail. Angie hung up.

Should she text Hayes and tell him she was going back to the city alone? The thing was, she didn't *want* to go back to

New York. She loved Nantucket more than anywhere else in the world. They always went in August, but Angie thought it was even more beautiful now, in June. She wanted to be with her brother and Laurel and Buck. She wanted people she could talk to, people who had known Deacon. And they were going to scatter the ashes; Angie couldn't miss that.

The sun was hot, and Angie could smell and hear the ocean. Living the life on Nantucket: Deacon should be here, fishing and swimming. Tonight, the sun would set off the back deck, and he wouldn't be here to raise his glass, or to clap as if for God: *Another day well done, Sir.* Deacon's days were over.

Angie screamed, as loudly as she could. *Aaaaaaaayyyyy-aaahhhh! Eeeeyyyyyaaahhh! Eeeeeeeaaaaayyyyyah!* She screamed so loudly, her throat hurt. There was no one to stop her. Could they hear her back up at the house? Probably not.

Aaaaaaaaeeeeeeeeeeeyyahhh!

If she screamed like this in Manhattan, her neighbors would call the police. She would be evicted or arrested. Or committed. One more thing Angie loved about Nantucket: she had the freedom to scream.

Yoooooooohoooeeeeahhh!

A car appeared around the bend, a silver Jeep Wrangler with the top down. The driver was a big, bearded bear of a man wearing Blues Brothers sunglasses. Instantly, Angie heard Deacon's voice in her head: *"It's a hundred and six miles to Chicago, we got a full tank of gas, half a pack of cigarettes, it's dark, and we're wearing sunglasses."* To which Angie had been trained to respond: *"Hit it."* But instead, Angie clamped her mouth shut and stared down at the road, willing the person to pass so that she could go back to losing her mind. Much to her enormous consternation, the Jeep stopped in front of her.

"Hey," the guy said. "Are you *okay?*"

Angie nodded at him mutely, thinking that if she pretended she didn't speak English, he might drive away. Then she noticed what looked like a mason jar of iced tea in his console. Or maybe it was whiskey over ice. Either way, she needed it. She was so thirsty.

"Could I possibly have a sip of that?" she said. "I'm parched."

Parched? she thought. What on God's green earth had made her say that? Customers ponied up to the bar at the Board Room all the time and announced to Dr. Disibio that they were "parched," and they all sounded like douche bags. Because of this, Deacon had put "parched" at number eight on the Stupid Word List.

The guy handed her the jar. "This? It's sun tea, unsweetened, with mint and lemon. I brewed it myself."

"That sounds really good," Angie said. "Do you mind?" She took the jar from him, and before she knew what was happening, she had downed the entire thing. Angie was so thirsty and the tea was so light and lemony that it was like drinking the nectar of the gods.

"Wow," the guy said. He grinned and held out his hand. "My name is JP Clarke. Are you lost? Do you need a ride somewhere? This is a pretty uptight neighborhood—actually, it's a private way, so . . . I wouldn't want you to take flak from any of the residents for wandering around."

"*You're* JP?" Angie said. She couldn't *believe* it. Deacon had talked about "JP this" and "JP that" all the time in recent years, but Angie had never met him, despite Deacon incessantly promising Angie that she would love him. *Great guy, real local, lives off the land, fishes, hunts, knows all the best spots. You two would really get along.* Deacon had met JP surf casting out at Great Point, and from there, the friendship had grown. JP had sent Deacon Nantucket bay scallops the past few Octobers, and Angie and Deacon always ate part of the shipment raw, with a squeeze of lime juice and a sprinkle of salt. Hobo seviche, Deacon called it. JP also sent backstraps of venison from the one buck he shot each November, and Deacon would marinate it for three days, then grill it to rosy, juicy perfection and serve it at staff meal.

Angie had thought JP would be older. She had imagined someone her father's age, but JP barely looked thirty.

"I *am* JP," he said. "Who might you be?"

"Angie," she said. "Angie Thorpe."

"Angie Thorpe," he said. He moved his sunglasses to the top of his head, as if he wanted to get a better look at her. "Oh my darling. Your father..."—here he trailed off and squinted out the windshield at the lighthouse beyond—"was a fine human being. Just...I don't know? An original. I can't seem to use my words here. He was super cool in his every aspect. I feel blessed to have known him."

"He felt the same way about you," Angie said. "He talked about you all the time. Okay...that jam you sent him? The Concord grape? He took one jar home to eat on toast, and the other jar he reduced into a sauce that he served with a pheasant special we ran—and it was the night Pete Wells came in to review for the *New York Times*. And what was the first dish Wells raved about? The crispy pheasant with the Concord grape sauce." Angie felt a flush thinking about that night. Joel was the one who had suspected the diner registered as Albert Emerald was actually Mr. Wells. He had come back to the kitchen immediately to tell Angie and Deacon, and Deacon had sent out the pheasant dish.

But then, suddenly, a less pleasant thought cut in. "Oh

God," she said to JP. "You're the one who found him." She closed her eyes, and the dark world spun.

"Yes," JP said. "I'm sorry."

"*I'm* the one who's sorry," Angie whispered.

JP nodded at the seat next to him. "I was just going up to the house to see if your family needed anything. And I brought some strawberries that my mother picked up at Bartlett's Farm." He nodded to a cooler in the back. "Let me give you a ride up to the house?"

"I'm not sure I want to go back there," Angie said.

"Things are that bad already?"

Angie nodded.

"Is Laurel your mother?" he asked. "Because she sounded really cool."

"She *is* really cool," Angie said. "But she's not my mother. My mother is...Belinda. Belinda Rowe."

"Ah," JP said. "Well, I liked her in *Brilliant Disguise*."

"You and every other man in America," Angie said.

"I'm not as typical as you might think," JP said. "I'm the ranger out at Coatue all summer. You could always come stay in my shack."

Angie smiled. This guy was terrific. She thought about spending all summer in a one-room shack out on the wild, deserted arm of beach that was Coatue. There was nothing out there but sand, water, and seabirds. "You'd be surprised how much I'd like that," she said.

"The offer stands," JP said. "You can help me protect the plover eggs and tow tourist Jeeps out of the sand."

Angie blushed.

"Maybe we shouldn't move in together right away," JP said. "Maybe you should just hop in. I'll drive you home, and you can surprise everyone with hand-picked strawberries."

"Deal," she said.

HAYES

He couldn't feel anything and so he had to pretend, or he would be discovered. His mother, in her job, dealt with junkies every hour of every day; she knew the signs. He couldn't scratch, and he couldn't lose his focus, or he would nod off.

He said to Laurel, "I'd love to get unpacked and maybe go for a swim before dinner. Or...? I don't know...is that bad? I mean, we don't have to sit shiva, right?"

Laurel studied him for a second, and he thought, *She knows.*

She started to cry soundlessly, and Hayes hugged her tight. His mom. She was still so pretty, still so *young,* only fifty-four. And still so cool, the coolest person Hayes had ever known. Hayes had loved his father, but he and Deacon had been more like casual, easygoing friends, and really, that was only later in life.

Hayes had carried around a fair amount of anger after his father left. He could remember Deacon flying home from L.A. one weekend a month to "spend time" with Hayes, which meant a Yankees game or kite flying in the park or checking out the dinosaurs at the American Museum of Natural History. All of this was fine except that Hayes, even at age eight or nine, could sense that his father was trying too hard. At least forty times over the weekend, Deacon would ask Hayes if he was having fun, and then would come the litany about his own father.

He didn't want me, Deacon would say.

But I want you, Deacon would say.

Kiss on the forehead, no matter who was watching.

The weekends in New York were better when Buck joined them. Buck had no children, and so he treated Hayes like an adult and Hayes flourished—they talked about the Knicks and the stock market; plus, it alleviated the father-son pressure. So things were sometimes okay, sometimes not, but every visit ended the same way: Hayes would have dinner at the Manchester Diner, down the street from Laurel's apartment, with both of his parents. His mother and father would hold hands, and Hayes could see the air shimmering with electricity between them. Usually his father would start crying first, then his mother, but sometimes it was the other way around. It was guaranteed that both of them would cry and run through a stack of paper napkins, blowing their noses and wiping their eyes, and, since no child wants to see either of his parents cry, Hayes hated the weekends with his father, purely for the way they always ended.

Things got better once Deacon and Belinda adopted Angie, because then Deacon got more on board with the family program, but even so, what Hayes remembered was spending time with Angie and Angie's nanny, who had been Scarlett, whom Deacon had eventually married.

Was it any wonder Hayes was addicted to drugs?

He squeezed his mother. He loved his mother; she had been his rock, his guiding light, his true north, his best friend for all his life. Hayes was in agony about his father's death, not to mention really *scared.* His father had had a bad heart, and so *what did that mean for Hayes?* Nothing good, he was sure. But if Hayes had lost his mother... well, that would have been a different story altogether. Hayes couldn't imagine a world without his mother in it. His last serious girlfriend, Whitney Jo, had told Hayes that he was *too* attached to his mother and that was why he was thirty-four and unmarried. Because no woman could ever measure up.

Laurel wiped her eyes on the collar of her shirt. "I've been trying very hard to be civil to Belinda."

"Oh," Hayes said. "Right." His mother and Belinda were not cool with each other—nope, not at all. It had made for some awkward family gatherings in the past. When Hayes was growing up, he wasn't allowed to watch any of Belinda's movies or play with the toys Belinda had bought him or even say her name—otherwise, his mother got this sad, spooky expression on her face. It was okay for him to talk about Angie, thank God; his mother had always liked Angie. Even Scarlett was okay in Laurel's book. Not great, Hayes thought—his mother had been "disappointed" that Deacon had done the "predictable thing" and fallen for the nanny. But, Laurel had said, *I'm sure she paid attention to him, and Belinda didn't.*

Was that what had happened? Probably. By the time Deacon had married Scarlett, Hayes had acknowledged to himself that Deacon was hopeless when it came to women. One reason Hayes hadn't married Whitney Jo was because he feared he would fail, just as his father had.

"Right," Hayes said. "Good for you, Mom."

"There's no point holding on to old anger," Laurel said. "Deacon is dead."

Hayes nodded. It had been six weeks, which was right around the time Hayes expected someone to announce it had all been a joke or a mistake and for Deacon to reappear somehow.

His mother still hadn't answered his question about swimming. He said, "So... the beach is okay? Not okay?"

Laurel said, "I went swimming yesterday, and it was very therapeutic. We gathered to honor Deacon's memory, and if I'm sure of one thing, it's that he doesn't want us to sit inside and cry."

Hayes breathed a sigh of relief. He knew they were here to *mourn,* whatever that meant, and they were going to spread the ashes on Monday—but that was two whole days from now. Two days was a *very long time* under circumstances such as these.

"We're not eating until seven thirty or so," Laurel said. "So you have time to unwind."

Hayes was down with that. He could refresh his buzz once he was alone. He needed a little bump; his tolerance had grown remarkably while he was in Bali—he and Sula were shooting up four or five times a day. But first he had to get past the land mine in the kitchen.

Belinda.

"Hello, Hayes," she said in that famous, famous voice. She gave him dual-cheek air-kisses, a greeting Hayes excelled at, thank God.

"Belinda, it's nice to see you," he said, not meaning it.

"And you," Belinda said, not meaning it either, he was sure.

"What happened to Angie?" Hayes asked. He congratulated himself for noticing that his sister was missing. The key to not letting the world know he was high was constantly monitoring his surroundings. Angie had been here; now she was gone. "Did she go upstairs?" This was Hayes's goal. Go up to his room, shut the door, pull out the precious H, which he was hiding in a secure spot. Shoot up. But just a bump. The mere thought set Hayes's teeth chattering.

Belinda said, "I heard you ran into Naomi at the Escondite last month."

Boom, just like that, he was lost. He repeated the sentence in his mind, looking for landmarks. The Escondite rang a distant bell. It was...a hotel? In the past month, Hayes had been to Bali, of course. Before that, he had been in Ecuador and Peru; before that...Vegas, where he had stayed at Aria. Before that...Shutters on the Beach in Santa

Monica. That was Belinda's part of the world. He tried to remember something, anything, about his time in California other than the sheer size of the muscles on the dealer he found in Venice Beach. And who was Naomi?

"Naomi Watts?" Belinda prompted. "She bumped into you at the Escondite? The rock club?"

Yes! Hayes thought. He had gone to the Escondite on the recommendation of the Shutters concierge to see a band called Pretty Little Demons. The place had a burger called the Fat Albert, which was a bacon cheeseburger with maple syrup served on a glazed doughnut bun—the concierge said it was so good, it made her want to punch someone in the face—and Hayes had ordered one but not eaten it. Naomi Watts was a blond, he knew, so she must have been the woman who grabbed his arm when he was coming out of the men's room. He hadn't been sure if it was her or Kate Beckinsale.

"Yes!" Hayes said. "I did see Naomi at the Escondite. Great burgers there. And we saw a phenomenal band. It was two little girls—they're in, like, *seventh grade,* but boy, do they rock!" He made a sloppy hand motion indicating drumsticks. He constantly impressed himself with the way he could pull stuff out of his ass.

Belinda narrowed her eyes at him. "Are you *okay,* Hayes?" she asked.

She knows, Hayes thought. Or she suspected.

"I'm fine," he said. "Other than the fact that, you know, my father is dead."

Belinda continued to study him in an unnerving way.

"Where's Angie?" Hayes asked. He couldn't remember if this question had been answered or not.

"Oh, she ran off," Belinda said, nodding at the front door. "She got a bee in her bonnet."

Bonnet? Hayes thought.

"Hayes, honey, come with me," Laurel said, saving the day. She swept Hayes past the ticking time bomb that was Belinda and up the stairs.

His room was the room of the little boy he had been when he first came to Nantucket with his parents. There was still the blue sailboat wallpaper, now dulled by years of sunshine, the blue muted and dusty but so familiar, as though the pattern had been embossed on Hayes's heart. The wallpaper had not been selected for him but rather for one of the Innsleys' children, but one of the unwritten rules of this house was that nothing was allowed to change. The porthole mirror encircled by nautical rope still hung over the dresser. Deacon was dead, never coming back, D.E.A.D.—and yet that stupid mirror had endured, unchanged. Was Hayes the only person who understood how patently unfair this was?

Hayes crashed on the bed that had seen him through childhood summers to teenager summers to adult summers, some of them with Whitney Jo—they had nearly broken this bed—to today.

Laurel sat down on the bed next to him and smoothed his hair off his face. "We're going to get through this," she said.

His mother needed comfort—Hayes could sense that much—and he knew he should be the one to administer it; he was her son. But he couldn't go down that long and winding road right now. He was too... tired.

His eyes fell closed. He worried he would never be able to get them back open. He wanted Laurel to step out of the room and close the door behind her with a definite click.

"Mom," Hayes said, "I'm sorry. The trip from overseas wiped me out. I just need a quick nap..."

"Of course, sweet—" Laurel said, but that was all he heard.

BUCK

He could barely bring himself to look at Belinda. The memory of earlier that afternoon was too disturbing. Had it even happened? Well, yes, there she was... wearing clothes now, at least, as she poured herself a glass of wine. She gave him a wicked smile.

"Beer?" she asked.

"No, thank you," he said. He'd gone through nearly a six-pack over the course of the day, and he was starting to feel dizzy. He had blown any chance of asking Belinda for financial help with the house, he realized. He could ask her for one favor but not two, and he needed her to keep quiet about what had happened that afternoon.

"Listen," he said. "About earlier..."

Belinda waved a hand. "Already forgotten," she said.

He breathed a sigh of relief while at the same time feeling offended. *Already forgotten?*

He needed air.

"I think I'll walk to the beach."

"Dressed like that?" Belinda asked.

He was still wearing half his suit. When he'd told his secretary, Margaret, that he was going to Nantucket for the weekend, her mouth nearly came unhinged. (Margaret had something of the marionette about her as it was—exaggerated makeup, long chin.)

"What are you going to *do?*" she asked.

"Say a proper good-bye to my best friend," he said, and this had made Margaret, who was a big Deacon Thorpe fan, weepy. All women were big Deacon Thorpe fans, Buck thought. It was the damnedest thing.

Margaret had gone to the Billabong store on her lunch

break and bought Buck a pair of board shorts. They were blue and red striped and sort of resembled a nautical flag. Buck had stared at them, baffled.

"You're going to an island," Margaret said. "You might want to swim."

Swim? he'd thought.

Before Buck left for his walk, he went upstairs and tried the board shorts on, then checked himself out in the mirror. He looked as though he were wearing clown pants, but oh, well. When in Rome.

He decided he would ask Laurel to come with him. Maybe he would try to kiss her on the beach. It could be like a scene from a Nicholas Sparks novel; Buck's ex-wife Mae used to gobble up those novels as if the pages were potato chips. She would always cry, and Buck had learned to comfort her and listen to her explain about how Noah loved Allie or whatever, and Buck would nod and pluck tissues—and then, he would nearly always get lucky.

He found Laurel in the kitchen, trimming asparagus. Belinda was out on the back deck reading a script, so Buck kept his voice low. "Hey," he said. "I'm going for a walk on the beach. Want to join me?"

"I'd love to," she said. "But I'm in charge of dinner tonight, and this is a crowd with high expectations."

"Do you want me to stay and help?" he asked.

"No," she said. "Enjoy your walk." She winked at him. "I never thought I'd see John Buckley in board shorts, but they look pretty good."

She was being kind. He had nice strong legs—forty-five minutes three days a week on the treadmill, and weights two days a week with his trainer, Lexi—but they were Irish-boy pale.

"Okay," he said. "I'll be back in a little while."

* * *

When he reached the road, his phone started to beep and ding and light up like a pinball machine. Three missed calls from a blocked number and two missed calls from Margaret. This was not a good sign. Margaret worked eight a.m. to noon on Saturdays, which was one of the reasons Buck paid her such a fortune. That, and the fact that she answered her phone whenever he called, twenty-four hours a day, seven days a week, Thanksgiving, Christmas, Mother's Day. Margaret's children were grown but had yet to procreate, so there were no distractions; she and her retired accountant husband, Del, rattled around their big house in Katonah. Whenever Buck called, Margaret was eager to help.

He didn't bother with the voice mails. He called her back. "Talk to me, Goose."

Normally, this set a lighthearted tone, but when Margaret answered, she was all business. "Scarlett called," Margaret said. "She's been trying to reach you."

"I have no reception out here," Buck said.

"Surprise, surprise, she's run out of money," Margaret said. "Visa declined, AmEx declined, six overdraft notices from the bank. She wants to know what the...expletive...is going on."

"Did you tell her the money is gone?" Buck said.

"I thought I would leave that up to you," Margaret said. "I'm just the secretary here."

Buck wished Margaret were the type of secretary who would do his dirty work for him—tell Scarlett that Deacon had wired a million dollars to save his restaurant after her uncle had pulled his funding, and tell her that she had better give up her projects and her get-rich-quick schemes and find the best job that a degree from University College could get her.

"I'll take care of it," Buck said. "Have we heard from either Harv or the accountant's office?" This was the last hope: that the Board Room was sitting on a gold mine and Buck might be able to claim some of Deacon's investment back.

"Not yet," Margaret said.

"Okay," Buck said, though it was not okay. Someday he was going to write a memoir entitled *Don't Shoot the Messenger.* "Thank you, Margaret."

"You're welcome," Margaret said. "Enjoy your weekend."

Enjoy his weekend. Fat chance of that!

Buck walked over the dune in his bare feet until he saw the water sparkling before him. It was so much more beautiful than the East River, or even the Hudson. The ocean was a wild, living thing. The beach was deserted except for gulls.

As Buck approached the water's edge, he thought about Scarlett. She had been justified in leaving; if Buck were she, he might have done the same thing. Deacon had gone on benders before, of course, but the one a couple of weeks before he died had been the worst ever—for many reasons. Scarlett had been away on a seven-night "silent retreat" at the Omega Institute in Rhinebeck, New York. It was one of her new things: yoga, mindfulness, a break from technology, finding balance, finding her center, cutting out all white noise and conflict. That was Scarlett's way of dealing with stress, while Deacon's way had been drinking and drugs.

It was a Tuesday, so the restaurant was closed. A phone call came to Buck's phone at five thirty. It was the headmistress of Ellery's school, Madame Giroux. Ellery hadn't been picked up, and the office had had no luck reaching either parent. It was understood that Madame Oliver was on a spiritual retreat and could not be reached, but all ten calls to Monsieur had gone straight to voice mail, and there had been no answer at his place of work. Madame Giroux then let a stream of very angry French fly, the gist of which, Buck gathered, was that she found the situation unacceptable. Mr. Buckley was listed as the emergency contact. Would he please come get the child? She had been quite traumatized.

Buck hopped in a cab to the school. Traffic was a trial at that time of day, so he didn't collect Ellery until nearly six fifteen, and she was, in fact, weepy and shivering, as though they'd kept her in a meat locker. Buck made his extreme apologies to Madame Giroux, with her chignon, her pencil skirt, her expression of French superiority, and then he whisked Ellery into his waiting cab. He called Deacon—voice mail. He called Angie, who answered and said that yes, she would meet Buck and Ellery at Deacon's apartment so that Buck could go on a manhunt.

Buck didn't know where to start, so he started with the obvious—McCoy's—but Sarah hadn't seen Deacon in weeks, she said. Buck considered checking downtown at Five Points and then stopping at every bar on the Bowery, but his good judgment told him to go back to his apartment and wait. The call would come, eventually, and meanwhile, Ellery was safe.

A little after ten, Buck received a call from an unfamiliar 646 number.

"Mr. Buckley?" a female voice said.

Oh dear, Buck thought. "Yes?"

"My name is Taryn Ross," the voice said. "I'm a dancer? At Skirtz Gentlemen's Club? Your friend Deacon passed out in my car, and I can't get him to wake up."

Buck had met Taryn Ross on the third level of a parking garage on Twelfth Avenue. She was dressed in cherry-red hot pants, high-heeled Mary Jane pumps, and a gray New York Giants hoodie that Buck recognized as belonging to Deacon. Deacon was slumped behind the wheel of a 1994 Saab convertible; Buck's first wife, Jess, had driven one exactly like it when he first met her. There was an open bottle of Billecart-Salmon champagne in the console.

"Whose car is this?" Buck asked.

"Mine," Taryn said.

"You were going to let him *drive?*" Buck asked.

"No," Taryn said. She jingled the car keys. "He said he was okay, he said he wanted to take me up to Nantucket so I could see it, but he was really, really drunk, and the two of us did a lot of coke."

"A lot, like how much?" Buck asked.

"Enough to make him think he could drive," Taryn said. "But then he just sort of fell over. At first I thought he was dead, but I checked, and he's breathing."

"Great," Buck said.

"I'm sorry," Taryn said. "When he came in, I was so *surprised.* I grew up watching his show. I made the clams casino dip once for my in-laws."

"You're married?" Buck asked.

Taryn nodded and stuffed her hands in the front pocket of the sweatshirt. Deacon had probably lent it to her because she was topless.

"Well, so is he," Buck said. "He has a wife and child at home."

"Nothing happened," Taryn said, shrugging. "He just wanted to show me Nantucket. He said we were going to take a ferry boat."

"I'm getting him out of here," Buck said. He eyed Taryn Ross, wondering if he needed to pay her to keep her from posting this on Facebook. He decided the answer was yes and handed her two hundred-dollar bills. "Thank you for calling me."

"Can I tell you one other thing?" Taryn said. "He seemed sad. Just really, really sad."

At two o'clock the next afternoon, when Deacon finally woke up, Buck filled him in on what had happened because he most certainly would not remember.

"First off, Ellery is okay. You forgot her at school, but I went to pick her up."

Deacon's expression collapsed into one of predictable despair. "No."

"Yes," Buck said. "You drank too much, you wandered into Skirtz, on Thirty-Second between Eleventh and Twelfth, you met a dancer there named Taryn. Blond. Any of this ring a bell?"

Deacon shook his head, but even that looked as though it hurt.

"Apparently, you and Taryn hoovered up most of an eight ball; then you told her you wanted to show her Nantucket, so you got in her car. With a nice bottle of bubbly."

Deacon closed his eyes. "Did I drive?"

"No," Buck said. "The girl was smart. She held the keys."

"Good," Deacon said. "Is Ellery okay? Does Scarlett know?"

"Ellery is fine. Angie took care of her. Scarlett is at the ashram or whatever, and so she may know, or this surprise may be in her future."

"Okay," Deacon said with a big exhale that smelled strongly of whiskey. "I'm sorry, Buck. Things are tough right now."

"It's like you have a death wish," Buck said.

"I don't," Deacon said. "I'm going to stop drinking."

Buck stared at him.

"I'm serious," Deacon said. "And no more drugs. I have to learn to live with myself."

When Scarlett got home, Deacon told her the PG-13 version of the story: McCoy's, lost track of time, completely spaced on picking up Ellery. He was beyond sorry, and he realized he had a problem. He was going to stop drinking.

I don't believe you, Scarlett said. She pulled Ellery out of school, she packed two suitcases, she flew to Savannah.

Now, Deacon was dead, and Scarlett was out of money. Initially, upon reading Deacon's will, Buck had been uneasy about informing Scarlett that she was only inheriting a third of the Nantucket house and that the other two-thirds were going to Laurel and Belinda. But now, that was a moot point. One third of nothing was nothing.

Buck trudged through the sand to the water's edge and let the waves lap at his feet. Then he shed his shirt and set it and his phone out of the ocean's reach. He charged into the water. *This is okay,* he thought as he paddled out, letting the waves swell up and over him. This was what he needed to clear his head and prepare for what lay ahead.

ANGIE

JP delivered Angie up to the house but declined to come inside. "I just wanted to drop off the strawberries," he said.

"I'm getting your family a boat on Monday so you can spread the ashes. I'll meet everyone else then."

Angie said, "Do you know who Dad's caretaker is these days? Nailor retired, but did someone else take his place? There's a rotten floorboard in the porch that has tried to kill me twice."

"Your dad hired my friend Tommy A.," JP said. "But he's flat out this time of year, and besides, I don't want him to see you, or there go my chances."

Angie smiled into her lap. The guys in the kitchen teased Angie all the time, but it had been a while since anyone had flirted with her. Well, except Joel.

JP said, "I can come fix the board myself tomorrow morning..."

Angie said, "You don't have to..."

"Angie," JP said. "I want to." He ran a hand over his beard. "It's hard not knowing what to do to help. It would be an honor if you let me fix the board."

"Okay," she said. "Thank you." She jumped out of the Jeep and headed up the front steps to the porch, stepping carefully around the board. She waved at JP as he backed out of the driveway.

Belinda was standing sentry right inside the front door.

"What are you *doing,* Mother?" Angie asked. She grabbed the handle of the suitcase and headed up the stairs.

Belinda followed her. "That friend of yours is *darling.*"

"He's not a friend of mine," Angie said. "He was a friend of Deacon's. JP was the one who found Deacon out back."

Belinda's voice fell flat. "Oh."

Angie ducked into her bedroom, where her eyes fell on her old dollhouse. She could remember rearranging the furniture again and again with Scarlett. She remembered setting out butter and eggs on the rough-hewn kitchen table and saving the three-tiered party cake and the tiny, tiny teacups for the formal dining room. The living room sofa was upholstered in rose chintz, with throw pillows the size of postage stamps. Angie had loved very few physical things as much as she had loved that dollhouse. She sighed.

"I'll switch rooms with you," Belinda said. "This room doesn't even have a closet. At least Clara's room has a closet. Of course, it's filled with skeletons."

"I don't need a closet," Angie said. "I didn't bring any couture."

"Please, darling, don't be nasty," Belinda said. "This is all hard enough for me as it is."

Angie lay down on her bed. The pillowcases smelled like home. At least that was comforting. "Go away, Mother."

Belinda shut the door, but she was still inside the room. This was *not* okay, but had Angie expected her mother to change? Here was her modus operandi. She was largely absent, away on location, but when she was around, she didn't leave Angie alone for one second. Angie was twenty-six years old, and Belinda was a helicopter parent.

"I think your father would want you to get a boyfriend," Belinda said.

"I have a boyfriend," Angie said. She squeezed her eyes shut. This always happened: she gave over precious pieces of information just to prove to Belinda that she didn't know everything.

"Who is it?" Belinda asked.

"No one," Angie said. *Joel Tersigni,* she thought. She longed to say his name out loud. The problem with conducting a secret love affair was that she couldn't talk about it with anyone. If Angie had had a close girlfriend, one she could have confided in, then the situation might be a tiny bit more bearable. Growing up, Angie had had Scarlett, who was the person she told the things she couldn't tell her mother. Then, in high school, there had been Pierpont Jones. Pierpont had been fun and wild but not great with secrets. In culinary school and in the kitchen at work, Angie's friends had all been men.

Could she tell Belinda about Joel? Angie wondered. Would it make things better between them, or would Belinda take the information and ruin it, the way she ruined everything?

Angie knew what her mother would say. She would tell Angie to call Joel and figure out what was going on. She would say, *You deserve to be treated with respect.* And she would be right.

Angie stood up. "Excuse me," she said. "I have to make a phone call."

She walked past her mother, out of the room, down the stairs, and out of the house. When she got a signal at the bottom of the driveway, Angie dialed Joel's number. There was no way he was going to answer. Joel was a coward. Why had it taken Angie so long to realize this?

The phone rang once, then a woman's voice said, "Hello, Angie."

Angie stammered. "I—I—"

"This is Dory Tersigni, Angie," the woman said.

Hang up! Angie thought. *Hang up!* Joel had handed his phone off to Dory—or, more likely, Dory had stolen Joel's phone and had been waiting for Angie to call.

"I know you've been having an affair with my husband," Dory said. "Since December twentieth, after the Christmas party. I know the affair took place primarily in your apartment on East Seventy-Third Street. I know there were texts—literally thousands of texts—as well as explicit photos, and hundreds of phone calls. I know everything, Angie."

Angie opened her mouth to speak. *Retaliate!* she thought. She knew things, too. She knew that Dory was an anorexic and a bulimic, that she was a corn-husk doll, dry and unappealing in bed, unable to meet Joel's voracious sexual appetite. She knew that Dory controlled Joel with money, and guilt about the boys. She knew Dory was a crackerjack attorney, a bulldog in negotiations, tough and unrelenting. *She never loses,* Joel had told Angie once, but he had made that seem like a negative. Now that Angie found herself in direct competition with Dory, Angie wished for a less formidable opponent.

"I'd like to speak to Joel, please," Angie said.

"That's not going to happen," Dory said. "Your little fling is over."

" 'Fling,' " Angie said.

"What?" Dory said.

"It wasn't a fling," Angie said. "I'm in love with him. And he's in love with me."

"Joel Tersigni doesn't know what love is," Dory said. "Do you know who he was sleeping with before you?"

"Excuse me?" Angie said.

"Karen, the hostess. And Winnie before that. You're just one in a long line. Although I have to admit, I'm surprised. He prefers blonds, the paler the better."

"Stop," Angie whispered.

"You're sleeping with my husband, and you want *me* to stop? I'll tell you who's going to stop. *You* are going to stop. If you call or text or email or smoke-signal Joel ever again, I will call the press and tell them about the disgusting shenanigans going on behind the scenes at Deacon Thorpe's restaurant. You're not just an anonymous citizen, Angie Thorpe. Your father was a celebrity, and your mother is an even bigger celebrity. I'm sure the tabloids would eat this up!"

"Please," Angie said. "My father is *dead.*" With those words, Angie started to cry. *Finally,* she thought. It felt like rain after a drought; it felt so *good,* and yet Angie hated that it was Dory who had elicited the tears. "My father is dead!"

"I didn't know Deacon well," Dory said. "But it's probably safe to say he would have been ashamed of you. Any parent would be."

The conviction of Dory's statement took Angie's breath away. Deacon *would* have been ashamed. He *would* have been disappointed. Deacon, no doubt, had known about Joel's affairs with Karen and Winnie, the two vapid blondes who had worked the front of the house with Joel. *Eye candy,* the guys in the kitchen called them. Winnie had been at the Board Room for only three or four months. Joel must have moved in on her right away, and possibly it was their breakup that had caused Winnie to quit without giving any notice.

"I'm sorry," Angie whispered. "Dory, I'm sorry."

She waited for a response, but there was none. Dory had hung up.

LAUREL

The first full day had been something of a roller coaster, and Laurel, for one, was relieved when she could pour herself a glass of wine.

"Another for me," Belinda said. "Please, Laurel."

"And one for me," Hayes said. "Please, Mom."

Laurel opened a new chilled bottle of the Cloudy Bay. She poured a glass for Belinda, who was wearing black jeans and a black silk blouse, as if she were about to see a foreign film at the Angelika. Hayes was in cargo shorts and a ripped Ramones T-shirt. He hadn't shaved in a week, and his eyes were rimmed in red. He smelled god-awful. Would it be too mom-like of her to suggest he take a shower before dinner, the way she used to when he was a teenager? In recent years Laurel had grown used to Hayes being well-coiffed and beautifully dressed. He liked his suits cut close to the body; he wore Robert Graham shirts in colorful patterns and expensive silk ties and Italian shoes. He had experimented with facial hair—goatee, soul patch, sideburns—but he had never looked messy or disheveled the way he did today. He looked, Laurel thought, like one of her clients at Social Services. And he was scratching the hell out of his arm, which set off a distant bell.

She thought, *Drugs?*

He had smoked weed in high school, and she assumed he'd experimented with cocaine and LSD at some point in college. She wished he were still dating Whitney Jo. Whitney Jo had been from the prairies of Kansas. She wore trucker hats over her braids. She had a wholesome, pearly-white smile and was utterly without guile.

Laurel had an urge to ask about Whitney Jo, but that would really be an annoying mom thing to do.

She raised her glass. "Cheers, honey," she said to Hayes. "I realize getting here was an epic poem."

They touched glasses. Hayes drank deeply, then scratched his arm.

He said, "I don't think I told you this, but the cabdriver who brought Angie and me here was the same guy who drove Dad from the ferry. He remembered the address."

"Did he know what had happened?" Laurel asked.

"He knew," Hayes said. "Safe to say, at this point, the

whole world knows." He scratched his arm. Laurel didn't like the scratching. *Narcotics,* she thought. *Opiates.*

Laurel ground fresh pepper over the steaks. "Tonight is going to be simple," she said. "Steaks and asparagus. Tomorrow night, Angie is cooking."

"Monday, after we spread the ashes, we should have pizza," Hayes said. "In honor of Dad."

"That's a wonderful idea, sweetheart," Laurel said.

"I thought so, too!" Hayes said enthusiastically. Too enthusiastically? Now Laurel was hypersensitive. "I'm going up to my room for a hit."

"*What?*" Laurel said.

"I'm going up to my room for a bit," he said. He picked up his glass and disappeared from the kitchen.

Leaving Laurel with...Belinda.

"How is Angie doing?" Laurel asked.

"I have no idea," Belinda said. "She tells me nothing. She let it slip that she has a boyfriend, but then she wouldn't say who it was. I think...well, I think maybe she was making it up."

"I used to ask Deacon periodically if she had anyone special in her life," Laurel said. "He told me she was too busy to date."

"Deacon and I talked about it when I saw him in New York last fall. I said I was worried; he told me to relax." Belinda buried her face in her wine. "That was the last time I saw Deacon—in September. How about you?"

"I saw him all the time," Laurel said. "Hayes and I went to the restaurant for dinner on Easter. Then I talked to him about two weeks before he died, right after he stopped drinking..."

"He stopped drinking?" Belinda said. "Deacon?"

Laurel nodded, but she wouldn't elaborate. Belinda didn't

need to hear about the stripper and the Saab. "And then he sent me a birthday card May second."

"He sent you a birthday card?' Belinda said. "In seventeen years, I don't think the man once remembered my birthday. September thirtieth. Forgettable, I guess."

"Deacon and I were friends," Laurel said.

"That's because you never remarried," Belinda said. "Bob wouldn't have tolerated me being friends with Deacon."

"You don't think so?"

"I know so," Belinda said. "Bob is a very jealous man."

"I'm sure he is," Laurel said. She looked toward the front door. "Buck has been gone for a while. Do you think he drowned?" She tried to keep her voice light and casual, but she was having some pretty overwhelming feelings about Buck since the almost-kiss on the deck. Every time Laurel thought about it, she felt light-headed and giddy.

"He's probably just avoiding me," Belinda said.

"Avoiding you why?"

"We had a little run-in this afternoon," Belinda said. She waved a hand. "It was nothing. Already forgotten."

"This afternoon?" Laurel said. "While I was in town?"

"Yes," Belinda said. "But, like I said, it was nothing. I'm sure he's embarrassed."

Laurel's stomach muscles tightened. She didn't like the expression on Belinda's face. "Why would he be embarrassed?"

"Well...," Belinda said. She leaned forward, as if in confidence, but the screen door slammed shut, and two seconds later, Buck walked into the kitchen, dripping wet and trailing in sand.

"Hey, we were just talking about you," Laurel said. She grabbed a cold beer from the fridge and opened it for him. "How was the swim?"

"Much needed," Buck said. "Thank you." He took a healthy

chug of the beer. "Listen, I'm going to need to talk to you two at some point about some legal matters."

"Belinda was just about to tell me about the run-in you two had this afternoon," Laurel said.

Buck's mouth dropped open. He looked at Belinda. "I have no idea what you're talking about," he said. He collapsed in one of the stools at the counter. "You're both aware, I assume, that Deacon had financial troubles?"

Laurel nodded, although this came as news to her.

"I wish Scarlett were here," Buck said.

"I don't," Belinda said.

"Well, like it or not, she was Deacon's wife, so this concerns her, too," Buck said.

"She's unstable," Belinda said. "And impulsive. If Deacon was having financial troubles, it was because Scarlett is a spendthrift."

Laurel felt her grip on her civility slipping. "Scarlett isn't here to defend herself. And how would you know about Scarlett's spending habits?"

"Have you forgotten?" Belinda said. "She was my *nanny*. I used to send her to Gristedes with a hundred-dollar bill to buy milk, and she would come home with pennies."

At that second, Angie walked into the kitchen. She tapped Belinda on the shoulder. "I heard you from upstairs," she said. "You think I'm making up the fact that I have a boyfriend?"

"Darling," Belinda said.

"You think I'm, what...a child with an imaginary friend?" Angie said.

"Well, you did have January," Belinda said. "January was around for years."

January, Laurel thought. She had forgotten all about it, but now she vividly recalled that Angie had invented a friend named January.

"January lasted for years because I was *young!*" Angie said. "And I was *lonely!* And you were *never around!*"

"Darling, please calm down," Belinda said.

"His name is *Joel Tersigni!*" Angie said. "He's the dining room manager at the restaurant."

"Good God," Buck said. "Please don't tell me you're involved with Joel. He's married to that battle-ax who works for Wilson and Oskam."

"Angie!" Belinda said.

"What, Mother?" Angie said. "You've never slept with a married man before?"

"I'm going to light the grill," Laurel said. She raised her eyebrows at Buck. "Maybe you can fill us in on the other stuff during dinner."

BUCK

Don't shoot the messenger.

Buck sat tight in his chair on the back deck, beer at the ready. Under the guise of helping Laurel "pull dinner together," he had opened every cabinet in the kitchen until he found the liquor, to the bottom right of the stove: Jameson, Tanqueray Ten, Mount Gay, Jack Daniel's, and a clear mason jar—Deacon's moonshine, which, he knew, would take the enamel off his teeth.

He waited until everyone was settled in their chairs and Laurel had set out the platter of steaks and asparagus, the bowl of salad, the basket of bread.

"I'm sorry this is so simple," Laurel said.

"Mom," Hayes said; then, at an apparent loss for words, he shook his head.

Hayes was *not* looking good, Buck thought. And he seemed to have misplaced his razor.

Buck raised his beer. He wasn't sure what to say. He had been raised Catholic, and he was pretty sure he alone felt a prayer was in order. They were, after all, sitting at the table where Deacon had been when his soul departed the earth. Should Buck acknowledge this? He considered himself a master of social graces—his career demanded it—but some situations had too many emotional potholes to be negotiated smoothly. He would speak as a friend first, he decided, then he would slide into agent mode.

"To Deacon," he said. "Husband, father, friend, chef, and a man like no other. I know I speak for all of us when I say a bright light has gone out."

"To Deacon," Laurel said. She touched her glass to Buck's beer.

Belinda heaped her plate with salad. Hayes took a roll, then stared at it on his plate as if it were a pterodactyl egg. Angie helped herself to steak and asparagus but didn't pick up her utensils. Only Laurel dug in. Deacon used to say Laurel ate like a three-hundred-pound long-distance trucker.

Food is like sex for her, man, Deacon had told Buck decades earlier. *She can't get enough.*

Buck blushed, remembering this. But he had to stay on point.

"So," Buck said.

Laurel turned to him, as did Angie. Belinda stabbed some greens. Hayes stared at the roll.

"Deacon ran into some financial trouble at the end of last year that snowballed quite a bit."

Hayes upended the contents of his wineglass into his mouth. Laurel let a soft breath escape as she watched him.

Buck said, "Let me start over."

"The suspense is killing me," Belinda said.

"Deacon left this house to Scarlett. And to you, Laurel. And to you, Belinda. Technically, each of you inherits a third."

Laurel gasped. "You're kidding!"

Even Belinda seemed taken aback. "That was very nice of him," she said. "He certainly didn't have to leave me anything."

"The idea was that the three of you would then pass your share on to your child," Buck said. "And the three of you would split time in a way that's deemed reasonable by the executor."

"Meaning you?" Belinda said.

"Me," Buck confirmed.

"So, let me guess...Laurel will get the summer, Scarlett will get the spring and fall, and I'll get February."

"Mother, stop," Angie said.

"Stop what, darling? I think we all know Buck is sweet on Laurel."

"Belinda!" Laurel said.

"There's a problem," Buck said. "The house is buried in debt. It's due to be repossessed by Nantucket Bank on July first if the estate doesn't come up with the arrears."

"How much is that?" Angie asked.

"Four hundred thirty-six thousand—"

"Good God," Laurel said.

"Two hundred ninety-two dollars and nineteen cents."

"I've got the nineteen cents," Hayes said. He gave the table a big grin.

"That's too bad," Belinda said. "It really is."

"Mother," Angie said.

"What?"

"You can afford it," Angie said.

"I can afford my third of the arrears," Belinda said. "A

hundred and fifty grand, give or take. But I'm not going to pay Laurel's or Scarlett's portion."

"No one is asking you to!" Laurel said.

"Well, there is a sense of urgency," Buck said. "We have less than two weeks."

"Bob warned me that the only reason you invited me here was to ask me for something," Belinda said. "I'm dismayed to find out he was right."

"No one is asking you for anything," Laurel said.

"But if we're going to lose the house...," Angie said.

"People lose houses all the time," Belinda said. "Every day, all across America, people default on their mortgages."

"You're going to lose the house unless the arrears are paid in full," Buck said. "Guaranteed. And there's also a fourteen-thousand-dollar-per-month mortgage."

"Whoa," Hayes said.

"No one is asking you for anything," Laurel said to Belinda. "But how typical of you to think so." She scowled at Buck. "I can't believe you brought this up over dinner."

"You..." Buck nearly said, *You told me to!* But he sensed that any words out of his mouth would only serve to make things worse. He cut a piece of steak. "This is delicious."

The rest of the table was silent.

HAYES

He felt like a dragonfly on a pond, skimming along the surface, hovering in one spot for a second or two to drink in reality, then alighting again. Hayes stared at his roll. He had a pretty good idea of how it would taste, but he was so high, he had a difficult time focusing on what to do with it. Break it in half? Ask for the butter?

The conversation quickly became a burning building that Hayes needed to escape. Deacon had money problems, and they were going to lose the house. The Nantucket house! That had to be wrong. Hayes had always been under the impression that Deacon had plenty of money. He was on TV! He got royalties and residuals. He was mentioned in *New York* magazine every month, practically—and he was always being quoted in *Bon Appétit* and *Saveur.* The Board Room was the hottest restaurant in America.

But Buck wasn't exaggerating, Hayes could tell. Deacon had died flat broke—worse, in debt. Hayes thought guiltily of all the money Deacon had given him over the course of the past few years. Probably close to forty grand. Deacon had allowed Hayes to live beyond his means, keeping an apartment in Soho where he stayed only four or five nights a month. Hayes felt monstrously selfish. He never thought to ask Deacon if the payments to Hayes's co-op board were a stretch. Deacon had offered! He was the dad. Was Deacon one of those people who gave and gave and gave, even when he was having a hard time? Apparently so.

Laurel asked about Deacon's cookbook. Was there any potential there? Angie laughed, saying the "cookbook" was a folder filled with disjointed notes and untested recipes.

Hayes decided to take a stab at the conversation.

"But Dad *wanted* to write a cookbook?" Hayes said. "There's something to work with?"

Angie shrugged. "I guess so, yeah."

Hayes wondered why his father hadn't asked *him* for help with the cookbook; he was the writer in the family. It could have been a father-son collaboration, with both of their names on the cover, both of their photographs on the cover. It would have made Deacon some money, and it might have been the thing Hayes needed to top the masthead at *Fine Travel* or make the leap, finally, to *Condé Nast Traveler*. Hayes loved his job, make no mistake, but there were a few rungs on the ladder above him, and every once in a while, ambition swirled in him like smoke in a bong and he thought about climbing up higher, higher, higher.

"He knew he was never going to get it done," Angie said. "It was killing him."

Everyone was silent after that. "Killing him" was no longer an appropriate euphemism. But the idea of the cookbook stayed with Hayes. What if he and Angie took Deacon's notes and wrote it together? She had the food knowledge, and Hayes the writing chops. It could be a posthumous tribute to their father, with both of their photos on the cover, a son and daughter, one white, one black, one biological, one adopted—it would be a public relations bonanza! But they probably couldn't get it done in time to save the house. Nope, definitely not.

Angie threw her napkin on top of her untouched food. "I don't know about anyone else, but I can't talk about this any more tonight."

Laurel reached over and rubbed Angie's back. "This too shall pass away," she said.

Hayes stared at his roll. Laurel had been saying that phrase since time immemorial, and, although it was meant to be encouraging in this instant—what felt bad today would be less painful tomorrow and even less so next month or next year—in general Hayes found the sentiment depressing. Everything would pass, the next thing would happen, we were alive now for an inconsequential thirty-four or fifty-four years of all of human history—then we died. It was going to happen to everyone; there would be no avoiding it.

He was no longer hungry. He stood up.

"May I please be excused?" he said. It was being in the presence of his mother, perhaps, that caused him to act like a nine-year-old.

"Honey, you haven't eaten any—" Laurel said, but Hayes didn't stick around to hear the rest. He carried his plate into the house and headed up to his room.

Later, when it was dark and the rest of the house seemed to have settled into some semblance of peace, Hayes called Pirate, the taxi driver. Could Pirate come pick him up? Could Pirate help him score some drugs?

There was a pause. Hayes panicked: had he called in over some dispatch line?

Pirate said, "Yeah, man, I'll be there in fifteen minutes."

Pirate showed up, as promised, in the '65 Lincoln, wearing his velvet coat and eye patch, his hair looking as though a raven had died on his head. "You ready to *party?*" he asked Hayes. He shouted the question with the enthusiasm of a meathead frat boy—John Belushi, perhaps, minutes before he overdid it.

"Yeah, man," Hayes said. He was, essentially, sneaking out of the house like a teenager. He had considered leaving Laurel a note saying he'd gone out, but then he figured she wouldn't know any better, and if he left her a note, she might worry. She had been giving him some suspicious looks, so if she knew he was out, she might search his room. She wasn't naive; she had made a career out of dealing with liars and thieves, drug addicts and miscreants.

Pirate took the Polpis Road—where streetlights were few and far between—at breakneck speed. Hayes looked over at him. His uncovered eye was focused with a maniacal intensity on the road.

"Are you already high, man?" Hayes asked.

"Yeah, man," Pirate said. "We've been partying down. I hope you're ready for a slammin' time." He took the next curve so fast, the Lincoln's tires screeched and Hayes feared he might get carsick. He should ask Pirate to turn around and take him home. He needed sleep and water and a string of clean hours. But then, that thought evaporated. What Hayes needed was to get high, higher, higher. Sad fact.

But Hayes was also looking for something else. He was looking for information.

"So, Pirate," Hayes said, his voice pitched low so as to be calming. "Dude, I have to ask. Do you remember any details about my dad? Do you remember anything he said or did, or what he was like?"

"Yeah, man," Pirate said. "I do."

Hayes waited for him to say more. A few moments of silence passed, and Hayes figured Pirate—there was *no way* this was his real name; Hayes should have asked—was collecting his thoughts, but then, when it seemed no answer was forthcoming, Hayes said, "What? What do you remember?"

"Oh," Pirate said. He shook his head as if awakening from a dream. "He was just really cool. I mean, it was *Deacon Thorpe,* man. I've been watching his show since I was... I don't know, a kid. And then, all of a sudden, he's climbing into my taxi."

"Right," Hayes said. He was used to fan dribble. Deacon was recognized everywhere, and he had married a woman even more famous than he was. Hayes had seen statements on Twitter from Mario Batali and Bobby Flay and Eric Ripert, and incessant use of the term "cultural icon." While all of that was gratifying, it wasn't what Hayes was after. He wanted something more personal. "How did he seem? When he climbed into your taxi, I mean? Was he upbeat? Was he quiet? Did he make any jokes?"

"He was cool," Pirate said. "He asked me to take him to Thirty-Three Hoicks Hollow Road. He said, 'Do not pass go, do not collect two hundred dollars.' It's from Monopoly. A board game."

"Well, yeah," Hayes said. Deacon had been a fiend about playing Monopoly. He had a tattoo of Rich Uncle Pennybags on the inside of his right forearm.

Pirate leaned forward against the steering wheel as if to see better, and Hayes thought, *If you want to see better, take off that stupid eye patch.* "He told me about the first time he ever came to Nantucket. The day trip, with his old man."

"He told you that?" Hayes asked. "Did he say anything about the house?" Hayes became transfixed by the glowing circles on the dashboard. They were only going forty miles an hour, but because the top was down on the Lincoln and it was dark and the road was winding, it felt as though they were about to hyperspace into another reality. "Did he say he was going to lose it?"

"Lose it?" Pirate said. "No, man. He was all excited when we turned onto Hoicks Hollow Road. He said it was his..."

"Home away from home," Hayes finished. "Right."

Pirate pulled over on the Polpis Road. He got out of the car, walked down the bike path, and made a phone call. Hayes rested his head against the seat. He should go home right now: *Do not pass go, do not collect two hundred dollars.*

American Paradise was going to be repossessed just like one of the little green houses in Monopoly, plucked off the board and placed back into the coffers of the bank. Hayes had to find a way to save it. But first, he needed drugs. At the rate he was going, he would run dry by tomorrow. Just thinking about it nearly brought Hayes to tears. How had he *gotten* this way? He had meant to be careful. He had meant to stay ahead of it.

He should get out of the car and call Angie to come get him. He could tell Angie the truth, and she would know what to do. She would be pissed, but she would come up with a plan.

Get out! Hayes thought. *Go now!* But he didn't budge.

Pirate climbed back into the car without a word.

"We good, man?" Hayes asked.

"Yeah," Pirate said. "We're good."

Pirate cut his speed as they approached the rotary. They took Hooper Farm Road, and then Pirate made a series of turns that Hayes tried to keep track of, but he closed his eyes for one or two seconds, and when he opened them, they were on a dirt road. *The road to Hell,* Hayes thought.

"Where we going, man?" Hayes asked.

"Party," Pirate said. "Private party."

He drove all the way out to the end of the road, past where the houses ended. All Hayes could see in front of him were skinny scrub pines.

Pirate pulled over and got out of the car. Was Hayes supposed to go with him? Yes. Pirate windmilled his arm.

They walked down a sandy path that led into the woods. Hayes took deep breaths, trying to calm his slamming heart.

They were on Nantucket. It was a fairy-tale summerland where nothing bad ever happened.

Hayes strained his ears for the sound of a party. He had been thinking of a large, finely appointed beach house with a young, polished crowd and pyramids of very fine cocaine. Or possibly a bonfire where a bunch of overprivileged kids in $300 jeans and Rip Curl T-shirts would be smoking Nepalese hash. But the woods were quiet.

Suddenly, a man stepped out of the shadows. He was huge, a Goliath. Hayes thought briefly of the guy he'd bought heroin from in Venice Beach. This guy made that guy look like the Little Mermaid.

Pirate put a hand on Hayes's shoulder. "Hayes Thorpe, I'd like you to meet..."

But Hayes didn't hear the Goliath's name, because at that second, the Goliath's fist, which was the size of a brick, met with Hayes's face. Hayes's head snapped back, and he thought, *Broken jaw.* Pirate pinned Hayes's arms behind his back with one hand and emptied Hayes's pockets with his other hand. Three hundred and fifty bucks, Hayes knew.

"Please," Hayes managed to say. He wished he had considered his present circumstances as a possibility; he would have brought a weapon. In his duffel bag was a *kris* knife, presented to him by Sula before he left Nusa Lembongan. It had once belonged to her grandfather and was invested with some kind of mystical energy, which was the reason Sula's family had become so wealthy and powerful, she said. Hayes would have loved to have pulled out the *kris* knife, with its wavy blade, and stuck it in Pirate's good eye.

"Junkie," the Goliath said. He drew his fist back and delivered the knockout punch square in the face, shattering Hayes's nose. His face was warm and wet with blood. Hayes hit the ground, taking in a mouthful of sandy dirt. Someone was kicking Hayes in the leg, but honestly, he could barely feel it. He was just going to lie here and drown in his own blood.

"How much?" Hayes heard the Goliath ask.

"Few hundred," Pirate said.

"I thought you said he was *rich,*" the Goliath said.

"I figured he'd have more," Pirate said. "I told you who his father is, right? His father is Deacon Thorpe, the chef."

Was, Hayes thought, before he lost consciousness. *Was.*

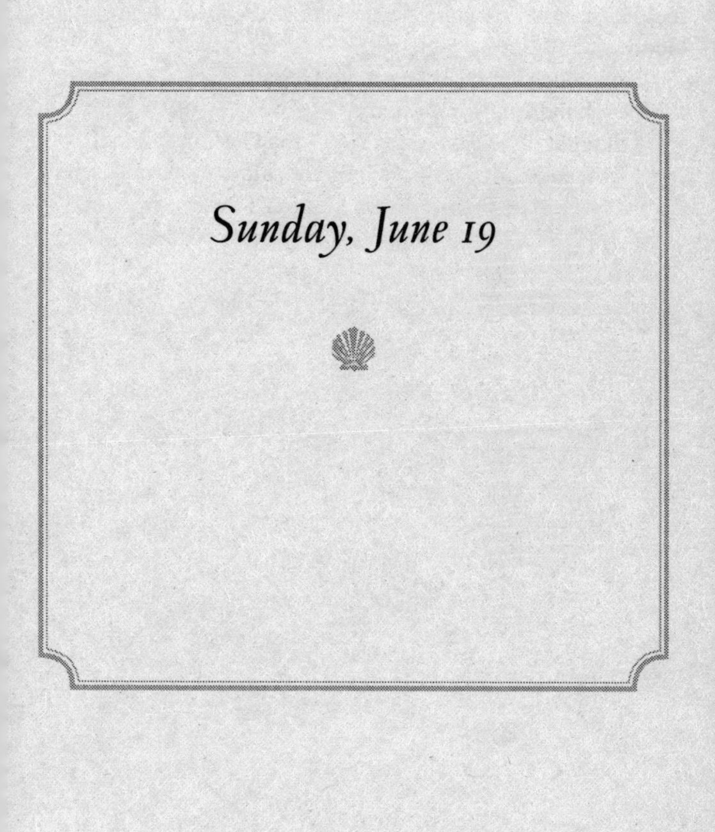

Sunday, June 19

BUCK

He woke up in the middle of the night and, again, didn't know where he was. Then he remembered: he was living the life on Nantucket, in Deacon's house, but Deacon was dead.

Pain like a stab to the heart. Buck had awakened to this same pain every day for the past six weeks. He had hoped that coming to Nantucket would make him feel better, but the opposite was true. Being on the island Deacon loved so much, in the house that was so dear to him, surrounded by his wives and his children, only made Buck believe that Deacon might walk through the door any second. It was easy to imagine that Deacon had gone to run an errand and was very, very late in getting home.

Buck's bed was two feet too short for him and had an unforgiving footboard.

Buck rose to use the bathroom. The house was old and creaky; the plumbing was loud. He was probably waking everybody up just by taking a leak.

He noticed a light on under the door of Laurel's room. Was she awake? He didn't think twice about it; he knocked.

"Come in," she said.

Buck slipped in and shut the door behind him. Laurel was

sitting up in bed. Her covers were white, smooth, and as neatly folded as origami paper; he loved Laurel's calm, orderly perfection. Buck's second wife, Mae, had never once made their bed. Every night it had been like sleeping in a pile of dirty laundry, and that, Buck supposed, had been their undoing—his desire for shipshape, hers for chaos.

Laurel was wearing a dove-gray scoop-necked pajama top and a pair of narrow, black-framed glasses. She was reading a book called...Buck strained his neck, trying to see, hoping it was one of the two novels he'd had time to read in the past three years...but no, it was *Euphoria,* by someone named Lily King. Buck had never heard of it, but the title seemed promising.

Euphoria.

"Am I interrupting?" Buck asked.

Laurel looked up and smiled. The glasses were incredibly sexy. "Not at all," she said. "I couldn't sleep."

"Me neither," Buck said. He looked around the room for a place to sit. The only chair in the room was a cane-bottomed rocker that would most definitely collapse under his weight.

Laurel patted the side of the bed. "It's okay," she said.

Buck perched on the edge of the bed next to her. She set the book down on the nightstand. "I'm devastated about the house," she said. "I wasn't even expecting a part of it to go to me. I just hate that the family is losing it. The kids..."

"I'm sorry I brought it up at dinner," Buck said. "I didn't know when I would have everyone all together."

"I wasn't angry at you," Laurel said. "I was angry at Belinda. I don't want her to pay for the house. I will not spend my life indebted to her."

"I'll state the obvious," Buck said. "She's the only one of us with that kind of money. You don't have a spare hundred and fifty grand, do you? And then five grand per month after that?"

"No," Laurel said. She peered at Buck over the tops of her glasses. "What did Belinda mean when she said the two of you had a run-in?"

His breath caught. *Belinda.* News of their awful interlude had nearly leaked before dinner, like a noxious gas. He considered lying. But Buck had gone to Catholic school and been educated by nuns; even now, his conscience spoke to him in the voice of Sister Mary Agatha. He heard her saying, *The truth always comes out.* She had been referring to Richard Nixon and Watergate, but it applied across the board. The truth always came out.

"I've been half in love with you since the first second I saw you," Buck said. "You realize this, right? Since way back—when you and Hayes came to that first meeting with me at the restaurant."

He thought back to those earliest days: Buck had been interning at William Morris during the day, and to pay the bills, he worked as the maître d' at Solo, in the Flatiron District, where Deacon Thorpe had just been named chef de cuisine. Buck was desperate for a client to call his own. As the maître d', he had handed out his card to every pretty potential-model face, thinking maybe he could transform beauty into talent, but it had yet to work out that way.

Buck's direct boss at work, an agent named Gus, suggested Buck break out of the usual mold. "Find an ice skater," he said. "Or a tennis player."

Or a chef, Buck thought. *Deacon.*

He thought of the potential *fortune* he could earn by turning shaggy-haired, foul-mouthed, twenty-two-times-tattooed, brilliantly named Deacon Thorpe into a star. Celebrity chefs weren't a phenomenon yet—but Buck sensed that they *could* be.

He'd set up a "meeting" in the hour before staff meal. Both Laurel and Hayes always came to staff meal—it was a deal that Deacon had set up with the restaurant owners—and so they also came to the meeting.

Deacon had said, "I'm not sure what you're after, man. I hope you're not thinking about me doing a cookbook, because I nearly flunked English in high school."

"Not a cookbook," Buck said. "I was thinking maybe... TV?"

"TV?" Deacon said. "You mean, like Julia Child?"

"And the other guy...," Laurel said. "The Frugal Gourmet." She smiled at Buck, and he felt his face grow hot. "Deacon could do for cooking what Bob Ross has done for painting. *Just a little indication of a tree over here*... I think it's a great idea." She leaned across the table and slapped her hand down. Her fingernails were filed but not painted. Buck could have peeked down the front of her white sundress, but there was nothing to see; she was flat chested. And lightly tanned, with long, sandy-colored hair. Laurel Thorpe was a natural, unvarnished beauty. "Can you make it happen?"

He had made it happen—for her. This many years later, John Buckley could admit, he had worked his ass off cold-calling and making a nuisance of himself with his superiors, all for Laurel. Deacon got a screen test at ABC, where the execs were looking for late-night material to launch opposite Johnny Carson. Deacon was offered a half-hour slot called *Day to Night to Day with Deacon*. Deacon had been young and savage in those days, real and hungry.

Now, Laurel smiled. "I remember how nervous you were. I thought you were just excited to sign your first client."

"It was you," Buck said. Laurel had belonged to Deacon—she was his wife—but Buck had been overwhelmed just by sitting across the table from her. He could remember wanting to sound professional, confident, impressive. "So anyway, the run-in with Belinda..."

"Yes?" Laurel said. "Did the two of you have an argument?"

"An argument?" Buck said. He *wished* they'd had an argument. They *should* have had an argument. "No." He sighed. "She, well...she hit on me. Do people even say that anymore? She came on to me...while you were in town this afternoon...and I let it happen."

"You *slept* with her?" Laurel asked.

"Not exactly," Buck said. "But close enough."

"You...?" Laurel waved a hand as if she were trying to erase him. "Don't tell me. I don't want to know. But you're saying something happened between the two of you? Something sexual?"

Buck nodded. He could picture Sister Mary Agatha, her pasty, white face strained in her wimple. "I had a weak moment."

"A weak...? Okay, wow." Laurel pushed her glasses up her nose. "Wow. I can't believe I'm hearing this. I'm... frankly, I'm disgusted."

"Laurel," he said.

"I understand you're grief stricken," Laurel said. "And maybe that's clouding your judgment. But I thought you and I had a connection. You almost kissed me on the deck, right? Or was I imagining that?"

"You weren't imagining it," Buck said. "I *was* about to kiss you. I *wanted* to kiss you. I've been thinking about kissing you all day long. Like I just said, Laurel, I've been half in love with you ever since I can remember."

Laurel picked up her book, and for a second, Buck thought

she was going to throw it at him, but instead she flung it across the room. So much for euphoria. "I've always thought you were different from everyone else, Buck. *Better* than everyone else. You're like a man from another age, with the suits and the handkerchiefs and the elegant manners. But, as it turns out, you're just like your friend Deacon. You have no self-control! Belinda bats her eyes at you, and you surrender? You *know* why she came on to you, right? She wanted to prove she could steal you from me. It's a *sport* for her, Buck!" Laurel's voice was quiet but furious. "This morning, when we went to the beach together, she told me I should date you. And then... what... a matter of hours later, she's unzipping your fly? She can't help herself, I guess. She has to steal what might be mine. And I'm supposed to sit back and let her because I'm the nice one. Do you know what happens to nice people, Buck? They lose. They lose every time."

"Laurel, no—" Buck said.

"*I'll* state the obvious," Laurel said. "I won't have Belinda paying for my part of this house. I will not allow it."

"Laurel, please..."

"Get out of here, Buck. I don't want to be part of a game where you sleep with every woman in this house!"

"Laurel, that isn't what I'm doing," Buck said.

"Belinda this afternoon, me tonight," Laurel said. "I know you didn't come in here to play Scrabble or have a discussion about Papua New Guinea. You came in here hoping to get lucky."

"No, I—"

"If Scarlett shows up, you'll go after her, too, I'm sure," Laurel said. "Hat trick."

"No, I—"

"And do you know why?" Laurel said. "Because all these

many years, you were *jealous* of Deacon. You wanted everything he had. Admit it!"

Laurel's hair was falling in her face; her cheeks were pink. The awful thing was that Buck had never seen her look more beautiful than she did at that moment, when she was confronting him with the truth. Yes, he had been jealous of Deacon. It had been impossible *not* to be jealous of Deacon. The man had a talent and a magnetism and a raw power that was unparalleled in anyone Buck had ever met.

"I was jealous of Deacon, yes," Buck said. "But that's not what this is about..."

"Get out of my bedroom, Buck," Laurel said. "Please."

Buck stood up to leave. This was officially the last time he would tell the truth to anyone. From now on, it would be all deceit and subterfuge.

Laurel's phone rang on the nightstand. Buck turned.

"Go on," Laurel said. "It's probably just my other lover." She looked at the display, then answered the phone. "Hello?"

Buck lingered at the door in case Laurel needed him, although it was doubtful that he would be able to do anything other than mess things up further.

"Oh God," Laurel said. "Buck?"

Buck swung around.

"It's the police," Laurel said. "Hayes is at the hospital."

Laurel wanted to drive, but Buck insisted. "You're too upset," he said. "Just tell me where I'm going."

"He's not dying," Laurel said. It sounded as though she was trying to convince herself. "He was assaulted, the police said. And robbed."

"Here on Nantucket?" Buck said. "I didn't know there was any crime."

"I read about a prostitution ring busted here last year," Laurel said. "It was run by a local real estate agent, and his clients were high-end businessmen here on vacation. Further proving to me that all men are depraved."

Buck pulled into the hospital parking lot, and Laurel rushed into the emergency room entrance without waiting for him. Should he go in? If Deacon were here, Deacon would go in, but Deacon was the father. Buck was a paltry surrogate. Was he anything more than a buzzard feasting on his best friend's leftovers?

Yes, goddamn it! He loved Laurel. He loved her more than he could remember loving any woman, including his two wives. How spectacularly he had blown it! He should have told Belinda to leave him alone. He should have pushed her away. Of course Laurel was hurt! Why had he expected otherwise?

At that second, the Jeep door opened and Laurel climbed in and Hayes crawled into the back with a groan. His face was swollen and bruised; his nose was bandaged, and he had a black eye.

"He won't cooperate with the police," Laurel said. "He won't tell them who did this."

"Mom," Hayes said in a nasal voice, "I don't *know* who did this."

"I don't understand what you were doing out," Laurel said. "I thought you went to bed, like the rest of us."

"I got antsy," Hayes said. "Cabin fever. I'm used to nightlife, Mom. That's how I roll."

"How did you get to town?" Laurel asked. "You certainly didn't walk."

"I took a taxi because I was drinking at dinner," Hayes

said. "The driver and I had an argument about the way he was taking me into town, so he stopped, and I got out. And then, I guess, I got mugged. I don't remember anything else."

"The police found him in the state forest," Laurel said to Buck. "All his cash is gone, and his credit cards and his driver's license."

"What did the doctor say?" Buck asked. "Anything broken? Concussion?"

"No," Hayes said. "My face is going to look like a Halloween mask for a while, and it's going to hurt, but it's okay. They gave me a bunch of painkillers."

Intermezzo: *Deacon and Belinda, Part I*

Los Angeles is all swimming pools and vodka martinis. When Belinda introduces Deacon to her friends and colleagues as a chef, they all, to a person, say, "Oh, like Wolfgang Puck?" Puck has the town locked up. *Everyone* eats at Spago. Is there even room for another chef?

In their new life in Los Angeles, Belinda pays for everything. She buys Deacon new clothes. She buys him Gucci loafers that pinch, but she insists they will stretch and conform to Deacon's feet. He doesn't tell her that he's never owned a real pair of shoes before. He has made it through life in Chuck Taylors, flip-flops, and kitchen clogs.

Belinda is renting a house in Beverly Hills that has a heated pool and a gym with a steam sauna and a screening room. The kitchen is bigger than Deacon and Laurel's entire apartment on

West 119th Street. This makes Deacon feel guilt at first, intense, piercing guilt that brings him down. He was busy in New York, but here in L.A., he has hours of unstructured time. When Belinda is busy or away—which is more often than he anticipated—he is at loose ends. There is a whole city to explore; he could go to the Getty Museum or to the beaches of Malibu or to Disneyland. He has never been anywhere Disney before, and it intrigues him. But instead, Deacon lies in bed watching TV, and then, when he gets up, he goes out drinking. He can't go anywhere stylish—not the Wilshire or the Beverly Hills Hotel—because someone will recognize him, and it'll get back to Belinda. And so, he seeks out dive bars. He goes to Compton and South Central. He goes to Anaheim.

When Belinda is around, Deacon is happier. They watch movies in the screening room and always end up making love in the extra-wide reclining seats. They lie by the pool—Deacon in the sun, Belinda under an umbrella. Deacon swims laps, but Belinda won't even dip her feet. Deacon teases her about this. It's like drinking decaf coffee or non-alcoholic beer, he says. The point of coffee is caffeine, the point of beer is alcohol, and the point of having a pool is swimming in it! Belinda won't budge.

They go to a Dodgers game; they ride the Ferris wheel on Santa Monica Pier. Belinda takes Deacon to a party on Mulholland Drive at the house of James Brinegar, who directed her in *Between the Pipes*. Jaime is a super-cool guy, intellectual and erudite, but fun, too. He's a huge fan of the Clash, and he takes Deacon to his man cave to show him his collection of memorabilia, including a picture of Jaime with Joe Strummer on the beach in Ibiza, and Deacon thinks he may have found a friend.

Jaime brings out a mirror and taps out two long lines of cocaine. Deacon starts shaking just looking at it.

"We'll race," Jaime says. "Whoever finishes first snorts what's left of his opponent's line."

"You're on," Deacon says, confident he will win. And he does.

Maybe Jaime is angry about being bested in his own home, because he turns to Deacon and says, "You know I used to bang Belinda, right?"

Cocaine turns Deacon into a monster under the best of circumstances. Upon hearing Jaime say the words "bang Belinda," Deacon punches Jaime right in the face and knocks him to the ground, where Deacon starts kicking the living shit out of him. Someone in the other room hears breaking glass and comes rushing in to save Jaime's life.

The police take Deacon off the property in handcuffs. Belinda is crying. She isn't allowed in the cruiser, but she follows Deacon to the police station in her Jaguar. She is famous enough and beautiful enough, he supposes, that he is only charged with drunk and disorderly, and not with assault and battery.

"He told me he'd banged my girl," Deacon says to the arresting officer. "What was I supposed to do?"

Belinda had said she would get Deacon his own restaurant so that he could be his own boss, but after his arrest and the attendant humiliation, Deacon can't bring himself to ask. Eventually, Belinda forgives him; she decides he was being gallant, defending her honor. She buys Deacon a Porsche 911—his own freaking Porsche. He should be the happiest man in L.A., and yet somehow, he's not.

It's always sunny, which depresses Deacon. He starts to long for the gloomy, overcast days of New York in November.

He yearns for a thunderstorm, something to match his temperament. He calls Laurel and Hayes every single day, sometimes more than once a day, but more and more often, Laurel doesn't answer. One weekend a month, Deacon flies back to New York to see Hayes, and every time, he considers staying. He and Laurel talk about getting back together, conversations that always end with Laurel saying, "You won't leave her. I know you won't. She's too strong, and you're not strong enough."

Deacon fears she's right.

A popular pastime in California is finding oneself, and Deacon gets swept along. He needs to find himself. He needs a job. Deacon and Belinda eat at Spago. They eat at the Ivy. Deacon toys with getting a job in the kitchen of one or the other, but how can he work as a line cook when he's dating the most sought-after actress in Hollywood?

When summer rolls around, Deacon persuades Belinda to go to Nantucket, although the second she agrees, he starts to worry. As much as he loves the house, when he looks at it through her eyes, he sees only what's wrong with it: a peeling linoleum floor in the kitchen, rooms that haven't been painted in twenty-five years, sand permanently embedded between the floorboards.

Matters are made worse when they arrive in the middle of a nor'easter—driving rain and wind gusts up to fifty miles an hour. Nantucket is the greatest place on earth on a sunny summer day, but in the rain, it's worthless. They've been in the house less than an hour—just enough time for Belinda to perfect her "brave face"—when the power goes out. Deacon figures this is either the best-case scenario or the worst. He lights a fire, he brings pillows and a blanket down from the bedroom, he makes a nest. He finds a bag of marshmallows in the cabinet—bingo!

"Cozy, right?" he says to her. He's afraid she's going to turn her nose up at him or start screaming, because in this kind of wind, the house feels like a cup of dice God is shaking. Life with Belinda, he's realized, is a prison of high expectations.

She surprises him by snuggling up and resting her head against his heart. "Right," she says.

It's in the rudimentary kitchen of the Nantucket house that Deacon starts to develop recipes. Belinda has a sweet tooth, so he makes a fluffy white champagne cake with champagne icing and champagne-candied strawberries.

When she tastes it, she swoons.

"Oh my God," she says. She says that she has never been as in love with anyone or anything as much as him...and that cake. "Let's make a baby."

It's six months later, and, although sex is now Deacon's cool second job, he can't get Belinda pregnant. She goes to the doctor and gets checked out and insists he do the same. He jerks off in a cup so that they can check the sperm count. His sperm count is fine. He already knew this, he tells Belinda, because he got Laurel pregnant without even trying. This sets Belinda crying. She feels like a failure, she says. She feels like she's less of a woman. With his own money, Deacon books a suite at the Four Seasons in Santa Barbara. He plies her with vodka martinis and gets to work.

Later that month, she gets her period.

Now he feels like a failure. But then, out of the blue, he gets a call from Luther Davey, owner of the TruBlue Entertainment Group, saying he wants to open tricoastal restaurants called Raindance, one in L.A., one in Chicago, one in New York, and he wants Deacon to be the executive chef of all three.

Yes, Deacon says right away. He doesn't ask Belinda her opinion, which is a mistake. She becomes hysterical when he tells her. She takes the clamshell that Deacon got so many years ago with his father on Nantucket, and which sits in a hallowed place on the mantel, and she throws it into the swimming pool. Deacon is so livid that he grabs Belinda by the forearm. Her arm is delicate; he could easily break it with just one hand. He could throw her into the pool and watch her drown. But then he comes to his senses. He lets Belinda go, and he dives to the bottom of the pool to rescue his shell.

He takes the job at Raindance.

He signs a forty-page prenup, after which he and Belinda are married by her yogi on a cliff overlooking the Pacific Ocean. Buck is the only other person in attendance.

Belinda decides she wants to adopt a baby. She somehow finds a newborn in an orphanage in the Australian outback, and the next thing Deacon knows, Belinda is flying to Perth to pick up their new daughter, Angela. They will call her Angie, after the Rolling Stones song that is their favorite.

When Angie is five years old and ready for kindergarten, Deacon lobbies to move back to New York. He is there half-time anyway, and he doesn't want L.A. to be all Angie experiences. She deserves better. She is the coolest kid that Deacon has ever known, and, despite the fact that Los Angeles is the second-largest metropolis in the country, it's not as racially integrated as New York. Look at Rodney King!

It's impossible for Belinda to argue about Rodney King. It's impossible for Belinda to argue that California is not, at its essence, a dominion of blond girls. Angie might not be discriminated against, but she could easily be ignored or overlooked.

Belinda succumbs. She will allow a move to New York. They will get an apartment in the Waldorf Towers. Angie will go to private school—at Chapin, Spence, or Nightingale-Bamford.

But...Belinda won't be around as much as she was in L.A. (Was she around in L.A.? Deacon spent all his days off with Angie, teaching her how to squeeze the juice out of a lemon, crack an egg, measure flour.) Belinda is in negotiations to play Mai Hanh in *The Delta*—a role she wants more than she wants to breathe—but this will mean three to six months of filming in Vietnam. It won't matter where Deacon and Angie are, because Belinda won't be home either way.

We have to get a proper nanny, Belinda says. Not a Mexican housekeeper, like they had in L.A., but someone professional and organized and whimsical and kind. A Mary Poppins.

Belinda interviews thirty girls. There are fat girls, Goth girls, British girls; there is a woman with a mustache who scares Deacon with her list of rules. There is a woman who has a graduate degree in molecular biology; there is a girl with red, chafed nostrils who clearly likes to party downtown.

And then, number thirty-one: Scarlett Oliver, from Savannah, Georgia.

Deacon happens to be in the apartment when Scarlett arrives. She is tall and slender, with dark hair to her waist and a pearly-white smile. *Too pretty,* Deacon thinks right away. Belinda will never hire her.

Scarlett reveals that she is a debutante from Savannah. Belinda will never hire her. This will be one of those interviews that lasts four minutes.

Belinda says, "What exactly does that mean, 'a debutante'?"

"Well," Scarlett says. "It means I had a debut. It's a ball where one is presented to society."

"I was presented to society half-naked in *Brilliant Disguise,*" Belinda says, then she laughs at herself. "Have you ever seen it?"

"Only about forty times," Scarlett says. "It's my favorite movie."

Oh boy, Deacon thinks. To a one, all the nanny candidates have been gushing fans. To a one, all have asked Belinda for her autograph, even the Goth girl.

"Let me introduce you to Angie," Belinda says.

What? Deacon thinks. Meeting Angie means Scarlett made it through the first gate. Is that possible? Deacon pokes his head out of the kitchen and sees Scarlett's lovely long legs in denim shorts. He doesn't know whether to pray that she gets hired or pray that she doesn't.

She gets hired. Frankly, Deacon can't believe it. She is way too beautiful, and Belinda, as famous as she is, finds other beautiful women threatening.

"What made you hire Scarlett?" Deacon asks.

"Gut feeling," Belinda says. "She was so good with Angie. Angie hung on to her neck when it was time for her to go. She hasn't done that with anyone else. I feel like she's meant to be in our lives."

What Belinda says, goes. Scarlett is around 24-7 in the apartment, wearing shorts and halter tops and half shirts that show off her perfectly flat, pale stomach. Deacon tries to make himself immune to her beauty and her innocence. And her Southern accent. She teaches Angie the phrase "Gimme some sugar." When Scarlett says this, Angie purses her lips and gives Scarlett a kiss. Then Scarlett says, "Now, give Daddy some sugar." And Angie gives Deacon a kiss while Deacon looks at Scarlett.

Belinda films in Vietnam for so long, Deacon forgets what she looks like. He is very busy at Raindance, but he manages to wrangle ten days off in August to go to Nantucket with Angie, who is six, and Hayes, who is fourteen. Deacon is under the delusion that Hayes will be able to watch Angie and earn some pocket money. But this notion is quashed in an email from Belinda.

Hayes is not a suitable babysitter, she writes. *If he goes chasing a girl down the beach or gets wrapped up in his skim-boarding, Angie will drown.*

Take Scarlett, please, Belinda writes. *I implore you. It will put my mind at ease.*

And so, the four of them go on vacation together—Deacon, Scarlett, Hayes, and Angie. Everyone on Nantucket assumes Scarlett is Deacon's mistress; he grows weary of explaining that he is still married to Belinda, but she is on location overseas, filming. Scarlett is just their nanny, like Mary Poppins. Eventually, he stops bothering.

Hayes is fascinated by Scarlett and follows her around as night follows day. Deacon can only imagine that Hayes is entertaining some pretty impure thoughts about Scarlett, which serves as a distraction from Deacon's own impure thoughts. Deacon sleeps in the master bedroom, and Scarlett takes the bedroom right next door. She is so close, he can hear her turning over in bed at night, which leaves him with an aching erection.

And then one evening, Deacon is lighting the grill on the back deck while Scarlett is in the outdoor shower. He hears her squeal as the water goes cold. She shuts the water off and says, "Deacon?"

He freezes. He feels caught.

"Yes?" he says. He's trying to figure out where the kids are. Angie is upstairs, he guesses, playing with her dollhouse, a pastime that occupies her for hours on end.

"Is there anything I can do to get the water hot again?" she asks.

"Nothing," he says. "Except to wait forty-seven minutes."

She peeks her head over the shower door. "You could come in here and wait with me," she says.

Here it is: the invitation. Inevitable, he supposes. Belinda is far away, and he and Scarlett have been masquerading as husband and wife, going grocery shopping together and sharing an ice cream cone when they take the kids to the Juice Bar—he licks first, then she says *Gimme some sugar* and she licks.

Plus, they are on vacation, on an island thirty miles out to sea; they have been plucked out of their usual roles. They feel removed, safe.

"Scarlett," he says. His tone hits halfway between stern (*How dare you!*) and pleading (*Please don't*).

She smiles at him. She is so, so pretty! So sweet! So helpful! But Deacon will not be that guy. He heads inside and decides to cut the vacation short. They leave Nantucket the next day.

Fluffy White Champagne Cake with Champagne Candied Strawberries

MAKES ONE 8 × 8–INCH CAKE

1¼ cups all-purpose flour
1 teaspoon baking powder
¼ teaspoon salt
½ cup unsalted butter
1½ cups white sugar
1 whole large egg plus 2 large egg whites
1 teaspoon vanilla extract
½ cup whole milk

Preheat the oven to 350°F. Grease an 8 × 8–inch baking pan with butter, then pour some flour in the pan and shake it around until the bottom and sides are covered. Dump the excess flour out.

In a bowl, whisk together the flour, baking powder, and salt.

In the bowl of an electric mixer, beat the butter on medium speed until creamy. Add in the sugar and beat until light and fluffy, about 3 minutes. Add the egg and egg whites in one at a time, beating for a minute after each addition. Add in the vanilla extract, making sure to scrape down the sides and bottom of the bowl if needed. Add in half the dry ingredients, mixing on low speed, then add in the milk.

Finish with the rest of the dry ingredients, beating until the batter is combined and smooth.

Pour the batter into the prepared pan. Bake for 27 to 32 minutes, or until a toothpick inserted into the center comes out clean. Let cool completely before frosting.

CHAMPAGNE FROSTING

½ cup unsalted butter
4 ounces cream cheese, softened
4½ cups powdered sugar
3 to 5 tablespoons champagne
1 teaspoon vanilla extract

Place the butter and cream cheese in the bowl of an electric mixer and beat on medium speed until creamy. With the mixer on low speed, gradually add the powdered sugar, beating until combined. The frosting will look crumbly, but continue to scrape down the sides and the bottom of the bowl until it's somewhat combined. Slowly drizzle in the champagne, 1 to 2 tablespoons at a time. You can do this in between additions of the powdered sugar if needed, but I find it works best at the end. Beat in the vanilla extract.

Beat the frosting on medium to high speed until it's thick and creamy and fluffy, about 3 to 4 minutes. If it becomes too runny, add more powdered sugar, ½ cup at a time. If it becomes too thick, add in more champagne 1 tablespoon at a time. Once the cake cools, frost it!

CHAMPAGNE CANDIED STRAWBERRIES

1½ cups sugar
¼ cup water

⅔ cup champagne
1 pint strawberries, hulled, some sliced, some kept whole

Place the sugar, water, and champagne in a saucepan over medium heat. Whisk constantly until the sugar dissolves and the mixture starts to simmer, then cook for 2 minutes. Add the strawberries to the mixture and simmer for 2 to 3 minutes. Remove the strawberries with a slotted spoon and place them in a bowl—they will be sticky! Additionally, you can store the strawberries in their syrup in the fridge until you're ready to serve the cake. I like to keep the syrup for drizzling and serve the strawberries on the side of the cake.

ANGIE

When she heard the hammering, she hurried to the window. JP's silver Jeep was in the driveway. He was downstairs, fixing the wonky board on the porch, just as he'd promised. At least he was reliable.

Unlike Joel Tersigni.

Angie pulled on clothes and headed downstairs.

The sun was in her eyes as she opened the door. "Good morning," she said. "Coffee?"

JP was on his knees on the porch with a jigsaw and a toolbox, a baseball hat on backward, his Blues Brothers sunglasses resting on the railing. Angie hadn't noticed his eyes before. They were brown—not deep brown like Angie's, but more like a reddish brown. He grinned at her. "I'd love some."

"You're here awfully early," she said.

"I have ranger duties today," he said. "But you were right: this board is an orthopedist's dream."

Angie nearly told JP that there was no point in fixing the board, or anything else, because they were going to lose the house. But JP didn't need to know about the miserable inner workings of the Thorpe family. He thought Deacon was a superhero; Deacon would remain a superhero.

Angie headed to the kitchen for coffee; she hadn't been able to eat anything after the conversation with Dory the day before, but she had set up the coffee because it was the one thing she couldn't live without. A house was a house was a house, she thought. People lost houses all the time, just like her mother had said. She could live without this house.

But she couldn't look at the door frame where she and Hayes and Ellery had all been measured. She wondered if the new owners of the house would paint over the hash marks or keep them. She took three deep breaths, then headed out to the porch with the coffee.

Just as she was about to step outside, Belinda descended the stairs.

This is not happening, Angie thought. It had been a long time since Angie had woken up in the same house as her mother, but she recalled that one of Belinda Rowe's trademark behaviors was sleeping in.

Apparently not today, however. Maybe the hammering had woken her, although she didn't appear disgruntled, merely a bit disoriented. She was in her white lace nightgown and white silk robe, and she had her sleep mask pushed off her face; it rested messily in her famous strawberry-blond hair. She had washed off her makeup. Angie was always surprised at how regular her mother looked with clean skin.

"Good morning, darling," Belinda said.

"Good morning," Angie said. "There's coffee."

"Wonderful," Belinda said, but instead of heading into the kitchen, she followed Angie out the front door, onto the porch. "Oh, hello," she said to JP, who was still on his knees. "No wonder I was dreaming about a giant woodpecker."

Angie rolled her eyes. JP jumped to his feet and offered Belinda his hand. "I'm JP Clarke," he said. "I was a friend of Deacon's."

"Hello, JP," Belinda said. "I'm Angie's mother."

Angie hadn't heard Belinda introduce herself as "Angie's mother" in more than ten years, since Angie was a student at Chapin. She had to admit, she was almost flattered that Belinda had identified herself as such. She just as easily could have said, *I'm Belinda Rowe,* and let JP think: *Academy Award–winning actress, former face of Chanel, and cover girl of* Vogue *(five times),* Vanity Fair *(twice), and* Time *magazine (in character, as Vietnamese heroine Mai Hanh).*

"It's nice to meet you," JP said. "I'm sorry for the ruckus. I wanted to get here first thing this morning to fix the board before somebody hurt themselves."

"Thank you," Belinda said. "I assure you, that would have been me. I brought very impractical shoes."

This caused both JP and Angie to stare at Belinda's feet, which were bare. Her toenails were painted baby blue.

Angie handed JP his coffee, which he accepted gratefully. Angie said, "There's coffee in the kitchen, Mother."

"So, JP, do you live on Nantucket year-round?" Belinda asked.

"I do," he said. "I'm the ranger out at Coatue."

"Now *that's* interesting," Belinda said.

"It is if you like nature," JP said.

"My mother doesn't like nature," Angie said.

"I like nature, darling," Belinda said. "So what does a ranger *do,* exactly?"

"I'm half-policeman, half-conservationist," JP said. "On the one hand, I keep track of the tourists. Make sure they stay in the designated areas, help people who get stuck in the sand. On the other hand, I keep track of the wildlife. I count plover eggs and report seal and shark sightings. I get a fair amount of fishing in, and some clamming."

"And then what do you do in the off-season?" Belinda asked.

"Mother," Angie said.

"I tutor middle and high school students in math," JP said. "I was a math major at MIT."

"Oh my goodness!" Belinda said.

"Before I dropped out," JP said. "I liked my classes, but I hated the city. I missed Nantucket, so I moved back after first semester junior year. The tutoring gives me time to do what I really love. In the fall, I scallop, and come November, I hunt."

"My husband hunts!" Belinda cried out.

"Bow or shotgun?" JP asked.

Belinda's shoulders sagged. "I have no idea," she said. "He keeps a hunting cabin in Tennessee. But I don't know what animals he shoots or how he shoots them."

Angie shook her head. Her mother sounded like a simpleton. She said, "There's coffee inside, Mother."

"Yes," Belinda said. "I heard you the first two times."

"It's probably only a matter of hours before the paparazzi discover you're here," Angie said. "You might not want to stand on the porch in your nightgown."

"It was nice to meet you, Angie's mother," JP said.

"And you…!" Belinda said. Her voice dropped off a

cliff, and it became clear that she had already forgotten his name. She disappeared inside, and JP got back to work.

Angie sat behind him on the top step and gazed at the water.

"How are you doing?" JP asked.

She was about to say "fine," but then she thought, *Why lie?*

"Been better," she said.

He hammered the new board into place with such force that the vibration traveled up Angie's butt and jarred her teeth.

"I'm almost done here," JP said. "Then, if you're free, I can take you on a little field trip."

"Field trip?" Angie said.

"It'll get your mind off things," JP said.

"I thought you had ranger duties," Angie said.

"I do," JP said. "But this will only take an hour or so, then I'll bring you back."

"But no people?" Angie said. "I can't do people."

"No people," JP said.

As soon as they climbed in the Jeep and backed out of the driveway, Angie felt the heady rush of escape.

"I'm sorry about my mother," she said.

"You don't have to apologize."

"We don't get along," Angie said. "I was much closer with my father."

"He used to talk about you all the time," JP said.

"Did he?" Angie said. She wanted to ask what Deacon had said, but the question got caught in her throat, and before she knew it, she was crying again. She thought it might be embarrassing to break down in front of a near perfect stranger, but she was beyond caring what anyone thought of her. There had been only two people who mattered—Deacon and Joel—and both of them had left her.

"Hey," JP said. He reached into the backseat of the Jeep and pulled out a clean, folded white T-shirt. The front of the shirt had a black oval with the word BOX written inside. Angie stared at it through her tears.

"The Box," she said. It was the greatest dive bar in the civilized world, and yet all she could think of were the rainy days that she and Deacon had spent in the dark grottiness shooting pool, drinking really cold beer, and playing songs on the jukebox. As with everything else on Nantucket, there was tradition: Angie always started out playing "Beast of Burden," and then Deacon played "Fool in the Rain."

"Yep," JP said. "You can feel free to blow your nose on the shirt."

She did just that. The T-shirt was soft and smelled like pine soap.

She said, "I feel bad defiling your T-shirt."

JP said, "I feel bad I don't have any tissues. I can wash the shirt." He took a right onto the Wauwinet Road, and Angie rested her head against the seat and tried to drink in the scenery. The land was a little lusher here than elsewhere on the island, with tall deciduous trees casting leafy shadows over the road. They passed the artist colony's barn, they passed the sailboats bobbing in Polpis Harbor, they passed Squam Swamp, home to the three-mile nature trail where Angie used to hunt for salamanders and frogs when she was young. Eventually, they cruised past the gatehouse operated by the Trustees of Reservations. JP waved at the woman manning the gatehouse and called out, "Hey, Maggie!"

JP shifted the Jeep into four-wheel drive as they headed out the sandy road that led to Coatue and Great Point. The landscape changed to wild, windswept beach and eel grass, with Coskata Pond on the left and the forever-blue ocean on the right.

"I forgot how unspoiled this place is," Angie said.

"You live in Manhattan?" JP said.

She nodded. "I have a studio on East Seventy-Third Street. Technically, that's the Upper East Side, but my apartment is just a square room with a bed and a sofa. My mother threatened to send her decorator, but I managed to hold her off."

"Good for you," JP said. "I'm not much of a city person, as I told your mom."

"It's about as different from this as a place can get," Angie said.

JP pulled up to a small, shingled cottage with a covered porch. "Here it is," he said. "My own square room with a bed and a sofa. Minus the sofa."

"Yeah, but look at your view," Angie said. The cottage was set in a sandy clearing that overlooked the slender, five-pointed arm of sand that was Coatue and the placid blue oval of Coskata Pond, which was ringed by tall grass and cattails. In the distance, Angie could pick out the Nantucket skyline—the church steeples and the mansions of Orange Street.

JP hopped out, and Angie followed him, albeit somewhat reluctantly. She wasn't sure what kind of field trip this was supposed to be. Angie wondered if JP was just one more typical male, preying on a girl who had absolutely no defenses left. He noticed she was lagging behind.

"This isn't what you're thinking," he said. "I swear. We don't even have to go inside."

"I'll take a peek," she said. She climbed the step to the porch, where JP kept a clam rake leaning against the railing and a wire clam basket filled with shoes—work boots, flip-flops, Chuck Taylors. A pair of board shorts flapped on a makeshift clothesline.

"Would you like some sun tea?" JP asked. "Brewed fresh this morning."

"You brewed tea *and* you came out to our house to fix the porch?"

"Sun rises at quarter to five," JP said. "And a dutiful ranger rises with it. I even had time to cast my fly rod a few times in the pond." JP stepped into the cottage, and Angie poked her head in. Bed, as promised, table stacked with math textbooks and topped with a copy of Peterson's *Field Guide to Eastern Birds,* and a galley kitchen. There was a cast-iron frying pan on the stove and row of mason jars on a shelf over the sink. JP took two glass jars, filled them with ice, then poured in the sun tea and added a fat wedge of lime to each. He noticed Angie checking the place out.

"It's primitive," he said. "Sort of like summer camp. There's a half bath behind that door and an outdoor shower off the back."

"What else do you need?" Angie asked. She had always envisioned Joel and Dory's house on Rosebrook Road in New Canaan as grandiose—with a circular driveway and white pillars and a swimming pool out back with a waterfall. Joel and Dory's bedroom would have a pencil-post bed, she supposed, that was sheathed in ten-thousand-thread-count linens; there would be a sunken Jacuzzi tub in the master bath. Something had to be keeping Joel there, something that was more desirable than Angie's body and her love.

JP was patiently holding out her jar of tea. She realized she'd gotten lost for a second. She took the jar, and together they stepped out onto the porch.

"I like your father's house," JP said. "It's a real old-school summer cottage. My grandparents' house was like that.

They lived at the end of Massasoit Bridge Road, way out in the hinterlands of Madaket. When I was a kid, I would ride my bike out there in the afternoons to swim in the waves and then play a few hands of euchre. My grandmother used to make an appetizer called the special. It was bacon wrapped around a Club cracker and put under the broiler until it was crispy golden brown. It sounds crazy, but it's, like, the most delicious thing I've ever eaten."

Angie raised her eyebrows. If she ever cooked for JP, she could do better than bacon wrapped around a Club cracker. But maybe not; he looked pretty keen.

"My father's house is..." Angie trailed off. "Well, Deacon always said it was our home away from home, but I just think of it as home. You know? It's the one place I feel at peace."

JP smiled wistfully. "I do know."

They stood together on the front porch in silence for a second, Angie inhaling the scenery, gorging on it. This insane beauty, which only yesterday would have brought her comfort, now caused pain—because she was going to lose it.

JP said, "Anyway, what I want to show you is out back. Come on." They walked around the cottage, past the outdoor shower, to a door that revealed a storage closet.

He pulled out a dense foam cube with a picture of a deer painted on it. Then he picked up a black case that looked as if it might hold an electric bass.

He opened the case and lifted out an elaborate contraption that did in fact look like some exotic instrument, but Angie soon realized it was a hunter's bow.

JP said, "Most women misunderstand hunting. They think it's brutal, a behavior left over from caveman days. But I love to hunt because it requires skill and it requires patience. It's not the killing that draws me to the stand at five o'clock in the morning; it's the thrill of the chase. The relationship between man and animal is older than recorded time."

Angie nodded. She could see how Deacon would have fallen head over heels in love with this guy. Deacon appreciated purists. He admired integrity in people and their pursuits. He liked things done the correct way, not the quick and easy way.

"You only shoot one buck a year?" she said.

"One buck a year," JP said. "I set up cameras, check them all summer, watch the deer grow. Sometimes I give them names." He grinned. "I'm sure I sound like a dope." He counted out a certain number of paces and set the target down in the sand. When he came back, he picked up the bow.

"This, Angie Thorpe, is a compound bow. The peep sight is here, and if you look through the peep sight, you'll see the pins. The top pin, the green one, is for thirty yards, so that's the one we're going to line up because that's how far away our target is. I'm going to put on this release"—here he strapped on a wristband that had a clip attached—"and nock the arrow in. And then I'm going to draw." He pulled back the string of the bow. Angie watched the muscles of his forearm jump. "And then it's as easy as pulling the trigger." The arrow whinged through the air with an audible *whoosh*. It hit the cube just below the deer.

"Aw!" JP said. "I'm sorely out of practice. And I think I got a little nervous because I'm trying to impress you."

Angie smiled at her feet. JP took the bow off his shoulder. "It's your turn," he said.

She said, "I don't know how."

"I'm going to teach you," he said. He gently positioned the bow over Angie's shoulder and pulled out an arrow with hot-pink fletching. "This is a field tip. It's not going to kill anything. We just use this for target practice." He secured the release onto Angie's wrist; it buckled like a watchband. He nocked in her arrow. "Now, draw back."

Drawing back the bow was nearly impossible. Angie's left arm pushed forward; it was trembling with the strain, and she got the bowstring back part of the way, but not far enough.

"Pull harder," JP said.

She was about to tell him she couldn't do it; she wasn't strong enough. But then she gritted her teeth and pulled the string back with all her might. She had learned to dice ten onions in fifteen seconds and fillet a Dover sole with the grace of Leonard Bernstein conducting the New York Philharmonic. If she could do those things, then she could shoot an arrow.

"There you go," JP said. "Now line up the pin, and when you're ready, pull the trigger."

Angie's arm gave way as she reached for the trigger, and the hot-pink arrow sailed about three feet over the target cube and ricocheted across the sand.

"Let's try again," JP said.

The second arrow sailed over the target. The third arrow hit the sand four feet in front of them. The muscles in Angie's forearm burned. The sun was in her eyes, and she was sweating through her white T-shirt. She thought about her Aboriginal ancestors prowling the dry, hot, bloodred terrain of the Australian outback. Surely they had archery skills that had atavistically been passed on to Angie?

The fourth arrow went wide left.

"You're taking your eyes off the target," JP said.

"No, I'm not!" Angie said.

"You are," JP said. "You need to line up the pin."

"I *am* lining up the pin!" she said. "Why am I even doing

this? You said this would take my mind off things, but it's making me feel like shit because I can't do it." She glared at him. "Was that the idea? To make me feel like a loser?"

"I thought it would give you something else to think about," he said. "Something else to want."

Angie laughed incredulously. "I don't *need* anything else to want!" she said. "I want my father back! I want Joel to call me and tell me what the hell is going on! And I want to keep our house!" She raised the bow over her head and thought about throwing it, but she suspected it cost a lot of money, and so she carefully brought it back to her side.

JP took the bow from her. He nocked an arrow, drew the bowstring back, and pulled the trigger. The arrow hit the deer in the heart.

"I'll take you home," he said.

"Wait," she said. "Let me try one more time." She had never thought of shooting a bow and arrow for any reason, but she hated to back away from a physical challenge. In the Board Room kitchen, she was the only one Deacon trusted to take on the fire. Tiny and Julio urged her to try out for one of the competitive cooking shows like *Iron Chef.* She would win, they said. She would dominate. But, unlike her father, Angie had no desire to cook in front of cameras.

JP went to collect the arrows while Angie stretched out her wrist. She felt embarrassed by what she'd said.

Angie drew back the bowstring. She lined up the pin.

"Pretend the target is my ass," JP said.

Angie was grateful for the light tone of his voice, but she lost her concentration; she had to relax her stance and start over.

"No input from the peanut gallery, please," she said.

JP made a motion of himself zipping his lip. Angie imagined Deacon up in the sky, in a wild blue heaven, gazing down on her. But then Angie dismissed this thought. She didn't believe in heaven. Or maybe she did, but she realized she wasn't shooting at this target to prove anything to Deacon—or to Joel, or even to JP. She was shooting to prove something to herself.

She pulled the trigger.

It missed the target, but only by a few inches.

"Better!" JP said. He pulled his phone out of his back pocket and checked the time. "I should get you back. I have tourists to save."

"Okay," Angie said. Reluctantly, she handed over the bow.

As JP drove her home, Angie said, "I have to ask. What did my father tell you about me?"

JP pushed his Blues Brothers sunglasses up into his bushy hair and stared out the windshield. "I guess the question is, What didn't he tell me about you?" JP said. "He told me you were smart, and tough, and a crackerjack chef. He told me you could drink every man he knew under the table. And he told me you were the finest surprise of his life."

"Surprise?" Angie said.

"He said..." Here, JP paused and ran a hand over his beard. "First of all, you have to take into account our circumstances. Most of our talks took place driving out to Great Point before the sun rose. We got reflective. It was something about the sun just coming up and the mist lifting, the sound of the waves hitting the sand and the cries of the gulls. If you were going to talk—and Deacon was a talker—you were going to say stuff that mattered."

"Yeah, but what did he mean by 'surprise'?" Angie asked.

"He was telling me about the first time he held you as a baby," JP said. "I guess he'd sort of gone along with the whole adoption thing for Belinda's sake, but he wasn't really a part of the mission of finding you and bringing you home. So Belinda plops you in his arms and says, 'Here's your daughter,' and Deacon said he looked down to see this dark-skinned baby who had nothing whatsoever to do with him."

"Great," Angie said. "You are failing miserably in your attempt to make me feel better, I hope you know."

"Just wait," JP said. "So I guess you grabbed his finger with your little baby hand, and you didn't let go. You had this relentless grip, apparently, and Deacon told me he felt something pass between you and him. Like you were choosing him, or accepting him, and he said to himself, *If you're not letting me go, Buddy, then I'm not letting you go.*"

Angie blinked tears. "He never told me that story," Angie said. "He never talked about when I was a baby."

"He said that every single day after that, it got better. He said when you were five or six, he taught you how to crack an egg. And you loved it so much that you insisted on choosing the egg from the carton, and you would say, 'I do it myself.' "

Angie laughed and wiped her eyes. She could see young Deacon so clearly in that instant: his dark, shaggy hair, the exact green-brown of his eyes, his three-day scruff, his inked-up arms, his smile, with the one tooth that overlapped his front tooth just a little. She could hear his voice: *Okay, Buddy. Do it yourself.*

JP said, "And then, by the time you grew up, he said, the two of you were best friends. He said, 'I would never have guessed that my daughter could be a friend of mine. But, man, there were some days when she was the only person I could handle. She was never too much. She was always just right. My girl Angie has been the finest surprise of my life.' "

Angie blew her nose into the Box shirt again just as JP pulled off the beach, onto the sand road that would take them back to the gatehouse and civilization. She never wanted this ride to end. She could spend all eternity driving around with JP, listening to the things Deacon had said about her.

"He told you a lot," Angie said.

"It was relevant at the time," JP said. "In this particular conversation, my girlfriend was pregnant. And your dad was talking about what it was like to have kids."

"Oh," Angie said.

"Molly miscarried," JP said. "And then, shortly after that, she broke up with me." He laughed a little, in a fairly good-natured way, considering. "She dates my friend Tommy A. now, which is another reason I didn't want him to fix the board of your porch."

"Oh," Angie said. She didn't know what else to say.

"Now I have to ask you something," JP said. "You said before that you wanted Joel to call. Who's Joel?"

Angie looked out her side window as they passed the Wauwinet. She caught a glimpse of herself in the mirror. She had only seen her hair look this frizzed and crazy when she got off the Cyclone on Coney Island. Her cheeks were pink, which either meant she had gotten some sun this morning or she was embarrassed. "Joel Tersigni." God, it felt good to say his name. "He's this man I've been seeing, a married man, who was going to leave his wife for me, he said. But something backfired, or he changed his mind. Anyway, Joel is gone. He bailed out at the exact moment I needed him most."

JP took a long, steady look at Angie. "Well," he said, "Joel is a fool."

She felt herself blushing. "And, listen, that thing I said about the house..."

"I know about the house," JP said.

"You do?"

"Deacon told me," JP said. "When he came up here the last time...he wanted to pack some things up. The clamshell his dad gave him, and your dollhouse. I was going to help him after we went fishing."

"Oh God," Angie said. The clamshell, the dollhouse, that stupid mirror in Hayes's room, the old map of Nantucket, the wooden cutting board with the half-moon burn where they always used to slice Bartlett's Farm tomatoes, the black, speckled enamel lobster pot, the picture frame made from scallop shells that she and Scarlett had hot-glued one rainy afternoon, the deck of naked-lady cards in the side-table drawer under the ugly lamp—Deacon would have wanted all of that. Most of the furniture had originally belonged to the Innsleys, and none of it was special, but there was something about the atmosphere of that house that Deacon would have wanted to bottle up and take with him. The way it smelled of sunblock and wet towels, the sounds it made when it settled at night, the view of the lighthouse as the sun was coming up. "My father didn't really die of a heart attack, did he? He died of heartbreak."

"Probably something like that," JP said.

They drove down the road in silence until JP turned left onto Hoicks Hollow Road, and Angie felt their time together coming to a close. "Thank you for the field trip," she said.

"You don't have to thank me," he said.

"Target practice was probably exactly what I needed," she said.

"I could come pick you up tomorrow morning, and we could try again?"

Angie was alarmed by how quickly her spirits rose at the invitation. She wasn't doing the predictable thing and falling for the very next man who showed her any kindness, was she?

"I'd like that," she said.

JP said, "Great, then, it's a date. I'll come get you at eight thirty?"

Date, Angie thought.

Angie was so distracted that it took her a moment to notice the woman in the straw hat strolling down the side of the road.

"Oh God," she said. "There's my mother."

JP pulled up to Belinda. "Can we give you a lift back to the house?"

"No, I'm fine, I'll walk," Belinda said. She looked upset. If Angie wasn't mistaken, there were tears in her voice.

"Mom, what's wrong?" Angie asked.

"Nothing," Belinda said. "You kids run along. I'll see you at home."

"You're sure?" Angie said.

Belinda nodded and waved them off.

JP pulled into the driveway. "Looks like you have visitors," he said.

"What?" Angie looked up to see a strange black car in the driveway. Her first thought was that they had been discovered by the paparazzi, which might explain why Belinda was upset and meandering along the road like a hobo. But the car didn't seem to be holding a ragtag band of scrappy tabloid photographers. It looked more dignified than that. Maybe it was the president, come to pay his respects? Deacon had cooked for both Bush and Obama. Or was it some elder statesman of the culinary world—Jacques Pépin, perhaps?

The driver of the black car stepped out wearing a black suit. He opened the back door, and Angie watched one long, shapely leg emerge, then another.

She gasped. Scarlett was here.

BELINDA

On Sunday morning, Belinda put on her wide-brimmed straw hat and her Tom Ford sunglasses, and she slipped her feet into Laurel's truly hideous turquoise flip-flops. She set off down the road in search of cell phone service so that she could call Bob.

She opted to wander toward town, even though the view in the other direction was more picturesque. She needed bars on her phone, not views of the rolling, green golf course and the peppermint-stick lighthouse. She trudged down the road, feeling every pebble and shell beneath the thin foam sole of Laurel's pathetic shoes.

Belinda's mind was swarmed with problematic topics, so many that she didn't know where to start.

Number one: the house. Deacon had gotten himself into a hole he couldn't climb out of, and they were going to lose the house. No one had come right out and asked her, but obviously they were all thinking the same thing: Belinda should offer to save the house. Angie loved that house, possibly more than everyone else put together. Belinda should save it and restore herself to her daughter's good graces. But

Belinda had a big, fat issue with paying for Laurel's portion—and never mind that she *would not for any reason* pay Scarlett's portion. But Belinda couldn't leave Angie without a house on Nantucket, so she had to come up with a plan.

Number two: Buck. Belinda had all but forced herself on Buck the day before. Really, what was wrong with her? She had noticed Buck looking at her, and she'd thought, *Why not?* Her self-esteem needed a boost. It was arduous being in the house with Laurel assuming the throne, even though Laurel was the empress of a nation overthrown long ago. But then again, so was Belinda. Laurel had made the strategic move of arriving first. She had assigned Belinda the least desirable bedroom—saving the "good" guest room for someone who wasn't even coming! Then she had said that Belinda was *beneath her consideration.* Well, Belinda wouldn't stay *beneath her consideration* now that she'd been intimate with Laurel's potential boyfriend. Belinda knew she was acting like a vindictive sorority girl, an even worse version than she'd played in her second movie role, Taffy in *Sophomore Slump.* Belinda had almost told Laurel all about it; she had wanted to prove that she wasn't so irrelevant after all. But, thank God, the matter dropped. Buck would get over it. Belinda needed to start setting a better example for…

Number three: Angie. Angie had, apparently, plopped herself in the middle of someone else's marriage. However, instead of breaking up the marriage, Angie had ended up getting broken. This came in addition to losing her father and the house. In some ways, Angie was very strong. She was smart, talented, mentally tough. She kept getting more and more beautiful—her skin was creamy, her eyes were bright, her hair was wild in its bushy ponytail, her body was lean and sculpted. She had full lips and long, graceful fingers and a little sexy rasp to her voice. But Angie wasn't confident the way other girls her age were. She didn't care about clothes or shoes or makeup or how to make a man do what she wanted. She was easy to hurt because she loved with her whole heart. She held nothing back.

Number four: Bob. Buck had said to Belinda yesterday, *I thought you were married.* Yes, Belinda *was* married. To Bob Percil, who was widely held to be the finest Thoroughbred trainer in the country, if not the world. Belinda had met him at the Breeders' Cup the October after she'd separated from Deacon. Bob was a ruggedly handsome, bourbon-drinking, cigar-smoking, Kentucky-born-and-bred good ol' boy who handled horses better than humans. He was gruff and occasionally humorless and intensely focused on his work, immune to most of Belinda's Hollywood charms and intolerant of her theatrics—and for all these reasons, Belinda had fallen in love with him. For years, Deacon Thorpe had served as the epitome of manhood for Belinda, but upon meeting Bob, Belinda realized that Deacon was as needy as a teenage girl.

Belinda had been happy to marry Bob and leave the emotionally fraught nonsense with Deacon behind. She moved to Louisville, Kentucky, and then she got pregnant, something she had thought was physiologically impossible. She took a year off filming, sat tight on the horse farm, and nursed her baby, Mary. Her very own baby! Belinda hired Mrs. Greene, and she got pregnant again. It was only after giving birth to Laura that Belinda realized Bob couldn't control himself around his young, female stable hands.

The first girl Belinda caught him with in the tack room was Carrie. That, when Mary was two and Laura nine months old. Since then, there had been Jules and now Stella. Were Bob and Stella screwing in the master bedroom?

Belinda wondered. She hadn't spoken to Bob once since leaving L.A.

No reception.

Belinda saw a vehicle approaching, a faded forest-green Jeep Wagoneer with woody sides and a row of colorful stickers on its bumper, a car Belinda recognized. It was Mrs. Glass. Was it possible the woman was still alive? Still *driving?* She had been an old lady back when Belinda used to come to Nantucket, years and years ago. The Wagoneer slowed down from ten miles an hour to five, then came to a rolling stop in front of Belinda.

Mrs. Glass cranked down her window. She was wearing cataract sunglasses.

"Excuse me," the woman said. "Who are you?"

Belinda offered Mrs. Glass her most winning smile. "Mrs. Glass? It's me, Belinda Rowe."

"I'm sure I don't know you," Mrs. Glass said.

"I'm Belinda Rowe," Belinda said in a louder, clearer voice.

"You're *trespassing,* is what you are," Mrs. Glass said. "I'm Mrs. Dustin Glass of Twenty-One Hoicks Hollow Road, and my husband, I'll have you know, was president of the association for eighteen years. This road is private. It's for residents only."

"I know your husband," Belinda said. "Dusty. I used to be married to—"

"I certainly don't recognize you," Mrs. Dustin Glass said. "I've lived on this private way since 1945, and before that I summered with my parents on Baxter Road in Sconset."

"I know," Belinda said. "I used to be married to Deacon, Deacon Thorpe, the chef…?" She paused, searching Mrs. Glass's face for signs of recognition, but her expression was immutable, her watery blue eyes defiant. "We live at number thirty-three. American Paradise?"

"American Paradise?" Mrs. Dustin Glass said. "That house belongs to the Innsleys."

Belinda smiled. "It did a long time ago," she said. "Then my husband bought it. I lived here with him in the nineteen nineties. I'm Belinda Rowe."

"I don't care if you're the queen of Sheba," Mrs. Glass said. "You are trespassing on a private way. I intend to get to the bottom of this." She cranked her window back up with purpose.

Belinda watched the Wagoneer until it turned into the driveway for number twenty-one. She couldn't believe Mrs. Glass didn't remember her. Hadn't Belinda signed autographs for her granddaughters once upon a time? Hadn't Deacon baked her and Dusty a triple-berry pie with a lemon-rosemary crust? But she supposed Mrs. Glass was right—Belinda *didn't* belong here. Not anymore. She belonged in Los Angeles, or in Louisville, Kentucky, with her daughters and her unfaithful husband.

She passed the Sankaty Head Beach Club, PRIVATE, and rolled her eyes. She and Deacon had sat on the waiting list for a membership throughout the entirety of their marriage, and by the time they were up for consideration, they had split. Belinda had forgotten about the way Nantucket was one big private, Yankee blue-blooded club where people drove old clunkers—even though they probably had enough money in the bank to buy a Shelby Cobra with a Lamborghini chaser—just to prove some kind of point about their frugality and restraint.

But maybe—maybe the beach club had something as newfangled as a booster. Because suddenly, Belinda had reception! She stopped dead in her tracks and dialed Bob.

"Bob Percil here," he said.

Belinda knew that Bob answered the phone this way

regardless of who was calling, but still, Belinda longed for the day when he would actually check his display and greet her with a "Hey, baby." He didn't even have to be faithful as long as he gave her the tender, sexy attention she deserved as his wife.

"Bob," she said. "It's Belinda."

No response.

"Bob?"

"I'm here."

"I'm on Nantucket," Belinda said.

"Oh yes," Bob said. "I know."

Belinda could hear the horses on the track—hooves on dirt, whinnying, whistles blowing. Bob was busy with his life. Belinda had thought marrying someone who had nothing to do with show business was a good idea—it had worked for Meryl Streep—but what, really, did she and Bob have in common?

"How are the girls?" she asked.

"They finished school Friday," Bob said. "And they've been trail riding with Stella ever since. They were out until dark last night and up at it first thing this morning."

Stella, Belinda thought. She knew she should be happy the girls were outside riding their very expensive horses. Girls who rode became interested in boys and makeup and cigarettes much later than their nonriding counterparts.

"Poor Stella," Belinda said. "That's not in her job description. You'll have to pay her extra."

"Nah," Bob said. "She's happy to do it. She loves the girls."

Great, Belinda thought. What Bob was probably saying was that Stella would someday become the girls' stepmother. She wondered if Mrs. Greene was turning a blind eye. Mrs. Greene didn't like it when Belinda went away—for work or any other reason. She was a firm believer in family meals and bedtime reading. Mrs. Greene was happy to *prepare* the meals—she was a traditional Southern cook, and Belinda had to constantly watch herself around the fried chicken, macaroni salad, collard greens, corn bread, and lemon chess pie—but she wanted both Belinda and Bob to sit down at the table in the formal dining room with the girls, who were to have their hair brushed and their hands washed. And Mrs. Greene wouldn't stay at the house past eight p.m., which meant that either Belinda or Bob was in charge of what Mrs. Greene called "stories and tuck-in," which she deemed vital to the girls' development.

When Belinda was away, she was pretty sure Bob let the girls eat chips and salsa and watch *Dance Moms* on Netflix until they fell asleep.

Belinda saw a dust cloud down the road; another car was approaching. Probably someone else to tell Belinda she didn't belong. She closed her eyes.

"Please give the girls my love," she said. "And tell them I miss them."

Bob cleared his throat. "Stella picked up a phone message off the main line for the stables," Bob said. "The call came in at four o'clock in the morning."

"Oh yeah?" Belinda said. She wasn't sure why Bob was telling her this. Half his owners lived in Dubai, Hong Kong, Macao. The phone at the stables rang all night long.

"The call was from Laurel," Bob said. He cleared his throat again. "Laurel Thorpe. She said there was something she wanted to tell me. Any idea what that might be?"

Belinda nearly dropped the phone on the road. *Hang up!* she thought. She could pretend she lost service. She needed to think!

Laurel had called Bob. She had something she wanted to

tell him. Something about Belinda, obviously. Had she found out what happened with Buck?

"Um...," Belinda said. "We had a discussion last night about the house. It's going into foreclosure. Deacon left me a third interest and a third to Laurel and a third to Scarlett. But the debt needs to be cleared."

"You're not going to do it, are you?" Bob said. "How much money are we talking?"

"A hundred and fifty grand, for my portion," Belinda said.

Bob whistled. "Deacon really got in over his head."

"Yeah." Belinda knew what Bob was thinking: *Deacon may have been a great chef, but he was a terrible business-person.* Whereas Bob was a great horse trainer and an even better businessperson. The stables turned a huge profit every single quarter.

"Let it go, Belinda," Bob said. "I don't want you sinking our money into a pile out there."

Our money. Ignoring advice from her accountant and Leif Larsen, her agent, Belinda had consolidated her finances with Bob's because that was how she had run things with Deacon: what was hers, was his, was theirs. Belinda wasn't naive, of course—she stashed all the money she'd earned in points from *The Delta* into an escrow account that Leif over-saw. Last time she'd checked, it was hovering just above five million. She kept it to the side, just in case.

"I know," Belinda said.

"So, I'm sorry?" Bob said. "Do you think Laurel was calling to ask me for money? Because somehow I don't think so. That wasn't how it sounded."

"Oh really? How did it sound?"

"Like something else," Bob said.

Like Laurel had found out about Belinda and Buck and she had called Bob to tell him.

Wow, Belinda had to hand it to her: that was an effective scare tactic.

"I would just forget about it," Belinda said. She tried to keep her voice modulated. "I'll handle Laurel. I'm sorry she bothered you."

"No bother," Bob said. "I have to admit, Belinda, my curiosity was piqued."

"Stay out of it, please, darling," Belinda said. "Things are tricky enough here as it is."

"Well," Bob said. She heard him exhale smoke. Was he going to let it go? *Oh please please please.* "When are you coming home?"

"Wednesday," she said. "I'll be home on Wednesday." She would, in truth, be home on Tuesday, but if she told him Wednesday and showed up on Tuesday, she would catch *him* at whatever *he* was doing. He was the philanderer here, not Belinda, short of one tiny indiscretion with Buck, which had lasted all of two minutes. Belinda *could not believe* Laurel had called the stables!

"We'll see you on Wednesday," Bob said. "Let me know when you're flying in, and I'll have Tenner pick you up at the airport."

Tenner was the driver; airport pickups and drop-offs were his job, but was it too much to ask to have Bob pick up Belinda, either with or without the girls?

"I love you," Belinda said.

"Okay then," Bob said, and he hung up.

Okay then. Bob wasn't effusive by anyone's standards, but he could normally be counted on for an "I love you, too," or at least a "You too." But not today. Today, Bob Percil was suspicious—or maybe he was just distracted by the gait of Shadow, his prize dappled gray. Belinda hung up the phone and stepped into the grass to get out of the way of the approaching car. As opposed to Mrs. Glass, who drove like a sloth on barbiturates, the driver of this car was moving *way* too fast.

Slow down! Belinda thought. The car was a sleek, black sedan, a car-service car, one step down from a limousine, and Belinda's mind came up question marks. But then she reasoned that someone on Hoicks Hollow Road might be an investment banker or a corporate attorney and would be used to employing this very un-Nantucket-like vehicle.

Belinda didn't much care. She moved Bob up in her worries from number four to number one. Tears sprang to her eyes. It wasn't fair! Belinda did one little thing, and now it was a federal case, whereas Bob had screwed around for years and years—and it was far worse than Belinda even suspected, she was sure. That was always how it worked, wasn't it? She thought he had been with three girls, which probably meant there were thirty.

Laurel! What had Laurel *done?*

Belinda heard another vehicle approaching behind her. Hoicks Hollow Road was becoming a regular autobahn! When Belinda turned, she saw a silver Jeep headed toward her. The Jeep stopped, and Belinda realized it was Angie and the cute, bearded ranger.

"Can we give you a lift back to the house?" the ranger asked.

Belinda very much wanted a lift back to the house. She was hot, nearly panting—this walk constituted the most exercise she'd gotten in months—but she was too upset for conversation, and she didn't want to explain why.

"No, I'm fine, I'll walk," Belinda said. "You kids go ahead."

The Jeep drove off.

By the time Belinda headed up the driveway of American Paradise, she was clutching her side. She saw the silver Jeep parked—and beyond that, the shiny black sedan.

What? she thought.

And then . . . . she saw them, all standing on the porch in a grotesque tableau. Angie, the ranger, Laurel, Buck, a little girl wearing a silver, sequined party dress, and a tall, striking woman with black hair cropped into one of those pixie cuts that were currently all the rage.

The pixie cut was what threw Belinda. *Who?* Then she figured it out.

Scarlett was here.

She had won the Academy Award for Best Actress in a Leading Role, and she'd been nominated for both Best Actress and Best Supporting Actress, and she'd won an Emmy for Best Actress—but she couldn't pull off the acting job that was required right now.

She turned around to face the road. She supposed she could walk back to the beach club and call a taxi. A taxi would take her to the airport; she would charter a plane to get off this godforsaken rock if she had to. She looked at her feet, in Laurel's flimsy flip-flops; they were one step up from the disposable flip-flops one received after a pedicure. And Belinda was hot and tired. She looked down the road in the other direction. Maybe she could go knock on Mrs. Glass's door. Mrs. Glass might know exactly who Belinda was five minutes from now; old people's memories were sometimes like that.

"Mom!" Angie called out.

Why had Belinda even come? She should have realized that Scarlett would show up. Scarlett had never found a career path, and so she liked to attract attention in other ways—like this dramatic appearance. She couldn't have taken a taxi, like the rest of the world; she had to hire a driver and that pretentious car.

Belinda would have none of it. Scarlett had slept with Deacon while he was still married to Belinda. After Deacon's appearance on *Letterman,* Belinda and Deacon had had an awful blowout, and Deacon had flown down to the Virgin Islands.

Belinda had seen the charge come onto the AmEx, for five nights at Caneel Bay, and then she'd gotten a phone call from Renée Zellweger's personal assistant, who swore she'd seen Deacon on a sailboat in Maho Bay with a blond in a bikini.

Blond, Belinda thought. The assistant was wrong about the blond; Deacon had taken Scarlett. Belinda's suspicions were all but confirmed when Deacon got engaged to Scarlett two months after his divorce from Belinda was final. Belinda loathed Scarlett Oliver. She would never forgive her.

"Mom!" Angie said again. She wheeled her arm. "Come on!"

Nope. She would just stand here in the road until she melted.

"Mom!" Angie said. "We can all see you!"

Belinda waved as if just noticing her daughter and—*Oh, look!*—other people Belinda knew gathered on the porch.

She had no choice. She trudged up the driveway and, with her last vestiges of energy, climbed the porch steps.

"Hello, all," she said.

"Belinda," Laurel said. "Look who's here!"

"Hello, Scarlett," Belinda said.

Scarlett said nothing. Her eyes were red and watery; she was crying. She engulfed Belinda in a stifling, Chanel-scented embrace. Scarlett had been wearing Chanel since she was eighteen years old; all the Southern debutantes wore it, she'd informed Belinda during their first interview.

"I can't believe he's *gone,*" Scarlett said. She was shaking in her ruby-red patent-leather ballet flats. Scarlett was six foot one; she always wore flats. As it was, Belinda's head met Scarlett at her half-an-A-cup bosom. She had been bigger breasted when she worked for them, but after nursing Ellery for three years—three years!—her breasts had nearly vanished. "I. Cannot. Believe. This. Happened. Did you know he quit drinking for me? The drinking and the drugs—he was finished with all of it. Then this!"

"It's okay," Belinda said. "You have to be strong for…" Here, Belinda tried to extract herself from Scarlett's embrace, but it proved to be as difficult as getting gum out of her hair.

"I shouldn't have left," Scarlett said. "But I was just. So. Angry. And what he did was inexcusable."

"Scarlett," Belinda said. "You have to be strong for your daughter." Belinda broke free and smiled down at Ellery.

"Hello, Ellery," Belinda said. "I'm Belinda."

"No," Ellery said. "You're Miss Kit Kat."

"That's right," Belinda said, trying not to sound startled. Belinda had starred in three seasons of the HBO series *Boarding,* about a group of precocious teenagers at an exclusive New England prep school; Belinda had been the slightly dotty headmistress, Miss Kit Kat. Did Scarlett allow Ellery to watch the show at the tender age of nine? "I am Miss Kit Kat."

"Ellery is destroyed," Scarlett whispered.

"Well, yes," Belinda said. She wasn't about to let Scarlett corner the market on grief. "We all are."

LAUREL

Things were happening very quickly, but Laurel, for one, was happy Scarlett had come. On the one hand, it felt *right*—Deacon's entire family was now assembled, which was as it should be—and on the other hand, Laurel had backup in her struggle with Belinda.

When JP left, the rest of them filed inside. Laurel put her hand on Scarlett's arm. "I have you and Ellery in the guest room."

"The *guest* room?" Scarlett said. "This is *my* house. I sleep in the master."

"I'm in the master," Laurel said. "Sorry about that. I got here first." *And I was married to him first,* she thought. *And I bought this house with him.*

"You're the guest here," Scarlett said. "You can move out of the master and take the guest room."

Laurel immediately retracted her sanguine feelings about Scarlett's arrival. Scarlett was making Belinda look like Glinda the Good Witch.

But then, as Scarlett stormed up the stairs, lugging her two monstrous suitcases behind her—*bump bump bump*—Belinda yanked Laurel into the living room.

"You called Bob?" she whispered. "You called my husband at his place of work and said you had something to tell him?"

Laurel closed her eyes. Yes, she had called Bob Percil. After she had gotten home from the hospital with Hayes, she had been *in a state.* Buck had wanted to comfort her, but she sent him away. He was half her problem! Once the house was quiet, Laurel had wandered down to the kitchen, and she'd poured herself a shot of Jameson from the liquor stash. One shot calmed her somewhat, and so she did another. After the third shot, she wondered if anything would make her feel better aside from more Jameson. That was when she'd decided to wander to the end of the driveway...wait for a signal...and call the famed Percil Stables in Louisville, Kentucky.

This message is for Bob, she'd said, her voice slurring despite her intention to sound sober, serious, reliable. *It's Laurel Thorpe. I'm on Nantucket, and there's something I want to tell you about Belinda.*

This morning, when she had woken up, her stomach roiled with regret. What had possessed her? She was the nice wife, the good wife, the altruist. She had made a career of helping people, *saving* people—but after twenty-four hours in Belinda's presence, she had become a vengeful bitch, unrecognizable even to herself.

"I did," Laurel said. "I called him."

"And what, pray tell, did you have to tell him?" Belinda asked.

Belinda thought she could get away with *anything. That's the problem,* Laurel thought. Some people were like that. They thought they couldn't be touched; they thought the rules didn't apply to them.

"What do you *think* I had to tell him?" Laurel asked.

Before Belinda could answer, they both heard the sound of things being thrown out into the hallway above, then Scarlett's voice. "The master bedroom is mine! This is my house!"

Is this happening? Laurel wondered.

Buck appeared in the living room. "Should I tell her that only a third of the house is hers?"

"Now is not the time," Belinda said.

"Right," Laurel said.

At that moment, Angie came flying down the stairs. She grabbed Laurel's arm. "Talk to you?"

Laurel followed Angie to the kitchen.

"Hayes got *mugged?*" Angie said.

"Yes," Laurel said, sighing. "He said he was in a taxi heading to town, and he and the driver had a disagreement about which way to go, so Hayes got out of the cab by the state forest. And then he got beat up and robbed."

Angie's eyebrows shot up. "Taxi?" she said. "He probably called the six-sided nut hut who brought us here. The guy was dressed like a pirate. Hayes asked him for his card."

"Hayes didn't tell the police anything," Laurel said. "He just wants to let it go."

"I asked what would make him feel better, and he said he wanted me to make Dad's chowder tonight."

"That'll be delicious. Thank you, sweetie," Laurel said. Tears sprang to her eyes, even though the last thing on her mind was what they would eat for dinner. But Deacon had made shellfish chowder at least once during each of those long-ago Nantucket summers.

"And I'll make an arugula salad with warm goat cheese, and a tri-berry crumble using those strawberries JP dropped off," Angie said. "And I'll get freshly baked baguettes from the Sconset Market. They come out of the oven at four o'clock." Angie grabbed a notepad and started making a list.

Ellery skipped into the kitchen. She studied the hash marks on the door frame and trailed her finger down, looking for her name.

"Do you want me to measure you, sweetheart?" Laurel asked. "I bet you've grown a lot since last summer."

"No," Ellery said. "I want Miss Kit Kat to measure me."

"Miss Kit Kat will measure you later," Scarlett said as she stormed into the kitchen. Belinda and Buck had now vanished, a fact that irked Laurel like an itch she couldn't reach. Maybe they were upstairs in Buck's room, consummating their sudden love affair. To Laurel, Scarlett said, "Listen, I'm sorry, but you have to understand, I am Deacon's wife, and the master bedroom is *my* bedroom, *our* bedroom. I didn't even sleep in the guest room when I came here as the nanny. Back then, I stayed in the room Buck is in."

Laurel had first met Scarlett on one of the Sunday nights when Deacon brought Hayes back to the apartment. *I thought the two of you should meet,* Deacon said. *Since Scarlett will be the primary caretaker while I'm working and Belinda's away.*

Laurel had been nonplussed; Hayes was then fourteen and could basically care for himself. But she had shaken Scarlett's hand and noted how beautiful she was. She could remember thinking, *I hope Deacon behaves himself.*

She had been shocked when, a few months later, Scarlett appeared at Laurel's office in the Bronx, crying. Scarlett thought she was pregnant, and she was afraid to tell Belinda.

Deacon told me you were a social worker, Scarlett said. *And he said you had Hayes at a really young age.*

Nineteen, Laurel said. She had given Scarlett literature about some of her options: adoption agencies, clinics where she could terminate the pregnancy. But then, a few days later, Scarlett called to say it had been a false alarm.

Laurel had never asked her who the father of the baby might have been.

Now, Scarlett dissolved into tears. "He left me with *nothing!*"

Laurel was tempted to say that that was how Deacon left people—with nothing. But then she remembered the birthday card he'd sent: *Forever love.* He had loved her, he had loved Belinda, he had loved Scarlett.

"How do you feel?" Laurel asked. "You look exhausted."

"I haven't slept in six weeks," Scarlett said. "How could I? I left Deacon, and I took Ellery away from him. I *wanted* him to suffer! I *wanted* him to be miserable without us! I had no idea he was going to die!"

"Of course you didn't," Laurel said softly. She cut a quick glance at Angie, who was scribbling down a list of ingredients. "None of us did."

Buck wandered into the kitchen wearing his board shorts. "I'm going to the beach," he announced. "Would anyone like to come with me?"

"Why don't you ask Belinda?" Laurel said.

"I don't *want* to ask Belinda," Buck said.

"Belinda doesn't know how to swim, anyway," Scarlett whispered. "All those years I came here with Deacon, Belinda, and the kids, she never went in the water."

Angie stood up to her full height, but she still wasn't quite as tall as Scarlett. "Watch how you talk about my mother," she said.

"Really?" Scarlett said. "You're taking *Belinda's* side? That's something new."

"There aren't sides anymore, Scarlett," Angie said. "Deacon is dead. The competition for who he loved best is over. We all lost."

"I was so angry with him, I wished him dead," Scarlett

said. "But I thought that the way people think it. I didn't mean it." Scarlett broke down in tears, collapsing on one of the bar stools.

Buck looked hopelessly to Laurel, while Angie shrugged, grabbed the keys to the Jeep, and left the kitchen, saying, "I'll be back. Dinner will be ready at seven."

Laurel reached out to touch Scarlett's arm. "Would you like to go for a walk? Or for a bike ride? We can go swimming at the pond. It's so pretty there."

"Pretty?" Scarlett said. "How can you care about pretty, or expect *me* to care? My husband is dead!" She screamed this last sentence at the top of her lungs, and Laurel bristled. She understood the bedroom issue—sort of—but she wouldn't allow Scarlett to throw a tantrum. Scarlett had a child in the house, and she was setting a terrible example. Laurel wasn't going to indulge Scarlett's sense of entitlement. Deacon *had* been Scarlett's husband, but he had also been Belinda's husband, and long, long ago he had been Laurel's husband. And he had left behind three children, not one.

Laurel said, "Well, I'm going to bike to the pond." She marched out the back door.

Like the rest of the house, the shed was exactly as Laurel remembered it. It held two bikes that Deacon had bought from the classifieds in the *Inquirer and Mirror*—the royal-blue one had been Deacon's, the silver one with the wicker basket, Laurel's. In addition to the two bikes, the shed held a riding mower, some rakes, a snow shovel, half a bag of potting soil, and a hose and sprinkler. Laurel wondered if hooking up the sprinkler would be fun for Ellery, but then she decided that she was finished thinking about other people. Her whole life involved thinking about other people—solving their problems, making their downtrodden lives slightly more bearable—but now, today, she was going to think about herself. She was going to go for a nice, long bike ride in the sun. She would swim in the pond. She would come home, take an outdoor shower, put on a pretty dress, and enjoy Deacon's chowder.

Make the best of things, she thought. Enjoy Nantucket while she still could.

Laurel took a few deep breaths of the cool air of the shed. It smelled comfortingly of gasoline and cut grass. Then she pulled her bike outside and adjusted the seat. It was like seeing an old friend. She wheeled the bike to the front of the house.

"Laurel!"

Laurel turned around. Scarlett was following her with Deacon's bike.

"I want to come," Scarlett said.

Well, now Laurel wasn't sure she wanted company, especially not the Southern diva variety. But Laurel was too nice a person to tell Scarlett no.

"Okay," Laurel said. She hopped on her bike and bumbled down the driveway; the wind and the motion were instantly exhilarating. "Let's go."

They pedaled out to the end of Hoicks Hollow Road, then took a right onto Polpis. The bike path was a mixture of sun and shade. At first, Laurel rode ahead, but eventually Scarlett caught up and they rode side by side. Scarlett had hitched up the skirt of her dress so that it didn't get caught in the spokes.

"I'm sorry I lost my temper," Scarlett said.

"It's fine," Laurel said. "Everyone's emotions are running high."

"Belinda makes me uncomfortable," Scarlett said. "She always has."

"You were her nanny," Laurel said. "She trusted you with Angie for years, and then when you ended up with Deacon, I'm sure she felt betrayed."

"I didn't start dating Deacon until after they were divorced," Scarlett said. "But Belinda has never believed that. When they had that big fight after Deacon went on *Letterman*? Deacon got arrested for drunk and disorderly, and *then* he flew down to the Virgin Islands for a week. Belinda was waiting for him when he got back and, I guess, knew he'd been with a woman, and she thought it was me. But it *wasn't* me; it was someone else. And then, about six months later, I bumped into Deacon at a club downtown. It was very late, I was with a group of my photography-school friends, and Deacon was too drunk to stand, but he took my number and called the next day. Belinda never believed that story; she thought we were fooling around the entire time they were married."

"Remember when you came to my office right after you started working for them?" Laurel asked.

Scarlett's gaze followed a butterfly flitting around the rugosa roses.

"Scarlett? Do you remember that? You thought you were pregnant. I've always wondered... if you *had* been pregnant, would the baby have been Deacon's?"

"No!" Scarlett said. "I see you don't believe me, either."

"I could never understand why you came to me," Laurel said. "You said you were afraid to tell Belinda, and I thought that meant..."

"I was afraid to tell Belinda because I *worshipped* Belinda. I mean, she was a *movie star.* So beautiful, so famous, so talented..."

Laurel couldn't help but chime in. "So dishonest," she said. "So completely unscrupulous."

"I didn't see any of that until later," Scarlett said. "At first, she was larger than life, and of all the girls she interviewed, she gave me the job. I didn't have any college, no early-education classes, I didn't know CPR, I wasn't qualified at all, but she chose me anyway. She chose *me.* She said she had a gut feeling that I was supposed to be part of their lives."

"Well," Laurel said, "you certainly ended up that way."

"I couldn't tell her I'd accidentally gotten pregnant," Scarlett said. "She would have been so disappointed in me. So that's why I came to you."

"Who was the guy?" Laurel asked. "You can tell me."

"It was my old boyfriend from home, Bo Tanner," Scarlett said. "He was engaged to my best friend, Anne Carter. If I had ended up being pregnant, I think he would have broken up with her and married me. My life would have been totally different."

Laurel turned right onto Quidnet Road. Scarlett pedaled faster to catch up. When she was back alongside Laurel, Laurel took a deep breath. There was no point in being anything but honest now. Deacon was dead.

"So...the woman Deacon took to the Virgin Islands? It was me."

Scarlett gasped. "It was *not!*"

"It was," Laurel said. She didn't like Scarlett's tone, conveying as it did that it couldn't have been Laurel because Laurel was the discarded first wife and therefore undesirable. "I realize I'm not as glamorous as Belinda or as young and sweet and pretty as you—believe me, I've spent way too many hours bemoaning that. But you don't have to sound so surprised."

"It's not that," Scarlett said quickly. "It's that you're so... good."

Laurel shrugged. The obsidian marble had escaped; Laurel imagined it rolling ahead of them. "I didn't have any qualms about Belinda," she said. "She stole Deacon right out from under me. But it wasn't like I'd been lying in wait all those years to seek revenge. When Deacon left me for Belinda, a part of me understood. I mean, here was this kid, abandoned by his parents, shipped up to his aunt in a strange town, a total outcast at school, who ends up finding his calling, becoming a chef, and then... *then*... he meets someone as famous as Belinda Rowe, and she falls for him. I saw how that would have been impossible for Deacon to resist. He thought she could help his career, and she did. He got the job with Raindance, and then the new show. He traveled all over the country; he cooked for the president and the prime minister. All of that was good for Deacon." Laurel shook her head, letting her hair fly out behind her. She couldn't believe how freeing it was to finally tell someone this story. "When Deacon got arrested that time after going on *Letterman*? He called me. I went downtown and bailed him out."

Laurel had seen all the bad press about the "teaspoon of crack cocaine" comment he'd made when Letterman asked him what was in his clams casino dip; she had read the statement issued by the Partnership for a Drug-Free America and had seen angry rantings against Deacon online, saying he was an emissary of Satan, glorifying drug use. Laurel acknowledged it was a poor choice of words, but, even as a social worker, she wasn't offended. *An emissary of Satan?* Laurel couldn't believe it when Deacon called saying that

Belinda had eviscerated him and told him he was devaluing her "brand"—all because of some quip he'd made on late-night TV. Laurel assured Deacon that Belinda would be back; she was, as ever, simply being dramatic.

Later that night, Laurel received a second phone call from Deacon. He was at the police station near Washington Square Park. He had been arrested at Mischief Night, the restaurant owned by Quentin York. Deacon had thought it was a good idea to get really drunk and then show up at Mischief Night, bust in through the back door of the kitchen, and start teaching York's staff how to cook. York had not been amused. He asked Deacon to leave, Deacon threw a punch, and York called the police.

Deacon said, *Buck is on his honeymoon. I didn't have anyone else to call.*

Laurel retrieved Deacon from the police station, paid his fines, signed his paperwork, and got him back to his apartment, where she made him a pot of coffee and gave him aspirin. Neither of them slept that night. They talked and cried and talked some more, and at some point, they concocted the plan to get away together, to someplace neither of them had ever been. They wanted to go somewhere warm, somewhere tropical, somewhere low-key—and they decided on St. John.

"Deacon needed a friend," Laurel said to Scarlett. "And I knew him best. Deacon was a very fragile man underneath it all."

"I can't believe it was you," Scarlett said. "I asked him more than once, and he would never tell me who he took."

This didn't surprise Laurel. Deacon was good at keeping secrets.

She turned onto the road that led to the pond. There was a wide, crescent-shaped beach and a place to lock up the bikes. Laurel turned to make sure Scarlett was right behind her.

"I'm going to swim," Laurel said.

"Me too," Scarlett said.

"Are you wearing a bathing suit?" Laurel asked.

"No," Scarlett said. "I'll swim in my dress. I don't care. I'm just so hot. And I'm so frazzled that I left my daughter in the care of a woman I don't trust."

"Ellery will be fine with Belinda," Laurel said. "Belinda has two little girls the same age."

"Who are being raised by a housekeeper," Scarlett said.

Laurel headed out onto the golden sand, past beached kayaks and dories. On the far side of the pond, the lighthouse winked. There were kids building sand castles while their mothers read novels and unwrapped thick ham sandwiches from wax paper. People here were enjoying summertime just the way Laurel used to.

Laurel stripped down to her bikini and waded in. Scarlett was right alongside her, leaving her ruby-red slippers in the sand. Laurel had to admit, she was impressed. She would have thought Scarlett too prissy to swim in her dress.

They swam out together, matching stroke for stroke, which was a nice change from landlubber Belinda. Scarlett's dress swirled around her in the water like blood. She came up with droplets of water caught in her long lashes.

"Why did you cut your hair?" Laurel asked.

Scarlett shrugged. "I did it as soon as I heard he was dead. He loved my hair, and what was the point of keeping it if he wasn't around to appreciate it?"

Laurel didn't know what to say. Scarlett Oliver's very long, very dark tresses were her trademark. Laurel couldn't believe she had butchered them. All she was left with now were her lashes, her cheekbones, her lips. Hayes had once made a comment about Scarlett being born in a male-fantasy factory. Laurel said, "You left for Savannah after . . . ?"

"After Deacon went out, got drunk, and forgot Ellery at school," Scarlett said. "Forgot his own daughter. He went to a strip club and persuaded one of the dancers there to let him drive her car up to Nantucket."

"He told you about that?" Laurel said.

"Yes," Scarlett said. "I knew there was no way he'd stayed at McCoy's. Sarah, the bartender, knew what time Ellery got out of school because of all the other Tuesdays that Deacon went there to drink. She, at least, would have sent him on his way. When I pointed this out to Deacon and told him I was going to check out his story with Sarah, he broke down and confessed."

"He told me nothing happened with the stripper," Laurel said.

"Nothing happened except he was going to drive her up to Nantucket," Scarlett said. "How could I not feel betrayed by that? And who knows if he was telling the truth? The whole time I was in Savannah, I kept waiting for him to call and say he'd gotten the girl pregnant. It was a betrayal, Laurel."

Laurel knew the feeling only too well.

She had been in the apartment on West 119th Street, hanging out with Hayes after school. They had been looking at the globe. Hayes had been only seven years old, but even then he'd been fascinated by faraway countries: Malaysia, New Zealand, the Sudan. Deacon had walked into the apartment midafternoon, as usual. He went to Solo in the mornings to supervise prep, then came home and napped or watched TV and made love to Laurel before returning to the restaurant at five. On this day, Deacon had stood in the doorway watching Laurel and Hayes for a while. Normally when he did this, he wore an expression of love and wonder, as if he could not believe his great good fortune. Laurel felt this way all the time. She marveled at how they had changed from awkward freshmen sitting at the lunch table at Dobbs Ferry High School, into a small, perfect family. Laurel had been wondering how to broach the topic of having another baby. She feared Deacon would balk at the idea. He had taped three seasons of his show, *Day to Night to Day with Deacon,* and because of this, the world was starting to notice him. He had been asked to guest-chef in Chicago and L.A. He had been courted to join an all-star lineup at the food and wine festival in Aspen, although the invitation hadn't included Laurel or Hayes. There was now the money for another baby, but maybe not the time.

On this day, Deacon's expression was sad. As he walked across the hardwood floors toward them, he started to cry. Laurel looked up at him in panic. Had something happened? Had he lost his job? Had someone *died?*

"What's wrong?" she said.

Deacon hugged Hayes. "Can you go in your room and watch some TV, buddy? I have to talk to your mom."

Hayes had squared his small shoulders; he was Laurel's sentinel, her guard. But he wasn't brave enough to disobey his father, and so he skulked to his room in the back of the apartment.

"What's wrong?" Laurel said again. "What happened?"

"Laurel," Deacon said. He sat next to her on the floor and took both her hands.

Laurel had known something bad was coming, but she had not predicted the nature of this *bad.*

I've met someone else, I've fallen in love, I didn't mean for it to happen, it just did. It's Belinda Rowe. I met her briefly in Los Angeles, and then a couple of weeks later, she came to New York to film and she tracked me down. I've been seeing her for four months. Now she's headed back to

L.A., and she wants me to go with her. I've thought long and hard about it, and I'm going to do it. I'm leaving, Laurel. I'm going to L.A. with Belinda Rowe. I want a divorce.

Laurel had studied her husband. He was wearing a black T-shirt, jeans, a pair of black Chuck Taylors. His dark hair fell into his eyes; he had a three-day scruff, which looked sexy on him, but then Laurel realized that he'd started maintaining the scruff about three months earlier. He also wore a heavy silver watch with a dark-blue, pearlescent face, a TAG Heuer, which Deacon said he had bought for himself, a splurge. Laurel had been puzzled and a little miffed at this spontaneous purchase. They had two mortgages—the apartment and the Nantucket house—and Hayes's private-school tuition to pay for. Their lifestyle didn't include spending three or four thousand dollars on a watch, but Laurel had eventually rationalized the watch as Deacon rewarding himself. He hadn't had any nice things growing up.

Belinda Rowe? Laurel said. She was utterly perplexed. *The movie star?*

Deacon's eyes lit up before he could help himself, and for this—then, and still now, almost thirty years later—Laurel hated him.

Yes, he said. *She wants me, Laurel.*

I want you, Laurel said. *You're my husband. You're my...* She couldn't even come up with a word. She had been with Deacon since she was fifteen years old. She had never even held hands with anyone else. He was her beginning and—she'd thought—her end. He was her everything... *My whole world,* she said. Then she realized how puny and small that made her sound. She didn't have a fraction of the sophistication of Belinda Rowe.

Deacon hugged her tightly, and Laurel let him as tears—the realest, saddest tears she had ever cried in her life—wet the front of his T-shirt. She faced the cruel reality that one person's want was more valuable than another person's want.

Laurel and Scarlett had swum out to the center of the pond, almost without Laurel's noticing. She rarely allowed herself to go back to that day in her mind. She thought, with renewed vigor, that she didn't have one iota of guilt about going to St. John with Deacon.

Laurel reached for Scarlett's hand and, although they were treading water, they embraced.

"I'm sorry," Laurel whispered. She telescoped up, up, up, like a camera taking an increasingly wide angle, until she pictured herself as Deacon in the sky, gazing down at the lighthouse, the golf course, the beach, with its crescent of golden sand, and Sesachacha Pond, in which swam two of his wives—his first and his last—comforting each other about the pain he had caused them.

Intermezzo: *Deacon and Belinda, Part II*

He can't stand the sight of her. She is imperious, selfish, and a control freak, even when she's half a world away. She is petty. She resents how close Deacon is to Angie, and so whenever she's home in New York, she takes Angie on exclusive mother-daughter outings—to the Village to buy jeans, to the theater to see *Rent,* to MoMA for a Van Gogh exhibit. Deacon suggests the three of them do something as a family, but Belinda will have none of it. She says, "The two of you will ignore me."

When Angie is eleven, Scarlett is twenty-four, and she tells Deacon and Belinda that she's quitting in order to pursue a career in photography. She's had a camera in her hand nonstop for the past few years, taking pictures of Angie to send to Belinda when she's on location. And now, she wants to turn the hobby into something more serious.

Belinda sets up an interview for her with Annie Leibovitz, and Annie gives Scarlett an internship.

"Good for Scarlett," Deacon says.

Belinda says, "She only took the job as our nanny so that I would help her when the time came."

"She was with us for six years," Deacon says. "She paid her dues and then some."

"She owes me," Belinda says, and Deacon sighs. Belinda keeps score in every relationship; it turns his stomach.

Angie is fourteen, a freshman at Chapin. She has a friend who lives on Ninety-Fourth and Fifth named Pierpont. Angie spends way too much time with Pierpont, who is a fast, privileged, egregiously snooty girl. Is there anything Deacon can do to get Angie away from Pierpont? When he is in New York, he brings her to work at the restaurant. She's a natural, always has been. She wants to be a chef just like him, she says.

One Friday night, Pierpont gets drunk on grain alcohol and loses her virginity to some douche bag named Chas, a senior at Collegiate. Pierpont shows up at the Waldorf Towers at two in the morning, crying. Deacon is home with Angie; Belinda is in L.A.

Deacon sits up with the girls all night. He makes omelets and lots of toast and listens to Pierpont weep—and then vomit. In the morning, Deacon calls Belinda and says there have to be some changes. Belinda has to put her career on hold; she needs to come home and parent. She wanted a baby so badly—but since Angie has been in their care, she has come second to Belinda's career.

Belinda is outraged. She can't come back to New York! She has just started filming the series *Boarding* for HBO, and she has a contract for three seasons. She is also playing opposite Philip Seymour Hoffman and James Gandolfini in a film called *Cryin' to the Devil,* which is being shot in Burbank. Moving to New York isn't realistic this year and probably not next year either.

"In a few years," Deacon says, "Angie will be gone. Come home while she's still a kid."

"Why don't you quit *your* job?" Belinda says. "I make a hundred times what you make."

Later that year, Deacon develops his recipe for the clams casino dip. He has never imagined that one recipe could make a difference in his career, but he is wrong about that. *Gourmet* magazine chooses it as the recipe of the year, and Deacon's career goes stratospheric. The *Wall Street Journal* runs a profile on him: working-class kid rising up from Stuy Town to the CIA to Solo to heading up the power franchise of Raindance. Then Deacon is asked to appear on *David Letterman.* When Buck calls to tell him this, they sit in stunned silence, and then they both laugh, as if they have pulled off some great caper. He is going on *Letterman*!

Deacon crows about this to everyone he knows except Belinda. Belinda has been on *Letterman* five times, *The Tonight Show* six times, and *Oprah* three times; she has hosted *Saturday Night Live.* Going on national TV isn't exciting to her; it's work.

When he does casually mention that he's going to appear on the show, she says, "Good for you. Back on late-night TV."

This feels different from *Day to Night to Day with Deacon,* though he can't quite explain why. Filming the show felt amateur and decidedly small-time, like a college kid's film project. This is *Letterman*!

The night before the show, Deacon can't sleep. He has persistent worries that he is somehow going to screw up. He is a profligate swearer—it has been said he makes Gordon Ramsay look like the Charmin baby—so he tries to self-hypnotize: *I will not say the word f***.* He worries he will forget how to make the recipe, even though the script will be posted on the teleprompter. He worries, most of all, that he will be boring. He can't quite wrap his mind around how many people will be watching—anywhere between 7 and 10 million, if you believe Nielsen—and who might be included in that group. Mrs. Glass from Nantucket might see him; Gary Decca, an offensive lineman from the Dobbs Ferry football team, might see him; his mother might see him. His *father* might see him! Deacon lies awake imagining his father in some shotgun shack in New Orleans or in a motel room in Reno, watching Deacon on *Letterman* and filling first with regret, then with amazement at the superstar Deacon has become.

The female producer at the studio—Nell is her name; she can't be more than twenty-five—is nonchalant and businesslike. Of course, this is her job; she does it every day, the way that Deacon reduces sauces. She smiles and brings Deacon to the green room, where there is coffee and a fruit-and-cheese platter and a TV hanging from the ceiling that is playing the show as it's being taped.

"Relax," Nell says.

Relax? he thinks. He had thought there might be a bar back here, or beer in the mini fridge, but there isn't, so he takes out his flask of Jameson and throws some back to calm himself.

When he is back in the green room after the filming is done, he takes another hit off the flask in relief. He did it! Somehow, he went out there and faced the cameras and was funny and articulate and poised. He and David had a witty repartee going (*"Repartee": stupid word,* he thinks), and David loved the recipe, or he appeared to.

Nell comes back to show him out.

"Did I do okay?" Deacon asks.

She gives him a tight smile, which seems to suffice as an answer. He decides to watch the show by himself—no Angie, no Buck. Belinda is in L.A. Deacon sits in his dark bedroom with a hefty glass of Jameson. He's afraid there's something wrong that might be imperceptible to him, sort of like the way he can't smell himself.

But the segment goes fine, he thinks. He looks scruffy and unpolished, but that has always been his trademark. He sounds confident. He makes Dave throw his head back and laugh, displaying that famous gap-toothed smile.

When the show cuts to commercials, his phone rings. It's Belinda. "What the hell is wrong with you?" she asks.

* * *

What follows defies the imagination. Deacon is all over the news. The clip of Dave tasting the dip on a garlic-herb-butter baguette, saying, "I literally cannot stop eating this. What's *in* it?" and Deacon saying, "A teaspoon of crack cocaine," is run again and again and again. Deacon is vilified in a statement from the anti-drug people and from the right-wing politician Avery Eubanks. There is a seething editorial in the *New York Times* that compares Deacon to D.C. mayor Marion Barry. And a man whom Deacon considers a friend, fellow Manhattan chef Quentin York, goes on record saying that Deacon has "single-handedly ruined the reputation of everyone in the food and beverage industry."

Deacon spends hours on the phone with Buck, trying to put the best possible spin on the situation.

Just tell them it was a joke! Deacon says.

But something more serious is required, something that addresses the insensitivity of the statement in today's day and age. Seventy blocks north of where Deacon lives, drugs are a plague of biblical proportions.

Buck uses the old adage that no publicity is bad publicity, and it's true that reservations at Raindance nearly quadruple in all three outposts, but that hardly matters to Deacon. Luther Davey calls to tell Deacon he is being put on leave until the brouhaha calms down. Deacon says, " 'Brouhaha' is a stupid word, Luther. And you don't have to put me on leave. I put myself on leave. I quit."

Deacon's day job isn't the only thing going down the drain. Belinda is *livid* with him. She says, "You weren't thinking about your brand when you made that comment."

Deacon says, "I don't have a brand."

"Okay then," Belinda says. "You weren't thinking of *my* brand."

This *infuriates* Deacon. All Belinda cares about is how things reflect upon her.

She says, "There are crack babies dying every hour at St. Vincent's."

Deacon laughs derisively. Everything Belinda knows about crack babies she learned from a six-show guest-star appearance on *High Street* back in the nineties.

"I've had it with you," Deacon says.

"What does that mean?" Belinda says.

"What do you *think* it means?" Deacon asks. He and Angie are supposed to fly to L.A. the next day for Angie's spring break, but Deacon doesn't want to go. He sends Angie out by herself—and there, at the airport, the second after he watches Angie's plane take off, he starts drinking, and he doesn't stop until he's kicking in the back door of Quentin York's restaurant and humiliating Quentin in front of his line cooks, an escapade that gets him arrested and—because Buck has just left for his honeymoon in Ireland—calling the only friend he has left in the world.

Laurel.

She answers on the first ring. *I'll be right there,* she says.

At five in the morning, after Deacon has been released, they go back to his apartment together. He thinks she might try to lecture him or give him a pep talk, but she does neither of these things. She lets him put his head in her lap, and she strokes his hair.

He says, *I just want to get away from my life.*

So get away, she says. *I'll go with you.*

They book flights to the Caribbean. Five nights in an oceanfront suite at Caneel Bay, in St. John. The suite has two bedrooms. They agree that one room will be for Deacon, one for Laurel.

Are you going to tell Belinda you're going? Laurel asks.

Definitely not. Angie will be gone until a week from Sunday, and the idea of stealing away to a Caribbean paradise with Laurel has taken up residence in his mind. Laurel is going to be the one to save him...again.

He remembers a night their senior year. Laurel is pregnant—she went to prom in a maternity dress and was still the most beautiful girl in the room by far—and she is helping Deacon write his final essay for English. He needs at least a C to pass the class and graduate, and they both know he can't get a C on his own. The book is Mary Shelley's *Frankenstein.* They stay up all night drinking Mountain Dew and eating Doritos while Laurel tells Deacon what to write and Deacon writes it. She says, "I'm trying to turn my words into your words." At four o'clock in the morning, they fall asleep together on the sofa fully dressed, Deacon's hand resting on Laurel's pregnant belly.

Deacon gets a C-plus.

Deacon and Laurel walk hand-in-hand through the town of Cruz Bay. They stop for rum drinks, they buy a mango, Deacon picks a hibiscus blossom and tucks it behind Laurel's ear. She is lightly tanned, she wears no makeup, it doesn't take her two hours to get ready, she is happy to hike the Reef Bay Trail to see the petroglyphs, which is something Deacon desperately wants to do. He wants to see something that has lasted thousands of years, something that has endured.

They make love. It's the same; it's different.

They swim at night under the stars, then climb into bed with sandy feet. When Deacon has a nightmare, Laurel wakes up with him. She scratches his back until he falls back to sleep.

"I love you, Laurel," he says.

"I know," she says.

ANGIE

She knocked on the door of Hayes's room. Scarlett and Ellery had arrived; Angie needed to give her brother fair warning.

There was a muffled groan from within that Angie assumed was an invitation to enter. She opened the door.

"Hayes!" she said. "What happened?" Hayes was lying flat on his back in bed. Half his face was covered in bandages, and the part that wasn't covered was black-and-blue. The colors were so dark and vivid, they looked like paint. Angie took a few steps closer. Hayes's lip had been sewn up, and his cheekbone was swollen. "What the fuck happened?"

"Got beat up," Hayes said, barely moving his lips. There was a tray of juice and toast, untouched, on the chair next to his bed—and on the windowsill, half a glass of water and a prescription bottle. She checked the label: *Percocet.*

"When?" she said. "And by whom?"

Hayes shrugged. "Last night."

Angie sat on the bed and studied her brother. He looked exactly like Deacon, but now like a Deacon who had been through the meat grinder.

"Did you call that taxi driver?" she asked. "The guy redefines 'lunatic fringe.' Is that who did this?"

"No!" Hayes said. The vehemence in his voice startled Angie. She thought, *Definitely the taxi driver.* But Hayes seemed keen for her to believe otherwise. Why protect the pirate? Had Hayes made sexual advances? Was Hayes gay? Angie considered this for a moment. Hayes had the ways of a dandy at times—he favored bow ties and bright shirts and fancy shoes. He used to be very particular about how he looked. That had all fallen to the wayside this week, but, of course, their father had died. In the past, Hayes had always had girlfriends, the most excellent of whom was Whitney Jo. Hayes and Whit went out forever, but she eventually left him because he wouldn't commit. Wouldn't commit because...? No, Hayes wasn't gay. He was protecting Pirate for some other reason.

"Were you robbed?" Angie asked.

Hayes nodded.

"What did they take?"

"Everything," he said.

"So... money, license, credit cards?"

Hayes nodded.

"I can't believe this," Angie said. "Have we not been through *enough?*" She gazed up at the ceiling, where she spied a gray watermark that sort of resembled an octopus. That would be the next thing: the roof would cave in. Hayes looked physically the way Angie felt emotionally. Joel Tersigni had mugged her; he had stolen her heart, her good faith, her confidence.

"Angie," Hayes said. She could tell he was in pain. "It's okay. I brought it on myself."

"Brought it on yourself *how?*" Angie asked. "Nobody deserves to be robbed and beaten, Hayes."

Hayes closed his eyes, and Angie felt sorry for yelling. Something was going on with him, but he didn't want to tell her what it was. Could she blame him? She didn't exactly feel like explaining how she had started an affair with a married man and had ended up a crash test dummy.

She eyed the prescription bottle. "Do you need a painkiller?"

He held up a hand. "I'm good."

"You sure?"

He nodded.

"What can I do?" she asked. "Anything to make you feel better?"

He rolled his head so that he was looking at her with his uncovered eye, which was shot through with red veins. He looked like Halloween on a bad acid trip. "You can make Dad's chowder," he said.

Angie had to admit: it was a relief to get out of the house, light a cigarette, and climb behind the wheel of Deacon's old pickup, a 1964 Chevy C10, which smelled like cigarettes and Big Red cinnamon gum.

Angie tried not to think about sitting in the passenger seat of Joel's Lexus. She tried not to think of his hands resting on the top of the steering wheel, or of the way he played "Colder Weather" every time he took her home. She backed out of the driveway and took off down the road.

She had gone through the drill with Deacon each summer—Sandole's for seafood and Bartlett's Farm for produce in the morning, and Sconset Market in the afternoon, their arrival timed for the exact moment when Sally, the baker, was pulling the first batch of baguettes from the oven. Last year, Deacon had discovered a new wine-and-cheese shop on Old South Wharf called Table No. 1, where he'd found both the Pagemaster, which were little buttons of goat-cheese goodness bathed in chocolate whiskey, and Pipe Dreams bouche, the ultimate goat cheese, so they added that stop to the lineup.

Sandole's would be first, at 167 Hummock Pond Road. Angie hit the gas. She was going to enjoy this, she told herself, even though her heart had split in half like a shell or a nut, one half of it containing grief and the other half rejection. She thought about what JP had told her about his girlfriend—pregnant, then not pregnant, then leaving JP for his best friend, Tommy A. Things changed that way, often without warning. Six weeks earlier, Angie had been working as the fire chief at the restaurant, basically a content and busy person, although with a question mark about Joel's greater role in her life and a persistent desire to find new ways to impress her father. Now, her life was something she needed to survive.

Angie turned on the truck's radio. The Clash was singing "Train in Vain." Angie was so overcome, she had to pull over. What were the chances that the first song she would hear while driving Deacon's pickup would be that song?

The lines had been tattooed on Deacon's biceps.

Did you stand by me? No, not at all.

Angie started to cry. Deacon had adored the Clash—this song was his favorite, "Lost in the Supermarket" his runner-up. And because Deacon had loved them, Angie had loved them. That was how it worked, Deacon once told her. First you love the music that your parents love—and then, later in life, you love the songs your kids love.

Angie closed her eyes and listened until the song was over. *It must be a sign,* she thought. Deacon was here with her. She looked over at the passenger seat—empty, but maybe not.

She wiped at her eyes, checked the road behind her, and took off. She hoped she wasn't the only person in the world ever to believe the car radio was trying to tell her something.

A bell jingled when Angie walked into the simple shack that was the fish market. A sign above the refrigerated cases read, *Anyone who asks if the fish is fresh has to go to the end of the line.* Angie gazed longingly at the thick, meaty swordfish steaks, the ruby-red tuna, the jumbo shrimp, the delicate cod fillets, the pile of cherrystone clams, the black, glossy shells of the mussels. There were cartons of smoked bluefish pâté and homemade guacamole; there were marinades, sauces, rubs, and compound butters.

The girl behind the counter smiled at Angie, revealing deep dimples. Angie remembered this girl, but she hoped the girl didn't recognize her. Angie had always loved coming back to Nantucket summer after summer and being remembered by people just like this. *Hey, you're back! How was your winter?* But, under the circumstances, such a conversation would be nearly unbearable. If Bill Sandole himself had come out to the front, there would have been hugs and tears and *I'm sorry for your loss*—all of which Angie wanted to avoid.

She was relieved when the girl simply asked, "What can I get you?"

"Everything," Angie said.

She walked out of the fish market with three dozen cherrystones, two dozen mussels, a pound of pearly-white sea scallops that the dimpled girl assured her had been sitting on the ocean floor the day before, and four bottles of clam juice. And a container of smoked bluefish pâté, because Angie couldn't resist.

Next, it was off to the market at Bartlett's Ocean View Farm, set amidst patchwork fields of corn and a particularly winsome field of flowers—gladiolas, cosmos, snapdragons, sunflowers, lilies. Angie slowed the truck down and feasted her eyes on the colors. She wanted to lie down in between the rows and never get up.

Inside the market, Angie was greeted by tall, galvanized buckets filled with cut flowers and an old tractor bed that had been repurposed as a table and now supported tall stacks of homemade pies—peach, blueberry, fruit of the forest. There was a refrigerator case filled with fresh salads, fried chicken, and one-serving portions of chocolate mousse and tiramisu. Angie wandered over to the produce. There were heads of romaine, chicory, radicchio, endive, and trays of herbs—basil, dill, mint—that filled the air with their fragrance. Angie chose dill, chives, parsley, and three heads of tender butter lettuce. She selected a bulb of garlic and two sweet onions.

At the Board Room, night after night, Deacon and Angie had dutifully marched out to the dining room to greet VIPs and to congratulate the people who were celebrating—college graduations, fiftieth birthdays, twenty-fifth anniversaries, retirements, engagements, a new baby, a first grandchild, a promotion, a book deal, a bon voyage. But one night, Joel had come into the kitchen and said to Angie, "There's a woman in the dining room with her daughter. The daughter said this is her mother's first meal out since her husband of fifty-two years died. She was wondering if you and Deacon would come out and say hello."

Deacon and Angie had met the woman, a well-heeled, silver-haired woman of about eighty who wore a raspberry-colored dress and a pearl brooch. Both Deacon and Angie had embraced her. A few tears were shed by the woman,

Rosemary, and her daughter, Kendall, who explained that Martin, the husband and father, had died three months earlier of congestive heart failure, and for his wife, dark times had followed. But then, about a week earlier, Rosemary had woken up and decided that she was ready to eat a fine meal. She had wanted dinner at the Board Room. It marked her return to the world of the living, she said.

Deacon had kissed Rosemary's cheek and said, "Welcome back."

Angie remembered thinking how good it had felt to know she was cooking not only for people in their high moments but also for people who were trying to climb out of their low moments.

That was what Angie would do tonight.

Wikipedia: Belinda Rowe, Actress

Early Life: Belinda Marjorie Rowe was born on September 30, 1964, in Iowa City, Iowa, to parents Calvin and Anne Rowe. Calvin Rowe was a pilot for the United States Post Office, and Anne was a homemaker. Belinda attended Iowa City High School, where she was a cheerleader and held a part-time job at Pearson's Drug Store on Linn Street.

In 1982, Miss Rowe moved from Iowa City to Los Angeles, California. Within a week of moving, Miss Rowe did a screen test for the director Donald Disraeli and was cast as the lead, Maggie Burns, in the movie *Brilliant Disguise,* about a midwestern girl who runs away from home and hitchhikes to Los Angeles to be in the movies.

"It was basically my life story," Miss Rowe told reporters at the movie's premiere. "I left Iowa, and I never looked back. I became someone else entirely."

Miss Rowe has also starred in *Charming Joe, Sophomore Slump, Daniella and Charlie, Excuses Excuses, Drought, Dire Emergency, Between the Pipes*—for which she was nominated for Best Supporting Actress—*Gypsy Red, Macbeth, Cleopatra on the Nile*—for which she was nominated for Best Actress—*The Prairie Sisters, The Delta*—for which she won the Oscar for Best Actress—*Cryin' to the Devil, Drama Queen, Drama Queen 2,* and *Bet On It.* She guest starred in two seasons of *High Street* and appeared as Miss Kit Kat in the HBO series *Boarding,* for which she won the Emmy for Best Actress. Miss Rowe has been the spokesperson for Lululemon since 2006.

Personal Life: Belinda Rowe married Chef Deacon Thorpe in a private ceremony in Beverly Hills in 1990. The couple adopted a daughter, Angela Thorpe, in Australia in 1990. Miss Rowe divorced Thorpe in 2005 and wed Kentucky horse trainer Robert Percil in 2006. The couple has two daughters, Mary and Laura, and they reside in Louisville, Kentucky.

BELINDA

Belinda was hiding in the dim, ascetic cell of Clara's room when she heard the little girl calling for her. Ellery. Or rather, Ellery was calling out for "Miss Kit Kat." Belinda considered ignoring her, knowing full well that Ellery wouldn't dare enter Clara's room; Deacon had taught all his children to be afraid of it. But Ellery's voice was clear and sweet, and Belinda missed her own girls—desperately, viscerally—and so Belinda emerged.

"Miss Kit Kat, at your service," she said, clapping her hands in the crisp, efficient way that Belinda had created for her character, a gesture that meant: *Let's go, girls! Grin and bear it!*

The smile on the child's face was priceless. Sometimes, Belinda thought, it felt good to just be nice.

"If you'd like," Belinda said, "I can do your hair like Ashland's on the show."

"In a double diagonal fishtail braid?" Ellery asked.

"Yes indeed," Belinda said. "Chop, chop! Let's find a brush."

It took the better part of an hour, but in the end, Ellery's braid didn't look half-bad.

"I'm finished," Belinda announced. Back in the last season of filming *Boarding,* Belinda had asked the show's stylist, Turquoise, to show her how to do the braids, thinking she would try the style out on Mary and Laura. But the girls were no-nonsense, like their father. They wore their jodhpurs to bed, practically, and were so eager to be on horseback that they couldn't be bothered with anything more complicated than a ponytail. It was almost as if Belinda had brought the wrong children home from the hospital. She had suffered through tomboy Angie and now had to endure the horsiness of Mary and Laura. Was it any wonder that Belinda was so enjoying this time with girly-girl Ellery in her silver, sparkly dress? Belinda knew that neither of her daughters would be caught dead in such a dress. Belinda cut the hanger straps from her black Stella McCartney and used them to tie up the loose ends of Ellery's braids. She pulled out her silver hand mirror and showed Ellery the final result.

Ellery clapped her hands in delight. She grabbed Belinda around the middle. "Oh, thank you, Miss Kit Kat!"

"You're quite welcome," Belinda said. It was slightly disconcerting the way Ellery seemed to believe that Belinda *was* Miss Kit Kat. The girl was nine years old. Could she handle learning that the woman she thought was Miss Kit Kat was actually the actress Belinda Rowe, who had been married to her father before her mother was? Could she handle knowing that Scarlett had once worked for Belinda as Angie's nanny?

No, probably not. Belinda smiled at Ellery in the mirror. Such a pretty little girl, more Scarlett than Deacon, but that might change as she got older. Belinda envied the child for being able to sustain an attitude of make-believe. If she wanted Belinda to be Miss Kit Kat, then Belinda would be Miss Kit Kat. It would be less painful or complicated than being Belinda Rowe, especially under the present circumstances.

"Shall we go look at the dollhouse in Angie's room?" Belinda asked. She had always thought of the dollhouse as Angie's, but for all she knew, it had passed to Ellery in recent years.

"I'm not allowed," Ellery said. "I'm not old enough."

"Oh, but you are this summer," Belinda said, and she led Ellery by the hand down the hall.

Belinda looked on as Ellery took all the fancy, delicate furniture out of the house to rearrange it. There was the canopy bed, its mattress the size of a playing card, and the porcelain claw-foot tub and the Venetian double-globed lamp. Belinda could remember sitting in this exact spot watching

Angie play with the house—although back then, Belinda always had a script in her lap and looked up only when Angie implored her. *Mama, look at this!* However, Belinda had paid Nailor, the old caretaker, to keep the house in climate-controlled storage for the winter. And look—the house had lasted!

Belinda recalled what Angie said about Belinda not caring about her own parents, which struck Belinda as painfully true. Belinda's mother had been an old-school Iowa housewife who made casseroles and put up jars of stewed tomatoes and pickled dilly beans. She always made way too much food, as if confronted with the daily surprise that she didn't have six children. Belinda's birth had had complications that precluded her mother from ever having another baby. Belinda's father was a quiet, balding man who blended in with the woodwork—except for Saturdays in the fall, when he put on his Iowa Hawkeyes sweatshirt and hat and cheered like a fiend at Kinnick Stadium.

Belinda's parents had always seemed small to her—not in stature, but in dreams and ambition. They didn't *want* anything; they didn't *aspire*. It had been their great misfortune to have given birth to a daughter who had wanted to escape them from the moment she could walk. They were strict with her. She wasn't allowed to date or, God forbid, bring boys home—which had forced Belinda to sneak out. When she was a sophomore, Craig Eskind used to wait for her at the end of Moyers Lane in his pickup. He had taught Belinda how to drive in the green F-100 with the finicky stick shift. Small girl, big truck—Belinda laughed now to think of what she must have looked like behind the wheel. And her parents had never found out!

Belinda left Iowa City right after graduating from high school—ostensibly on a summer road trip with her best friends, Judie and Joanne Teffeteller, from which she never returned. Now that Belinda was a parent, she could see how unspeakably *cruel* that had been. Angie was right: Belinda had never loved either of her parents the way that Angie loved Deacon.

"Look!" Ellery said, pointing to the commode. It had a pull chain.

Belinda gave her a smile. "That's funny, isn't it?" She rarely had time for introspection like this, which was a good thing, she realized, as it nearly always led her to dwell on the ways she had failed the most important people in her life.

Craig Eskind. It had been ten million years since Belinda had even thought of him. She had once cut his lip with her braces.

Belinda clapped her hands. "Downstairs you go, now," she said in her Miss Kit Kat accent, which was half-British, half–Locust Valley lockjaw. "Find Mummy, show her your new 'do, and ask her to make you some lunch."

"Aren't you coming downstairs?" Ellery said. She grabbed Belinda by the hand. "Please?"

Belinda smiled. This was a new feeling: someone in this house wanted to be with her. "Well, if you insist," she said.

Mummy was nowhere to be found. The only person in the kitchen was Buck, who was sitting at the counter, holding Deacon's clamshell in one hand, running his finger over the swirl of blue inside.

"Where is everybody?" Belinda asked.

Buck barely looked up. "Laurel and Scarlett went for a bike ride," he said.

"They did?" Belinda said. This was unsettling news.

Most likely, they were talking about Belinda. At that very instant, Laurel would be describing Belinda's indiscretions, and Scarlett would be on the phone to the *New York Post.* Belinda broke out in an unpleasant sweat. "How long will they be gone?"

Buck shrugged.

It was nearly noon. Belinda was starving, and she was sure Ellery was hungry, too. Who would make Ellery's lunch? Was *Belinda* supposed to do it? She noted the reversal here, and she didn't like it one bit: Scarlett had left Ellery in Belinda's care, as though Belinda were Ellery's nanny!

Belinda regarded Buck. He was lost in thought, preoccupied with the shell. They had barged in on his private moment of mourning. Belinda remembered that shell from the day Deacon had moved out of his apartment on West 119th Street and into the St. Regis with Belinda. He had come with one duffel bag and the canvas satchel that held his knives. When he'd unzipped the duffel, the clamshell had been on top. Belinda had picked it up.

What's this? she'd said.

He had all but snatched it away from her. *It's mine,* he'd said. *It goes where I go.*

Belinda wanted to apologize to Buck, but she didn't know how to do so with Ellery right there. She lightly touched his back. "You finally look relaxed," she said. He jumped. Belinda retracted her hand immediately. She had lost her right to touch Buck even casually, even in friendship. "Would you like some lunch?"

"I'm all set," Buck said.

Belinda opened the fridge. At home, Mrs. Greene had food prepared and waiting. Before Mrs. Greene came into her life, there had been Deacon to cook for her and, when she was on location, catering crews. Before Deacon, Belinda had sustained herself on Tab and saltines. She had been terrified of gaining an ounce.

There was a whole roast chicken that had been basically picked clean, some green grapes, a box of Velveeta—oh, how Deacon had *loved* Velveeta, the greatest of all melting cheeses!—milk, butter, beer and wine. When Belinda checked the cabinets, she found bread, cereal, peanut butter, jelly.

Belinda spun around to Ellery. In her best Miss Kit Kat voice, she said, "You can have cereal, my darling pet, or you may have that timeless classic, peanut butter and jam."

"I eat toast with brown sugar," Ellery said.

Toast with brown sugar. Belinda could only picture the look of Mrs. Greene's extreme disapproval. Belinda wasn't much of a cook, but she knew Scarlett was even less of one. The woman didn't eat at all, and now she was passing her poor habits along to her daughter. But Belinda wasn't going to argue. She could do toast. She checked the cabinets again for brown sugar.

"We have white sugar," Belinda said. "That will have to do."

Just then, Angie burst into the kitchen, loaded down with bags. She eyed Belinda holding the bread knife.

"Let me do that," Angie said.

"I can handle it," Belinda said. "It's toast."

"Mother," Angie said. If Belinda wasn't mistaken, there was a playful note in Angie's voice. Belinda looked up. Angie was giving her a warning look, but with amusement in her eyes. "If you want to help, you can put these groceries away."

Belinda stared at the bags on the counter.

Angie said, "If it's cold, put it in the fridge. Otherwise, set it next to the stove."

Buck stood up. "I'm finally going to go for that swim," he said. "Anyone else want to go?"

"I'll meet you in a little while," Angie said.

"I'll go!" Ellery said.

"You have to eat lunch first, El," Angie said.

"And then you must wait an hour for your food to digest," Belinda said.

"No," Angie said. "That's an old wives' tale."

"Is it?" Belinda said. She was certain Mrs. Greene would disagree.

At that instant, Buck's phone rang. "Hello?" he said. "Hello, hello, *hello?*" He jabbed his finger at the display. "Gosh darn it! I'm going down to the end of the driveway. When I get back, we can go for a swim."

"Deal," Angie said.

Buck disappeared. Belinda pulled mussels and clams from the bag. "These go in the fridge?"

"Yes," Angie said. "It's *fish.*"

"Right," Belinda said. She didn't like her daughter talking to her as if she were the class dunce, but at least Angie was talking to her. She set the mussels, clams, and scallops in the fridge. She would quit while she was ahead.

"I'm going upstairs for a while," she said. "To Clara's room."

"But that room is haunted," Ellery said.

"It's okay," Belinda said. "I'm not afraid of ghosts."

Upstairs, Belinda heard a groan coming from Hayes's bedroom. For a second she thought she had caught him in a private moment—*Oh no, awful!*—but then Belinda realized he was groaning in pain. She tapped on the door. "Hayes?"

Another groan, but one that contained a "come in."

Belinda cracked open the door. The sight of Hayes's face—beaten to a bloody pulp, half of it swathed in bandages, half of it discolored and misshapen—startled her even more than being faced with the apparition of Clara Beck.

"Hayes!" she said. "What happened?"

"Beat up," he said. "Can you please... reach my... pills?"

"Of course," Belinda said. She had played a nurse once in a terrible film called *Dire Emergency* that had nearly won her a Razzie and ended her career. Belinda picked up the bottle of pills—Percocet—and shook out a few in her hand.

"How many?" she said.

"Three," Hayes said.

Belinda checked the prescription bottle: *1 to 2 pills every six hours.* And Hayes wanted three. Belinda sighed. When Hayes was little, she had tried to mother him, but he had been obstinate. He had spent an entire year alternately throwing tantrums, complete with flailing limbs, and ignoring every word Belinda said, nose turned defiantly in the air. Belinda had cried about it to Deacon. She had wanted the three of them—and then, after they adopted Angie, the four of them—to be a family. But Hayes would have none of it. How many nights had he cried for his mother? Deacon had told Belinda not to worry, to just concentrate on being his friend, but Belinda didn't know how to make friends with a little boy, and so she had resorted to giving in and bribery.

Hayes had once thrown a keg party in her and Deacon's apartment in the Waldorf Towers, when Belinda was filming *Macbeth* and Deacon, Angie, and Scarlett had come to Scotland to visit. Hayes had allowed the girls at the party full access to Belinda's closet, which was how he'd gotten caught. Belinda came home to find her Valentino and YSL gowns in silk puddles on the floor, beer spilled all over her dressing table, and vomit in her Birkin bag.

Then there was the time Hayes had come to L.A. during his spring break from Vanderbilt and gotten into an accident in the parking lot of Paradise Cove while driving Deacon's Porsche.

Those incidents were long ago. Hayes was an adult now, a successful man with an enviable career and a loft in Soho that he rarely stayed in because he was so busy globe-trotting. But Belinda feared there were vestiges of the little boy who knew how to swindle her.

Should she give him three pills, or only two, as the bottle instructed? She recalled what Naomi Watts had told her. *He was on something. Like, really on something.*

But Hayes was in legitimate pain, not out partying. Belinda gave him three pills. He reached for his water glass, which was empty.

"Here, let me freshen that," Belinda said. She was being nice again, and it felt wonderful! She took the glass to the bathroom and brought it back full. Hayes slugged back the pills, then collapsed on the bed with the effort.

"Thank you."

"Do you need anything else?"

He shook his head.

Belinda said, "If you think of something, just shout. I'll be in my room, resting."

She turned to leave, and as she did, she saw something on the floor by the other bed, where Hayes's duffel gaped open. She bent down to pick it up. It was a glassine packet filled with a brown powder, like so much dust. *Cocaine?* she thought. It was too dark to be cocaine. It was . . . ? She peered inside the duffel bag and saw the shiny, sinister point of a hypodermic needle. He was shooting something. It was . . .

heroin? She blinked and froze in her tracks. *Heroin.* When she checked on Hayes, his eyes were closed.

She slid the packet into her pocket, then stepped out of his room, closing the door behind her. Her insides went liquid with panic. Hayes had looked awful even before he met with foul play; she had indeed thought that. She had chalked it up to Deacon's death...but he was using.

Okay, okay, Belinda thought. *What do I do?*

There wasn't time to consider this question, however, because Belinda heard footsteps coming up the stairs, and a second later, Laurel appeared, wearing only her flowered bikini, her hair hanging in damp strands down her back.

When she saw Belinda, she gasped and put a hand to her chest. "Jeez!"

"Sorry!" Belinda said.

"I wasn't expecting anyone to be up here," she said. "I just have to grab a towel for the outdoor shower..." A sudden change came over Laurel's face as she registered that Belinda was standing outside the door to Hayes's room. "What are you doing?"

"I..." Belinda said. The glassine packet was burning a hole in her pocket. Should she show it to Laurel? Hayes was an adult, but he was also a child, Deacon and Laurel's child, Belinda's stepchild. She should show Laurel the packet and let Laurel deal with it. If Deacon had been there, Belinda would have handed it right over, no question.

"Were you in Hayes's *room?*" Laurel asked, with the voice of a dragon lady. "Did you...? Belinda Rowe, please tell me you did not just step out of *my son's room!*"

Belinda's mouth dropped open. Laurel was...what? Accusing Belinda of...? Being inappropriate with Hayes? Of *sleeping* with him? Belinda felt a wave of nausea.

Eeeeeeeee! She had made *such* a mess of things. She fled past Laurel, down the stairs.

She needed to get rid of the heroin. At the bottom of the stairs, she ducked into the powder room, a sad little bathroom with a sour smell. She would flush the packet. But then common sense warned her that the plumbing in the house was ancient and temperamental, and flushing something like this might cause a backup or a flood or a housewide contamination. She could just pitch the packet into the trash, but someone might see it. In the end, Belinda stuck the packet of heroin in the mason jar filled with beach glass that was sitting on the back of the toilet. At the top of the jar was the dark-brown, frosted, nearly round bottom of a beer bottle with a curled lip. The piece was so frosted, it looked as if it were encrusted with sand. Belinda had found this piece on the beach herself years ago, back when Angie was ten or eleven and collecting beach glass had been her life's purpose. Both Deacon and Angie had been impressed by this piece—*Not bad for a prairie girl!*—and Angie had awarded it the top spot in the jar.

Now Belinda would use it to conceal Hayes's heroin.

Belinda flushed the toilet, let the water run in the sink for a second, then emerged from the powder room in time to hear Scarlett shepherding Ellery upstairs for a nap. She heard Ellery say, "Do you like my hair, Mommy? Miss Kit Kat braided it."

Scarlett said, "You know, honey, she's not really Miss Kit Kat."

"Yes, she is," Ellery said.

"No," Scarlett said. "She just played her on TV. A long time ago. That's what an actress does for a living. She pretends to be other people."

Pretends to be other people? Belinda thought. Up until

five seconds ago, Belinda had been a person pretending to be civil to her ex-husband's other wives—but no longer. That comment, delivered in the most condescending of tones, was the final straw. Belinda had *had* it.

She entered the kitchen to find Angie at the sink, scrubbing clams.

"I need to get out of the house for a while," Belinda said. "Do you think I could use your father's truck?"

Angie spun around. She had become so, so beautiful, Belinda thought. Belinda loved the curve of her neck, the length and thickness of those eyelashes. She and Deacon couldn't have made a child this beautiful in a thousand tries. "Is everything okay?"

Belinda smiled, but she was acting. She loathed nothing more than sympathy. *If I want sympathy,* she had once said to Deacon, *I'll look it up in the dictionary between "shit" and "syphilis."* She didn't want Angie feeling sorry for her, but the events of the day had taken their toll.

"There's an errand I'd like to do in town," she said. "May I take your father's truck?"

"Sure," Angie said. "Keys are in it."

"Thank you," Belinda said. "I'll be back."

Belinda climbed into Deacon's antique pickup, a worthy successor to his beloved Willys jeep. Deacon had loved old cars, and what had Belinda bought him? A brand-new Porsche. If she'd been paying attention, she would have gotten him something like this.

Oh, regrets!

Belinda took off down the road.

She was so fed up with Laurel and Scarlett that she had

half a mind to drive to the airport and fly home. But that would be like quitting a movie in the middle of filming. She'd put effort into being a part of this weekend, and she had gotten embroiled in the family drama. She couldn't leave. She had to fix things.

Besides, she had an idea.

She drove into town on Pleasant Street, then took a left up Main. She remembered everything: the yellow house on the corner with the magnificent planters on the porch, the Three Bricks—one for each of the Starbuck sons—and the royal-blue Victorian for the daughter, which was prettier, anyway. The truck bounced over the cobblestones, jarring Belinda's teeth. She passed the Civil War monument and continued on Main until she reached number 141, the George Gardner House, built circa 1835. Everyone who had ever spent time on Nantucket had a favorite house, and this one was Belinda's. She idled on the street out in front, admiring the white-clapboard symmetry of the house, the decorative railings of the roof walk, the Ionic portico, the ornamental balustrade, the four crisp brick chimneys. The house was simple, elegant, and distinctive all at once. The front landscaping was lush, the hydrangeas in glorious lavender bloom, the boxwood meticulously pruned. It was divine! It evoked a gracious age, summer parties with men in straw boaters and women carrying parasols, everyone drinking spiked lemonade and sloe gin fizzes. Belinda caught a glimpse of the glassed-in porch off the back and a slice of the azure swimming pool. The white spire of the Congregational church was visible in the distance. Belinda was completely charmed.

She was going to do it.

She parked the truck in front of the house and walked up the brick path to the front door. She knocked.

"Mom!" a young man's voice called from inside.

"Answer it!" a woman's voice said.

The door swung open. A boy of about sixteen stood before Belinda. He was wearing American-flag swim trunks and a white T-shirt that said BUCKNELL WATER POLO in orange and blue letters. He was eating a nectarine.

"Hi," he said to Belinda. "Are you here for my mom?"

"Well... ?" Belinda said. He was too young to be a fan, or even to recognize her, she supposed. He would recognize Jennifer Lopez. He would know Reese Witherspoon. But not Belinda Rowe. She would bemoan her advanced age later; right now, she was on a mission. "Yes, I suppose I am."

He held the door open. "She's in the kitchen, making sandwiches."

"I would expect nothing less," Belinda said. "And the kitchen is..."

"That way," the boy said, pointing down the hall. He then galloped up the stairs two at a time, leaving Belinda to wander in.

The inside of the house was even more captivating than the exterior. This—this!—was how people were meant to live: with Persian rugs and antiques and Scalamandré fabrics, with clean fireplaces behind gleaming brass andirons and thoughtfully chosen window treatments. Belinda walked slowly, soaking in the impeccable white wainscoting and the chandeliers and the soft Mozart piped in through unseen speakers. She popped her head into the kitchen, where a woman stood at the counter with slices of bread in a row on the butcher block before her. The air smelled vaguely of celery and herbs.

"Chicken salad," Belinda said. "My favorite."

The woman's head snapped up. "Oh!" she cried. She was

pleasant looking—pretty, even—with a mass of light-brown curls secured to the top of her head and large, brown eyes. She blinked about forty times as she looked at Belinda.

"Am I going crazy?" she said. "Or did Belinda Rowe just walk into my kitchen?"

"Yes," Belinda said. So far, so good: the woman hadn't screamed or threatened to call the police. The woman recognized her. "Hello. Your name is...?"

"Marianne," the woman said. "Marianne Pryor. Are you...? Are you lost? Or...did my husband send you as a... prank? Am I on TV?"

"No, no," Belinda said. "I'm so sorry. I didn't mean to startle you. I just sort of wandered in off the street because... well, I wanted to talk to you about your house."

"My house?" Marianne Pryor said.

"Yes," Belinda said. "I'd like to buy it."

One hour and two glasses of chardonnay later, Belinda climbed back into Deacon's truck, her spirits crumpled like yesterday's newspaper.

The house wasn't for sale, not even to Belinda Rowe, not even for $6 million cash. It wasn't that Marianne Pryor wasn't a lovely or accommodating woman—she had been both. She gave Belinda a tour of the entire house and then the guest house and then the pool area, complete with shaded cabana and home gym. Every step Belinda took made her fall more deeply in love.

This is exactly what I want, Belinda thought. It was the polar opposite of Deacon's house. *It has style and taste; it has modern conveniences—a dryer, bathtubs that function, Wi-Fi, a warming drawer in the kitchen, a microwave!*

The last place they toured was the basement, completely finished, with full windows. There were cedar closets and a pine-paneled bunk room for kids; there was a family room with big, comfy couches and a big-screen TV. The walls were decorated with movie posters: *Rocky, Any Given Sunday, Fargo,* and... *Brilliant Disguise.*

Now Belinda was the one doing the blinking. The poster for *Brilliant Disguise* featured Belinda at age seventeen, standing on Route 66 with her thumb out. Belinda stared into her younger face.

"You...?" she said, turning to Marianne.

Marianne shrugged. "I'm a huge fan. *Brilliant Disguise* is my favorite movie of all time."

Victory! Belinda thought. She had been able to see herself in this house—and now she was actually *seeing herself* in this house.

She would pay anything, she decided. She would do anything. She would give the son, or one of the pretty daughters who had been sunbathing by the pool, a cameo in her next movie.

"Please!" Belinda had said close to the end of her second glass of wine. "Sell me this house!"

"I can't," Marianne Pryor said. "My husband's mother grew up in this house, my husband grew up in this house, and my kids are growing up in this house. My husband proposed to me on the widow's walk. We got married in the backyard."

"I'll give you six million dollars," Belinda said.

Marianne had rested her hands on Belinda's shoulders. Marianne had nice skin, lightly tanned, with just a few laugh lines around her eyes. She exuded a certain calm and wisdom and centeredness. Belinda could tell her life had been privileged but she didn't take it for granted. She probably practiced yoga, gave thanks every day, made soup from scratch, took an annual weekend someplace warm with her college roommates, chaperoned school dances, and loved Christmas.

"Belinda," Marianne said. "It's not a house to us. It's a home. And it's not a home, it's a way of life. Our summertime happens here. This house is part of our past, it's our present, it'll be our future. It's who we are. It isn't for sale."

"But you could buy a house on the beach," Belinda said. "You could buy a house on Hulbert Avenue fronting the harbor."

"I can see you're not understanding me," Marianne said. "We don't want to move anywhere else. We couldn't. You might as well have walked in and asked to adopt one of our children." She finished her own wine. "It's nothing personal. If I were going to sell this house, I would most definitely sell it to you."

Belinda had smiled, but she was acting. "I get it," she said. "Thank you for letting me see it." More acting. She should never have knocked. She should never have come inside.

"It was really nice to meet you," Marianne said. "Having you walk into my kitchen is one of the most exciting things that's ever happened to me."

"But I can't change your mind?" Belinda said.

"I'm sorry," Marianne said. *But now she's acting,* Belinda thought.

They said their good-byes, and Marianne waved from the portico as Belinda pulled away.

Back to Hoicks Hollow Road, she thought. And all the joys that awaited there.

BUCK

It was Margaret on the phone.

"Talk to me, Goose," Buck said. It was nearly noon on a Sunday. Margaret should be out puttering in her garden.

"Are you sitting down?" Margaret asked.

"No," Buck said. He eyed the rock painted with the green *33* that marked the end of the driveway. "Is it that bad?"

"I heard from Harv," Margaret said. "That restaurant runs on a hundred-thousand-dollar-a-week budget. Food costs, rent, payroll, the hickory wood, the cleaners, the flowers, the linen service, heat, water, electricity...the list goes on. They spend seventy-five hundred a week on caviar alone. And all of those precious little farms Deacon loved so much? They must have been selling him eggs made from gold bullion."

"But the restaurant charges a fortune," Buck said.

"It doesn't cover costs," Margaret said. "The restaurant operates at a deficit, and don't forget, they closed for a month after Deacon died, but the staff still got paid, and they took a huge loss due to food spoilage."

"So there's no chance of getting any of Deacon's money back?" Buck said. In his heart, he had known this, but he'd thought...well, the prices *were* astronomical. To have a martini at the bar set you back twenty-eight bucks! He had thought maybe there was a refrigerator filled with cash.

"None," Margaret said. "Deacon was the last investor in, so even if the restaurant were turning a profit, he'd be the last of the six to see any money."

"There goes the house," Buck said.

"Have you told them?" Margaret asked.

"I've only told Laurel and Belinda," Buck said. "Scarlett got here just this morning."

"Scarlett *showed?*" Margaret said. She sounded gossipy, as she did when she and Lanie, Buck's intern, discussed the plot twists of *Ray Donovan.*

"She did," Buck said.

"Wow," Margaret said. "So now it's you and the three wives. How are you handling *that?*"

Badly, Buck thought. He needed to make things right with Laurel—but how?

"Just fine, Margaret, thank you."

"Okay," she said, in a tone that indicated she knew things were anything but okay. "Call if you need me."

"Will do," Buck said, then he hung up.

At that moment, he gazed down the road to see two figures bicycling toward him—Laurel and Scarlett. He waited for them to approach. They were both wet. Scarlett's red dress was plastered to her body, but Buck made a concerted effort not to look.

"Hi, Buck!" Scarlett said. Her mood had markedly improved. "We biked to the pond, and I swam in my dress."

"How very Becky Thatcher of you," Buck said. He smiled at Laurel. Her damp hair fell over her tanned shoulders. She seemed to be staring off in the direction of the lighthouse; most likely, she was simply avoiding Buck's eyes. Still angry.

"I was just on the phone with my secretary," Buck said. "I have some business issues I need to discuss with Laurel. So if you'll excuse us, Scarlett...?"

Scarlett's mouth dropped open. "Business issues to discuss with *Laurel?* That makes no sense. I was Deacon's wife. Someone here needs to acknowledge who the widow is. It's me."

"You're the widow, yes, you are," Buck said, hoping that sufficed as acknowledgment. "But right now, I need to talk to Laurel."

"I'm starving," Laurel said. "Can it wait until after I eat something?"

Scarlett hopped off her bike. "'Business' means 'money,'" she said. "So I think I'd like to be in on the conversation."

"We *will* have a conversation, I assure you," Buck said. "But first I need to talk to Laurel."

"Unbelievable!" Scarlett said. She huffed as she pushed the bike up the rocky incline of the driveway.

When she was out of earshot, Buck said to Laurel, "Let me take you out to lunch."

"No."

"Laurel, please."

"You don't seem to understand," Laurel said. "I'm not sharing a man with Belinda. I did that once, and I'll never do it again. You had a chance with me, Buck, but you blew it."

He looked up. There was so much sky here, whereas in Manhattan, one got only slices. "I know I messed up," he said. "I'm not interested in Belinda, and she most certainly isn't interested in me. What happened yesterday"—God, had it been only yesterday? It seemed like three years earlier—"was as random as an asteroid strike. And as insignificant as..." Buck rummaged through his mind, trying to think of something insignificant. "As an ant's shoelaces."

Laurel didn't even smile. "It was significant to me," she said. "I need someone I can trust."

"I'll earn your trust back," Buck said. "I'll spend the rest of my life doing it. But right now, let me take you to lunch. Please?"

Laurel's expression softened. "Okay," she said. "But only because I'm hungry and there's a place I've been wanting to go."

In town, Laurel parked the Jeep in front of a restaurant called Black-Eyed Susan's, with a big plate glass window and window boxes bursting with candy-striped petunias. Buck's stomach rumbled at the alluring smell of frying bacon emanating from within. He had changed from his board shorts back into half of his suit. He ran his free hand over his face. He hadn't seen his razor since leaving New York, so he was now sporting gray whiskers. There was nothing worse; he felt like his grandfather. But who cared? He was with Laurel. He had to make this count.

"This will be more like breakfast," Laurel said. "Is that okay?"

Buck wanted to say he would eat his Gucci loafers as long as he could do it across the table from Laurel, but he didn't want to sound like a stooge.

Buck and Laurel were seated at the two-top in the big plate glass window, where they could watch the day unfolding out on the street. Laurel ordered a latte, the veggie scramble with pesto, the Yucatán chicken sausage, and the Santa Fe hash browns with extra sour cream.

"Sorry," she said. "I'm starving."

Buck felt abstemious by comparison: black coffee and the corned-beef hash with two poached eggs and rye toast.

"Can you throw a ladle of hollandaise on top of that?" he asked the waitress.

"*Now* you're talking," Laurel said, rubbing her hands together. "You are *definitely* giving me a bite of that."

Buck couldn't believe he had just added seven hundred calories to his breakfast solely to impress a woman. But then again, it wasn't just any woman.

Buck relaxed in his chair and inhaled the scent of bacon and coffee. Black-Eyed Susan's was a homey place, a sort of farm-to-table diner where everything was prepared by line cooks on a griddle that ran the length of the bar. There was music playing, a mellow country band. How long had it been since Buck had noticed *music?* He and Deacon had gone to see the Rolling Stones on a reunion tour, but that was before Ellery was born. Buck wished he knew the words to this song; he was so happy to be with Laurel, he felt like singing.

A mother and daughter in matching toile sundresses sat on the bench outside; an older gentleman in bright-yellow Bermuda shorts walked a French bulldog. A young couple—in high school, maybe? college? Buck could no longer gauge anyone's age—stopped right in front of the window and started to kiss as though peace had just been declared after a decades-long war. Buck watched for a second before looking away. He wanted to kiss Laurel like that.

"Do you think people assume we're a couple?" he asked.

"It doesn't matter, because we're not," Laurel said. "I'm here for the hash browns."

"You know, I've tried everything in my power to save the house," Buck said. "If I had the money myself, I would hand it over to you, and you would never have to pay me back, I swear."

"I know, Buck, it's okay." She frowned. "I thought Deacon was doing well financially. He lived like a rock star—that apartment on Hudson Street, the fancy school for Ellery—and I know he's been helping Hayes out."

"He ran through his income. I mean, don't get me wrong—as of last December, he had a million dollars in the bank. But once that was gone, he started to sink. The TV royalties made him money, but after my commission and losing forty percent in taxes... I mean, it's a cooking show; it's not like he was hosting *American Idol.* I found a canceled check for a hundred grand made out to something called Skinny4Life. Ever heard of it?"

"No."

"It sounds like one of Scarlett's schemes," Buck said. "But unless there's something I don't know, it hasn't paid off yet. One of the reasons she came to Nantucket was because she ran out of money—credit cards denied, checks bounced."

"Oh jeez," Laurel said. "What about Scarlett's parents?"

"Brace declared bankruptcy last year," Buck said. "Deacon paid for his lawyer."

"Who else do we know who has money?" Laurel asked. She caught Buck's gaze. "I refuse to ask Belinda."

"She has the money."

"I don't care," Laurel said. She took a sip of her coffee, then wrapped both hands around the mug. "I caught her standing outside Hayes's room."

"Doing what?"

"Looking guilty."

"Even Belinda isn't that warped," Buck said.

"I put nothing past her," Laurel said. "And I'm not taking her money."

"Okay then," Buck said. "Pray for a miracle."

"Have you told Scarlett yet?" Laurel asked.

"No," he said.

"Oh boy," Laurel said. "She won't be happy."

"Put mildly."

Their food arrived. Buck dug into his hollandaise-drenched corned-beef hash. It was Deacon worthy: the kind of bite that made Buck's eyes roll back in his head. He took another greedy bite, then he glanced out the window at the gentleman walking the bulldog. Yellow shorts. Could *he* do yellow shorts?

"I think I need some new clothes," Buck said.

Thirty minutes later, Buck and Laurel wandered into a store called Murray's Toggery, which was an old-fashioned clothier, so preppy it would have made Lisa Birnbach pop a wheelie (Lisa had nearly been a client, once upon a time). The men's section of Murray's was a profusion of madras and bold-colored prints. There were spinning racks of whimsical ties—yellow with pink anchors, navy with lavender dolphins—piles of cable-knit sweaters, and a whole wall stacked with dusty-pink pants. *Home of the Nantucket Red,* a sign said. Whatever that meant.

"I have always loved this store, but I couldn't get Deacon within a hundred yards of it," Laurel said. "He didn't like shirts with collars. Do you mind if I start picking out things for you?"

"Go crazy," Buck said.

In the dressing room, Buck tried on polo shirts—light blue, navy blue, Kelly green, and pink—and khaki shorts in three different shades. He modeled each outfit for Laurel, who was sitting in what he thought of as the judging chair, giving him the thumbs-up or thumbs-down.

"You look fantastic!" she gushed. "You look twenty years younger! You look like a completely different person."

Their salesman, named Wyatt, was extremely enthusiastic about Buck acquiring something called the "on-island look." He brought Buck a pair of madras shorts and a pair of navy shorts embroidered with white whales.

Buck scoffed at the whale shorts, but he agreed to try them on with—*Why the hell not?*—the pink polo shirt. He spoke to Deacon in his mind. *It would serve you right if I wore this getup to spread your ashes.*

Then Buck thought, *Why not?* He would buy the whale shorts and the pink polo.

Buck poked his head out from the dressing-room curtain. "I'm buying this combo," he told Laurel. "I'll wear it tomorrow when I say good-bye to our old friend."

Intermezzo:
Deacon and Scarlett, Part I

The age of the celebrity chef is upon them. Mario Batali and Bobby Flay, Daniel Boulud and Anthony Bourdain, and the biggest gun of them all—Thomas Keller—are household names. No sooner does Deacon quit Raindance, and no sooner do he and Belinda officially separate—both developments land Deacon on the front page of the tabloids—than the Food Network calls to offer Deacon a new half-hour show called *Pitchfork*. The producers want to capitalize on Deacon's bad-boy image while it's still fresh in everyone's minds. The show will spotlight his diabolical recipes—the caramelized foie gras pudding, the striped bass cooked in cigar smoke, the lobster *momo*s with the creamy *sriracha* dipping sauce.

Buck is over the moon. Deacon's shameful behavior has turned out to be his salvation—once again.

Only two weeks after his divorce from Belinda is final, Deacon resumes his old ways. He tapes the show every afternoon, and then he goes out drinking. His haunts include McCoy's, McSorley's, the Cupping Room, Spring Lounge, Mother's Ruin, Fish, the White Horse Tavern, and El Teddy's. Sometimes he meets Buck at Ryan's Daughter because Buck doesn't like to go below Fourteenth Street, and especially not since 9/11.

Having Angie helps keep Deacon in check. He's home by seven or seven thirty to make her dinner and see that she's at least pretending to do her homework. One weekend per month, however, Belinda comes into town, and Angie is required to stay with her. Belinda has given Deacon the apartment in the Waldorf Towers, and now she stays at the Standard, in the Meatpacking District.

The first time Belinda fulfills her maternal duties, Deacon is at loose ends. Angie keeps him honest, but now she's with her mother, and the way Deacon feels about Belinda, a city of nine million people isn't big enough.

He goes on a bona fide bender: Spring Lounge, Gatsby's, White Horse, Jekyll & Hyde, the Ear Inn, the Four-Faced Liar. At the Four-Faced Liar, he bumps into a bachelor party for two gentlemen getting married, one of whom used to be a sommelier at Raindance, a guy named Morgan. Morgan lassoes Deacon into their group, and down they go to Soho, to places that are so exclusive, they don't even have names—private lounges, supper clubs, speakeasies. They are dimly lit and filled with beautiful people. Deacon is underdressed and unprepared, but it doesn't seem to matter. Everyone knows him. Free drinks appear wherever they go—or maybe the drinks aren't free, maybe Morgan's future husband is paying; Becker is the in-house counsel for Merrill Lynch. Deacon is confused, disoriented, drunk, and growing more depressed by the minute. The downtown partying life is empty and hollow; it's filled with poseurs, pretenders, charlatans, and actors like him. He's a chef, but something about cooking in makeup makes him feel like a fake. He longs to be back in a real kitchen, but not at Raindance. Raindance was too corporate. He longs for his days at Solo, back when things were immediate and real. Back when he was with Laurel.

It's nearly three o'clock in the morning. Should he call Laurel? When they got home from St. John, she returned to her life saving souls in the Bronx—and he went back to his.

He hasn't spoken to her since their return, and he's pretty sure she doesn't want to receive a drunken, late-night phone call.

He has lost the bachelor party, which is a blessing and a curse. Morgan, at the very least, would have seen him into a cab. Deacon doesn't know the name of the place where he presently finds himself, so even if he calls Laurel or Buck, he wouldn't know where to tell them to come. He locates a banquette upholstered in what appears to be black mink. There's a glass of ice water on the table. Deacon drinks it gratefully down and thinks he'll probably just sleep here, and when he wakes up, he'll stumble home.

Someone slides into the banquette next to him and puts a hand on his leg. He startles awake. It's a young woman with a shiny curtain of long, dark hair. She smiles at him. He knows the smile somehow.

"Deacon," she says. "Is it you?"

It takes him several seconds to figure out who this is and how he knows her and if this is real or if he is dreaming. The voice is *so familiar,* a voice he knows intimately, he thinks, and yet he can't place it. The Jameson has gobbled up all the brain cells necessary for him to interact appropriately.

He nods. He can say with relative certainty that he is Deacon.

"You don't recognize me, do you?" she says. "It's me, Scarlett!"

Scarlett? Deacon blinks. Last he heard, Scarlett was still pursuing her dream of becoming a photographer. She latched onto the entourage of Pilly Dodge, whom Deacon knows because Pilly once shot Belinda for the cover of *Vogue,* and Belinda came home crowing about what a genius he was—better than Weber and Demarchelier combined.

"What are you doing here?" he asks.

"I live here," she says. "I have a studio apartment on Sullivan Street." Deacon nods and feels relieved that Scarlett didn't move to Brooklyn, like all the other cool and smart people in New York.

"But what are you doing *here* here?" he asks, indicating the club around them.

"Here at Yukio's?" she says. "My friends and I popped in for something to eat. I'm starving. Are you hungry? They have the most amazing edamame with sea salt, and word is that they take more calories to digest than they actually have, so you lose weight eating them. Do you want me to order you some?"

"Yes," Deacon says.

He won't lie; there's no point in it now. He has fantasized about making love to Scarlett Oliver since she first walked in the door to interview for the nanny position. He sometimes thinks back to the time on Nantucket when she invited him into the outdoor shower—she was right on the other side of the door, wet and naked—and castigates himself. He blew his chance! Other times he congratulates himself for his restraint. Despite his hundreds of other sins, he wasn't the guy who seduced the nanny.

But now, things are different. Scarlett is no longer the nanny. She is a woman who can make her own decisions. She decides *not* to take Deacon up on his offer to come home with him, but she does agree to have dinner with him the following night at Le Bernardin.

The dinner at Le Bern is twelve courses with wine pairings and all kinds of luscious treats sent out by Chef Eric Ripert. Scarlett looks absolutely ravishing in a red dress, her hair straight and long, framing her pale face and wicked red lips. She is exquisite.

But she isn't much of an eater, he notices. Nothing like Laurel or Belinda. When Scarlett worked for them, she used to carry around a book that told her how many calories were in a grape (eight) or a chocolate éclair (ten thousand), but even then, she used to indulge in the occasional treat. She loved grits, and she never turned down an ice cream cone. Now, she lets most of her very expensive courses sit untouched until their server whisks them away.

Can Deacon pursue a relationship with someone who doesn't enjoy food? Normally he would say no, but he is so swayed by her beauty that he says yes.

They go on three dates—Le Bernardin, Blue Hill, and Per Se—before she sleeps with him. The sex isn't quite as explosive as he'd hoped—Laurel and Belinda were both unbridled in their lovemaking—but again, he doesn't care. She is so beautiful, it's like making love to a Michelangelo. He loves to watch her walk across the room naked.

"Have you dated anyone seriously?" Deacon asks. "Were you involved with Pilly?"

"For a little while," Scarlett says. "Everyone who works with him sleeps with him eventually, I guess."

But…she still really loves Bo Tanner, she says. Bo is her former boyfriend from the Savannah days. He's an attorney down there, married to Scarlett's best childhood friend, Anne Carter.

"Still Bo?" Deacon says. He logged in a lot of hours listening to Scarlett pine away for Bo the football star, Bo the president of Delta Chi at the University of Georgia. Deacon feels more jealous of Bo Tanner than he does of the ostensible genius Pilly Dodge.

"Sort of, yeah," Scarlett says. "He sends me letters when he gets into the bourbon. Anne Carter has no idea about that."

Deacon can't believe the jealousy that consumes him. He gathers Scarlett up in his arms. He wants her to be his. How can he make her his?

The very next day he heads to Harry Winston and blows $90,000—his entire savings, basically—on a diamond solitaire engagement ring. Ninety grand: the number makes him shake, but he's still not sure the diamond is big enough.

That night, he invites Scarlett to his apartment for dinner. He tells Angie only that there will be a surprise visitor eating with them; he doesn't say who. Deacon makes a cold curried zucchini soup, a roasted red pepper and smoked Gouda quiche, a delicate mâche salad—Scarlett tries to eat vegetarian when she can, she's confided—and he makes the champagne cake with champagne icing and champagne-candied strawberries. He feels a little squinchy about this because it was a cake he created for Belinda, but he convinces himself that if it worked on Belinda, then it will work on Scarlett.

When Scarlett rings the bell and Deacon ushers her in, Angie's face falls. She glares at Deacon. "You're kidding me, right?"

Scarlett doesn't seem to hear this. "Angie!" she says. "I can't believe how big you are! Come here and give me some sugar!"

"You're dating my father?" Angie said. "You're *dating* him?"

Scarlett's arms drop to her sides.

"Angie," Deacon says. "Stop with the theatrics."

"I think it's disgusting," Angie says. She grabs her jacket, purse, phone. "I'm going to Pierpont's."

"No, you're not," Deacon says. "You will stay right here and eat with me and our old friend Scarlett."

Angie opens the door to the hallway and steps out without another word.

Scarlett is suddenly teary. "She hates me."

"It was a bad idea to surprise her," Deacon says. "I should have told her you were coming. I should have explained what all the fuss was about."

"Fuss?" Scarlett says.

Deacon pours two glasses of Billecart-Salmon rosé champagne. He's just going to do it, no point in waiting. Angie is fifteen years old; she will get over whatever imaginary problems she has with this.

Deacon pulls out the velvet box. Scarlett's eyes widen; they are a kaleidoscope of green, blue, gray. He opens the box, revealing the ring. "Will you marry me?" he says.

Now that he is back on TV, he is tabloid fodder. News of Deacon's engagement to his former nanny, Scarlett Oliver, a scant two months after his divorce from Belinda Rowe hits the front of *Us Weekly* and the *National Enquirer*—complete with paparazzi photographs of the ice cube on Scarlett's finger.

Belinda calls in a rage. She says, "Did you take Scarlett to St. John? I can only assume that you did. You were probably banging her the entire time she worked for us!"

Deacon doesn't want to talk about St. John. To deny that

Scarlett was there seems to put him at risk of admitting that he took Laurel.

He says, "It's none of your business, Belinda."

She says, "We were married when you went to St. John, Deacon. It is absolutely my business."

He says, "Scarlett and I are in love, and we're getting married."

Belinda says, "She's too young for you. And too shallow. Mark my words, you'll be miserable."

Deacon hangs up.

Deacon and Scarlett are engaged for nine months, and those months cost Deacon a fortune. Scarlett doesn't want to move into Deacon's apartment in the Waldorf Towers because that's where he lived with Belinda, and her apartment on Sullivan Street is a studio that she *shares.* Deacon enlists the help of a real estate agent who also happens to be a gourmet cook and a fan of his show. Veronika has an inflated sense of Deacon's net worth, however, because it takes her five tries to show him something even remotely in his price range, and that is the spacious, light-filled two-bedroom apartment in a newly renovated doorman building on Hudson Street.

"If you don't like this," Veronika says, "we can cross the bridge and look in Brooklyn."

Deacon takes the apartment, even though it feels like swallowing a crab apple whole.

Next, Scarlett wants to enroll as a photography major at University College. She's learned all she can from Pilly, she says, and from Dexter Candis before him, and from Annie Leibovitz before Dexter. What she needs now is schooling, a foundation in the basics.

Deacon is dying to point out to Scarlett that she has done this whole photography thing *completely backward.* What if he had interned with Marco Pierre White before learning to chop an onion? He wouldn't have become a chef, that's for sure. He also has hesitations about University College, which, ironically, is neither a university nor a college but rather a very expensive "institution of higher learning" whose sole reason for existence seems to be indulging the many, many dilettantes in Manhattan with money to burn on courses that won't get them credits or a degree.

But Scarlett is dead set. She rattles off the names of the "professors"—*ooh*ing and *ahh*ing after each one—though Deacon has never heard of any of them. She insists they're all talented, all masters of the craft, and reluctantly, Deacon gives in, but this time it feels as if he's swallowing a grapefruit whole.

It would be nice if she learned the basics, he thinks. All she has seemed to have learned during her years with Annie, Dexter, and Pilly is how to party. She knows the names of all the bouncers at all the clubs, but after going downtown with her a few times, he gives it up. Deacon can't *stand* the crowd Scarlett hangs out with, and besides, he has to be home to supervise Angie. He is also pursuing a dream of his own: he wants to gather a group of investors and open his own place in midtown called the Board Room, which he envisions as a groundbreaking restaurant, even here in Manhattan, where nearly all ground has been broken.

He's so excited by the concept of his new restaurant that he secretly wonders if getting married is a good idea. Once this restaurant takes off, Deacon will be working around the clock. He fears there might also be something to Belinda's argument that Scarlett is shallow. She works out three hours a day, and she barely eats a thing. Deacon can't feed her; he has tried and failed. She talks about Sue, a new dermatologist she goes to for facials; Mikey, the trainer she's hired at the gym; and a DJ at Club Barcelona named Go-Go; she talks about someday working for *Vogue, Cosmopolitan, Elle,* French *Vogue.* She talks about traveling to Africa, the Philippines, Tokyo. When Hayes lands his job with *Fine Travel,* Scarlett begs him to put in a good word for her with the photo editor. Meanwhile, she's only three weeks into her classes.

Deacon decides he's going to break the engagement, and he has to do it soon, because wedding plans are in the works. The nuptials are to be held in Savannah in July, in the backyard of Scarlett's childhood home. Her uncle, a judge, will do the honors. A week before the invitations are to go out, Scarlett says she needs to talk to him. She has been acting strange and distant. Deacon assumes she feels as he does, and wants to break the engagement.

He says to her, "Scarlett, is there something you want to tell me?"

"Yes," she says. "I'm pregnant."

The Board Room opens to rave reviews when Ellery is six months old. Scarlett has decided to take a year off from University College to nurse the baby and work on getting her figure back.

Everything is going smoothly.

Deacon has a $2,000-a-week coke habit, and he goes through a bottle of Jameson every three to four days. He tells himself it's medicinal: he needs the coke to stay awake and the whiskey to fall asleep. Anyone who thinks he has a "problem" has never opened a restaurant before.

* * *

Ellery is six years old and wears her hair in two braids. She joins the Brownies, and the local troop meets in the basement of the Cowgirl, a bar in the West Village. Deacon takes Ellery every week and sits up at the bar with moms Janelle and Greta Rae and dad Potter. They drink a few beers and mow through bowls of peanuts, dropping the shells on the floor. They talk about their kids and schools and a little bit about their lives. Deacon regales his new friends with the names of the celebrities who have come to eat at the Board Room—Beyoncé, Clint, Kiefer. Potter is a financial columnist for the *Huffington Post;* Janelle does hair and makeup on *CBS This Morning;* Greta Rae is married to an advertising mogul.

Deacon never wants Brownies to end. It's the happiest hour of his week.

And then, one week, Potter doesn't show up, and Janelle and Greta Rae come in red-eyed and weepy.

Haven't you heard? they ask.

What? he says.

Potter was high on crystal meth and jumped in front of the F train, Janelle says. *He's dead.*

Deacon swears he will never drink or smoke or snort again, a vow that lasts until midnight.

LAUREL

She wanted to stay in the outdoor shower for the rest of her natural life. There was something about being naked outside, with the sea breeze and the open sky above and hot water cascading down her back at a luxurious pressure, that put Laurel back in touch with her center. And this would be one of the last times she would get to use it.

Laurel was unhappy about her conversation with Scarlett. Laurel should *never* have told Scarlett about St. John.

Scarlett had wanted to revisit the topic on the way home. "So what you're telling me is that after the big Deacon-Belinda fight, Deacon called you, and then the two of you went to St. John?"

Oh, how Laurel had wanted to retract the whole story, but she couldn't. She nodded.

Scarlett said, "I guess I can see that. Deacon probably wanted someone he was comfortable with."

As though Laurel were an old shoe, a song he knew by heart, a bowl of rice pudding with raisins. It may have started out that way...the plans had fallen into place without either of them thinking about what it meant. Deacon had said something about "owing" Laurel a "really nice" vacation.

Laurel had said, *You don't owe me anything, Deacon.* And Deacon had said, *We'll get a suite at Caneel Bay. You deserve the best.*

The hotel had been glorious, the finest place Laurel had ever stayed. Deacon had booked an oceanfront suite on Honeymoon Beach. They had risen out of bed only to pour more Laurent-Perrier rose and eat ripe mango and crispy conch fritters with curry aioli. They swam in the middle of the night, naked, under a blanket of stars. One night, there had been wild donkeys on the beach, which had scared them both, then sent them into paroxysms of laughter. They took a sailboat over to Jost van Dyke and drank painkillers at the Soggy Dollar. One night they had ventured into the town of

Cruz Bay and drank rum punch and danced to a steel drum band.

You are so sexy, Deacon had said. *You are so much fun.*

Laurel emerged from the outdoor shower wrapped in a towel. It was almost worse to know that a third of the house they were going to lose would have been hers. If Buck hadn't told her, she would have left on Tuesday morning feeling grateful that she had gotten one last chance to stay in the house, but she wouldn't have carried this sense of *loss.* However briefly it had been that she had believed the house to be hers—a minute? Two?—the mere concept had struck her like a sky filled with dazzling, colorful fireworks. The house on Nantucket, the place where she had spent the happiest days of her fifty-three years, would have been hers to share with Hayes and Angie and, someday, their children.

Laurel sighed. Deacon had always been terrible with money. He had grown up without any, so when he finally started making a decent salary—after he landed the job at Solo, followed quickly by the first TV show—he spent it lavishly. He was generous, sometimes irresponsibly so—buying a round for everyone at the bar, that kind of thing. If Deacon had money, everyone around him had money. Laurel wasn't surprised to hear he'd paid for Scarlett's father's bankruptcy attorney. That was what he did.

Laurel sat on the deck for a moment, gazing over the golf course and the pond; the lighthouse winked at her like it had a secret. Buck came out wearing just his bathing trunks and a towel around his neck. He was holding a beer and a glass of wine.

"This is a send-out from Chef Thorpe," he said. Laurel squinted up at him. "Chef Angela Thorpe." He handed Laurel the wine. "You look quite fetching in that towel."

"Buck."

He took the seat next to her. "The thing with Belinda was a mistake. I'll regret it the rest of my life, especially if it means I've lost my chance with you."

Laurel sipped her wine. *Let it go,* she thought. Things were tough for everyone. Then she heard the voice of Ursula.

Men cheat. That's what they do.

Laurel wanted to believe there were men who *didn't* cheat. She wanted to believe Buck was one of them.

"Why did your marriages end?" she asked him.

Buck laughed. "Wow, are we really doing this?"

"I'm curious," Laurel said. She had known Jessica a little. Back at the beginning of Buck and Deacon's friendship, the four of them had gone out in the city together on the rare nights that Deacon and Buck both had off and Laurel could find a babysitter. So, probably three times. Jessica had been a bit Upper East Side pretentious. She had gone to Nightingale-Bamford with Buck's cousin, Macy; that was how she and Buck had met. When she heard Laurel was from Dobbs Ferry, she'd assumed Laurel had gone to Masters, and her face had fallen when Laurel said, "No, just regular Dobbs Ferry High School."

Jessica had been one of many people to completely drop Laurel and join Team Belinda when Deacon did. Laurel had bumped into Jessica at the Frick Museum and Jessica had breezed right past her without a word or a wave.

Laurel had met Mae briefly at Hayes's graduation from Vanderbilt, but by the time Hayes had found a job and moved to Soho, Buck was filing for divorce.

Buck said, "Well, Jessica wanted children and I didn't. That ended marriage number one. And Mae never made the bed, she flooded the bathroom every time she took a shower, and she chewed with her mouth open. That ended marriage number two."

"You weren't unfaithful?" Laurel asked.

"Work is a cruel mistress," Buck said. "Most women can't handle coming in second place."

"I bet I'm busier than you are," Laurel said.

"You might be," Buck said. "So we can both be busy and neither of us will get mad about it and we'll live happily ever after."

"Buck."

He reached for her hand. "I like you, Laurel."

Her heart fluttered, despite herself. She hadn't felt this way since she was a freshman in high school and Deacon had asked to walk her home, and then they stopped in the parking lot of the Grand Union and Deacon had kissed her for the first time. Laurel had thought that because he was from the city, he might be self-assured, but both of them had bumbled through the first kiss—lips, tongues, teeth, hands.

Laurel was thinking of this first kiss as Buck leaned in, and suddenly it was Buck's lips on hers, and he was a lot more skilled than Deacon had been back in 1977. This kiss was lovely; he tasted like the sea. His mouth opened, his tongue found hers, soft yet insistent, and Laurel thought, *Wow, chemistry.* There was nothing like the electric jolt of kissing someone for the first time.

But then an alarm went off in Laurel's head, shrill and piercing. She wasn't going to do this. She pulled away.

"I'm sorry," she said. "I can't."

"Laurel...," he said.

She shook her head and stood up, clenching her towel tight. Part of her knew she was being stubborn and probably also daft. She shouldn't let Belinda poison something as sweet as that kiss.

"I like you, too, Buck," Laurel said. "But I have principles." And with that, she entered the house, closing the sliding screen door gently behind her. She had stuck to her guns, but the kiss had lit her up like a constellation, with stars in her head, her chest, her legs.

One good thing, she thought, was that she no longer felt like an old shoe.

ANGIE

At quarter to four, it was time to go to Sconset to get the baguettes. Belinda had brought the truck home in one piece, which was, frankly, a relief, although she was acting a little tipsy, and she smelled like wine.

"Where did you go?" Angie asked. "A bar?"

"Don't be silly," Belinda said.

It was silly. Angie tried to picture Belinda sliding onto a bar stool at the Nautilus or the Starlight and drinking by herself on a Sunday afternoon. Maybe she had poured her heart out to Johnny B. at Ventuno: *Stuck in a house with my ex-husband's other wives and their children.*

"You went drinking somewhere," Angie said. "And you don't have any friends here. So you must have gone to a bar."

"It's none of your business, Nancy Drew," Belinda said, and she headed upstairs.

* * *

Angie squeezed behind the wheel of Deacon's truck and moved the seat way back. By the time she reached the bottom of the driveway, her phone started to beep. She turned onto Hoicks Hollow Road, and, since the speed limit was ten miles an hour and there was no one on the road, she checked her phone.

She gasped and pulled over.

There was a missed call from Joel Tersigni.

He had called at 2:05, nearly two hours earlier. Two o'clock on a Sunday afternoon. Dory didn't work on weekends, so she would be home—or maybe at the boys' lacrosse game. Or maybe Dory was still in possession of Joel's phone, and it was Dory who had called. Maybe she had come across more texts or photos; maybe Joel had shared more intimate details. Angie wanted to call back—God, did she want to call back—but if Dory answered... No, Angie couldn't risk it. Angie imagined drawing back the string of the bow, lining up the pin through the peep sight, and letting go. *Wheeeeeeeeee!* She imagined spearing both Joel and Dory through the heart. Kill shot.

She thought about JP in his hat and his sunglasses, with his easy smile and his passion for the outdoors. Would it be easier to love someone like JP, someone her own age, someone who had time to spend with her and an interest in showing her things? Someone who had been hurt himself and could teach her a thing or two about survival?

As she pulled into the parking lot of the Sconset Market, the smell of warm, freshly baked bread hit her. Angie loved bread. She and Deacon used to play a game called Final Meal. Their answers changed according to season and mood, but Angie always started with Parker House rolls and sweet butter. And Deacon always started with pizza.

The market was tiny and quaint, not unlike small-town markets elsewhere, except this one had a sophisticated selection of French cheese—Angie plucked out a soft, gooey Langres, which was difficult to find, even in New York. Angie got in a line forming at the register, where a straw basket was piled high with baguettes.

"Two please," Angie said. "And the Langres."

She paid the cashier and carried the warm loaves and the cheese out to the Chevy. As she started the ignition, she considered driving out to Coatue to find JP so that she could invite him to dinner. But then she decided against it. Laurel, Belinda, and Scarlett were going to sit down to eat together for the first time ever. No stranger should be subjected to that.

Back at the house, Angie pulled out the blue and white checked bistro tablecloth from the pantry and four matching napkins and three linen napkins that evoked the goldenrod crayon in Angie's long-ago box of Crayolas. She set the table. The wide, shallow bowls in the cabinet were impractical for cereal but perfect for chowder, and Angie put a dinner plate underneath each; and, although none of the dishes matched, it still looked okay. Sort of. She shook her head, thinking about how extravagant Deacon had been when selecting dishes for the Board Room. Four of the nine courses had their own custom-made dishes, most of these one of a kind, purchased from individual artisans throughout the Northeast. The caviar sets cost more than $200 apiece. Deacon argued that for most people, dinner at the Board Room would be a once-in-a-lifetime experience, and he wanted every aspect of it to be inimitable, unforgettable.

Tonight would be a once-in-a-lifetime experience, Angie was pretty sure, but no one would care about the dishes.

She set out a wooden laminate bowl for shells and claimed two hideous candlesticks from the living room that were made out of industrial spools. They held candles that might once have been ivory colored but were now yellowing like teeth.

She set out silverware, which was also a bit of a hodgepodge. Angie and Deacon had joked that the Innsleys must have gone to a lot of potlucks and brought home utensils from each one.

Angie softened the butter, then sprinkled it with sea salt and garnished it with a sprig of tarragon from the farm.

Angie turned around to see Hayes, half his face mummified but his uncovered eye reasonably bright and focused, sort of hunched over and yet upright, hobbling into the kitchen. "Fancy," he said, nodding at the butter.

"I'm just trying to make things as nice as I can," Angie said.

He touched her back and gave her a kiss on the cheek with the undamaged half of his mouth. "Thank you. Do we have wine?"

At seven o'clock, they assembled on the deck for a proper cocktail hour. Angie had set out the bluefish pâté, crackers, grapes, the Langres, and a bowl of Goldfish for Ellery. Angie had also made Ellery a Shirley Temple, complete with three maraschino cherries.

"Maraschino" was going on the Stupid Word List, Angie decided. What did it even mean? Unnaturally red and sickly sweet? And yet Deacon had loved maraschino cherries. He'd developed a recipe for roasted-pineapple bread pudding with maraschino-cherry ice cream while he was at Raindance, but that was before ironic retro was cool, and Luther Davey made him take it off the menu.

Laurel wandered out in a white sundress; Buck followed in a pair of khaki shorts and a kelly-green polo shirt. They joined Hayes, who was hunkered down in one of the supremely uncomfortable deck chairs with a brimming glass of wine. He was cold, he said, *freezing,* despite the fact that it was the end of a sticky, hot day. He had bundled himself in a crocheted afghan that he'd pulled from a trunk in the living room; the afghan smelled strongly of old age.

"I think that used to be Clara's blanket," Angie said, but Hayes didn't even crack a smile.

"Look at this spread!" Laurel said, helping herself to a cracker and an impressive hunk of the Langres.

Belinda sauntered out onto the deck in a flowing baby-blue one-shouldered number that wouldn't have been out of place at the Met costume ball.

"Well," Angie said, shaking her head, "it matches your toes."

"Armani Privé," Belinda said. "I bought it for awards season but didn't end up wearing it. Where's Scarlett?"

Laurel said, "She and Ellery went upstairs to nap a while ago. Should I wake them up?"

"Wake them up," Angie said. "I made enough food for a marching band."

"Let them sleep," Belinda said.

"Mother," Angie said. "This was meant to be a family dinner."

"I'll wake them up," Laurel said.

Scarlett and Ellery stumbled into the kitchen just as Angie was ladling the chowder, spooning in the creamy broth, rich with smoky, sweet chorizo, translucent onions, and fragrant herbs. She put the same number of mussels and clams and just-opaque scallops into each bowl. Next, she pulled the panko-crusted goat cheese out of the oven. The disks were golden brown, and Angie knew they would be lusciously melty in the center, perfect against the peppery arugula and the firm, ripe peaches.

Ellery was whimpering, and Scarlett wasn't much better, moaning and groaning as she collapsed in her chair. She set a tall can down by her plate. The can was amethyst purple, and in pink, girly cursive, it said *Skinny4Life.*

"I don't want anything to eat," Scarlett said. "I have this."

"What *is* that?" Laurel asked. "Skinny4Life? Is that some kind of new diet product?"

Scarlett threw Laurel a withering look but didn't answer. Angie couldn't believe how rude Scarlett was being. When someone went to the trouble to make you a home-cooked dinner, you ate it. You didn't show up with a can.

"Wine?" Angie asked, barely concealing her impatience.

Scarlett crossed her arms and shook her head. "No, thank you."

"Well, *I* want wine," Belinda called out.

You mean more *wine,* Angie thought.

"Angie, it looks beautiful," Laurel said. "Thank you."

"You outdid yourself, Ange," Hayes said.

"Your father would be very proud," Buck said.

A sob escaped from Scarlett. Laurel raised her glass. "Here's to our chef."

Angie lowered herself gingerly into her chair. She was afraid of something, but she wasn't sure what. She touched her glass to Belinda's glass, Laurel's, Buck's, and Hayes's.

Scarlett stood up. "I'm sorry," she said. "I can't do this."

"Scarlett, just sit with us, even if you're not going to eat," Laurel said. "Please?"

"Don't tell me what to do!" Scarlett said. "You ruined my day, Laurel Thorpe, with that disgusting story about St. John."

"St. John?" Belinda said. "What disgusting story about St. John?"

Scarlett said, "I know you always thought it was me that Deacon took to St. John when things were so bad between the two of you. But I found out today that he went with Laurel."

"What?" Belinda said.

"Scarlett!" Laurel screamed. Angie's head snapped back. She had never heard Laurel raise her voice like that before. "What is *wrong* with you? I told you that in *confidence!*"

Belinda raised her chin. "Am I understanding this correctly?"

Scarlett said, "Laurel was the one who went with Deacon to St. John. It wasn't me. I told you it wasn't me, but I knew you never believed me."

"You have got to be kidding me," Belinda said. "Laurel?"

Laurel sat with her hands in her lap, her head bowed. Then she raised her eyes to Scarlett and said, "I trusted you. I told you a secret I have kept for over a decade, and not eight hours later, you reveal it to the person it would hurt the most. I can't believe this."

Angie couldn't believe it either. She had slaved over this dinner in an attempt to bring everyone together, but before anyone had taken a bite, accusations were flying about something that had happened a dozen years earlier.

Angie remembered when Deacon had disappeared to St. John; she had been a freshman at Chapin. It was a year that had been ruined by her parents' marital problems.

Hayes reached into his bowl with his fingers and plucked out a mussel. "Really good, sis," he said.

Angie stared at him. He was completely oblivious!

"*You* went with Deacon to St. John?" Belinda said. "It was *you?*"

Laurel nodded. "I'm sorry, Belinda." But, Angie noted, she didn't sound sorry.

"Renée's assistant *told* me Deacon was with a blond," Belinda said, "but I didn't believe him."

"Because you thought it was me," Scarlett said.

"You do realize we were still *married,*" Belinda said. "I mean, things were tough between us, but that didn't give him the right to vanish to the Caribbean and screw somebody else." She laughed. "But, now that I think about it, it makes sense. You mooned over him for all those years. You never dated anyone else, you never got remarried. I'm sure when he asked you to go with him, you jumped at the chance. You never got over him."

"Maybe you're right," Laurel said. "Maybe I never did get over him. I had been with him since we were *freshmen in high school.* We grew up together. We learned to drive together, we registered to vote together, we got pregnant and had a child together. I made him the man he was, and he made me the woman I was. I never had an affair. I was faithful to that man, and in many ways, I still am, because I have never and will never love anyone the way I loved Deacon. Maybe that is pathetic. But the other thing I never got over is the way you sashayed into our lives and stole him away. Deacon was *married* when you invited him up to your room at the St. Regis. We had a young child."

Hayes raised his hand. "Affirmative. That was me."

"So the trip to St. John was what...?" Belinda asked. "Your *revenge?*"

Laurel shrugged.

"Oh, I get it," Belinda said. "It was just one more instance when I was beneath your consideration."

Angie tore off a hunk of baguette and slathered it with butter. She realized now why she had felt afraid. Food was food; food wasn't magic. It couldn't change the past. It couldn't right old wrongs.

Scarlett said, "The reason I went home to Savannah is because..." Here, she paused and looked down at Ellery, who had fallen fast asleep in her chair. "Deacon got drunk, went to a strip club, and decided he was going to drive one of the dancers up to Nantucket. He completely abandoned Ellery at school. Instead of picking her up, he climbed behind the wheel of the Saab that belonged to some floozy who was half his age."

Buck choked on his chowder. "He told you that?"

"He told *me* that nothing happened with the stripper," Laurel said. "And what does it matter now, Scarlett?"

"I don't want Angie or Hayes to think I left for any other reason," Scarlett said. She glared at Angie. "I'm sure your father told you I went to Savannah because of Bo Tanner."

"Bo Tanner?" Angie said. It took her a minute to recall who Bo Tanner was: Scarlett's old boyfriend, back in her nanny days. But Bo Tanner had married someone else, a friend of Scarlett's. Angie could remember Scarlett crying about it.

"Your father was very jealous of Bo," Scarlett said. "For absolutely no reason." She bent over and shook Ellery awake. "Come on, darling, we're going upstairs to bed, and you're too big to carry."

Ellery rubbed her eyes. "I want Miss Kit Kat to read to me."

"Maybe when I'm finished eating, angel bear," Belinda said.

"I'll read to my daughter, thank you very much," Scarlett said.

"But I want Miss Kit Kat!" Ellery said.

"You'll see Miss Kit Kat tomorrow," Scarlett said. "We are going up to bed right this instant." She shepherded Ellery off the deck and into the kitchen, where she made a point of slamming the sliding door so hard, Angie was surprised it didn't fall off the runner.

"I'm sure she *is* sleeping with Bo Tanner," Belinda said. "She pined for him the entire time she worked for us. Plus, we never get over our first loves, do we, Laurel?"

"Mother," Angie said. "Please, let's talk about something else."

Laurel forked a scallop in half. "No," she said. "I suppose we don't."

Deacon's Shellfish Chowder

24 baby (no more than ¾ inch in diameter) new potatoes or fingerling potatoes
1 tablespoon extra-virgin olive oil
2 tablespoons unsalted butter
1 medium onion, peeled and minced
3 cloves garlic, minced
4 ounces mild Spanish chorizo
1 tablespoon minced fresh tarragon
1 cup dry white wine
1 cup heavy cream
Sea salt and freshly ground black pepper, to taste
¾ pound fresh sea scallops, side muscles removed and halved vertically

2 pounds fresh littleneck clams, rinsed well under cold running water
1 pound fresh mussels, scrubbed and debearded if necessary
2½ tablespoons minced fresh parsley

Place the potatoes in a saucepan and cover generously with water. Bring to a boil over medium-high heat, reduce to a simmer, and cook until just shy of being tender, 12 to 14 minutes.

Meanwhile, heat the olive oil and butter together over medium heat in a 12-inch straight-sided skillet that has a matching lid. Add the minced onion and garlic and sauté until soft and translucent, 5 to 7 minutes. Add the diced chorizo and continue cooking, stirring occasionally, until the chorizo has released its paprika-colored fat and begun to crisp, 5 to 7 minutes. Stir in the tarragon and cook 1 minute more. Pour in the wine and let simmer until it has reduced by half, 3 to 5 minutes.

Drain the potatoes and cut in half. Add to the skillet and toss gently to coat with the sautéed onions, chorizo, and wine. Pour the cream into the skillet, bring to a simmer, and let simmer until lightly thickened, 4 to 5 minutes. Season all to taste with salt and pepper.

Scatter the halved scallops evenly over the ingredients in the skillet. Artfully arrange the scrubbed clams and mussels, hinged sides facing down, over the top of the chowder base. Cover the skillet and increase the heat so that the liquid comes to a gentle boil and the clams and mussels steam open, 5 to 6 minutes. Discard any clams or mussels that have not opened. Sprinkle the parsley over the top. Ladle the chowder into wide bowls, taking care to distribute all the wonderful components evenly. Serve at once with crusty bread or rolls.

SERVES 4

BUCK

Buck fidgeted in his chair while Angie served the berry crumble. He should go upstairs and tell Scarlett the news about the house. He should do it now, get it over with, and give her all night to process the situation.

Buck poised his fork over the deep-red berries, covered with golden dough and topped with vanilla-scented whipped cream. He decided to wait until morning.

Hayes struggled to push himself up in his chair. "I have to go upstairs," he said.

"You don't want your dessert?" Buck said.

"You've barely uttered a word all night, Hayes," Belinda said. "Are you all right?"

Laurel leaned forward. "Honey?"

Hayes's head fell forward on his neck, and he started snoring.

Laurel said, "Poor guy, he's been through so much. Buck, will you help me get him up to bed?"

Buck reluctantly abandoned his crumble and took Hayes under one arm as Laurel moved the chair and tried to rouse him. "Hayes, honey, upsy-daisy."

Hayes got to his feet, but it was slow moving into the house, through the kitchen, and up the stairs. Once they got Hayes to his room, he crashed onto the bed like a falling tree. Laurel tucked him in, smoothing his hair and kissing his bruised forehead. Then she and Buck tiptoed out to the hallway and shut the door.

Laurel looked at Buck in the dim light. "Do you think there's something going on with him?"

Buck didn't want to offer an opinion. He was no expert with women, and less of an expert with children, even when the child was thirty-four years old. If pressed, he would say, *Hell yeah, something is going on with Hayes.* Granted, the guy had just lost his father, so nobody expected him to be his best self, but Hayes was exceptionally off. Just off. Even before he'd ventured out on his own and gotten the shit kicked out of him.

"Everyone is grieving," Buck said.

Laurel stepped into Buck's arms and raised her face to him. He wondered if that was an invitation to kiss her. He wanted to so badly, but she had been clear about her wishes, so instead he gave her a hug, rubbed her back, and led her back down the stairs, where, he hoped, his crumble still waited.

Tri-Berry Crumble

1 quart fresh strawberries, hulled and halved
1 pint whole unsweetened blueberries, fresh or frozen
1 pint whole unsweetened raspberries, fresh or frozen
¾ cup granulated sugar
3 tablespoons all-purpose flour
⅓ cup cassis

TOPPING

1 cup all-purpose flour
½ cup granulated sugar
½ cup light-brown sugar, lightly packed
¾ teaspoon ground cinnamon
¼ teaspoon salt
1 cup quick-cooking (not instant) oats (I like to use McCann's, from Ireland)

12 tablespoons (1½ sticks) chilled, unsalted butter,
cut into small pieces
Vanilla ice cream or whipped cream, for serving

Preheat the oven to 350°F.

Combine all the berries, sugar, flour, and cassis in a large mixing bowl and toss gently until all the ingredients are evenly combined. Spread the berry mixture evenly over the bottom of an 8 x 11–inch ceramic baking or gratin dish.

To make the topping: Place the flour, granulated sugar, brown sugar, cinnamon, salt, and oats in the bowl of a stand mixer fitted with paddle attachment. Blend together on low speed. Add the chilled butter, and continue mixing on low to medium-low speed until the dry ingredients have become moistened and crumbly. Sprinkle the topping over the berries, covering them almost completely.

Bake the crumble until the fruit juices are bubbling and the topping is golden brown, 50 to 60 minutes. Serve warm or at room temperature with a scoop of vanilla ice cream or dollop of whipped cream.

SERVES 6 TO 8

ANGIE

At least dinner tasted good, Angie thought as she emptied the disgusting, gluey, gray contents of the Skinny4Life can down the drain. The conversation—well, that had been out of her control.

Laurel and Buck offered to clean up. Belinda excused

herself with a headache. Angie followed her mother out of the kitchen.

"Are you okay?" Angie asked.

"You know, Laurel Thorpe isn't the saint you think she is," Belinda said. "She had a clandestine tryst with your father while you were still a child, while we were still a family. The whole do-gooder thing is a front. She called Bob last night…"

"What?" Angie said. "Who called Bob?"

"Laurel did," Belinda said.

"What for?"

"To tell on me," Belinda said. "I had a little run-in with Buck…"

"With Buck?" Angie hissed. Her head was spinning. She could no longer keep track of the treachery. Laurel with Deacon, Scarlett with Bo Tanner, Belinda with…Buck?

"She blew it way out of proportion," Belinda said. "It was nothing. She called Bob so he would have the upper hand."

"I don't want to hear any more," Angie said. "You baffle me."

"I baffle you?" Belinda said. "I'm the only one here looking out for you, darling. Do you know where I went today? I went into town to buy you a house."

"What?" Angie said.

"I tried to buy One Forty-One Main Street," Belinda said. "The one with the white pillars and the glass porch? I knocked on the door and made them an offer."

"Oh my God, mother," Angie said. She tried to imagine what that scene had been like. "You're crazy, you know that?"

"I was trying to help you, darling," Belinda said. "I did it for you. I wanted to buy you another house. A better house."

"I don't want you to buy me another house!" Angie

said. "I want *this* house; don't you get it? This house and this house only. This is where I lived with Deacon. That room right there is where we used to play Monopoly when it rained. I was the shoe and Deacon was the wheelbarrow and Hayes was that stupid little Yorkie. This house is where I tasted my first clam, it's where I used to catch fireflies in the yard, it's where we sat on the back deck and pointed out the Big Dipper. That sofa is where we fell asleep doing our summer reading for school. Your room, Clara's room, is where we got punished when we stayed out at bonfires until two in the morning. This house is Deacon. There is no such thing as a 'better' house. Please don't pretend like there is."

"Okay, okay, calm down," Belinda said. "I was only trying to help."

"If you want to help," Angie said, "then start getting along with everyone else."

"Or," Belinda said, "they could start getting along with me."

"That's right, I forgot," Angie said. "The world revolves around you." With that, Angie stepped out onto the front porch to have a cigarette. She ran her bare foot over the board that JP had replaced. Deacon had come to this island with Laurel first, then Belinda, then Scarlett, but he had certainly never meant for the three of them to be here *at the same time*—even after he was dead.

As Angie blew out a stream of smoke, a car pulled into the driveway. It was a minivan with a bright-orange top hat: All Point Taxi. A man stepped out onto the driveway.

It was...Joel Tersigni.

Joel! Angie tried to breathe, but she coughed.

Joel.

Angie took the last drag of her cigarette and flicked it into the grass, which was so brittle and brown, Angie feared it might catch fire, but the ember burned softly out.

She raised her eyes to Joel. There were all kinds of panicked emotions stirring in her gut, but she tamped them down.

"Angie," he said.

"What are you doing here?" she said.

He paid the driver and pulled out the black nylon Nike bag that he usually took to the gym. That was what he had brought for luggage.

"Dory threw me out," he said. "I went to your apartment first, but then I remembered you were here, so I drove up and took the ferry. I have nowhere else to go."

"I called your phone, and Dory answered," Angie said. "She said horrible things to me."

"Babe, I know," Joel said. "She stole my phone. She made me tell her everything."

"Made you *how?*" Angie said. "I thought the plan if we ever got caught was to *deny deny deny.*"

"She had access to my cell phone records, detailed records that you can only get if... well, if you're an attorney or a spy. She knew a lot, but I wasn't sure how much—and she tricked me into filling in the blanks. Then she threatened to go public with it—to the press, to your mother, to our friends in New Canaan, to my *parents.*"

Joel's parents, the owners of the Biblical Dinner Theater in Pigeon Forge, Tennessee. Adultery wouldn't be looked kindly upon by them, Angie supposed.

"She said if I left quietly, if I left without taking anything, she would tell everyone I'd gone on vacation, and then, after the summer, when the boys were home from camp, she would say we decided to separate. She would say it was a mutual decision."

Joel and Angie both turned to watch the cabbie back out of the driveway and take off down Hoicks Hollow Road. When Joel faced Angie again, she could see how rattled he looked. He held out his arms. "Come here."

She hesitated, thinking about JP nocking an arrow for Angie to shoot. She heard JP say, *Line up the pin.*

But she wasn't strong enough to resist Joel. She loved him. Forty-eight hours of silence hadn't changed that. She stepped forward, and he grabbed her up.

"There's my girl," Joel said in her ear. "I missed you. I've been trying to find a way to get out of my marriage without blowing my life to bits. Dory is tough, Ange."

Angie nodded against Joel's chest. She had missed the way her face rested right against his heart; she had missed the way he smelled. And she understood what he meant. She, Angie, was an island—especially now that Deacon was dead. She wasn't responsible for anyone; she didn't own anything. Joel had a wife and kids, a house, a car, a community, friends. On Tuesday nights, when the restaurant was closed, he had a poker group. He was a member of the Lions Club, and he ran the Toys for Tots drive at Christmastime. His life was more than just the restaurant and the city and her. A lot more.

Angie lifted her face to Joel's, and he kissed her, their first kiss since she was in his car on Seventy-Third Street. She let herself get lost in it. He whispered, "Where can we go?"

"The house," she said, pulling his hand.

"Is your mother inside?" he asked.

"Unfortunately, yes," Angie said. "You'll meet her in the morning."

Angie led Joel up onto the porch. She stepped over the board that JP had replaced; she couldn't think about JP right now. The front hallway was empty. Angie led Joel up the stairs, to her room. She put a finger on her lips and shut the door. Joel scooped Angie up in his arms and laid her down on the bed.

Mouth, neck, breasts, tongue, nipples, ribs, belly, the curve inside her hip...ohhhhhh. Joel. *Joel!* He had to sandwich the side of his hand in her mouth so she wouldn't scream and set off alarms. Sex sex sex sex sex. It meant nothing, Angie thought. And it meant everything.

BELINDA

A little girl in a sparkly silver dress with double diagonal fishtail braids empties the jar of glass onto the floor and begins to sort it by color: white, brown, green, blue, lavender. The glass is broken but not sharp. It has smooth edges and frosted surfaces. It's beach glass—shards pulled from the ocean after years and years of tumbling through the sand and salt water. Among the pieces of glass, the girl finds a packet of something that looks like brown sugar. The girl loves brown sugar; she eats it on toast. The girl opens the packet and empties it into her mouth.

Belinda woke up with a start.

No!

She looked around the dark room—Nantucket. Belinda was in Clara's narrow, uncomfortable nursemaid's bed, under one thin sheet. She'd had a bad dream about... about...it slipped down the drain. Gone. She couldn't remember what the dream had been about. It was something bad, something with a hole or a cavern.

Then she had it back. It had been about Ellery. Ellery mistaking the heroin for sugar, Ellery eating the heroin.

Good God, Belinda had just *left* the heroin downstairs in the powder room. After a glass of wine and the disturbing conversation at dinner, Belinda had forgotten all about it.

She slipped out of bed and crept down the stairs to the powder room. The packet of heroin was exactly where she'd left it, tucked under her special piece of beach glass. She plucked it out and carried it back upstairs.

She sat on her sorry excuse for a bed with the heroin in her lap. What to do?

She tiptoed down the hall to Hayes's room and tapped on the door. No response. Certainly he was fast asleep. Well, Belinda didn't care. She opened the door and stepped in.

Hayes was in bed, snoring. The duffel, which had been agape that afternoon, was now zipped up tight. If Belinda opened it, she knew what she would find: more packets, needles, rubber tubing, a spoon, a lighter. She wouldn't go through Hayes's things while he slept. But she did want to talk to him.

She sat on the edge of his bed and shook him awake. He opened his eyes and saw her and most likely thought he was the one having a bad dream. He tried to sit up. Belinda put a hand on his arm to reassure him, and a finger to her lips. The last thing Belinda wanted was Laurel rushing in and finding Belinda in Hayes's bedroom *again*.

"Hayes," she said. "I need to talk to you."

"Now?" he said. His voice was froggy. "In the middle of the night? What the hell for?" He scooted his body toward the wall, away from Belinda.

She held up the packet. "I found this on the floor when I came in here earlier," she said. She shook it. "This is heroin, yes?"

Hayes reached up to grab it, but Belinda snatched it away. "Answer the question, Hayes. Is it heroin?"

"It's mine," Hayes said. "Give it to me."

"Hayes," Belinda said. "Is it heroin?"

Hayes let his arm fall to the bed. "Yes."

Belinda nodded. She felt pleased with the admission. He had said it was his. There was no denial.

"How often are you using?" she asked.

"It's none of your *business,*" Hayes said. "Now give me that, and get out of my room, please."

"It *is* my business," Belinda said. "You're my stepson. I care about you, and I don't want to see you doing this to yourself."

Hayes grabbed the packet out of Belinda's hand. "You know nothing about it," he said. "You know nothing about my life. You know nothing about me."

"I've known you for nearly thirty years, Hayes," Belinda said.

"Get out, please," Hayes said.

"I could just tell your mother," Belinda said.

"Why would you burden her with this?" Hayes said. "She has enough to worry about."

"If it were my child, I'd want to know," Belinda said.

"Yeah, well, I'm *not* your child. Angie is a good kid. You got lucky."

"I won't tell Laurel," Belinda said. "But you have to. She knows people who deal with this in the city, I'm sure. Treatment facilities, programs, methadone clinics..."

"My mother has *enough* on her plate," Hayes said. "Anyway, it's not as bad as you think. It's a casual habit."

"A casual heroin habit," Belinda said. "I see. I assume the reason you look like you went fifteen rounds with Floyd Mayweather is because you went out looking for drugs?"

Hayes rolled away from her to face the window, the packet clenched in his hand. "Good night, Belinda," he said.

"Tell your mother before the end of the day tomorrow, or I will," Belinda said. "She loves you." With that, Belinda stood up. "We all love you, Hayes."

HAYES

We all love you, Hayes.

He closed his eyes. Sleep was right there, like an ocean. All he had to do was jump in.

Tell your mother. His mother would be disappointed. No, delete that. She would be destroyed. She had only one child, Hayes, her golden boy. Laurel had been nineteen when Hayes was born, twenty-eight when Deacon left. Deacon's life had become very populated—with Belinda first, then Angie, then Scarlett and Ellery, and always Buck—but Laurel had just been Laurel. She had dated here and there, and she threw herself into her career, but somehow she'd always made Hayes feel as though her first job, above and beyond everything else, was being his mother.

Belinda had him backed into a corner. She was going to tell Laurel if he didn't. But maybe she was bluffing? She was a pretty good actress.

Hayes had heard that coming off heroin was a living hell, that you got violently sick, you vomited and wet yourself, you went into painful convulsions, you experienced jonesing like you'd never known. Grown men cried, screamed, begged, and groveled for a hit. Hayes didn't think he could do it. He was smart, and he was sophisticated—but he wasn't strong. Quitting heroin was apparently like climbing a greased pole—impossible to find purchase, with a chance to slip every second. And when you slipped, it was like falling into a hole with no bottom.

The heroin had been an accident, a trip-up, something Hayes had meant to try once, as a cultural experience. The opium pipe had been offered to him in a three-hundred-year-old teak house in a deep green valley in a part of China that few Westerners saw. That weekend had been so foreign as to be surreal, as if Hayes were a character in a storybook. He had been trying to abide by local custom—when one was offered the opium pipe, one smoked. Hayes had never imagined it would lead him directly to a street habit back in New York.

There was no way Hayes could describe how tremendous a feeling the high was. It was better than sex, better than a cold beer after a long day at the beach, better than a promotion at work with a huge pay raise, better than caviar on blini with a dollop of sour cream, better than love. Heroin equaled euphoria, a cloud walk, a feeling of superhuman power and complete peace at the same time. He couldn't give it up.

How had he *gotten* this way? He was *addicted*. How had he allowed this to happen? He had meant to be careful, but he had not been careful. Belinda, with her hard, cold eyes like pieces of blue flint, had discovered him. Would he be paranoid to think that Belinda had been out to get him ever since he was a child? She had wanted Hayes to love her; he remembered the deals and the bribes. She had taken Hayes onto the set of *The Truman Show* to meet Jim Carrey; she had let Hayes and his high school girlfriend, Shauna, stay in the house in L.A. without any supervision; she had handed over the keys to Deacon's Porsche whenever he asked. But Hayes had never bought into the whole Belinda worship, and she was painfully aware of this and probably hated him a little. She had started off this weekend by mentioning Naomi Watts, whom Hayes had bumped into while he was high as a kite.

Hayes had messed up so badly! He should have married Whitney Jo. He should have taken a job with a different magazine, one that required less travel; he should be a father by now. But the idea of a sedentary life—of daily routine, home ownership, a mortgage, a wedding ring, holiday dinners, a lawn sprinkler, bagging leaves and trips to the dump with the recycling; of back-to-school nights and entire Saturday afternoons spent at the soccer field—was suffocating. He might as well wrap a dry-cleaning bag over his head.

At the end, with Whitney Jo dropping hint after hint, leaving magazines in the bathroom open to De Beers ads, complaining that she had been a bridesmaid seven times in twelve months, Hayes had gotten queasy. He couldn't do it. He was a traveler; he suffered from wanderlust and a bad case of Fear of Missing Out. He liked airport security, a stiff vodka and tonic in the VIP lounge; he enjoyed harmless flirting with flight attendants; and he loved the thrill of visiting a place he'd never been before. Kathmandu, Marrakech, Dakar, Dubai, Sydney, Tahiti, Vienna, Shanghai. Check in, check out: that was the life he had cultivated. Having no home was his home.

And now Belinda was threatening to bring it all down. He tried to picture himself at rehab. He tried to imagine himself entering a methadone clinic. No, he couldn't do it. He didn't want to talk to a counselor or sit in a circle of other addicts and confide the ways he'd been wronged growing up. He hadn't been abused or ignored. He had been nurtured and loved—even by Belinda. Threatening to tell Laurel but allowing time for him to do it himself was Belinda showing him love. She cared about him.

His mother. Tell his mother? He couldn't.

But maybe Hayes wasn't as bad off as he thought. He had been surviving just fine on the Percocet alone—plus a bump around noon. Nearly twelve hours earlier. Although now, after the interaction with Belinda, he wasn't going to lie—he could use a hit, a full hit, not a baby half hit like he'd been limiting himself to since he'd gotten here.

He clenched the packet and went to his duffel bag for his spoon and his needle. He was shaking a little as he cooked the heroin, as he drew it up into the needle, as he grabbed the rubber tubing in his teeth until his vein popped. As he shot.

Ahhhhhhhhh.

LAUREL

She and Buck did the dishes together. They bagged up the leftover salad and wrapped a heel of baguette and covered the butter. Laurel picked up the empty can of Skinny4Life that was by the sink.

"Here's the answer to one mystery," she said.

Buck was elbow deep in sudsy water at the sink. "He invested a hundred thousand dollars in that stuff."

"She probably got a lifetime supply," Laurel said, pitching the can in the trash.

"I can't believe Deacon was such a sucker," Buck said.

"He knew he was going to lose the house," Laurel said. "I'm sure he was grasping at straws. Then he came up here to say good-bye to it."

"I'm sure he knew when he went out that night and ended up at the strip club," Buck said. "He wanted to drive that girl to Nantucket. That was the act of a desperate man."

"I wonder what he was thinking about at the end," Laurel said. "He was supposed to go fishing with JP the next morning, so maybe he was thinking about that—casting a line, feeling a tug, getting that rush you get when there's a fish on." She started to blubber. Of everyone in the house, only Laurel had known Deacon as a child. He had never believed himself worthy of any of the good things that had come his way—starting with Laurel. He used to say to her, *You are the first good thing that ever happened to me.* God, she hadn't thought of that in years and years. When they were in high school, he used to squeeze her hard when he walked her to her door, as if he was afraid she would disappear overnight. So... when he found out he was going to lose the Nantucket house, he might have seen it as his fears finally coming true. He was going to lose the thing he loved the most.

"The ashes come tomorrow," she said, wiping her eyes. What remained of Deacon Thorpe would fit in a shoe box. The chef and the swearer and the incredible kisser and the proud, loving father were now chunks and silt that they would throw in the water. It was inconceivable. It was wrong. And yet, everyone died. Laurel herself—with all her thoughts and feelings and all her love and compassion—would someday cease to be, and once she was gone, she would never be back. Never was a long, long time.

She dried the dishes that Buck had set in the drainer, then

replaced them in the cabinet. Existential thinking terrified her. She preferred to believe that she would have another thirty or forty years in relative good health, with some meaningful companionship.

She threw down her dish towel and hugged Buck around the middle from behind as he hosed the scraps out of the sink.

"Would you take me upstairs and make love to me?" she asked.

He shut off the faucet. "What did you say?"

Laurel laughed, embarrassed at herself. "Never mind," she said.

"No, I'm sorry. The water was running, and I didn't hear you." He took her by the chin. "What did you say?"

She could retract her statement now, or amend it, but it felt as if she were being spurred on by some invisible force. "I asked you to take me upstairs and make love to me," she said.

"You did?"

She bit her lower lip. Should she explain that she was all of a sudden very afraid to die?

No need to explain to Buck. He took her hand and led her up the stairs, and it felt natural and meant to be, as though it would be the first time of many, many times, thirty or forty years' worth.

Monday, June 20

ANGIE

There was a knock on her bedroom door. Her eyes flew open. Sunlight filtered into the room through the bottom of the window shade; it was morning. Joel lay splayed across the bed, buck naked. Angie hastened to cover him up with a sheet and the meager chenille blanket. The last thing she wanted was Ellery marching in and seeing Joel in Angie's bed. Angie scrambled to put on shorts and a T-shirt. She opened the door. Laurel was standing there in her bathrobe, her hair mussed, her eyes at half mast behind a pair of glasses that Angie had never seen her wear.

"Sorry to bother you, sweetie," Laurel said. "But JP is downstairs? He said you two had plans this morning?"

Angie gasped. "What time is it?"

"Eight thirty," Laurel said.

Eight thirty already? JP, being reliable and prompt, had come to collect Angie for her archery lesson. But now that Joel was here, Angie didn't want to go. She didn't need to go. She didn't have to prove anything to herself or anyone else. Joel had shown up. She, Angela Thorpe, was desired; she was loved.

Oh, how she wanted Laurel to go downstairs and break the bad news to JP, but that was unfair. Angie would do it.

She hurried down the stairs in her bare feet and squinted at the burst of sunlight pouring in through the front door. JP stood respectfully outside, wearing his visor and Blues Brothers sunglasses, grinning.

"Look at you, Sleeping Beauty," he said. "Get your shoes on. I have coffee for you at my cottage."

Angie smiled ruefully. She felt awful about this. If Joel hadn't shown up, she would have been happy and grateful to have gone with JP. It would have made the sad day in front of her bearable.

"I'm going to have to take a rain check," she said.

"Oh," he said. He took his sunglasses off so that he could study her. "Is everything okay?"

"Everything is great," she said. She lowered her voice. "My boyfriend, Joel? The one I told you about? He showed up last night. He's upstairs."

JP's face fell into an expression halfway between dejection and skepticism.

"I didn't know he was coming," Angie said. "He literally just appeared." Then she said, "I can't believe I just used the word 'literally.' "

"Okay," JP said. He didn't bother hiding his frown, and Angie wondered what exactly he was unhappy about. Angie had wasted his time, making him come out here from Coatue, but only twenty minutes at the most. Maybe he didn't approve because Joel was still married. Or maybe... maybe JP had been looking forward to spending time with Angie. She sort of thought this last thing was it, and she felt really bad, but she hadn't lied to JP—and she certainly hadn't made him any promises.

She said, "I'm sorry you had to come all the way out here."

"Don't worry about it," JP said. "I'll see you tonight on the boat."

"Right," Angie said. She wondered if Joel would want to come out with her family to spread the ashes. She wondered if her mother or Laurel or Scarlett would have a problem if he did. While she was thinking about this, JP turned and walked down the driveway to his Jeep. Angie wasn't sure why, but she followed him.

"Listen, JP, I'm sorry," she said. "I feel terrible. Honestly, I forgot you were coming this morning."

JP laughed. "This guy must be pretty terrific if you forgot about your shooting lesson," he said. He gave her a genuine smile. "I'm glad he showed up. You deserve to be someone's everything, Angie."

For some reason, tears pricked Angie's eyes. "I was someone's everything," she said. "But he's dead now."

JP reached out and wiped away the tear that fell. Then he climbed into his Jeep, started the ignition, and gave her a wave as he backed out of the driveway.

"Wait!" Angie shouted. She waved her arms for him to come back. She would get her shoes on; she would go with JP, strap on the bow, nock an arrow, line up the pin, and—*whoosh!*—hit the target.

But JP didn't see or hear her. He took off down the road, and after he was out of sight, Angie turned around and made her way back to the house.

Joel was sitting up in bed. The window shade had been raised.

"Who was that?" Joel said.

"Who?" Angie said.

"Um...the guy in the Jeep in the driveway? The guy you chased? The guy who touched your face? Who was that guy?"

"That was JP," Angie said. "He's the ranger out at Coatue."

" 'The ranger out at Coatue'?" Joel said. "Am I supposed to understand what that means?"

"No," Angie said. "You're not. I'm sorry."

"Are you hiding something from me?" Joel said.

"No," Angie said. On the one hand, she wanted to tell Joel all about JP: *He spends the summer in a shack out on a deserted stretch of beach, he gets up at dawn and fly-fishes on Coskata Pond, he goes clamming and scalloping, he makes a mean Concord grape jam, he reports shark sightings, he rescues sunburned tourists whose Jeeps are stuck in the sand. He's a bow hunter, and he's teaching me to shoot.* But on the other hand, Angie wanted to keep JP to herself. "He's a friend. A friend of mine."

BUCK

His morning dreams were about pizza. He was awake enough to know he was dreaming, awake enough to remember that he hadn't really slept because he had spent most of the night making love to Laurel Thorpe, awake enough to feel Laurel rise from bed and to think, *No, please, don't go anywhere,* awake enough to see the promise of morning sunshine—another beautiful day, living the life on Nantucket—and yet, he was also still asleep and dreaming of pizza.

He had been born and raised in New York City, so to him, the only real kind of pizza was pizza with a very thin, crispy crust, tomato sauce, and loads of gooey mozzarella cheese. Buck had to have his cheese gooey; he lived for pulling the strings and winding them around the tip of the triangle before popping it into his mouth. Deacon had liked his pizza well done, hard and a little brittle, which was not a preference Buck was ever able to understand. When they went out for pizza—maybe two or three hundred times over thirty years—they each got their own pie, because two men so particular and opposite about their cheese could never share. Buck was a purist about toppings—pepperoni only. Deacon would throw on anything—meatballs, onion and mushrooms; olives, green pepper, sausage. Deacon accepted white pizza as pizza, which Buck did not. Deacon would eat square Neapolitan slices and the "tomato pie" that people from Philadelphia called pizza, which Buck did not.

In Buck's dream, he and Deacon were at Ray's on St. Mark's Place, and there was one pie in front of them, with gooey cheese. Buck looked up at Deacon, who was smoking a cigarette, and said, "Are you actually going to eat this?" And Deacon said, "No, man, I'm out." He crushed the cigarette in the crappy black, plastic ashtray, stood up, and walked out the door of Ray's with a jingle. Buck wanted to follow him, but in the weird way of dreams, he couldn't follow. Something kept him from rising from his chair. He stared at the pizza for a moment; then he reached for a piece and wound the mozzarella strings around the tip and stuck it in his mouth.

Buck woke up just as Laurel was climbing back into bed. She had shed her bathrobe and was deliciously naked.

"I heard someone at the front door," she said. "It was JP. He was looking for Angie, I guess."

Buck collected Laurel in his arms. There had been a

couple of times the night before when he had experienced pangs of guilt about making love to his best friend's ex-wife. Buck wondered if this most recent dream was meant to put his mind at ease. Deacon had left; Buck couldn't go with him. Buck should stay and live on, live as fully and happily as he could. That was what Deacon would have wanted him to do. If Buck was wrong and Deacon didn't want that....oh, well. Buck kissed Laurel's shoulder.

Laurel wanted to sleep a little longer, so Buck slipped down the stairs by himself to make coffee. The rest of the house was quiet—nobody could have been too enthusiastic about having another scene like the one last night; therefore, Buck was startled to find the coffee already made and Scarlett, wrapped up in a red kimono with a white stork embroidered on the back, sitting out on the back deck. She looked at peace as she took in the view—fog was just lifting off the moors—and Buck thought he'd better leave her be.

But then he realized that this was his chance.

He stepped out onto the deck. Scarlett turned, saw it was him, and gave him a small, relieved smile.

"Mind if I sit?" he asked.

She held out a showcase hand, indicating the seat next to hers.

Buck took a moment to sip his coffee. He wanted to cultivate the right tone of voice for this conversation—comforting but not indulgent.

"Scarlett," he said, "I need to talk to you about a few things."

She arched her eyebrows but did not speak. This was sort of like communicating with a mime.

"I've sifted through Deacon's affairs," Buck said. "The first thing you need to know is that in his will, Deacon left a third of this house to you, a third to Belinda, and a third to Laurel."

Scarlett didn't move, didn't speak. Dread gathered in Buck's gut. Did she understand?

"Do you understand what I'm telling you?" he asked.

Scarlett nodded.

"Now, that's a moot point, because this house is going into foreclosure at the beginning of next month." He checked his watch. "Eleven days from now. Deacon had three mortgages on it, and he'd let them all slide since January. At the end of December, he had an investor pull out of the restaurant—your uncle, as it happens—and Deacon replaced your uncle's money with a million dollars from his brokerage account. He owes over four hundred thousand dollars on this house, and the estate just doesn't have it. The estate doesn't have much of anything, other than a one-sixth interest in the Board Room. And he left a two-hundred-and-fifty-thousand-dollar life-insurance policy that listed you and Ellery as the beneficiaries. That quarter million is yours. It should be enough to get you through until you figure out something else." Buck stopped and reminded himself to breathe. He had done it. He had told her. Suddenly, he perked up. "I saw the canceled check made out to Skinny4Life. Is that something he invested in that might pay off?"

"No," Scarlett said. "The company folded. All I ended up with was one of the huge suitcases I brought with me, filled with product."

Buck closed his eyes. The last hope popped like a soap bubble.

Scarlett pivoted in her chair to face him, adjusting the kimono around her legs. She was barefoot, and her toenails were painted crimson. Red was her signature color—Buck understood this—but it always put him on edge. "I trapped him, Buck."

"He believed in you," Buck said. "He wanted you to find a career that would make you happy."

"That's not what I'm talking about," Scarlett said. "I mean, back in the beginning."

Buck waited. He wasn't sure which beginning she was talking about.

"We'd been engaged for a while," Scarlett said. "But when he started working on the restaurant, when he got all the investors in place, I felt him slipping away from me. He was going to break the engagement, I could tell. And I loved him so much. I had wanted him for so long. I had a terrific crush on him the entire time I worked for him and Belinda. He was so talented, so funny, so...irreverent. And sexy, with the tattoos and the brooding looks on the one hand, and the sweet daddy persona on the other. I used to catch him looking at me, and I wondered if there was any way I could steal him from Belinda. From *Belinda Rowe,* whom I had grown up *idolizing.* You can't imagine what a rush it was to fantasize that I could have what she had, that I could, in a way, become her. I had to keep him. And so...I threw my diaphragm in the trash. I got intentionally accidentally pregnant."

"Oh," Buck said.

"And he stayed."

"Of course he stayed," Buck said. "He loved you."

"Did he?"

"Yes," Buck said.

"He told me about the girl at the gentlemen's club, and he said he was going to stop drinking and stop the drugs, and I told him I didn't believe him. I told him it was too little, too late, and that he'd lost me and it was his own fault. I knew he was mad that Uncle Cal pulled his money out, and I knew he thought it was because Bo Tanner and I were having an affair and my uncle knew about it and didn't want to keep his money in Deacon's pockets. But I didn't realize that Deacon had replaced my uncle's money with his own money. He told me he found another investor, someone who shared his vision."

"Were you?" Buck asked. "Having an affair with Bo Tanner? *Are* you?"

Scarlett shrugged, and the kimono slipped to reveal her shoulder. Was that supposed to be an answer or a distraction tactic?

"It's so obvious in retrospect!" she said. "Deacon became obsessed, all of a sudden, with writing his cookbook, but it wasn't going well. You would have thought he was working on some insane deadline. He was pulling his hair out about it, losing sleep, telling the same story over and over again about how he nearly failed English in high school, but somehow he passed, somehow he squeaked by. And then this woman at my gym approached me with the Skinny4Life proposal, and I thought, *Deacon is never going to go for it.* But when I brought it up, he jumped on it. He invested a hundred thousand in January, thinking we would have double or triple that by the end of June. But that failed. Like everything else I've tried."

"Scarlett...," Buck said.

"I bled him dry, Buck," Scarlett said. "I treated him horribly. I *was* having an affair with Bo Tanner, and I'm pretty sure Deacon knew it, and that *did* contribute to my uncle pulling his money out. So really, all of this is my fault."

"You didn't know he was going to die," Buck said. "None of us did. You think there aren't things I would have done differently?"

"You didn't need to do anything differently," Scarlett said. "He loved you. You two were Oscar and Felix."

Buck smiled. "I would have watched him more closely. I

would have negotiated better on his behalf. I would have pushed for merchandising. Gosh, there are a lot of things I would have done differently. I would have made him quit smoking."

"At least he knew you loved him," Scarlett said. "I can't say the same."

"Scarlett, come on..."

"Buck," she said, and she gazed off in the distance. "I think I'd like another minute alone out here."

"He knew you loved him, Scarlett."

"Please," she said.

Buck stepped inside the screen door and nearly ran smack into...Joel Tersigni, who was standing in the kitchen, downing a bottle of orange Gatorade.

Joel Tersigni?

Buck opened his mouth to speak, but Joel stuck out his hand first and said, "Buck, man, how you doing? This weekend couldn't have been easy."

Buck shook Joel's hand and watched as Angie approached with a shy expression on her face. Then Buck remembered that Angie was involved with this creep. If Joel's wife caught wind of this, there would be death threats. Because when it rained, it poured! Deacon wouldn't have liked Angie being involved with Joel. Nope, not one bit.

"Good to see you," Buck said to Joel. It was a total lie. Buck couldn't believe Angie had invited him here.

"Good morning," Belinda sang out, coming down the stairs wearing a leopard-print sheath dress, looking as though she were about to go out shopping on Rodeo Drive. She eyed Joel Tersigni. "Who is *this?*"

"Mom," Angie said, "this is Joel. Joel, my mother, Belinda Rowe."

Joel took Belinda's hand reverently, as if she were the queen mother. "Pleasure to meet you, ma'am."

" 'Ma'am'?" Belinda said. "I'm hardly older than you are."

"He's only forty, Mom," Angie said.

"*Only* forty?" Belinda said. "That's fifteen years older than you."

"Fourteen," Angie said.

"She always was a hair splitter," Belinda said to Joel.

Laurel entered the kitchen, followed by Hayes.

"Who wants avocado toast?" Laurel asked.

"I'll have some," Hayes said. "I'm starving." He eyeballed Belinda. "I had a rough night."

Scarlett stepped in off the porch.

"Do you want avocado toast, Scarlett?" Laurel asked. "It's vegan."

"No, thank you," she said. "I have my breakfast upstairs."

And with that, she flew from the kitchen, her kimono waving out behind her like a red flag.

LAUREL

She would not let herself get swept away.

But it was tough.

Whether or not she had admitted it to herself, she was lonely, probably because her standards were so high—and, let's face it, St. Ann's Avenue in the Bronx wasn't a great place to meet eligible men. But John Buckley met her standards, every single one of them, and the best thing was, he already knew her. There would be a discovery period, she assumed—what she liked, what he liked, where those likes intersected—but they had thirty years of friendship to build on. What a relief! Laurel was fifty-four years old, and the biggest deterrent to starting a new relationship at her age was all the explaining that would have to be done with a new suitor.

She wouldn't let herself get swept away, however. If being married to Deacon Thorpe had taught her anything, it was that the people you cared about the most would hurt you the worst, no matter how pure their intentions at the beginning. Laurel would not fall too hard or too fast. True, Buck had spent eight hours making love to Laurel the night before—kissing her eyelids, rubbing her hip bone, tucking the sheet up over her shoulder when they finally tried for sleep—but that didn't mean she could trust him. The only person she could trust was herself.

When Buck went downstairs to make coffee, Laurel tried to go back to sleep, but she was too dialed up, and so she picked up her novel, *Euphoria*—"euphoria" had a brand-new meaning now—but she couldn't concentrate and barely made it through one chapter. She decided to make the very messy bed and then head downstairs to resume her role as den mother.

She was surprised to find nearly everyone in the house awake. Hayes trailed Laurel down the stairs, and in the kitchen they found Belinda, Buck, Angie, and a man Laurel immediately thought of as Tall, Dark, and Handsome, introduced to her as Joel Tersigni, the dining room manager at the Board Room. This, then, was Angie's boyfriend, the married boyfriend.

Laurel reached across the counter and said, "I'm Laurel Thorpe. Wife number one."

"I'm sorry for the intrusion," Joel said.

"No need to be sorry," Laurel said, but her smile felt forced. She had to admit, she had preferred it when it was just family. But now that there was a stranger among them, maybe everyone would be a little more careful before speaking.

There was a knock at the front door. Laurel strode down the hallway to see a cute young guy in a brown uniform standing on the porch. UPS. He was holding a package about the size of a bread box.

"Delivery for Laurel Thorpe?" he said.

"That's me," she said. She wondered what on earth it could be. Thinking about St. Ann's Avenue and her clients' rent made Laurel worry that her assistant, Sophie, had shipped her a stack of files. She took the package, signed the electronic receipt, and then it dawned on her: These were the ashes. This box, handed over like a sweater from J. Crew, was what was left of Deacon.

Naturally, Scarlett chose this moment to descend the stairs, holding a purple can of Skinny4Life. She had changed into white shorts and a skimpy red tank top that showed how painfully thin she was. With her shorn head, she looked like a teenage boy.

"What's that?" she asked.

While Laurel was thinking of what to say, Scarlett figured it out.

"Let me?" she said.

Laurel handed her the box, thinking, *Be careful with it!* Scarlett had been so uneven since her arrival that Laurel could easily imagine Scarlett flushing the ashes down the toilet.

But Scarlett balanced her can on the newel post of the banister and cradled the box like a days-old infant—then she kissed it, leaving behind red lip prints. She handed the box back to Laurel and headed to the kitchen.

She loved him, Laurel thought.

Laurel stared at the box. Scarlett's handing it back had seemed symbolic. Laurel would be Deacon's keeper in the end, it seemed.

Joel Tersigni came down the stairs wearing a pair of green and black board shorts.

"Going for a swim?" Laurel asked.

"In a minute," Joel said. "I want to catch up with Scarlett. Pay my respects."

"Of course," Laurel said. Joel seemed cordial enough, maybe a bit practiced, maybe a bit insincere in the manner of Eddie Haskell, or maybe Laurel was just looking for flaws. It was Joel's job to be smooth and polished. Laurel could see how Angie would have fallen for the guy; he seemed like a professional heartbreaker.

All men cheat. That what they do.

Laurel took the opportunity to go upstairs and find Angie and Hayes. Angie was in her room, straightening up, and Hayes was sitting on the side of his bed, staring at his hands.

"Come into my room," Laurel said. "Both of you."

They obediently followed Laurel into her room, where she shut the door. She held out the box. "The ashes came."

"Oh," Hayes said, backing up as if she were holding a box of rattlesnakes. "Whoa."

Laurel used a pen from the nightstand to slice open the top of the box. There were several layers of bubble wrap to cut through, but swaddled in the center was a plastic urn about the size of a pineapple.

Plastic? Laurel thought. She had heard the word "urn" and thought it would be ceramic or, because Deacon was a chef, perhaps cast iron. She smiled, thinking of Deacon's ashes being held in a Le Creuset urn; that would have been fitting.

Angie lifted the urn, opened it, peered inside. "Is this happening?" she said. She seemed to genuinely be asking. "Every time I think I've wrapped my mind around it, it hits me again like it's the first time. He's dead." Angie shook the urn. "This is him."

Laurel thought back to the very first time she had set eyes on Deacon Thorpe. He had always believed it was at lunch in the cafeteria, but the truth was, Laurel had seen Deacon first thing that morning, getting off the school bus. Word had gone around among the girls of Laurel's class that there was a new boy coming, a boy from New York City, and Laurel had held out hope for someone interesting. When she'd seen Deacon, her heart had broken a little. Even way back then, she had had a tender spot for the marginalized. She had then sought him out at lunch, assuming he would be eating alone.

She had wanted, so badly, to save him.

ANGIE

You promised to take me for a swim," Ellery said. She stood in a pink lamé bikini in the door of Angie's bedroom, where Angie was starting to straighten up so that she could eventually pack. At the same time, she was trying to collect her wits. The ashes had messed with her head.

"I will," Angie said.

"I want to go now," Ellery said.

"I hate to say this," Angie said, "but you sound like a brat. And we both know you're not a brat. Who's the only brat in this family?"

"Hayes," Ellery said.

Angie smiled and held out her arms. "Come here."

Ellery hugged Angie, and Angie inhaled the sweet smell of her hair, which was slipping out of its braids.

Angie had initially resented Ellery's existence in the world, much as she resented Mary and Laura's presence. Angie didn't understand why both of her parents had to go and have other children. Wasn't Angie enough? Angie's relationship with Mary and Laura was pretty much nonexistent; she had last seen them a year and a half earlier, at Thanksgiving, and her preeminent emotion then had been bemusement. Both girls looked exactly like Bob, and they were quiet and horsey like Bob; it was as if Belinda had never been part of the equation. But because Ellery lived in New York, and because Deacon had encouraged Angie to make an effort to spend time with her sister, Angie and Ellery now had a close relationship. Angie was seventeen years older, so there were times when Angie felt like Ellery's mother or her aunt instead of her sister.

Angie had expected Ellery to cry and carry on about Deacon's death far more than she had, but what Angie realized was that nine-year-old children were too young to process the concept of "gone forever." Ellery and Scarlett had been away in Savannah for nearly two months; probably, in some part of her imagination, Ellery believed that when she finally got back to New York and the apartment on Hudson Street, Deacon would be there.

"Let's go get Joel," Angie said. "He'll want to swim, too."

"I didn't know Joel was coming here," Ellery said.
"No, me neither," Angie said.

When Angie and Ellery went out on the deck, Angie found Joel standing behind Scarlett's chair, massaging her shoulders. Scarlett lolled her head back and groaned with delight, saying, "Oh God, don't stop. That feels *so good.*"

Angie was hit by a wave of disgusting, ugly jealousy, the likes of which she had never experienced, even when thinking about Joel with Dory.

"You have magic hands," Scarlett said. "I didn't realize how tight I was."

"You've been through a lot," Joel said. He continued to knead her shoulders and upper arms. "You're in knots." He took a deep inhalation. "Are you wearing Chanel, by any chance? That is my favorite scent on a woman."

"We're ready to go swimming!" Angie said.

Scarlett's eyes popped open. "Baby, you look *edible* in that bikini. Honestly, I could eat you!"

Angie rolled her eyes. Scarlett constantly announced how *edible* Ellery looked, as though Ellery were a cookie, or a muffin, which was all tied in with her deep-seated fear of and desire for food—or so Angie and Deacon had surmised on one of their Tuesday-night dinners.

"Joel?" Angie said. "Are you coming with us?"

"Can you *believe* Joel is here?" Scarlett said. Years in New York had sanded away Scarlett's Southern drawl, but when she wanted something, she turned it on heavy and sweet, just like her namesake from *Gone with the Wind.* "Here" became "he-ah." Angie watched a dopey expression cross Joel's face.

Yes, I can believe it, Angie nearly said. *Joel is my boyfriend.*

But Angie wasn't confident enough to make this announcement. She wasn't even sure it was true. She had never had the freedom to call Joel her boyfriend. And now that he was free of Dory, Angie realized, he could go after any woman he wanted. Angie might have been good for him while he was attached, but what if he now found someone more desirable? What if he bided his time, then moved in on Deacon Thorpe's new widow, Scarlett Oliver? Scarlett obviously had no idea why Joel had turned up. Possibly she believed he had come solely to comfort her.

"Are we going swimming or not?" Angie asked. Her voice was harsher than she'd intended. If there was a brat in the family, it was now her. But really, the time had come for Joel to step up. If he had come to Nantucket because he loved her, she wanted him to say it. If he had shown up here because he had nowhere else to go, then he could go pound. She thought these words with bitterness, just like the tough girl everyone believed her to be, but the truth was, she wasn't equipped to deal with this situation at all.

"I'm going to stay here with Scarlett," Joel said.

Angie blinked, thinking she had misheard.

"Thank you," Scarlett said. "I could use a friend right now."

"So you're not coming with us?" Angie said.

Joel smiled at Angie patiently, as if she were a slow student. "I'm going to stay here with Scarlett."

"But you came here to be with me, right?" Angie said. "You came here because we've been lovers for six months."

"Angie," Joel said. He nodded toward Ellery, and Angie felt an immediate sense of shame. The girl had lost her father and didn't need the extra baggage of hearing about her sister's sex life. Joel's hands moved down Scarlett's back, and she moaned; she was so delirious with his touch that she didn't seem to have heard Angie's words.

"Can *we* go?" Ellery asked, tugging on Angie's arm. "You and me?"

"Thanks for taking Ellery," Scarlett said, her eyes closed and her head falling forward on her neck. "I really appreciate it."

"I'm sure you do," Angie said, with as much venom as she could muster. "Enjoy that back rub." She turned and all but lifted Ellery off the ground in her attempt to get away.

"See?" she heard Scarlett say. "They all hate me. I think even Angie hates me."

As they walked down the driveway, Ellery said, "Why are you crying?"

Angie wiped at her tears. She *hated* Joel Tersigni! Hated him!

"Daddy is dead," Angie said. She stopped and crouched down so that she could look Ellery in the eye. Ellery had green eyes, like Scarlett, pretty and clear, with dark rings around the irises. Her nose was dusted with freckles. She was a pretty girl—not beautiful, but cute and pretty, and Angie was glad for this. "You understand, right? Daddy is dead, and he isn't coming back."

Ellery nodded solemnly, and her eyes filled with tears. Angie felt like a monster. Who talked this way to a nine-year-old child? She, Angie, was hurting, and she wanted Ellery to hurt as well. Angie gathered Ellery up in her arms. "I'm sorry," she said. "I'm sorry, baby."

Ellery patted Angie on the back, as if she was the one who needed comforting. "It's okay, Buddy," Ellery said. "It's not your fault."

Intermezzo:
Deacon and Scarlett, Part II

Scarlett is having an affair, and Deacon can't blame her. They have nothing in common except for Ellery. Deacon works all the time, and when he's not actually running the kitchen, he's developing recipes for his cookbook. Tuesday nights, when the restaurant is closed, he eats dinner with Angie because Scarlett doesn't eat dinner, ever. Lately, on Tuesday nights, Scarlett has gotten a sitter and "gone out with the girls." But then, at some point, Deacon realizes that she's not going out with the girls; she's going out with Bo Tanner. Bo, the old beau.

The way Deacon discovers this is an old story. He's looking for tweezers because he has a piece of cucumber skin jammed up his thumbnail, and his thumb has grown hot and is starting to throb. Scarlett keeps tweezers in her nightstand drawer. Also in Scarlett's nightstand drawer is a stack of notes, letters, and cards from Bo Tanner, the last one dated three days earlier.

Deacon sighs deeply and looks up at the ceiling. He is happy, in a way, that he didn't come across emails or text messages. Letters seem old-fashioned; they seem Southern and genteel. They seem sincere, and, although he doesn't sit down and read them through, the glimpses he does catch tell him the story. Bo loves her, he has always loved her; he should never have married Anne Carter. The only reason he did was because Scarlett came north while Anne Carter stayed behind.

He puts the letters back. He finds a pair of tweezers in the bathroom.

* * *

Six weeks later, Scarlett starts crying at the drop of a hat, and when Deacon asks what's wrong, she says she has her period and she's gained three pounds. Deacon suspects Bo has broken things off, but he doesn't ask.

It's December 21, the night after the restaurant's holiday party, and Scarlett's uncle, the Honorable Calhoun Oliver, is coming to the restaurant with his wife, Abigail, and Scarlett. Judge Oliver is one of the six investors in the restaurant, although he has never eaten there—mostly because he doesn't like to travel north of the Mason-Dixon Line. But Abigail has long wanted to see New York at Christmastime—the Rockettes, the windows at Bergdorf's—and, since the judge isn't getting any younger, they decide to make the trip.

Deacon can sense things going wrong before the judge even arrives. First of all, his entire staff is hungover, tired, cranky, irritable, and half a step off. Lily, who is normally Deacon's nomination for Best Server in the Five Boroughs, had been dancing on the bar until five that morning, and she dozes off as Deacon gives them the night's specials, then naps all through staff meal. Joel Tersigni has dark circles under his eyes, and Deacon considers sending both him and Lily home, but there isn't time for last-minute changes.

That's it, he thinks. They will never have another holiday party.

When the judge arrives, Joel comes rushing back to the kitchen. They have an extra guest in their party, and Joel is caught in a quandary. He can either squeeze the four of them at a table meant for three, or he can put them at a four-top in

Siberia, the table that is treated to a frigid blast of air every time the front door opens.

"There's nowhere else?" Deacon asks.

"Nowhere," Joel says.

"Put them in Siberia," Deacon says. With nine courses and wine pairings, they'll never fit at the three-top. "Give them each two cashmere throws. Who's the extra guest?"

Joel shrugs. "Some guy."

Deacon comes out to greet the table just after they've received their first amuse-bouche: a simple Nantucket bay scallop poached in lime juice and sprinkled with sea salt. The judge's scallop sits untouched, as does Scarlett's. Deacon notices this before he takes stock of the fourth guest. "Some guy" is a tall, sandy-haired man in a navy blazer and an old-school blue and red striped rep tie.

"Greetings, all!" Deacon says.

The judge stands. "Chef Thorpe," he says. "You remember my wife, Abigail. And I'd like to introduce you to my attorney, Robert Tanner."

The attorney, Robert Tanner, stands. He and Deacon shake hands. "Call me Bo," he says.

Deacon turns to look at Scarlett. Her head is bowed over her uneaten scallop as if she's saying a prayer.

Deacon goes back to the kitchen and shuts himself in his office. He can't believe the rage that consumes him. He knew about Bo Tanner, and he made the adult decision to ignore it and let it run its course. Bo Tanner is married;

he's wearing a ring. And Scarlett is married. Scarlett has also proved to be flighty in her adult life. She can't stick with anything for more than a few months; as soon as a project or interest loses its shine, she's on to the next thing. Hence, it stands to reason, she'll lose interest in Bo.

Except that...she's loved him since she was in high school. Or maybe even before that; Deacon can't remember. This is a love that will haunt her forever. Deacon should just let her go. He considers sending her a text right that second that says *I want a divorce.* It pains him to think of the relief and the joy that such a text would bring her. It pains him to contemplate failing at marriage a third time.

There have been critical junctures in Deacon's life when he has needed his father: when Hayes was born, when he was about to leave Laurel, when he messed up so egregiously on *Letterman*...and right now. Deacon has toyed ten thousand times with hiring a private investigator to find Jack Thorpe. He'll do it tomorrow, he decides. He doesn't care how much it costs. He wants to know what's become of his father.

In the meantime, Deacon takes a bottle of Jameson out of his bottom desk drawer and pours himself a shot. He can't believe Scarlett brought her lover into *his restaurant!* It's beyond the pale. It breaks every code of human decency. Deacon doesn't care if the judge insisted; Scarlett should have put a stop to it somehow.

Harv knocks, Deacon doesn't respond.

Angie knocks, Deacon doesn't respond.

Lily knocks, then says through the door, "The judge's table refused the sexy scorched-octopus course, Chef. He took offense at the name."

Deacon pours another shot.

* * *

When Deacon goes back out to the dining room, he's drunk. It's the middle of course six, the salmon, and Scarlett's food is uneaten on her plate. Fury rises in Deacon's throat.

How does it look when even the chef's wife won't eat the food? Then he remembers that Scarlett is doing a juice cleanse. He had asked her that morning to abandon the cleanse, for him. Who in their right mind starts a juice cleanse four days before Christmas?

He bares his teeth to the table. The judge has hardly touched his food. Only Abigail and Bo Tanner are enthusiastically eating.

"How is everything?" Deacon asks.

The judge clears his throat to speak, but Deacon doesn't want to hear it. The judge is a long-winded, pompous ass who doesn't appreciate anything Deacon is trying to do on the plate.

Deacon sidles up behind Bo Tanner and whispers in his ear, "Stay the hell away from my wife."

"Deacon," Scarlett hisses. "You're being rude."

Deacon straightens up. "Enjoy your food," he says. He marches back to the kitchen and passes Angie and Joel Tersigni, standing too close together in front of the walk-in fridge.

"Get back to work!" Deacon shouts at them. He goes into his office and locks the door.

Joel and Angie? he thinks. Over his dead body.

He pours another shot.

The next day, the judge calls Deacon and asks for his initial investment of a million dollars back. Deacon is hungover and contrite. He apologizes for his behavior. "Let me make it up to you tonight, Your Honor. I promise the meal of a lifetime." Every restaurant has an off night, he says. The judge has to understand: the holidays are a fraught time for everyone.

The judge does not understand. Deacon will return his money, as per the clause in the investment contract. The judge had been the last investor Deacon needed in order to start construction nine years earlier, and in his eagerness, he granted the judge a legal rip cord, a get-out-of-jail-free card, and the judge wants to use it now—otherwise, Deacon will be hearing from the judge's counsel, Bo Tanner.

"Yes, sir," Deacon says.

Deacon spends the week between Christmas and New Year's calling every regular diner he knows in hopes that one of them will want to invest in the restaurant. But these guys are savvy; they know how much the restaurant costs to run and that they likely will never see a return on that investment.

Deacon needs to find someone who cares about the restaurant for the restaurant's sake. The only person he can think of is himself. He wires a million dollars from his personal account to the restaurant coffers. He'll deal with the ramifications later.

He hires a private investigator named Lyle Phelan, a former NYPD detective. Lyle Phelan charges a flat fee of $30,000 for missing persons, no matter how long the search takes. He will find Jack Thorpe, he tells Deacon. Guaranteed. Detective

Phelan reminds Deacon of Officer Murphy, who came to their apartment in Stuy Town so long ago. Deacon writes the check.

In the ensuing months, Deacon's financial situation goes straight downhill. He doesn't have a royalty check due until August, so he works on getting a proposal together for his cookbook. Buck has put him in touch with a literary agent named Kim Witherspoon, who is eagerly awaiting a submission. *I'm thinking part cookbook, part memoir,* she says. *The world is dying to know about your personal life.* She sees a bidding war in his future and an advance in the mid six figures.

Envelopes come from Nantucket Bank, but Deacon doesn't open them. He knows the news isn't good. Notices come from the management of his building, as he's behind on the rent. The building's business manager, Debi, is a huge fan of Deacon's, and he offers her dinner for two at the Board Room, on the house, if she will give him another month's leeway. He can't ignore his kids, however. He writes a check to Hayes's co-op board and pays the second half of Ellery's school tuition.

He's going under. By the time his royalty payments come, he will have spent the check three times over. The notes for his cookbook aren't anything he's willing to show anybody. Writing is hard! The world is dying to know about his personal life, but Deacon has serious reservations about discussing it. He'll need Belinda to sign a disclaimer and she will never agree to it. Writing is really hard! He nearly failed English in high school. The notes sit in a red folder on top of his desk at work, along with the envelopes from Nantucket

Bank. They are too awful now for Deacon to even look at, so he puts the envelopes away in a drawer and sends the red folder to Kim Witherspoon. Can she work with this?

Probably not, she says. He's sent her nothing except a bunch of disjointed notes and the recipe for the clams casino dip, which has been published and reprinted nearly a dozen times over the past decade.

Maybe you should hire a writer, she says. *Lots of people do it.*

But that costs money he doesn't have. He should just give the people what they want: the details of his love life, starting way back in the Dobbs Ferry High School cafeteria.

No, he can't. He'll stick to food.

Scarlett has been well behaved since the fiasco at dinner. Deacon checks her nightstand table: all the letters, notes, and cards have been removed, and no new ones appear. Scarlett notices him slaving over his cookbook, and she asks, *Why the rush?* He tells her they're a little strapped for cash and the cookbook will likely bring in a nice advance.

Scarlett hears "strapped for cash" and comes to him with a proposal for a diet-supplement company called Skinny-4Life. The prospectus suggests investors will triple their money in 90 to 120 days.

"Do we want to do this?" Scarlett asks. She sounds as though she's expecting him to say no, but he is so desperate at this point that he needs a miracle, and who's to say Skinny-4Life isn't that miracle? Scarlett has been drinking the stuff for weeks, and she is, in fact, very, very skinny. Deacon writes a check for a hundred thousand dollars, the last of his cash. Scarlett is elated! While he's in a good mood, she asks if she can spend eight thousand dollars to go to the Omega Institute in Rhinebeck, New York, for a week of silent retreat in April. Deacon says yes and tells her to put the charge on his American Express.

On the ides of March, Lyle Phelan appears at the front door of the restaurant. Joel Tersigni shows him back to Deacon's office.

Detective Phelan drops a sheaf of papers on Deacon's desk. Jack Thorpe was living in Flanders, New York, working as a cook at a Denny's. He rented a room, kept to himself, drank at a bar called the Alibi, and died in a one-man car crash on October 11, 1997.

"Looks like he had a heart attack behind the wheel," Detective Phelan says. "I'm sorry I couldn't give you better news."

Deacon nods. Flanders, New York, is on Long Island. *He was so close,* Deacon thinks. *So close all those years.* Deacon shows Detective Phelan to the door of the restaurant; then he goes back in his office, locks the door. *One perfect day with my son. That's not too much to ask, is it?* Deacon starts to cry.

Scarlett has been on her silent retreat for a day and a half when Deacon gets a funny feeling. Participants are not allowed to use their cell phones, so he can't call her. He calls the office of the Omega Institute and says, "I'd like to leave a message for my wife, Scarlett Oliver. It's urgent."

"Who?" the receptionist says. She tells him there is no Scarlett Oliver registered at the institute for that week.

"How about Scarlett Thorpe?" he asks. He's grasping at straws: Scarlett rarely uses that name.

"No, I'm sorry," the receptionist says.

Scarlett has bought herself a week away without a phone. Where has Bo Tanner taken her? To a far-flung Caribbean island? Deacon remembers his time in St. John with Laurel. *What goes around, comes around,* he thinks. Scarlett isn't doing anything that Deacon himself hasn't done.

The next day, Deacon gets a call from a number he doesn't recognize, and, thinking it's Scarlett, he answers it.

It's Julie from Nantucket Bank, whom Deacon has always thought of as Supremely Capable Julie. She's a fan of Deacon the chef and Deacon the person, and he knows the only reason the house hasn't been foreclosed on yet is because of her.

She says, "You're running out of time, Deacon. The wolves are at the door."

That afternoon, a Tuesday—the restaurant is closed—Deacon starts drinking at his apartment at noon. He leaves his apartment and goes to the only place he feels he can be anonymous: Times Square. He drinks at TGI Friday's, then at Olive Garden. This, he thinks, is rock bottom. At Olive Garden, his credit card is declined, so he pays cash, then walks over to the Board Room, unlocks the door, and grabs a bottle of Jameson from behind the bar. Dr. Disibio will notice right away—he runs an impeccably tight ship—so Deacon leaves an IOU scribbled on a cocktail napkin. From the restaurant, he walks west and ends up at an establishment called Skirtz. He meets a dancer named Taryn, who recognizes Deacon from his TV show. Deacon asks if she has a car. *Yes,* she says, *in the garage across the street.* Deacon asks if he can use it. *You can come with me,* he says. *We'll go to Nantucket.*

Deacon wakes up in Buck's apartment, on the unforgiving leather sofa. Deacon's first thought is that Buck's decorator is a sadist. His second thought is a confused jumble of broken promises and unfulfilled obligations. He has forgotten something—but what?

He has forgotten to pick up Ellery from school. Buck painted a pretty grim picture of how sad and cold Ellery was when he went to fetch her in a taxi, and an even grimmer picture of that bitch Madame Giroux, with her stern French disapproval. Deacon's imagination, however, is far crueler. He can see Ellery with her heavy, dark hair—hair he has brushed since she was very small—swept back in the required navy headband. He can see her plaid uniform skirt, her crisp, white blouse with the Peter Pan collar underneath her navy cardigan. Ellery hates her uniform because, even at nine years old, she has developed fashion sense, and the sameness with the other girls is an identity crusher. Scarlett adores the uniform and the school; both are reminiscent of *Madeline,* a book she read as a child.

Ellery would have had her backpack loaded with her assignments and library books. She would have been in the front courtyard playing tag or jacks with the other girls. One by one, the mothers would have arrived—Eleanor Rigby, Proud Mary, Runaround Sue (Deacon has spent the past four years coming up with rock-and-roll nicknames for each one)—and bringing up the rear was the mother Deacon thought of as Layla. Layla was a disheveled mess—depressed for certain and possibly also an addict—but she had a sleepy beauty that Deacon, perhaps alone, appreciated. On occasion, he beat Layla to the courtyard by only a moment or two, half a block.

Yesterday, Ellery would have seen Layla arrive to pick up her daughter, and the realization would have hit her: Deacon wasn't coming.

The expression Deacon imagines on his daughter's face—beyond dejection, beyond melancholy—is what vaporizes Deacon's soul.

There is no excuse for what happened. Scarlett calls in from "the Omega Institute in Rhinebeck" and gives him holy hell. She is home in New York the very next day, packing her things, pulling Ellery out of school, telling Deacon she's leaving for good.

He could tell her he knows she wasn't in Rhinebeck. He could tell her he knows all about Bo Tanner. But what would that do, other than further traumatize Ellery?

He will stop drinking, he tells Scarlett. And drugs, all drugs.

I don't believe you, Scarlett says.

I'm done, Deacon says.

I don't care, Scarlett says. *I'm sorry, Deacon. I simply don't care.*

BELINDA

She only had to last one more day without Mary and Laura, but something about being around Ellery made being without her daughters nearly unbearable, and so Belinda put on Laurel's flip-flops and made the trek to the end of the driveway. Calling Bob was useless; it was Monday morning, so he would be at his weekly meeting with Dr. Mary Ellen Plume, the large-animal vet. Belinda would have to call the house.

Mrs. Greene answered on the first ring. She was reliable that way, the last person in America who believed in landlines.

"Good morning, Percil residence."

"Mrs. Greene, good morning," Belinda said. She wandered down the road toward the beach club, hoping the signal would grow stronger. "I was hoping to talk to the girls."

"Oh goodness," Mrs. Greene said. "They've been out on the trails since the sun came up."

"Shoot," Belinda said. "Are they with Stella?"

"Yes, and Mr. Percil," Mrs. Greene said.

"Bob went along?" Belinda said. "I'm sorry, are you telling me Bob went on the trail ride this morning with Stella and the girls?"

"That's what I'm telling you."

"I see," Belinda said. "Has Stella been staying at the house since I've been gone?"

"That I wouldn't know of course," Mrs. Greene said. "All I can say for certain is, she's here when I leave at eight o'clock in the evening and here when I arrive at seven in the morning."

Belinda bit her tongue. *Is she staying in my room?* she wanted to ask. *Is she sleeping in my bed?*

"Mrs. Greene?" Belinda said. "Is there anything else I should know?"

"If I were you," Mrs. Greene said, "I would get home."

"I can't possibly leave until tomorrow," Belinda said. "We're spreading Deacon's ashes this evening."

Mrs. Greene was respectfully silent at this, and Belinda harkened back to a time when the girls were little—Mary a toddler and Laura an infant. It had been nap time, which was when Belinda practiced her lines, and she had wandered into the kitchen to get some of Mrs. Greene's banana pudding, script in hand. Mrs. Greene had been watching TV, and it took only a second for Belinda to recognize Deacon's voice. Mrs. Greene was rapt with attention, watching *Pitchfork*. Deacon had been making the clams casino dip; it was the classic episode.

As Belinda opened the fridge, she said, "Have you invited my ex-husband into our kitchen, Mrs. Greene?"

Mrs. Greene had turned to Belinda, and in a softer, more sincere voice than usual, she said, "What is he like?"

"Who, Deacon?" Belinda said.

Mrs. Greene gave a schoolmarm nod.

Belinda could have issued any number of answers. *Deacon is sweet, he's charming, he's a wonderful father, he's great in bed.* But Mrs. Greene could probably have deduced those things on her own.

"He's broken," Belinda said. "He was broken when I met him, but I didn't help."

Now, Mrs. Greene said, "I'm sure that will be very difficult for you."

"Thank you, Mrs. Greene," Belinda said. "For everything."

"Indeed," Mrs. Greene said, and she hung up.

Oh, how Belinda wanted to believe that Bob had gone on the trail ride because he wanted to spend quality time with the girls. But Belinda knew better. It was Stella, with the tits and the ass and the accent.

Belinda trudged back to the house; then she slipped upstairs to Clara's room, where she popped an Ativan. She wasn't that much better in the controlled-substance department than Hayes.

Would she have to divorce Bob? The notion was sad and exhausting.

The Ativan put Belinda to sleep. There was something nearly hedonistic about napping on a summer afternoon with the windows open, the sea breeze blowing the filmy white curtains, the sound of people coming and going downstairs, Angie's voice floating up, Buck's, Laurel's. Today was their last day. Belinda would miss Angie desperately. And Buck and Laurel, too, she realized, and Hayes and Ellery.

And Deacon, of course.

Belinda awoke at four o'clock, when she heard footsteps on the stairs and a general busy-bee atmosphere pervading the house like an impending storm. Was something happening? Then Belinda heard the word "boat," and she realized it was time to go out on the harbor and spread Deacon's ashes.

Boat. Harbor.

Belinda shook two more Ativan from the bottle into her palm and threw them back. She had known from the get-go that the plan was to spread Deacon's ashes in Nantucket Sound, but somehow she had ignored the fact that she, Belinda Rowe, would have to get in a boat.

Terror seized her. It was like asking someone afraid of heights to stand on a diving board at the top of the Burj

Khalifa and bounce. She wouldn't make it. She couldn't go. She would go downstairs and break the news: she was staying home. She would offer to watch Ellery. Should a nine-year-old child really be asked to spread her father's ashes?

Belinda sat on the edge of the bed, practicing her yoga breathing.

"Mom!" Angie yelled from the bottom of the stairs. "Let's go! We're leaving!"

She had meant to renege, offer her regrets, to say, *I'm sorry, but there's just no way I'm getting in a boat.* But for some reason, maybe the quieting effect of the Ativan, she allowed herself to be herded forward like a sheep. The ranger, JP, had arrived in his silver Jeep; he would drive half of them to the harbor, and Buck would drive the rest. Laurel climbed in with Buck, of course, and then Scarlett and Ellery climbed in the back.

Joel Tersigni said, "Move over. I'll go with you guys." He climbed in next to Scarlett.

Belinda caught the poisonous look that Angie gave Joel.

"We'll go with you!" Belinda said brightly to the ranger.

The ranger, too, was watching Angie. "You okay?" he asked her.

She shrugged and started to climb in the back of JP's Jeep, but Belinda said, "No, no, darling. Hayes and I will sit in the back. You get up front."

Hayes touched his face, as if making sure it was still there. He gallantly helped Belinda into the back of the Jeep, then smiled at her and said, "And how are you?"

She studied him. High or straight? It was impossible to tell. High pretending to be straight, most likely, but Belinda was grateful for his normalcy and that he didn't seem to be holding her midnight visit against her. But he did remember that she knew his secret, right?

"Never better," she said.

She had expected a garden-variety powerboat, white and utilitarian, but the boat JP steered toward the dock was an antique wooden launch with a hull the color of burnt honey. It was sleek and breathtaking and reminiscent of one of Bob's Arabian horses. Even Belinda, who could write what she knew about boats on her thumbnail and still have room for the Lord's Prayer, could tell this one was special.

Buck whistled.

"Her name is the *Lena Marie*," JP said. "She's a lapstrake mahogany harbor launch and was custom built in Denmark in 1950. She belonged to my grandfather."

"What a beaut," Buck said.

The boat was elegant. If Belinda was going to get into a boat—and she still hadn't made a final decision—it would be this boat. An American flag waved off the back.

"JP, this is more than I ever could have hoped for," Laurel said. "Thank you."

Thank you, *Laurel, our spokesperson,* Belinda thought. She stole a quick glance at Scarlett to see what Scarlett thought about Laurel taking the number-one pole position or about Laurel clenching the urn of Deacon's ashes as if it contained her own beating heart. Scarlett was holding on to Ellery with one hand and on to Joel Tersigni's impressive forearm with her other hand.

"Yes, *thank* you," Scarlett echoed. She let go of Joel and offered JP her hand. "I'm Scarlett Oliver, Deacon's widow."

JP nodded. "Nice to meet you. I'm sorry for your loss. Deacon was a good friend of mine."

"And this is our daughter, Ellery," Scarlett said, ushering Ellery forward.

"What do you say, Ellery?" JP said. "Want to help me drive the boat?"

"Yes!" Ellery said. She was in another party dress, this one a navy scoop-neck number with a handkerchief hem.

"Excellent!" JP said. "The person who assists the captain is called the first mate."

Belinda smiled. She should have known the ranger would be good with children.

"I'm Joel Tersigni," Joel said, stepping forward to shake JP's hand. "I manage Deacon's restaurant in Manhattan."

"The dining room," Angie said. "You manage the dining room, not the restaurant."

Joel ignored Angie's comment and stepped off the dock, into the boat, which Belinda thought was presumptuous. There should be some sort of hierarchy for who boarded first, and it certainly shouldn't be Joel. However, he stood at the side and reached for Scarlett's hand, then he lifted Ellery up and in. The boat had a horseshoe of seating around the front and two bench seats, one midboat and one in the back by the motor, which was where JP sat. Joel settled with Scarlett and Ellery on the middle seat, as though they were a family unit.

What is going on *here?* Belinda wondered. She was appalled at how this Joel person was ignoring Angie. Had they had a fight? Or was Joel simply abandoning Angie for Scarlett the way he had abandoned his wife for Angie? Once a cheater, always a cheater—look at Bob Percil. Belinda said, "Joel, I would really like to sit next to Scarlett, if you don't mind."

"Mother," Angie said.

"Scarlett and I haven't had a chance to catch up," Belinda said. She took the ranger's hand and stepped gingerly down into the boat. It rocked under her, and she wondered if she was going to do the predictable thing and faint, or vomit. But she felt spurred on by indignation. Joel Tersigni might be a heartbreaker, but he wasn't going to humiliate Angie in full view of her family. Belinda simply would not have it. She lorded her five-foot-two frame over Joel until he got up and with obvious reluctance gave Belinda his seat.

Laurel sat with Buck along the horseshoe, and Joel sat on the other side of Buck. Hayes stood in the front of the boat like some kind of damaged figurehead. Angie ended up sitting next to Ellery, who was next to JP.

"Are we all ready?" JP asked.

Belinda clenched the bench beneath her with one hand and the side of the boat with the other. The harbor was flat, and they cut smoothly through the water. The sun was hitting that place in the sky where it ceased to be hot and was merely warm as it cast a golden glow on the surface of the water and on the sails of the other boats. What did Deacon used to call it? The golden hour.

Sailors manning other boats waved and called out to the *Lena Marie.*

"She's beautiful!" one man called out. "And so are her passengers!"

Belinda smiled, though it was wrong to assume they were speaking of her when Scarlett, Laurel, Angie, and sweet Ellery were all on the boat. And Buck, wearing a pink shirt and a pair of shorts embroidered with whales. He had certainly bought into the whole New England summertime fashion disaster.

JP maneuvered around the other sailboats and power yachts. He headed toward Brant Point Lighthouse. Hayes sat down next to his mother and leaned his head on her shoulder. Laurel clutched the urn to her midsection and put her arm around her son. Belinda closed her eyes and imagined herself on dry land.

Belinda had had no intention of "catching up" with Scarlett, or of even speaking to her. But almost involuntarily, she said, "How far out do you think we'll go?"

Scarlett didn't answer. When Belinda looked at her, her lips were set in a grim line.

"Oh, come on, Scarlett," Belinda said.

"Come on, what?" she said.

"We need to get past our past," Belinda said. "You, Laurel, and I are all in the same boat." She laughed at her own joke. "Ha! We are literally *in the same boat.* We're scattering the ashes of the man all of us were married to. Not just you, my dear. All of us."

"I had a child with him," Scarlett said.

"So did I!" Belinda said.

Scarlett sniffed. "That's not the same."

The breeze was blowing from the back of the boat, so it wasn't likely that Angie was overhearing any of this exchange, but still, Belinda was... well, "furious" and "indignant" didn't begin to cover it. She was egregiously offended. She leaned into Scarlett's shoulder and lowered her voice. To everyone else, they probably looked like a couple of women sharing a trusted confidence.

"If you're trying to tell me that Angie is any less Deacon's child because she was adopted..." Belinda trailed off. "Or, even worse, because she's *black and adopted,* then you are revealing just how ugly you are on the inside, Scarlett. Maybe I should have been more wary when I interviewed you in the first place."

"I love Angie," Scarlett said. "And I was good to her all

those years you left her in my care. I practically raised her. Deacon and I raised her like a husband and wife."

Belinda clenched the seat beneath her so hard, she felt the nail on her middle finger snap, but she was too afraid of letting go to inspect the damage. They were out of the harbor now, puttering around the stone jetty.

"The boat isn't really built for this," Belinda heard JP say to Angie, behind her. "But your dad wanted his ashes scattered in Nantucket Sound, so that's where we'll go. Besides, it's a flat night."

A *flat* night? The boat was now a Mexican jumping bean every time they hit a wave. Would it get any worse? Belinda imagined the front of the boat rising so high that the whole thing flipped over, dumping all of them in the drink.

Drink. When this was over, Belinda was going to have a big, fat glass of wine. Or, better still, a margarita.

All of these thoughts served to distract her from Scarlett's last statement—but only for a matter of seconds.

"I didn't leave my daughter for you to raise," Belinda said. "You were her nanny. You watched her while I was working."

"You were never around," Scarlett said. "Ever."

"And when you say that you and Deacon raised her as a 'married couple,' what does *that* mean? Were you sleeping with Deacon back then, Scarlett? I know now that it was Laurel he took to St. John, but that doesn't mean you and he weren't carrying on years before that. When I was in Scotland? When I was in Vietnam?"

"We were not," Scarlett said. "But when I reconnected with him, he admitted to me that he fantasized about me all the time. So it's probably safe to say, when he was making love to you all those years, he was thinking about me. Pretending you were me."

Belinda wanted to slap her. She wanted to throttle her.

"How dare you say that to me, Scarlett. How dare you." Belinda stood up. She had to get away—but she was trapped. Belinda made her way to the back of the boat, where she lost her thoughts in the drone of the motor and the sharp smell of diesel fuel. The Ativan made her hazy and mixed up; she shouldn't have taken so many pills.

But desperate times called for desperate measures.

ANGIE

The boat ride would have been excruciating without Joel present, but Joel was making it a thousand times worse. Angie should have told him to turn around the second he arrived. She could have talked to Joel later, back in New York, where she wouldn't have had to witness him trying to make sweet love to Scarlett.

It didn't matter, she told herself. He could pursue Scarlett, but he would end up falling on his face.

It did matter. It hurt. It was humiliating.

She tried to focus on the task at hand. JP maneuvered the launch over the building swells and into the sound, and then, just off the coast from the Cliffside Beach Club, he cut the motor.

Laurel stood up and held the urn out to Buck.

Buck said, "Are we ready?"

No, Angie thought. She would never be ready.

Hayes stood up. Belinda stood up. Scarlett stood up and took a few wobbly steps across the boat until she was tucked under Joel's arm. Angie *could not* believe it. She felt a hand on her arm: JP.

You okay? he mouthed.

Angie got to her feet and gave JP a weak and defeated smile. It was both comforting and mortifying to know she wasn't the only one who'd noticed Joel's unbridled pursuit of Scarlett. JP had been through this. His girlfriend was now dating his best friend, and he had survived just fine.

Buck said, "I feel like I should say a few words, but I don't know what those words might be."

Hayes took a stumbling step forward and reached into the urn. He brought forth a handful of remains—chunks of bone, Angie supposed, and a powder that looked like talcum.

"I love you, Dad," he said. Then he flung his handful into the water.

"I want to try!" Ellery said, darting forward. She reached into the urn, took a prodigious handful, and tossed it overboard.

Scarlett sobbed into Joel's shoulder.

JP nudged Angie forward. She reached into the urn, thinking, *This is not Deacon.* Deacon was the man who had lifted her up onto his shoulders so she could feed leaves into the hungry mouth of the giraffe. Deacon was the one who had played endless games of Monopoly with her, in which his favorite strategy was to put up houses and hotels right away and then half the time watch himself fall into foreclosure while Angie cleaned him out. Deacon was the one who always saved Angie the last glass of wine. Deacon was the one who called her when a new Jamaican jerk place opened on Avenue C. *We have to go! Can you meet me in five minutes?*

He was my father, Angie thought. *But, more than that, he was my friend.*

She took a handful of remains and let them drop into the water, then she dusted off her hand on her shorts. She turned back to look at JP. He was wearing his sunglasses, but she saw the shine of one tear run down his face. He smiled at her. *I thought it would give you something else to think about, something else to want.* Certainly, JP had realized that nothing would trump what Angie wanted now and what she would want for the rest of her life: five more minutes with Deacon, so she could hug him and say good-bye.

Laurel threw a copious handful of ashes with exuberance, as though she were a passenger on the deck of the *QE2* throwing confetti at well-wishers on the dock. Buck followed suit because, as Angie realized in that instant, Buck was besotted with Laurel and would do anything to make her happy.

Buck handed the urn to Scarlett, but Scarlett turned her face away and wailed, "I can't! I just can't!"

Belinda staggered over and reached her hand into the urn. She bent all the way over the side of the boat as if she was afraid to throw Deacon's ashes, as if she preferred to simply set them down on the surface of the water. "Good night, sweet prince," she said. Angie rolled her eyes. Of course her mother would quote Shakespeare.

BELINDA

After the ceremonial moment had passed, they idled a bit. Belinda returned to the back of the boat, as far away as possible from Scarlett.

"It's a lovely night," JP said. "We'll turn around in a minute."

Scarlett stood up. At first, Belinda thought she had changed her mind about the ashes, which was a good thing. If she didn't scatter them now, she would always regret it. But instead of asking for the urn, Scarlett headed for Belinda with her arms outstretched.

"Belinda," she said. "Listen to me."

"No," Belinda said. She backed up. In that moment, Scarlett became Stella, or maybe just a younger Scarlett, maybe the Scarlett who *had* occupied Deacon's fantasies even while he was married to Belinda.

"Stay away from me, please," Belinda said. Belinda took another step back and instantly realized her mistake. There was nothing behind her except—after a moment of suspended time, which was at once instant and endless—the water.

ANGIE

Splash.

There was a beat of stunned silence. If it were anyone else, Angie might have laughed. But it was Belinda.

Angie said, "She can't swim! JP, my mother can't swim!"

JP jumped up onto the bench, and from there, he dove over the side of the boat. A few seconds later he surfaced and said, "I don't see her!"

Buck dove into the water. Laurel dove into the water. The boat bounced around, and Angie gripped the side to keep herself upright. JP went down again. Ellery wrapped her arms around Angie's legs.

"Miss Kit Kat?" she said.

"She'll be fine," Scarlett said.

"She can't swim!" Angie said to Scarlett. "You know she can't swim!"

"I was just trying to apologize!" Scarlett said. She turned to Joel. "I wanted to say sorry."

Joel peered over the side of the boat into the water, but he did not jump in, Angie noticed.

Mom! Angie could not lose both her parents. She could not. Belinda was a fighter. *Swim!* she thought. *Find the surface!* Wasn't everyone born with an innate sense of what to do in the water?

JP's head popped up. He dragged Belinda to the surface. Belinda sucked in air, coughed, and choked. Then, once she had oxygen, she started to howl. Angie, too, started crying.

"Mom!" Angie said.

Buck climbed aboard, and together he and JP managed to get Belinda back onto the boat. Laurel followed, then JP. Hayes was sitting with his head in his hands. "Man," he said. "I just cannot handle this."

From the launch, JP radioed the harbormaster, who sent one of his assistants to meet them on the dock with towels and blankets. Belinda was in full-on teeth-chattering, goose-bump mode. Angie walked her mother over to JP's Jeep, and Hayes helped Belinda get settled in the front seat.

They had to wait for JP to tie the launch back up, during which time Angie watched Joel, Scarlett, and Ellery climb into the back of the red Jeep, with Laurel and Buck in the front.

"Who *is* that guy with the goatee?" Hayes asked. "Do we know him?"

"He's my boyfriend," Angie said. Hayes was *so* oblivious! Angie wanted to snap in his face and say, *For Pete's sake, Hayes, pay attention!* But she didn't want to be the instigator of any more family strife, and besides, she envied Hayes his ability to block everything out.

"*Your* boyfriend?" Hayes said. "I thought he was Scarlett's boyfriend."

"Exactly," Angie said.

"But I guess that wouldn't make sense," Hayes said. "Because she was married to Dad, and he's only been dead a few weeks."

"Exactly," Belinda mumbled. Angie put a hand on Belinda's shoulder and kept it there until JP climbed into the Jeep.

"Back to Hoicks Hollow?" he asked.

"Yes, please," Angie said. She wanted to somehow apologize for her family, but she didn't know how.

Back at 33 Hoicks Hollow, there was a commotion in the driveway. Belinda had regained some color and some life. She sat forward.

"Someone is here," she said. "Is it Bob?"

"It might be?" Angie said. That would be a nice surprise for her mother. The red Jeep was already in the driveway, as well as...the Lincoln. Pirate's taxi.

"What does that guy want?" Hayes asked.

"What *does* that guy want?" Angie asked Hayes. "Do you owe him money?"

"More like the other way around," Hayes said.

JP said, "Pirate is the scourge of this entire island. He

moved here last year and parades around in that asinine costume like he owns the place. And it's no secret he deals drugs."

Angie saw a man—tall and lean, with sandy blond hair, wearing a coat and tie—climb out of the back of the taxi. Not Bob.

"Who's that?" she said.

Scarlett jumped out of the red Jeep and launched herself into the man's arms.

"Well," Belinda said.

The man was Bo Tanner. Angie unfolded herself from the back of JP's Jeep just in time for Scarlett to introduce her.

"Bo, this is Angie, Belinda and Deacon's daughter. Angie, this is Bo Tanner."

He held out his hand. Angie wasn't sure what she was supposed to do. Deacon's ashes probably hadn't even settled on the ocean floor yet, and already Angie was meeting his replacement. She shook Bo's hand. "I've heard a lot about you."

This, at least, was true.

When Angie turned around, she saw Joel waiting for her.

"You should go," she said. "Get your stuff out of my room and have Pirate here take you to the ferry."

Joel reached out for Angie's arm, but she swatted him away. "Don't touch me."

"Ange."

His voice, with its smoldering, sexy, ragged edge, nearly undid her resolve. She wanted to go to him and rest her head on his heart. The nonsense with Scarlett she could forgive; he had probably just felt uncomfortable putting his feelings for Angie on display. But then she thought of JP's words, *You deserve to be someone's everything.* She would never be Joel's everything. He might not leave her for Scarlett Oliver, but he would leave her for someone, the way he'd run through Karen and Winnie. Angie drew on some strength way down in the pit of her stomach that she didn't even know she had; it was even more difficult than drawing back the string of the bow. "Leave, Joel," she said. "Oh, and by the way, you're fired."

"You can't fire me," Joel said. "Only Harv can fire me."

"Okay, then wait for Harv to tell you," Angie said. "But you're fired."

Angie and JP helped Belinda from the car into the house.

"I can walk," Belinda said. "I'm fine, really."

Angie looked at JP. "We're ordering pizzas for dinner," she said. "Dad's favorite. Can you stay?"

"Let me run back to my shack and get changed," JP said. "Then, yes, I'd love to join you."

"My hero," Belinda said.

JP left, and Joel was gone. Laurel, Buck, Hayes, and Ellery were in the kitchen when Belinda and Angie walked in, followed by Scarlett and Bo.

"Bo is going to join us for dinner!" Scarlett announced. She beamed at Laurel. "Is that okay with you?"

Laurel opened her mouth, but no sound came out. Finally she managed: "It's Deacon's farewell dinner, Bo," she said. "Do you feel like you *want* to be here?"

Bo smiled. "No," he said. He held his palms up as if to

show he meant no harm. "I'll head back to my hotel, I think." To Scarlett, he said, "I'll let you enjoy your time with everyone tonight, and I'll come get you and Ellery in the morning. Good-bye, y'all," he said, excusing himself with half a wave.

"I'm hungry," Ellery said.

"I'll order the pizza now," Laurel said.

"I don't get it," Hayes said. "Who was that guy?"

LAUREL

They had four pies delivered from Sophie T's—three with three toppings each and the cheese well done, and one with just pepperoni and the cheese gooey.

"That one's for Buck," Laurel said after they'd spread the boxes out on the counter.

"Anyone is welcome to a slice," Buck said as he chose the largest piece for himself and wrapped the strings of mozzarella around the pointy end.

JP said, "Yeah, man, I'll have a slice of that."

"Me too," Ellery said. She was sitting on Angie's lap.

"Hey, shall we measure you, finally?" Angie asked.

"Yes!" Ellery said.

"I think we forgot to do it last year," Scarlett said. She was drinking a can of Skinny4Life and a glass of wine. "I can't remember. All the years run together."

Angie stood Ellery up against the door frame and checked the hash marks. "There's one here for Ellery from 8/12/15. It's in Dad's handwriting."

"He must have done it, then," Scarlett said. "I don't know

what I was thinking—he never forgot. It was one of his rules."

"Like the clothesline," Belinda said. "And showering outside."

"Living the life on Nantucket," Buck said.

"On Hoicks Hollow Road," Hayes said. "Our home away from home."

Angie marked the doorframe right above Ellery's head. "My, my, how you have grown," she said.

Later, after dinner, Laurel stood on the front porch with Angie, Hayes, and JP. Angie was having a cigarette, and the rest of them were gazing up at the emerging stars. Buck was cleaning up in the kitchen, and Belinda had volunteered to go upstairs and read to Ellery.

"Well, it wasn't pretty, but we survived," Angie said. She crushed the butt of her cigarette against the sole of her clog. She turned to JP. "Thank you for having dinner with us."

"Thank you for asking me," JP said. "But I should get home."

"I'll walk you to the car," Angie said.

Laurel and Hayes watched Angie and JP head down the porch stairs to the driveway.

"They would make a cute couple," Laurel said. "Don't you think?"

Hayes turned to her. "Mom," he said. "I have a problem."

"A problem?" she said.

"With drugs, I think?" Hayes said. His eyes filled with tears. "I'm sorry, Mom."

Laurel led Hayes up the stairs. They went into his room, where Laurel closed and locked the door so that they wouldn't be disturbed.

"I tried to be careful," Hayes said. He was openly crying now, her handsome, accomplished son, so worldly, so sophisticated, the same little towhead that she tucked into this bed after a long day of sun and sand, half-asleep before his head even hit the pillow.

She let him cry in her lap. She stroked his hair, which was how she used to comfort Deacon.

"What is it?" she asked. "What are you addicted to?"

"Heroin," he said. "It was an accident, Mom."

Heroin, Laurel thought. She closed her eyes.

BELINDA

Belinda read Ellery a picture book called *A Penny for Barnaby.* In the book, Barnaby Bear is on Nantucket and doesn't want to leave...so he follows the old tradition of throwing a penny off the side of the ferry as it passes Brant Point Lighthouse, to ensure his safe return.

Belinda was Barnaby: she didn't want to leave.

She lay next to Ellery in the gathering dark and tried to recall her own self as a little girl. She had been skinny with red hair and freckles, intent on learning how to do a one-handed cartwheel and then an aerial; she had practiced after school in the field behind her backyard. She had been obsessed with TV, which her mother called "the boob tube." Belinda watched *I Dream of Jeannie,* and *That Girl,* and *The Partridge Family,* and she dreamed of being like Barbara Eden, Marlo Thomas, Susan Dey. Then, in high school, she and her girlfriends Judie and Joanne Teffeteller, identical twins, used to spot one another for backflips. It was their dream to become cheerleaders for the Iowa Hawkeyes. Belinda worked the soda counter at Pearson's Drug Store after school. She wore a polyester dress and a name tag and a hairnet. The soda counter served sandwiches—tuna salad, ham and pickle, chicken salad, and egg salad—and single-serving Campbell's soup cans that came shooting out of a dispenser when Belinda pulled on the arm. She worked every day except for Thursday; on Thursdays, she and the Teffeteller twins went to the movies. It had been raining, she remembered, on the afternoon they went to see *Ordinary People.* It had been the first movie to break Belinda's heart, and she had sat in the theater long after the twins had left to have burgers at the Fieldhouse, reflecting on what she'd just seen.

The summer after they graduated from high school, Belinda and the twins had driven out to California, and Belinda had stayed, using her Pearson's savings on a motel room on Santa Monica Boulevard and showing up at the ICM offices without an appointment. It could easily have gone the other way; Belinda could have been forced to hitchhike home, or call her parents for bus fare, but she had been lucky because Sally Bloom had been on her way to lunch as Belinda was standing at reception, and Sally had stopped to take a closer look at Belinda. Within a week, Belinda had been cast in *Brilliant Disguise.* And that, as they say, was that. Belinda had spent her entire adult life pretending to be other people.

Once Ellery was asleep, her breathing deep and steady, her pretty face at peace despite the tumultuous adult day, Belinda slipped from the room and down the hall to Clara's pathetic excuse for a room. Belinda owned a 750-acre horse farm in Louisville, on which sat the sprawling 5,600-square-foot residence, as well as six barns, four outbuildings, three rings, and a racetrack. She kept a penthouse suite at the Standard in New York and the presidential suite at the Beverly Wilshire. But somehow, she felt more comfortable here in the spartan quarters of Clara's room, which had nothing to offer but the view from the window. *Simplicity,* Belinda thought as she lay down on the bed. *It's underrated.*

LAUREL/BELINDA/SCARLETT

Laurel couldn't sleep. She lay in bed next to Buck—he had been wonderfully supportive and, with a few phone calls, had gotten Hayes admission to Eagleville Hospital, about two hours south of New York City, for a twenty-eight-day rehab program—but even after Buck descended into slumber, with snores as regular and soothing as rolling waves, Laurel fidgeted. Legs under the sheet, one leg under and one leg over, pillow one way, pillow the other way, left side, right side, back. She ordered herself to put her concerns about Hayes aside. He would get help. They were leaving tomorrow; he would be in professional hands by the evening. There was nothing more she could do, but still the question lingered: why? Had it been her fault? Had she not given him enough love or attention? He told her he'd first smoked opium on his trip to inner China a year ago, and from there it had gotten out of hand. Was it Deacon's fault? Was it a result of Hayes growing up in a broken home? Laurel knew she was being ridiculous, but the questions presented themselves. *Stop thinking about it,* she told herself. It was nobody's fault.

She decided to go down to the kitchen. She needed a cup of chamomile tea or a shot of Jameson—or maybe both.

Scarlett had been in love with Bo Tanner for most of her life—ever since she saw him across the room at Miss Louisa's etiquette classes when she was in fifth grade.

But that was a story for another time.

At ten o'clock, Scarlett checked on Ellery: fast asleep. Scarlett slipped onto the back deck, tiptoed through the yard, and rolled a bike out of the shed. She pedaled down Hoicks Hollow Road by the light of the stars and half a moon, then turned left onto the Polpis Road. The night air was warm enough that she could ride without a jacket, and it was filled with cricket chatter.

Bo was staying at the Wade Cottages in Sconset. When Scarlett pulled into the shell driveway, she saw him standing in the moonlight, waiting for her. Ever the gentleman. He led her inside.

Scarlett was so distraught about losing the Nantucket house that she nearly asked Bo if he might loan her the money to save it. But she had asked quite a lot of him recently. She had asked him to leave Anne Carter—who had been Scarlett's friend since her earliest memories—but then, when Bo said he would, Scarlett hadn't been able to leave Deacon. When Scarlett decided that her marriage to Deacon was over, she again asked Bo to leave Anne Carter, and again he said he would, and he did. While Bo was moving out, Deacon had died.

Bo made a good living as an attorney for wealthy Georgia

gentlemen—mostly Savannah based, but some in Atlanta as well—who had business interests up North. But he would be paying alimony to Anne Carter, and besides, Nantucket wasn't his summertime place. He had always been a Folly Beach boy.

Scarlett bicycled home just after midnight; the dark was velvety and nearly opaque. Anywhere else in the world, Scarlett would have been afraid, but here she felt safe. She shed a few tears on the way home because endings were sad and the day had been filled with emotional fireworks. She had only wanted to apologize to Belinda for the atrocious things she'd said; the others, she feared, might have thought she'd meant to push Belinda off the boat. When JP had surfaced the first time without her, Scarlett's limbs had turned leaden, and a pool of cold dread had collected in the pit of her stomach. She had her problems with Belinda, but that was a far cry from wanting her dead.

When Scarlett tiptoed back into the house, she saw a light on in the kitchen. There, at the counter, sat Laurel—with a steaming mug of tea and a shot of Jameson sitting before her.

"That looks good," Scarlett said.

Belinda awoke in the night, certain that she heard voices below her. She strained her ears, but she couldn't be sure. She gave herself a case of the willies wondering if the murmuring she heard was the ghost of Clara Beck. She squeezed her eyes shut, willing sleep to take her.

The voices stopped, then started again. Belinda sat up.

They're probably going to ask you for something. Money, or a favor. Or both.

Technically, no one had asked; Belinda would make sure to point that out to Bob later. In fact, Laurel had been adamant about *not* accepting Belinda's money. Belinda might have a struggle with her—although Laurel probably felt as Belinda did: anything to save this house. Belinda recalled what Marianne Pryor had said: *It's not a house to us. It's a home. And it's not a home, it's a way of life. Our summertime happens here. This house is part of our past, it's our present, it'll be our future. It's who we are.*

Whether Belinda liked it or not, the Thorpe summertimes happened here, at American Paradise.

She would save it—for Angie's sake and Hayes's sake and Ellery's sake. She wouldn't bother with the arrears; she would pay off all three mortgages, whatever that cost. And during her weeks in residence, she would take the master bedroom! Although she might just sneak down to Clara's room every once in a while for a secret nap.

Belinda rose from bed and crept down the stairs. The voices grew louder and more distinct. There were people in the kitchen. Belinda poked her head in: Laurel and Scarlett were sitting together at the kitchen counter, each with a cup of tea and a shot of Jameson before them.

"Oh, hello," Belinda said.

They both looked over. Without a word, Scarlett rose, pulled a shot glass out of the cabinet, and poured Belinda some whiskey.

"Tea?" Laurel asked.

"Not necessary," Belinda said.

Scarlett and Laurel raised their shot glasses.

"Here's to us," Laurel said.

"To us," Scarlett said.

"To us," Belinda said.

The glasses clicked, and they drank.

A second shot followed. Then a third...before Belinda announced that she was paying off the mortgages.

"I don't want you to argue with me. And I don't want you to thank me. I'm not doing it for the two of you. I'm doing it for our children."

Laurel welled up with tears. "And our grandchildren."

"Thank you, Belinda," Scarlett said.

Belinda glared at her. "What did I just say?" She wandered over to the door frame. "I want to know why the kids are the only ones to be measured," she said. "Why not us? I, for one, would like my own hash mark."

Laurel stood up. "Me too."

Scarlett pulled a pen out of the junk drawer.

"You first, Laurel," Belinda said.

Scarlett measured Laurel. She was almost an inch taller than Hayes had been at thirteen.

Laurel then measured Belinda. She was a smidge shorter than Angie had been at twelve.

And Belinda, standing on the step stool that Mrs. Innsley had probably used to reach the high cabinets and shelves, measured Scarlett. She was taller than everyone.

When they were done, the three of them stepped back to admire their names on the door frame of American Paradise: LAUREL 6/20/16, BELINDA 6/20/16, SCARLETT 6/20/16.

My, my, Belinda thought. *Look how we have grown.*

Tuesday, June 21

ANGIE

She had thought she would be the first one awake; JP was coming to get her at eight. He had volunteered to give her another shooting lesson.

Joel had left behind a T-shirt. Angie had held it for a moment; she'd even brought it to her nose and inhaled his scent. It pained her to remember him holding her, his face buried in her neck, or the way he tugged on her ponytail. She had fallen for him, and he had disappointed her. Her first adult relationship had taught her what? That men were wily and opportunistic. That people used the word "love" without thinking. Real love existed—about this she was optimistic—but she hadn't found it having hurry-up sex in the dry pantry or in her apartment in the stolen hours between Joel leaving work and heading home.

When she entered the kitchen for coffee, she found Laurel, Buck, and Belinda already sitting at stools, deep in a hushed conversation.

"What's up?" Angie asked.

The three of them stared at her.

"I'm taking Hayes to rehab," Laurel said.

Angie nodded, trying to process these words. *Hayes.*

Rehab. "He's agreed to it? Or we're doing an intervention? What is he addicted to?"

"Heroin," Laurel said. "He's agreed to go. There's a place in Pennsylvania, about two hours south of New York. We're leaving later this morning."

"Oh, wow," Angie said. Heroin. She thought about how Hayes had looked the first time she saw him, sitting outside her door. *Like any tweaker plucked off Ludlow Street.* He was going to rehab; this was a sign of hope. But it was too much to think about, and so Angie deferred to considering the logistics of this new development.

"How am I getting home?" Angie asked.

"You are home," Belinda said.

As Angie stood aiming the arrow at the target, she felt herself relax. JP noticed, because he said, "There you go. You're breathing. Now, line up the pin."

She didn't have to hit the target today. Now that she was staying on Nantucket for the rest of the summer, the pressure had been lifted. She could work on getting her stance and form right, and if she missed, she missed.

She could always come back tomorrow and try again.

"I have to admit," Belinda said, "I'm jealous."

"You should be," Angie said. She couldn't believe how excited she felt about staying; nor could she believe how close she'd come to losing Nantucket altogether. Her mother had saved the day. Belinda! Now Angie would go to the beach every day, and she would work on Deacon's cookbook; it would be a dream summer. Only one thing would be missing. "Did I tell you that JP is teaching me how to use a bow and arrow?"

"He's adorable," Belinda said.

He was adorable, but Angie wasn't about to discuss her brand-new friendship with her mother.

"I think I'll come back after the Fourth of July," Belinda said. "Mary and Laura will be away at riding camp for three weeks. Would it be okay with you if I came for three weeks?"

"What would you do for three weeks?" *Other than drive me crazy?* Angie thought.

Belinda got a wicked glimmer in her eye. For an instant, Angie understood how her father had fallen so profoundly in love. "I'm going to take swimming lessons," she said.

Publishers Weekly

Legacy: The Recipes of Deacon Thorpe,
Foreword by Quentin York

Fans of Deacon Thorpe's TV shows, *Day to Night to Day with Deacon* and *Pitchfork,* and guests lucky enough to have secured a coveted reservation at Mr. Thorpe's midtown Manhattan restaurant, the Board Room, will rejoice that the legacy of the late chef—who passed away in May 2016—lives on through the voices of his talented children. His daughter, Angela Thorpe, graduated from the Culinary Institute of America in Hyde Park in 2010 and worked for the past four years as the fire chief at the Board Room. His son, Hayes Thorpe, was until June 2016 an editor at *Fine Travel* magazine. Together, the Thorpe offspring provide a host of the most popular recipes from the

TV shows and the restaurant, as well as some treasured family recipes and some original recipes developed by Ms. Thorpe. Interspersed throughout is an unflinchingly honest and often humorous portrait of their father. According to his eldest two children (Thorpe also fathered a daughter, Ellery, age 10, with his third wife, Scarlett Oliver), Deacon Thorpe fought the demons of drugs and alcohol most of his life, but he was buoyed emotionally by the women he loved—his childhood sweetheart and first wife, Laurel Thorpe, his second wife, Academy Award–winning actress Belinda Rowe, and the aforementioned Ms. Oliver. *Legacy* is more than a cookbook; it's a touching tribute to a cultural icon many Americans miss. It celebrates Mr. Thorpe's greatest legacy, which is love.

New York Times *Wedding Announcements*

OLIVER–TANNER

Scarlett Oliver and Robert "Bo" Tanner were married yesterday at the Cathedral of St. John the Baptist in Savannah, Georgia. The Reverend Clarence Meets officiated.

Ms. Oliver, the widow of the late chef Deacon Thorpe, was attended only by her daughter, Ellery Thorpe. Ms. Oliver is the daughter of Bracebridge and Prudence Oliver of Savannah, Georgia.

Mr. Tanner is a private wealth management specialist in Savannah, Georgia, and New York City. He's the son of Beulah Tanner and the late Harrison Robert Tanner. Mr. Tanner's first marriage ended in divorce.

Deacon and Angie's
Stupid Word List (reprised)

1. protégé
2. literally
3. half sister (brother)
4. oxymoron
5. repartee
6. nifty
7. syllabus
8. parched
9. brouhaha
10. doggie bag
11. giddy
12. unique
13. condolences/ sympathy/pity
14. maraschino

National Enquirer, *August 31, 2016*

Belinda Rowe divorces horse-trainer husband... her ex, Chef Deacon Thorpe, advises her from beyond the grave, "Get rid of him!"

LAUREL SIMMONS THORPE and
JOHN EDWARD BUCKLEY JR.,
along with their families,
invite you to join in the celebration of their marriage.
September 17, 2017
Nantucket Island, Massachusetts
American Paradise, 33 Hoicks Hollow Road
RSVP by August 10.

EPILOGUE: ONE PERFECT DAY

He's going up to Nantucket to say good-bye.

He has seen this coming for months now, but it feels like a fresh wound. It was either the restaurant or the house, and to lose the restaurant would mean putting forty-seven people out of work and watching his life's dream go up in smoke. There really wasn't a choice.

He has also blown his third marriage. Deacon knows he should be proud that his union with Scarlett has lasted as long as it did, and that they created a being as exquisite and clever as Ellery. And now, he is sober. The strongest thing about him is his willpower.

He plans a trip out of the city, one last visit to Nantucket. He wonders if he can make the time as sweet and pure as the day his father first took him to the island. He will try.

He decides to take the slow ferry, the way he and Jack did so many years earlier. Forty years have passed, but he can still recall his wonder. Deacon buys a cup of coffee and takes it up to the top deck. Over the years, people have maligned the slow ferry—it's easier and faster to take the fast boat or to fly—but Deacon enjoys it. The trip feels like an old-fashioned adventure. He pays close attention as the island comes into view, and then, as they grow closer, he squints. Are there seals lounging on the jetty? Yes, one. Deacon waves his empty cup; the seal barks.

He has brought no luggage, just his sunglasses, his phone (the battery about to die), and his wallet. He longs for his old Willys jeep, but it gave up the ghost the summer before. The mechanic that Deacon called to resuscitate it said it was a lost cause. The frame was rusted through, the engine shot. It would have cost Deacon $15,000 to replace and repair it, which was far more than the beater was worth.

Be grateful for all the years she gave you, the mechanic said.

The old, funky pickup he bought to replace it is at the house, and so Deacon has to take a taxi. The first one in line is an incredibly sweet 1965 Lincoln Continental with suicide doors—with a driver who is dressed like a pirate. Who is this guy? He seems a little theme-parkish to Deacon, but maybe the kid's just a scrappy entrepreneur. Deacon will give him the benefit of the doubt.

Deacon says, "Take me to the end of Hoicks Hollow Road, please."

The driver is wearing a long velvet coat despite the warm day, and his dark, greasy hair hangs to his shoulders. He's wearing an eye patch too, of course, so with his one beady eye, he stares at Deacon for a long moment in the rearview. He says, "Are you Deacon Thorpe?"

"Afraid so," Deacon says, and he nearly laughs. A pirate who watches cooking shows! "Now, to Hoicks Hollow, please. Do not pass go, do not collect two hundred dollars."

"Huh?" the driver says.

"It's from Monopoly?" Deacon says. "The board game?"

Blank look.

"Never mind," Deacon says.

The air on Nantucket is rich the same way that heavy cream is rich. Is there more oxygen in it? Deacon wonders. It smells of pine and salt. Today is a drop-dead stunner with plentiful sunshine and a sky so blue, it breaks his heart. It's beauty, ultimately, that hurts Deacon—his inability to match it, his inability to be worthy of it, his inability to hold it in his heart.

Pirate heads out the Polpis Road, past farmland and split-rail fences. They pass the tiny, rose-covered cottage that sits at the bend in the road. Tourists stop to take pictures of this cottage all day long, which means that Deacon, as a seasoned islander, should be immune to its beauty. But the cottage, draped in a lush blanket of 'New Dawn' roses, is too pretty to ignore. Seeing it fills Deacon with joy.

Pirate drives past Sesachacha Pond.

"It's taken me thirty years," Deacon says, "but I finally learned how to pronounce the name of this pond. *Seh-sack-a-ja.*"

Pirate barely nods; he probably couldn't care less, but Deacon is proud of himself. For decades, Deacon has stumbled over the name, sounding as though he had a mouth full of marbles. But JP broke it down into syllables, and now Deacon sounds like a Wampanoag native. JP is an ace with things like that: he can identify every shorebird, every species of tree and shrub and he can tell what kind of fish is on the line—bluefish, striped bass, or bonito—just by the way it tugs. The guy is frankly amazing, and Deacon would love nothing more than to somehow hook him up with Angie. He can't choose Angie's life for her, but how miraculous would it be if she fell in love with JP and moved to Nantucket year round? She could open her own restaurant here, take winters off to travel, and maybe give Deacon a grandchild.

Deacon spots Sankaty Head Light. When Ellery was little, he used to tell her it was a giant peppermint stick. He misses Ellery desperately—the way she smells after a bath, the freckles that dust her nose.

Pirate puts on his turn signal and takes a left.

Good old Hoicks Hollow Road, Jack had said. *Used to be my home away from home.*

When Pirate drops Deacon off, Deacon gives him money for the fare, plus a twenty-dollar tip. "Get yourself a parrot," Deacon says with a grin.

Deacon changes into a bathing suit and a long-sleeved T-shirt and grabs a beach towel from the linen closet. He pulls a bike out of the shed—*Laurel's bike* is how he always thinks of it—and throws the towel in the basket. He pedals down Hoicks Hollow Road to the Sankaty Head Beach Club. He and Belinda languished on the wait list for more than ten years, and then, the summer after they split, Deacon received a letter of acceptance, which he turned down because the application had Belinda Rowe's name on it, and it was no secret that private clubs preferred whole families to broken ones.

Ray Jay Jr. had still worked at the beach club when Deacon and Laurel first bought American Paradise. Deacon used to see him occasionally coming and going in a little white Ford Escort, smoking a cigarette—but Deacon had never been comfortable enough to reintroduce himself because he didn't want to tell Ray Jay Jr. that Jack Thorpe had left shortly after their visit to Nantucket and Deacon had never seen him again. Then Deacon read in the *Inquirer and Mirror* that Ray Jay Jr. died of a heart attack—and there went the last person on Nantucket who had remembered Jack Thorpe other than Deacon. It was sad but also something of a relief.

Deacon walks into the beach club through the swinging front doors, and he feels an old, familiar sense of not quite belonging. He has no idea if this part of his plan is going to be successful, but what the hell, he'll give it a shot.

The blond, round-faced teenager at the check-in window is too young to be a fan, and she turns a skeptical glower on Deacon when he admits that he's not a member but rather a person on a nostalgic mission, and that he'd love to have lunch. He says he's an old friend of the former manager, Ray Jay Jr.

"I don't know who that is," the teenage girl says. "I'll get my boss."

The boss is a young man—about Hayes's age—with a trim beard and rectangular glasses. Deacon nearly laughs. Now he has seen it all—hipsters have infiltrated the Sankaty Head Beach Club! But from ten yards away, Deacon notices a look of recognition cross this fellow's face.

"Hi there, I'm Claude," he says, offering a hand. "What can we do for you, Chef Thorpe?"

Deacon shakes Claude's hand. "Nice to meet you, Claude. I came here for lunch forty years ago with my father, and I'd love to do it again today."

Claude nods. "The pool just opened for the season on Monday. It would be our honor to have you as a guest of the house for lunch."

The Sankaty Head Beach Club has changed very little in forty years, although there are now new chaises and new canvas umbrellas and new towels—yellow and white striped. Deacon sits at a table overlooking the pool, which is smaller and paler than he remembers. He orders a double cheeseburger, fries, and a frosty Coke.

"Are you sure I can't get you a beer?" Claude says.

"I'm sure," Deacon says. As soon as Claude leaves to put in Deacon's order, Deacon takes off his shirt and walks to the edge of the pool. At the far end is a woman with twin girls a few years younger than Ellery, both of them wearing water wings. The lifeguard is a strapping college kid wearing red trunks and a gray hooded sweatshirt, spinning his whistle. The sun goes behind a cloud, and Deacon shivers, but he tells himself to toughen up. He has bigger worries than cold water.

He dives in.

After lunch, he thanks Claude profusely and signs autographs for the two line cooks in the back—and then he's back on his bike, and it's off to the beach in Sconset.

The weather is still fine and sunny, but it's spring, not summer, and Deacon isn't sure how long he'll last at the beach. He sets his towel in the sand and charges into the water. It makes the pool at Sankaty feel like a bathtub, but Deacon isn't deterred. He swims out, letting the waves crest over his head. *This is it,* he thinks. His last day on Nantucket for the foreseeable future. Of course, one never knows what will happen. Maybe a big investor will pop up, maybe Deacon will finally finish his cookbook, maybe, bit by bit, the Board Room will become more profitable and Deacon will be able to buy another house on Nantucket.

But it won't be the same; this he knows. American Paradise was where he raised Hayes and Angie and Ellery. That was the house where he lived with his three wives, the most beautiful, complicated women he has ever known.

Deacon swims until his limbs are numb with the cold. He's having some stomach pains; possibly he swam too soon after eating. He climbs out and collapses on his towel in the mellow late-afternoon sun.

It's the golden hour. Deacon can remember watching his father walk toward him from down the beach; he can still picture the inscrutable expression on his father's face. It was sadness and regret, Deacon supposes. His father might have wished he'd lived his life another way or been a more noble man—a better husband, a better father.

Deacon is overcome with emotion. Everything comes to an end—the day ends, the summer ends, an era ends. In a minute or two, Deacon will get on his bike and pedal back to American Paradise, where he will sit on the back deck, smoke a cigarette, drink a cold Diet Coke, and watch the sun go down.

But before he does that, he will stay and enjoy the last of the day's warmth and the sound of the waves hitting the shore.

He thinks of the words he wanted to say to his father so many years earlier.

Let's stay here, Dad. Please, let's just find a way to stay.

AUTHOR'S NOTE

As most of my longtime readers know, I love to write about food. This novel, *Here's to Us,* features four actual recipes that were developed specifically to fit my plot. They are real recipes that we can all make at home.

The first two recipes, Deacon's Clams Casino Dip with Herb-Butter Baguettes and the Fluffy White Champagne Cake, come from the person who is currently my culinary obsession, Jessica Merchant. Jessica is the author of the cookbook *Seriously Delish,* in which every recipe is... seriously delish. And she is the founder of the website How Sweet It Is (howsweeteats.com). When you check out her website, you will thank me because it is gorgeous and brilliant, and all of her recipes feel like they've been plucked out of the pages of one of my novels (and now, that's true). She is also the mother of the cutest baby of all time, who I like to pretend is my baby.

The second two recipes, Deacon's Shellfish Chowder and the Tri-Berry Crumble, were developed by my friend of over twenty years, the doyenne of the Nantucket food world, Sarah Leah Chase. Sarah's culinary career began on Nantucket in the early 1980s when she opened Que Sera Sarah, a specialty food shop and catering business. She has written seven cookbooks, including the bestsellers *Nantucket Open-House Cookbook* (this, the cookbook that has shaped my food sensibilities for the past twenty-three years) and *Cold-Weather Cooking.* Sarah's most recent work of genius is *New England Open-House Cookbook,* published in the summer of 2015. Sarah posts scheduled events and epicurean undertakings on her Facebook fan page: facebook.com/sarahleahchase.

ACKNOWLEDGMENTS

I want to start by thanking the two people to whom this novel is dedicated. Anne and Whitney Gifford have been friends since I moved to Nantucket. Not only did they hunt for a baby swing for my son Maxx (now sixteen) in the middle of a fondue party, but they also allowed me to use their second home as my own personal writing studio through five chilly winters. In the red library on Barnabas, I wrote *A Summer Affair, The Castaways, The Island, Silver Girl,* and *Summerland.* More recently, Anne and Whitney were instrumental in helping me purchase my new house. They are as close to me as family, and I treasure our friendship and value their unconditional love.

Joe Gamberoni taught me everything I needed to know about hunting on Nantucket. Let the record show that (unlike Angie) I was not strong enough to draw back the string of a bow (it's a lot harder than it looks). Joe's knowledge of hunting and deer is comprehensive, and he patiently answered all my questions.

Thank you to Mark Goldweitz for "lending" his boat, the *Lena Marie,* to my characters so they could spread Deacon's ashes in style.

Michael May, executive director of the Nantucket Preservation Trust, was a hero at the last minute and sent me Betsy Tyler's comprehensive and elegant house history of 141 Main Street, allowing me to write what is my favorite scene in this book.

Reagan Arthur did it again. She is, quite simply, the most talented editor in the business. She is the true superstar here, consistently making the magic happen by encouraging my best writing and teasing out the most engaging storyline. Every Elin Hilderbrand fan should also be a Reagan Arthur fan.

I am the luckiest novelist in America to have Michael Carlisle and David Forrer of Inkwell Management as my agents—and even luckier to have them as my friends.

Anyone who has ever read any of my novels can probably tell that Nantucket is a special place. Nothing makes it so more than the people who live there. Thank you to all of my friends, my children's friends, and my friends' children. I can't possibly name everyone who touches my life and makes the island home for me, but this year, I'll say Here's to you: Rebecca Bartlett; Wendy Rouillard; Wendy Hudson; Debbie Briggs; Beau and Elizabeth Almodobar; Heidi Holdgate; Shelly Weedon; Matthew and Evelyn MacEachern; Marty and Holly McGowan; Mark and Gwenn Snider and everyone on staff at the Nantucket Hotel; Angus and Melissa MacVicar; Mark and Eithne Yelle; Helaina Jones; Kevin, Sheila, Liam, and Paddy Carroll; Jeff, Liza, Kai, and Dylan Ottani (Pura Vida!); Manda Riggs; David Rattner and Andrew Law; Norm and Jen Frazee; Jen and Steve Laredo; Martha and John Sargent; Jessica Hicks; the incomparable Erin Frawley; and last but not in any way least: Chuck and Margie Marino.

Thank you to my sister, Heather Osteen Thorpe, for everything, always.

Finally, thank you to three of the coolest human beings I know—whom, it so happens, I have also had the privilege to raise: Maxwell, Dawson, and Shelby. I love you more than I love breathing.

ABOUT THE AUTHOR

Elin Hilderbrand first discovered the magic of Nantucket in July 1993. Her recipe for a happy island life includes running, writing at the beach, picnics at Eel Point with her three children, and singing "Home, Sweet Home" at the Club Car piano bar. *Here's to Us* is her seventeenth novel.

...AND *THE IDENTICALS*

Harper and Tabitha Frost are identical twins who couldn't look more alike... or live more differently. Laid-back Harper can't hold down a job and lives in their father's old house on Martha's Vineyard, while fashionable Tabitha runs an ailing boutique on Nantucket. After more than a decade apart, Harper and Tabitha switch islands—and lives—to save what's left of their splintered family. But the twins quickly discover that the secrets, lies, and gossip they thought they'd outrun can travel between islands just as easily as they can.

Following is an excerpt from the novel's opening pages.

NANTUCKET

Like thousands of other erudite, discerning people, you've decided to spend your summer vacation on an island off the coast of Massachusetts. You want postcard beaches. You want to swim, sail, and surf in Yankee-blue waters. You want to eat clam chowder and lobster rolls, and you want those dishes served to you by someone who calls them *chowdah* and *lobstah*. You want to ride in a Jeep with the top down, your golden retriever, named Charles Emerson Winchester III, riding shotgun. You want to live the dream. You want an American summer.

But wait! You're torn. Should you choose Nantucket... or Martha's Vineyard? And does it really matter? Aren't the islands *pretty much the same?*

We chuckle and smirk at the assumption, shared by so many. Possibly you're not familiar with the bumper sticker (a bestseller at the Hub on Main Street and proudly displayed on the vehicles of nearly every islander of distinction, including the director of the Nantucket Island Chamber of Commerce) that reads: GOD MADE THE VINEYARD...BUT HE LIVES ON NANTUCKET.

If you're not swayed by that kind of shameless propaganda, then consider the vital statistics:

Nantucket Island

Settled: 1659
Original inhabitants: Wampanoag Indians
Distance from Hyannis: 30 miles
Area: 45 square miles
Population: 11,000 year-round; 50,000 summer
Number of towns: 1
Famous residents: Prefer not to be named

Martha's Vineyard

Settled: 1642 (We say: "Age before beauty")
Original inhabitants: Wampanoag Indians
Distance from Woods Hole: 11 miles (We say: "It's practically the mainland!")
Area: 100 square miles (We say: "Twice as big")
Population: 16,535 year-round; 100,000 summer (We say: "Twice as many")
Number of towns: 6 (We are speechless [!!!]—and can someone please tell us what is up with Chappaquiddick?)
Famous residents: Meg Ryan, Lady Gaga, Skip Gates, Vernon Jordan, Carly Simon, James Taylor, and... John Belushi, deceased and buried off South Road (They have Bluto; we say: "So what?")

Is there any part of Martha's Vineyard that can compete with our cobblestone streets or the stately perfection of the Three Bricks, the homes that whale-oil merchant Joseph Starbuck built for his three sons between 1837 and 1840? Does the Vineyard have an enclave of tiny rose-covered cottages—as whimsical as dollhouses—as we do in the picturesque village of 'Sconset? Does "MVY" have a protected arm of golden-sand beach, home to piping plovers and a colony of seals, as our northernmost tip, Great Point, does? Does it have a sweeping vista like the one offered across Sesachacha Pond toward the peppermint stick of Sankaty Head Lighthouse? Does it have a dive bar as glamorously gritty as the Chicken Box, where one can hear Grace Potter one week and Trombone Shorty the next? You might not want to get us started on the superiority of our restaurants. If it were our last night on earth, who among us could choose between the cheeseburger with garlic fries from the Languedoc Bistro and the seared-scallop taco with red cabbage slaw from Millie's?

We understand how you might confuse those of us here with our compatriots there—after all, our region is lumped together as the Cape and the islands—but we are two distinct nations, each with its own ways, its own means, its own traditions, histories, and secrets, and its own web of gossip and scandal. Think of the two islands as you would a set of twins. Outwardly, we look alike, but beneath the surface... we are individuals.

MARTHA'S VINEYARD

There is a bumper sticker—a bestseller, according to the owner of Alley's General Store—that reads: GOD MADE NANTUCKET, BUT HE LIVES ON THE VINEYARD. Some of us would have edited that bumper sticker to say BUT HE LIVES IN CHILMARK—because who wants to be lumped in with the honky-tonk shenanigans happening down island?

However, in the interest of keeping this a foreign war and

not a civil one, let's celebrate the reasons we're superior to Nantucket. The Vineyard has diversity—of races, of opinions, of terrain. We have the Methodist campground, with its colorful gingerbread houses; the Tabernacle; Ocean Park; Inkwell Beach; Donovan's Reef, home of the Dirty Banana—and that's only in Oak Bluffs! We have dozens of family farms that harvest an abundance of organic produce; we have the Jaws Bridge and the cliffs of Aquinnah; we have East Chop, West Chop, the Katama airstrip, and a neighbor in Edgartown who keeps llamas on his front lawn. We have Chappaquiddick, which is a lot more than just the place where Teddy Kennedy may or may not have driven Mary Jo Kopechne to her death off the Dike Bridge. After all, there is a Japanese garden on Chappy! And if we let the air in our Jeep tires down to eleven pounds and pay two hundred dollars for a sticker, we can enjoy the wild, windswept beauty of Cape Poge.

We have rolling hills, deciduous trees, and low stone walls. We have Menemsha, the best fishing village in the civilized world, where one can get the freshest seafood, the creamiest chowder, and the crispiest, most succulent fried whole-belly clams. Have you never heard of the Bite? Larsen's? The Home Port? These are iconic spots; these are legends.

We have the best celebrations: Illumination Night, the Ag Fair, the August fireworks. We aren't sure what anyone celebrates on Nantucket other than being able to land a plane successfully at the airport despite the pea-soup fog or finally being able to find the correct shade of dusty pink on a pair of dress pants.

But what really makes the Vineyard special are the people. The Vineyard boasts a large and active population of middle- and upper-class African Americans. We have a Brazilian church. We also have celebrities, but you would never recognize half of them because they have to wait in line at "Back Door Doughnuts" and sit in traffic at Five Corners in Vineyard Haven just like everyone else.

Most of us have only been to Nantucket for one reason: the Island Cup. We won't say anything about the football game itself, because no one likes a braggart, but every time we visit to cheer on our high school players, we can't help wondering how our fellow islanders can bear to live on such a flat, barren, and foggy rock so far out to sea.

Still, there is a connection between us that's hard to refute. Geologists suspect that as recently as twenty-three thousand years ago, Martha's Vineyard, Nantucket, and Cape Cod were all part of one landmass. It might be easier to think of us as sisters—twins, even—birthed by the same mother. We like to think of Martha's Vineyard as the favorite.

But then, of course, Nantucket likes to think of herself as the favorite.

MARTHA'S VINEYARD: HARPER

Reed Zimmer isn't on call at 7:00 p.m. on Friday, June 16, when Harper Frost's father, Billy, draws his final breath. Dr. Zimmer is at a picnic at Lambert's Cove with his wife's family; apparently they hold the same party every year at the start of summer—bonfire, potato salad, chicken blackening on the portable Weber grill. Sadie Zimmer's brother, Franklin Phelps, is one of the Vineyard's favorite guitar players—Harper always goes to hear him when he's playing at the Ritz—and Harper imagines Dr. Zimmer, his feet buried in the cold sand, singing along with Franklin to "Wagon Wheel."

Harper is still at her father's bedside when she sends Dr. Zimmer a text. It says: *Billy is gone.* She imagines his shock followed by his guilt; he promised Harper it wouldn't happen tonight. He told her that Billy still had time.

"Check in on him as usual," Dr. Zimmer had said that afternoon when he rose from Harper's bed, the white sheets tangled from their lovemaking. "But feel free to enjoy your weekend." He had looked out her window at the lilac bush, which overnight, it seemed, had exploded into a show-offy bloom. "I can't believe it's all starting again. Another summer."

Feel free to enjoy your weekend? Harper had thought. She hated when Reed talked to her as though she were merely his patient's daughter, a virtual stranger—but isn't she a stranger to him, in a way? Reed only sees Harper when she's sitting by her father's hospital bed or when they're making love in her duplex. They don't go on dates; they have never bumped into each other at Cronig's; Reed claims he has never noticed her driving the Rooster delivery truck, even when she waves at him like a woman drowning. Harper and Reed have been sleeping together only since October, and so she isn't sure what 'another summer' means to him. Today offered the first clue: his wife's parents, the elder Phelpses, are now in residence at their house in Katama, recently arrived back from Vero Beach. There will be family obligations, such as this picnic, when it will seem as though Reed is living on another planet.

Harper waits a few moments before texting anyone else. Her father is right here, but he's gone. His face is slack; it looks *vacated,* like a house where there's no one home. Billy died while Harper was talking to him about Dustin Pedroia of the Red Sox; he took one great shuddering breath, then another, then he looked right into Harper's eyes, into her heart, into her soul, and said, "I'm sorry, kiddo." And that was it. Harper put her ear to his chest. The machine issued its sustained beep. Calling the game. Over.

Reed doesn't text back. Harper tries to remember if there is cell reception at Lambert's Cove. She is always making excuses for him, because of the three men now remaining in her life, he's the one she's in love with.

She sends the same text—*Billy is gone*—to Sergeant Drew Truman of the Edgartown Police Department. Harper and Drew have been dating for three weeks. He asked her out while they were both on the Chappy ferry, and Harper thought, *Why not?* Drew Truman belongs to one of the most prominent African American families in Oak Bluffs. His mother, Yvonne Truman, served as a selectman for more than ten years. She is one of the five Snyder sisters, all of whom own brightly colored, impeccably maintained gingerbread cottages facing Ocean Park. Harper remembered Drew back when he was a high school athlete featured every week in the *Vineyard Gazette* sports pages. He then went to college and the police academy before coming home to Dukes County to serve and protect.

Harper had thought that dating someone new might ameliorate the agony of seeing a married man. She and Drew have gone out six times: they've eaten Mexican food at Sharky's four times (it's Drew's favorite, for reasons Harper can't quite comprehend), they had lunch once at the Katama airstrip diner, and their most recent date was a "fancy" night out at the Seafood Shanty—surf and turf, water views, singing waiters. Harper knows that Drew expected sex at the end of the night, but Harper has been able to hold him off thus far, citing her dying father as the reason she can't be intimate.

Drew is keen to introduce Harper to his mother, his brother, his brother's wife, his nieces and nephews, his aunties, his cousins, his cousins' children—the whole extended Snyder-Truman family—but this, too, is a step Harper isn't ready to take. Part of her does yearn to be taken in, fussed and clucked over, cooked for, admired and petted, even argued with and looked askance at because her skin is white. In short, there is appeal in being "official" with Drew. But the harsh reality remains: Harper loves Reed and only Reed.

Harper sighs. Drew is working the beat tonight. He makes double time on weekends, but with all the bozos out drinking too much and enjoying the first days of the summer season, is it worth it? He'll go on thirty calls, she bets, and twenty-seven of them will be drunk and disorderlies and three will be accidents involving taxi drivers who haven't learned their way around yet.

The third man remaining in Harper's life is her precious, damaged friend Brendan Donegal, who is exiled over on Chappy. Harper wants to let Brendan know that Billy has died, but Brendan can't manage texting anymore. Like twenty-six killer wasps, the alphabet swarms him. He uses his phone only to tell the time.

Nothing from Dr. Zimmer. Will Harper be forced to call? She calls Dr. Zimmer all the time because she has had many legitimate questions about her father's condition—liver failure, kidney failure, congestive heart failure. Billy Frost's end has been a series of failures.

Surely no one will fault Harper for calling Reed *now,* after her father has *died.* But she has an uncomfortable premonition. She waits.

Billy Frost is dead at the age of seventy-three. Harper takes a stab at writing his obituary in her mind as the nurses come in to clean him up and prepare him for the fun-filled ride to the morgue. *William O'Shaughnessy Frost, master electrician and avid Red Sox fan, died last night at Martha's Vineyard Hospital, in Oak Bluffs. He is survived by his daughter Harper Frost.*

And...his daughter Tabitha Frost...and his granddaughter, Ainsley Cruise...and his ex-wife, Eleanor Roxie-Frost, all of Nantucket, Massachusetts. What will surprise people the most? Harper wonders. That Billy has a daughter identical to but completely different from the cute screw-up who delivers packages for Rooster Express? Or that Billy used to be married to the famous Boston fashion designer Eleanor Roxie-Frost, more commonly known as ERF? Or will the shocker be that the other half of Billy's family lives on the rival island—that fancy, upscale haven for billionaires? Harper's twin sister, Tabitha, hasn't set foot on Martha's Vineyard in fourteen years, and Harper's mother, Eleanor, hasn't been here since her honeymoon, in 1968. Harper's niece, Ainsley, has *never* been here. Billy had been sad about that; when he wanted to see Ainsley, he had to go to Nantucket, which he did, religiously, every August.

You sure you don't want to come with me? he used to ask Harper.

I'm sure, Harper would say. *Tabitha doesn't want me there.*

When will you girls learn? Billy would reply, and Harper would mouth along with him. *Family is family.*

Family is *family,* Harper thinks. That's the problem.